ANDY McNAB

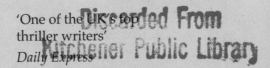

'One of the UK's top thriller writers'
Daily Express

'Like his creator, the ex-SAS soldier turned uber-agent is unstoppable'
Daily Mirror

'Could hardly be more topical'
Mail on Sunday

'Other thriller writers do their research, but McNab has actually been there'
Sunday Times

'Sometimes only the rollercoaster ride of an action-packed thriller hits the spot. No one delivers them as professionally or as plentifully as SAS soldier turned author McNab'
Guardian

'McNab's great asset is that the heart of his fiction is non-fiction'
Sunday Times

'Proceeds with a testosterone surge'
Daily Telegraph

'When it comes to thrills, he's Forsyth class'
Mail on Sunday

'Nick Stone is emerging as one of the great all-action characters of recent times'
Daily Mirror

'Andy McNab's books get better and better'
Daily Express

ANDY McNAB

▲ **In 1984** he was 'badged' as a member of 22 SAS Regiment.

▲ **Over the course** of the next nine years he was at the centre of covert operations on five continents.

▲ **During the first** Gulf War he commanded Bravo Two Zero, a patrol that, in the words of his commanding officer, 'will remain in regimental history for ever'.

▲ **Awarded both** the Distinguished Conduct Medal (DCM) and Military Medal (MM) during his military career.

▲ **McNab** was the British Army's most highly decorated serving soldier when he finally left the SAS in February 1993.

▲ **He is a patron** of the *Help for Heroes* campaign.

▲ **He is now** the author of over twenty bestselling thrillers, as well as four Quick Read novels. Following the success of the perennial bestseller *Bravo Two Zero*, McNab continues to write non-fiction too. Most recently, he joined forces with Professor Kevin Dutton on *The Good Psychopath's Guide to Success* and *Sorted! The Good Psychopath's Guide to Bossing Your Life*.

BRAVO TWO ZERO

In 1991, Sergeant Andy McNab led eight members of the SAS regiment on a top-secret mission in Iraq that would send them deep behind enemy lines. Their call sign: Bravo Two Zero.

IMMEDIATE ACTION

The no-holds-barred account of an extraordinary life, from the day McNab was found on the steps of Guy's Hospital as a baby to the day he went to fight in the Gulf War.

SEVEN TROOP

The gripping true story of serving in the company of a remarkable band of brothers. But he who dares doesn't always win. Every man is pushed to breaking point, some beyond it.

THE GOOD PSYCHOPATH'S GUIDE TO SUCCESS

As diagnosed by Professor Kevin Dutton, McNab is what they call a 'Good Psychopath' – he's a psychopath but he's also a high-functioning member of society. Learn how to be successful the McNab way.

SORTED! THE GOOD PSYCHOPATH'S GUIDE TO BOSSING YOUR LIFE

Together, Andy McNab and Professor Kevin Dutton are here to show you how to dial up your inner 'Good Psychopath' to get more out of life.

THE NICK STONE SERIES

Ex-SAS trooper, now gun-for-hire working for the British government, Nick Stone is the perfect man for the dirtiest of jobs, doing whatever it takes by whatever means necessary…

REMOTE CONTROL

◢ WASHINGTON DC, USA

Stone is on the run with precious cargo, the only person who can identify a vicious killer – a seven-year-old girl.

CRISIS FOUR

◢ NORTH CAROLINA, USA

A beautiful young woman holds the key to a chilling conspiracy that will threaten the world as we know it.

FIREWALL

◢ FINLAND

At the heart of a global espionage network, Stone is faced with some of the most dangerous killers around.

LAST LIGHT

◢ PANAMA

Caught in the crossfire between Colombian mercenaries and Chinese businessmen, Stone isn't comfortable.

LIBERATION DAY

▲ CANNES, FRANCE

Behind the glamorous exterior, the city's seething underworld is the battleground for a very dirty drugs war.

DARK WINTER

▲ MALAYSIA

The War on Terror has Stone cornered: the life of someone he loves or the lives of millions he doesn't know?

DEEP BLACK

▲ BOSNIA

All too late, Stone sees he is being used as bait to lure into the open a man who the West are desperate to destroy.

AGGRESSOR

▲ GEORGIA, FORMER SOVIET UNION

An old SAS comrade calls in a debt that will challenge Stone to risk everything in order to repay his friend.

RECOIL

▲ THE CONGO, AFRICA

A straightforward missing persons case quickly becomes a headlong rush from the past.

CROSSFIRE

▲ KABUL, AFGHANISTAN

The search for a kidnapped reporter takes Stone to Afghanistan – the modern-day Wild West.

BRUTE FORCE

◣ **Tripoli, Libya**

An undercover operation is about to have deadly long-term consequences.

EXIT WOUND

◣ **Dubai, UAE**

This one's personal: Stone is out to track down the killer of two ex-SAS comrades.

ZERO HOUR

◣ **Amsterdam, Netherlands**

A terrorist organization is within reach of immeasurable power – but not for long.

DEAD CENTRE

◣ **Somalia**

When his son is kidnapped by pirates, a Russian oligarch calls the only man he can think of, Nick Stone.

SILENCER

◣ **Hong Kong**

Stone must return to a world he thought he had left behind in order to protect his family.

FOR VALOUR

◣ **Hereford, UK**

Called to investigate a death at the SAS base, Stone finds himself in the killer's telescopic sights.

DETONATOR

▲ THE ALPS, SWITZERLAND

When someone Stone loves is murdered, he can no longer take the pain. He wants vengeance at any cost.

COLD BLOOD

▲ THE NORTH POLE

Accompanying a group of veteran soldiers on an expedition to the North Pole, Stone learns quickly that it isn't just the cold that might kill him.

LINE OF FIRE

▲ LONDON, UK

The Nick Stone series comes closer to home in more ways than one.

THE SERGEANT TOM BUCKINGHAM SERIES

RED NOTICE

Deep beneath the English Channel, Russian terrorists have seized control of the Eurostar to Paris and are holding four hundred hostages at gunpoint. But one man stands in their way. An off-duty SAS soldier is on the train, his name is Tom Buckingham.

FORTRESS

Ex-SAS and working for a billionaire with political ambition, Buckingham will have to decide where his loyalties lie as he is drawn into a spiral of terrorism, insurgency and, ultimately, assassination.

STATE OF EMERGENCY

Undercover inside a frighteningly real right-wing organization, Buckingham uncovers a plan to kill the party leader. But beneath that lies a far more devastating plot to change the political landscape of Europe for ever.

Andy McNab and Kym Jordan's novels trace the interwoven stories of one platoon's experience of warfare in the twenty-first century. Packed with the searing danger and high-octane excitement of modern combat, it also explores the impact of its aftershocks upon the soldiers themselves, and upon those who love them.

WAR TORN

Two tours of Iraq have shown Sergeant Dave Henley how modern battles are fought. But nothing could have prepared him for his posting to Afghanistan. This is a war zone like he's never seen before.

BATTLE LINES

Sergeant Dave Henley returns from Afghanistan to find that home can be an equally searing battlefield. The promise of another posting to Helmand is almost a relief for the soldiers but, for their families, it is another opportunity for their lives to be ripped apart.

ANDY
McNAB
COLD BLOOD

CORGI BOOKS

TRANSWORLD PUBLISHERS
61–63 Uxbridge Road, London W5 5SA
www.penguin.co.uk

Transworld is part of the Penguin Random House group of companies
whose addresses can be found at global.penguinrandomhouse.com

First published in Great Britain in 2016 by Bantam Press
an imprint of Transworld Publishers
Corgi edition published 2017

A CIP catalogue record for this book
is available from the British Library.

ISBN
9780552170949 (B format)
9780552174398 (A format)

Typeset in 11/14pt Palatino by Falcon Oast Graphic Art Ltd.
Printed and bound by Clays Ltd, Bungay, Suffolk.

Penguin Random House is committed to a sustainable
future for our business, our readers and our planet. This book
is made from Forest Stewardship Council® certified paper.

MIX
Paper from
responsible sources
FSC® C018179
www.fsc.org

1 3 5 7 9 10 8 6 4 2

COLD BLOOD

1

Longyearbyen
Latitude: 78.2461 North
Longitude: 15.4656 East

The American gripped the armrest between us so fiercely with his gloved hand that I thought he was going to rip it from its moorings. 'Holy Mother of fuck!'

He breathed rapidly through clenched teeth. His eyelids were clamped shut and, though the cabin was unheated, beads of sweat raced each other down his forehead. The heat supply was on the blink so we'd all kept our coats on. Mine was a thin duvet jacket with a high neck and sleeves. It wouldn't be all I needed out on the ice, but you didn't hear me complaining. His padded parka was fresh out of its wrapper and he had no hat under his hood, which told me he was an Arctic virgin. If you didn't keep head, hands and feet warm, it would fuck you up just as much as the turbulence that was about to make the pilots fuck up our landing.

The wooden houses of Longyearbyen came into view below us, like brightly coloured decorations on a giant Christmas cake. Appearances could be deceptive from the air. This far north, I knew there'd be little more to the airport than a runway surrounded by peaks.

The ice-glazed tarmac leaped up to meet us as a fresh blast of wind buffeted the port wing. The starboard undercarriage of the Scandinavian Airways flight from the mainland slammed down, then bounced away and scrabbled for height.

A shout went up from the Russians a few rows in front of us. They immediately unbuckled so they could turn round and fuck about with their mates seated behind them. They'd been necking their vodka since take-off and were loving the rollercoaster ride. Engines screamed and the nose lifted sharply. We were climbing again. The ever-so-cool Danish flight attendants did their best to get them to buckle up, but their best wasn't good enough.

Another air pocket dropped the aircraft twenty metres. The American's hand shifted to my forearm and gripped it like he was about to pull the whole thing off at the elbow. I shifted sideways as the strip disappeared again beneath a wash of cloud. A fresh weather system was coming in fast, swatting the plane about like an invisible King Kong.

The sound system crackled as the captain blabbed on in Norwegian and Russian, but the shriek of the engines blotted out whatever he was saying. I didn't give a shit. I didn't do praying, but a voice inside my head demanded more flying and less talking, so the dickhead next to me would calm down and leave me the fuck alone.

'I guess he's making another circuit. Third time lucky, eh?'

The American's head shot round towards me and his eyes snapped open. They were so wide apart they almost didn't fit on his face. Surrounded by the fur ruff on his hood, they made him look like an owl. A very frightened owl. I might as well have told him, 'Phone your loved ones. We're going down.'

The engines were still at full throttle as we made a tight, steeply banked turn.

'Jeez, I hate this shit. If God had meant us to fly he'd have—'

'Given us jet packs.'

Then the plane stabilized and his grip relaxed. His mouth cracked into something approaching a grin as the blood supply returned to my fingers. 'You Brits . . . The stiff upper lip thing, I envy you that.' He patted my duvet-covered forearm.

The Owl had that cosy home-cooked apple-pie Midwest accent that would invite you into his home but not really mean it. He leaned closer, enveloping me in coffee breath with a hint of vomit. 'I hate flying. I hate the cold.' He nodded towards the front of the cabin as another yell exploded from the vodka-fuelled contingent. 'But y'know what I hate most? Russians. Having to fly with these people just rubs our noses in it, don't you think?'

I didn't, but he took my silence as permission to continue.

'Those guys, they're headed to the coal mines.

Svalbard is infested with them. The whole place is still owned by Russia. Work there is about ten rungs down from sewage collector, but the fuckers come in every spring, work like dogs, then drink their pay cheques through the winter. That's if they don't die in a gas blast or a cave-in.'

He shuddered.

'You been to Barentsburg? No? Then thank your lucky stars. All they got there is one big hole in the ground, the hotel from Hell, with some Ukrainian skank if you get lonely, and an ER for when you try to leave without paying.'

He laughed. The Owl was obviously a man who was never ashamed to enjoy his own lame jokes.

'And the coal is low-grade brown lignite they can't sell for beans, so it's starved of investment.' He leaned close again. 'They say there's way more coin to be made there selling blow to the workforce.'

I raised my eyebrows enough to indicate the minimum possible interest. Whenever I was tempted to blank a talker, I remembered a lesson I'd learned the hard way: never discard information freely given – it sometimes came in handy later. Besides, right now any distraction was welcome.

'You in oil?'

I shook my head.

'Gas?'

Same again.

'Me, I'm oil *and* gas. Not the shitty end of the stick – I do the legals. Contracts, negotiations, that kinda thing.'

He spread a vast paw across his laptop and let out another wheezy laugh. 'This is my coalface. Out there . . .' he waved towards the porthole '. . . is *waaay* out of my comfort zone.'

When it came to stating the blindingly obvious, this lad was way ahead of the field.

I had to ask. 'So why you here, then?'

Spitsbergen was the only permanently populated island in the Svalbard archipelago, deep in the Arctic Circle. Longyearbyen, with just over two thousand inhabitants on a good day, was its biggest settlement – which made it the world's most northern city, if you could call it that. Whatever, it was a fuck of a long way from Kansas.

He nodded at the icefields that reappeared fleetingly through a crack in the wall of cloud. 'Forty per cent of the world's untapped oil is sitting under that ice, my friend.' He licked his very fleshy lips. 'And that makes for a shitload of very expensive paperwork.'

He gestured in the direction of the partying Russians and lowered his voice to a conspiratorial whisper. 'Gives the term "Cold War" a whole new meaning, don't it?'

'I guess.'

He was focusing on me now. 'So what about you, my friend? Weather too warm for you in good old London Town?'

'Vacation.'

He let out a series of staccato clucks that reminded me of a single-cylinder cement mixer on a building site where I'd once worked. 'For real?'

I nodded, with more confidence than I felt. I could have said 'job', but that didn't seem real either. Nothing much did right now.

5

Cauldwell's call had jolted me out of the flat in Moscow where I'd been trying, and failing, to finish packing up our things. I'd got as far as putting Anna's clothes into plastic charity sacks before I'd seen Mishka the teddy and crumpled onto Nicholai's bed. I'd stayed there I don't know how long, pinned down by the weight of pain and grief. My one-time CO's voice had been an unexpectedly welcome escape. He didn't explain how he'd got hold of my number, and I didn't much care.

'Stone? I'm calling in a favour.'

I didn't ask what type of favour he thought he'd ever done me. After leaving the Regiment he'd set up a private security firm, as so many of them did, then sold it and invested in one that made kit for oil rigs, but hit a rock when the bottom dropped out of the crude market. Since then he'd been trying to claw his way back, touting himself around as a consultant, advising on security for companies mad enough to want to drill in war zones. Last I'd heard, he was doing the business for a Scandi energy company called Armancore.

'I've got something for you – if you're available.'

His tone suggested he knew I was, somehow.

'There's ten grand in it.'

I came close to telling him to go fuck himself right there. I wasn't for sale and I didn't want his money. I had more than he would ever be able to lay his hands on in a lifetime, not that it mattered.

'Oh, and . . . sorry for your loss,' he added, as an afterthought. That was Cauldwell's version of a heart-to-heart and mercifully brief.

'Thanks.'

'I thought you might welcome a distraction.'

He wasn't wrong there. A stint in a Nigerian tin mine would have been welcome.

'My lad's set on doing some madcap tab to the Pole and I need someone to be there in case he finds it harder than he thought.'

Babysitting and freezing my nuts off. I told myself I wasn't *that* desperate. For about thirty seconds. 'Which one?'

'North.'

2

I'd first met young Jacobi when he was maybe thirteen. Cauldwell would bring him into the Lines and ask one of us to put the kid through his paces in the gym, get him ready for his army career – whether or not he was on board with the idea. He was a nice enough boy, but I couldn't see him in uniform, and I wasn't sure he could either.

Next I heard, Jack had made it through Sandhurst. No idea how. He must have been in his late twenties by now and, from the sound of it, was still in his father's shadow. It was a position he'd occupied most of his young life.

'He's . . . he's not had the best time of it since Helmand. Maybe you know . . .'

I did. News travelled. Three weeks into his first tour the boy had lost half a leg to an IED.

'He's roped in some of the other walking wounded he met at Selly Oak.' I could feel him shuddering down the phone. 'A right crew. Basket cases, the lot of them,

8

but he seems to want to make a go of it. I just wish he had the sense to let me help him.'

Cauldwell's attitude didn't help, except to remind me of what a twat he could be. In his world there were only two sorts of men, winners and losers. Seeing as the vast majority of us were somewhere in between, it made him pretty unpopular, but he'd never given a shit about that.

'So I need someone sensible in there, to make sure the wheels don't come off. You in?'

Normally I would have demanded a lot more information: Jack and the team's mobility level, how much training they'd had for the venture, his – and their – mental condition, who were the guides. But normal was no longer part of my life.

'I'll think about it. Give me a call tomorrow.'

'I haven't got time. It's yes or no. Now.'

That was Cauldwell all over. No pissing about. No grey, just black or white. I heard myself say yes.

Four minutes later I got a text saying a ticket to Longyearbyen via Oslo was waiting for me at the check-in counter, Terminal D, Sheremetyevo airport. Five minutes after that another appeared, asking for my account details for the transfer of five thousand GBP as an advance on ten and a booking at the Radisson.

That had been thirty-six hours ago.

'So how in God's name d'ya take a vacation in the *Arctic*?' The Owl was staring at me in dismay.

'It's more of an . . . expedition. Walking to the Pole.'

'On your *lonesome*?' His eyes rolled.

I shook my head.

'So how d'you get there? You got people who know the way?'

'We just head north, I guess.'

'No shit, Sherlock!' He slapped his forehead. 'How many on the team? I mean, how many of you heading up there?'

I didn't know how many 'basket cases' Jack was bringing with him, but I didn't feel like summoning the energy to explain. 'A few. Not sure yet.'

'Jeez, I hear it's over a hundred thousand bucks apiece, start to finish. You guys own a bank?'

'We have a sponsor.'

A giant in a faded parka and an equally well-worn Glacier Pilots baseball cap suddenly took up all my new best mate's attention and saved me having to give a more detailed answer. He picked his way down the aisle and jutted his chin at us as he drew level. 'Sam. It's OK, we'll be down soon.' It was more of a growl than a few words of comfort.

'Hey, Munnelly, I'm good. This Brit here's making the journey a pleasure. Getta loada him, will ya?' The Owl jabbed a thumb in my direction. 'He's only takin' a hike to the North Pole!'

Munnelly's mouth was hidden beneath a hedge of black beard but it didn't take a genius to spot that he didn't share his buddy's interest in strangers, or their madcap adventures. He commanded the space around him with the stillness and intensity of a man who was used to getting his own way. He totally ignored the flight attendant who came up behind him and tried to usher him politely back to his seat.

His dead eyes swivelled in my direction, like

10

howitzer muzzles, beneath his rock-shaped brow. His weathered complexion was a Native American's grizzly-bear brown.

The Owl grabbed my forearm again. 'Munnelly here's the real deal. Cut him and he *bleeds* oil.'

The grizzly still didn't move a muscle. I had a stab at being impressed, but didn't put too much effort into it. I undid my belt. 'You two want to sit together for the ride in? We can swap.'

Munnelly raised his hand. 'I'm with people.' He tilted his vast head in the direction he'd come from, then leaned down and whispered something in the Owl's ear.

My forearm was pushed to one side. 'Sure. You betcha.'

Munnelly gave me a faraway stare and retraced his steps, a very happy flight attendant in tow.

The Owl waited until Munnelly was back in his seat. 'Heck of a guy. Part Inuit.' He swallowed. 'They say he can *smell* the black gold under the ice cap. And he knows the ocean floor like the back of his hand. Don't hardly need sonar or any of that shit.'

The grey fog outside the window gave way to a blanket of white cotton wool lit briefly by a low sun, until we vanished into the next tower of cloud. The plane creaked and groaned as it tumbled into another air pocket. Several overhead lockers slammed open and the Owl clawed at my forearm again. His face whitened. I fished around for a sick bag as we were treated to a fresh burst of babble over the intercom.

He took a gulp of air. 'They might try to give us the bad news in English.'

'He's just telling us to go back to our seats.'

'Really? How d'you know Norwegian?'

'I don't. He's talking Russian.'

'Wow – like, you know it because you learned some, like you live there or something?'

I reached across with my free hand and unclamped his. 'Now, slow right down.'

'Excuse me?'

'Breathe. Slowly. Holding your breath pushes up your anxiety levels. And if you breathe too fast, like you're doing now, you suck in too much oxygen. You'll hyperventilate and feel faint. Then you'll think you're having a heart attack.'

He looked at me in surprise and let out a longer breath, like a small industrial bellows. 'You some kind of lifesaver?'

Up until a few weeks ago, I'd have thought that was really funny.

3

The pilot made another approach. The wind had slackened, the cloud cleared and suddenly I was looking at the primary-coloured houses close up. The visibility was pin-sharp. That was the thing about the Arctic. One minute you could see no more than a few inches, even when the sun was out, the next you could see for miles.

I'd never been a big fan of fucking about on ice. I hadn't even liked watching Torvill and Dean on TV when the rest of the world couldn't get enough of them. It was just easier to start off hot and try to cool down, instead of the other way round.

When I became a squaddie, NATO was shit scared of the Russians pulling a fast one and invading Europe from the top while we were busy looking east. Every couple of years we were issued with Arctic warfare kit – extra-thick socks, a woolly hat and a pair of mittens – and sent off to Porsangmoen, a Norwegian training area. We would spend two months each year freezing our bollocks off in the Arctic Circle in temperatures of −45° centigrade when the wind picked up. Some of the lads loved playing snow soldiers, but the idea of sliding along with a twenty-five-kilo Bergen and a fifty-kilo sledge never did it for me – especially when I was trying to steer clear of big white bears that could smell us from miles away and thought we were meals on skis.

Immersion training was what I hated most. We all had to ski through a hole in the ice into the water below. The cold took your breath away, and even with quick-release buckles, it was unbelievably hard to get your Bergen off your back with fingers that were so fucking cold they no longer did what you told them to.

Once the thing was off – and hopefully floating – we had to drag ourselves out before we froze to death. There were always safety guys nearby in case someone was in the water for too long, but it wasn't just the cold that could kill – the shock could literally take your breath away so you asphyxiated instead.

Even when you'd scraped yourself back onto the ice, that wasn't the end of it. We had to stand at attention, shout our name, rank and regimental number, then yell an even louder *Sir!* to confirm our minds were still in gear. Afterwards we were pushed into a steaming hot shelter, stripped, shoved into sleeping bags and given hot drinks before we got very dead.

That wasn't my idea of happy camping, and neither was being an appetizer at the polar bears' picnic. But as with pretty much everything in my life, when it was done I'd told myself it really hadn't been *that* bad – then tugged on the mittens and the extra-thick socks twenty-four months later and started honking about the Arctic all over again.

And playing soldiers on ice taught me one thing I was never going to forget: in the Arctic Circle, mistakes were only made once.

4

The wheels finally dropped onto the ice-coated tarmac with little more than a squeak and the aircraft taxied towards the low-level, rectangular and quite new-looking terminal.

The Owl looked as though he'd just been sprung from Death Row. As soon as we started taxiing he was out of his seat and reaching for the overhead locker, budget-airline style. The Russians all had the same idea and the aisle filled with padded coats and vodka fumes. The flight attendants threw their hands into the air and let everyone get on with it.

The Owl wrestled out an oversized bag and let it fall onto the seat beside me. The colour had returned to his cheeks for the first time since the aircraft had started bouncing around in the sky.

A low sun glinted off the runway. I knew it could really mess up your vision, even if there was some cloud cover. I put on my Julbo CAT 4 gigs and watched a ragged queue of big men with bloodshot eyes and broken veins stumble down the steps into the place they'd call home for the next six months.

I reached inside my day sack and pulled out the thick Rab Expedition duvet jacket I'd picked up in Oslo. My arms stood out from my sides like the new kid in the starched uniform once I'd put it on over my inner layer of padding.

The flight attendants had their jackets on, fur hoods pulled up, and were getting impatient. Fair one: they wanted to get us drunken noisy shits off their aircraft. I had my thermals in place and could pull on the padded trousers later.

They cracked a series of identical smiles as I passed through the door: we both knew what was about to hit me. A second later, I was being shoved into a deep freeze at the same time as having my face sandpapered by someone bent on revenge. I coughed with the shock of it, and as I breathed in it felt as if a claw made of ice-coated iron was reaching down my throat and into my lungs. I coughed again and bent forward.

'Will ya look at that?' The Owl's yell was almost lost in the driving wind. 'Last time I was here, back in the fall, ours was the only plane.'

Parked up on the apron were a couple more Antonovs, several private jets and an Airbus A330 freighter in blue livery that called itself 'Skyship'.

'Why the build-up?'

'Everybody wants a piece of what's down there.' He pointed at the ground. 'Like I said, it's the black-gold rush.'

Munnelly cruised up alongside and steered the Owl away towards a frosted black Chevy Suburban waiting on the apron. No formalities for those guys. Even in this security-conscious age there were always some with enough muscle and money to cut their way through the red tape.

'Nice meetin' you,' the Owl called over his shoulder. 'And watch your back out there. Ain't no trees, but it's a jungle.'

5

Cauldwell was waiting under the Arrivals sign, greyer and a little more lined than he had been the last time I'd seen him, but he still carried himself like a Rupert, all six-five of him towering over the throng. He was very much a Queen-and-country man. I saw it as a crutch, something to lean on, a bit like religion, because something else was missing. Any soldier at the bottom of the food chain would be very wary of Cauldwell's type of commitment, and I was no different.

He gave me a stiff handshake. 'Thanks for coming.'

'How could I resist?'

'How was the flight?'

'Interesting.'

I realized I didn't know how to address him. I'd never called him 'sir', and wasn't about to start now, but couldn't imagine us on first-name terms either. In the Regiment he'd been called various things, but none to his face.

Outside a sign said: 'Oslo 2046, London 3403, Tokyo

6830'. It was exactly the kind of place I needed: a long way from everywhere.

He started to lead the way to a Merc G-Wagen, then pulled up. 'That all you're carrying? Where's your kit?'

I shrugged.

He carried on walking. 'Stupid question. Well, you'll be able to sort that out here. They've got everything you'll need. Been this far north before?' He didn't give me time to answer. 'Because up on the ice it's at least ten degrees colder.'

He put on his sun-gigs and fired up the engine, then slammed the shift into Drive and moved off. I checked the temperature display on the dash: –14°C.

He'd gone all quiet, like he was concentrating hard on the road, except it was almost empty. At least the signs were keeping me entertained. The wildlife warning triangle didn't have a silhouette of a deer. It had one of a bear.

After greeting us briefly on the tarmac the sun had vanished again almost immediately, leaving nothing more than a ghostly glow on what might have been the horizon. In a couple of weeks it would be spring, or 'light winter', as they called it, then summer – when the temperature reached a sweltering six degrees – and the sun wouldn't set again until late August. The months of no light followed by months of no darkness were said to drive you mad. And the lack of decent broadband.

The moisture in the atmosphere was freezing into fairy dust. The coloured houses came into view again, and I could now see the stilts holding them all a metre or so proud of the ground.

Cauldwell followed my gaze. 'The permafrost is up to forty metres thick – the soil's frozen all year round. The top layer melts in the summer, so the stilts keep these places from sinking into the sludge.'

Behind them, the forbidding Arctic terrain surrounded the town, looming over it in a way that, if you were the nervous type, you might find unsettling.

We passed a couple on foot, rifles slung casually over their shoulders.

'It's the only place I know where you get into trouble for *not* carrying. The bears get quite bold when they're hungry, and when they see something edible they don't hang about. There are more of them here than there are people.'

Cauldwell moved to the centre of the road to avoid the pedestrians. 'Fuck knows why anyone wants to stay here. It's the constant daylight.'

'I don't mind the idea of eternal dusk.' It suited my current state of mind.

He looked at me as if I'd completely lost it. 'Well, wait until you try getting to sleep. You'll remember why people keep prisoners awake under interrogation. It's bloody torture all right.'

If he was trying to sell this trip to me he was making a pig's breakfast of it. Except for that last thing. I hadn't wanted to go to sleep much lately.

'So where's Jack now?'

There was a pause before he replied. 'You'll catch up with him in due course.' He chewed his bottom lip. 'Something you need to know from the start. We've not been on the best of terms, him and me. The usual father–son stuff. You know how it is. It's nothing,

21

really, but children can be a major fucking . . .'

I gave him a look that said all I needed it to.

'Sorry, forget I said that. Bit distracted.' He gave me a sidelong glance, then, seeing I hadn't broken down in floods of tears, decided to press on. 'I haven't seen the lad for the best part of a year . . . This tab, I was all for it. After lying around moping, he finally seemed to be pulling his finger out. It's just what he needs – something to focus on, a challenge.'

He let out a long, despairing sigh that probably said more about what he thought of his son than any words could.

'But he . . . he's been hell bent on going his own bloody way on it. Kept me pretty much in the dark, despite my offers to help. Anyway, there is one detail that I didn't have time to explain to you.'

He took a breath, ready to give me the bad news. Stuff that there was never time to explain was always bad news.

'His sponsorship's gone tits up. Cold feet – if you'll pardon the pun – about the condition of some of his fellow travellers.'

He misread my silence for lack of interest. It wasn't that. Either the trip was off or it was on. Either I had a couple of days to distract myself or I had a whole lot more.

'It's all right, Stone, you're being handsomely rewarded.'

That was the last thing I was thinking of. I was reminding myself of what a fucking awful judge of character Cauldwell was.

He was interrupted by the sat nav, telling him to

turn left. He swung the wheel. 'Anyway, I've pulled a few strings and put something together to help save the expedition so he can get it back on the rails.'

His face brightened. 'Quite a coup, frankly. Proper Arctic expertise, proper backup and kit. No arsing about. But he has to get going. It's now or never.'

'Why the hurry?'

'Well, they can't just sit around here freezing their arses off.'

That didn't sound like the real reason. 'But Jack's pleased, right?'

'He doesn't know yet. That's where you come in. You're going to give him the good news. He won't accept anything from me.'

I was starting to get pissed off. He'd lied to get me there. Then I took a breath too. Fuck it, so what? 'How's that going to work? What happens if he tells me to piss off?'

'Then he's fucked. He can't go without backup, decent kit, or the funding for the round trip. He needs cash for the flights – and do you have any idea how much fuel costs up there? There's the transport cost, the distance, the difficulty of transferring barrels of aviation fuel from one transport to another, the quality of the fuel. It has to be perfect because it powers everything up there, not just the aircraft.

'Getting aviation fuel this far is expensive enough. Further north it can be anything up to six hundred dollars a litre. That's expensive flying to get where they need to go, and it'll cost even more if they have problems and need airlifting out. They simply do not have that kind of money.

'I'm handing him all he needs on a plate. It's his last hope. Without it, the whole thing's off.'

He hit the brakes too hard and the wagon started to slide. He cursed, released them, and the tyres bit again.

'And all I ask from him in return is that you go with him.'

'He doesn't know about that either?'

'Look, I moved Heaven and Earth to make the going easy over the years. He'd never have got into Sandhurst if I hadn't pulled a few strings. He's never been what you'd call leadership material, and based on his all-too-brief time in the field, I can't exactly vouch for his judgement. So I need a grown-up watching he doesn't put his remaining foot in it.' He gave a half-hearted laugh.

'You mean getting blown up counts against him?'

He glared at me. 'For God's sake, you're starting to sound like his mother. What I mean is, he and his crew of— Well, they've all had a few bits knocked off them. But the deal is they have to get there. I've put a lot of effort into making this happen and I don't want it fucked up because one of them can't manage to put up a tent.'

Great. Hired for a job, by someone who didn't believe in it, to babysit someone who probably wouldn't want me anywhere near him. For money I didn't need. I guessed it was a bit better than spending my life working in a job I didn't like to buy things I didn't need and impress people I didn't give a fuck about.

Or maybe not.

I should have opted for the Nigerian tin mine.

6

Cauldwell gave me a big shit-eating grin, willing me to believe that some of the old can-do conviction was coming through, but I heard more than a hint of desperation in his voice, as if he had more riding on this than he was letting on. 'You'll convince him it's the right thing, Stone. I know you will.'

Either he had an absurd amount of confidence in my abilities or he really was even more desperate than he sounded. 'How do you think Jack will take it?'

'If he's got any sense he should bloody welcome this option with open arms. Without the sort of expertise and resources I'm bringing to the table, the whole thing's dead in the water so he should be over the moon. All the more so because it's coming from you.' He nodded enthusiastically, willing me to agree. 'You'll be the bearer of very good news. It should go down well. Extremely well.'

Or like a cup of cold sick, I couldn't help thinking. Something about the way Cauldwell was selling this suggested there was more than a mountain to be climbed before anyone set foot on the Arctic ice. But I decided to give him the benefit of the doubt. At least for now. After all, Jack was his son. He should know how his mind worked. And the fact that the sponsorship had gone south should make it a no-brainer for him.

A black Chevy Suburban swept past, empty now, heading back towards the airport, lights blazing, owning the road.

'Fucking Americans.'

'I met a couple on the way up. That was probably their wagon.'

Cauldwell let out one of his trademark sighs. 'They think they can waltz in here like it's D-Day all over again, behaving as if they own the place, winding everybody up. Frankly, I think it's only a matter of time before the Russians bite back.' He turned a corner without indicating, so a knackered two-door Toyota was now skidding along the ice, horn blaring, its driver fighting to keep moving in a straight line.

Cauldwell thought about what he had just said. 'Well, they are already. This is the third year they've conducted Arctic exercises. The Chechen Airborne jumped onto the ice last week. They flew directly from Murmansk. Not just troops, but heavy drop. Full support, very impressive.'

It was. Airborne was not just about getting boots on the ground. It was about having the kit and heavy-support weapons to keep the force there, if needed. The Brits could no longer do it, and until recently only the USA had had that capability. Now the Russians wanted everyone to know that was no longer the case and, to rub it in, their Murmansk military base was within spitting distance of Norway's northern border.

After the Russian Army had kicked Georgia's arse in 2008, its generals had told Putin it was completely due to Russian numerical superiority, not the quality of their troops or weapons. Because the invasion had given his country a sense of pride and dignity, Putin had had no problem with putting plenty of its new-found oil and gas wealth into rebuilding the military, moving from a largely conscript army to a professional one with world-beating kit.

'I know Norway are impressed, but in a bad way. They're flapping big-time about Russian power in the region, what with the Russians upgrading their air-strips to take heavy military, and making claims on old territories left, right and centre. I bet Norway's very happy it's in NATO. There's even a Norwegian TV show about Russia invading Norway.'

'Really?' Cauldwell never liked being told stuff he didn't know. And I doubted he'd even heard of Netflix. 'Hmm. Interesting.'

'The reality's more complicated than that, but the same idea. Russia in charge.'

'So you know about what's happening up here?'

'A little. The Moscow news covers a fair amount, and there are religious services on TV praying for the return of the Federation's power. The footage of the two flags being planted on the seabed under the Pole is still an audience-pleaser. It's a big deal for them. Putin keeps pumping out the message that the Pole belongs to them and the West is trying to fuck them over by taking all the oil and gas away.'

Cauldwell knew all about that. 'It's the new Great Game.' He was clearly pleased to be back in the lecturer's chair. 'That's what's being played up here, Nick. They aren't messing about and are getting very aggressive about "owning" the Arctic. They want what's under the ice, and global warming is going to make it easier to get it.'

'Is that why you're in bed with Armancore?'

He frowned. He hadn't expected me to have heard of it. 'That's none of your business.'

'OK, just making conversation. Who gives a fuck?'

'Well, I'd stay focused on the job in hand, if I were you.'

I tried very hard not to punch him. 'So how is Jack, physically?'

'Oh, he gets around all right, if that's what you mean. We got him a bloody first-rate leg, practically as good as his old one. Better, possibly. State-of-the-art. None of that NHS rubbish. It cost more than – well, an arm and a leg.' He snorted yet again. Maybe he felt safer in the world of the really crap joke.

'And how's his head?'

His grimace told me I'd just crossed a line. 'How the fuck am I supposed to know? They make far too much of that sort of thing these days.'

Hardly an answer. I stared at him, waiting for more.

'He took his time to get well, that's for sure. But this project seems to have given him something to aim for at last.'

It was hard to avoid the conclusion that he didn't

really know his son. 'What about his mates? Specifically.'

'A motley crew. But you know how men bond and get intense when they're thrown together.' Cauldwell threw his eyes skywards in exaggerated despair. 'One's a domestic health hazard, banned from seeing his family after he beat up their mother. Another's still on industrial quantities of painkillers – can't come off them. Then there's an older chap, nearer your age, I gather, and quite sensible, who crashed his Puma. Should have known better than to get tangled up with this lot. The only one who didn't get through the medical was Adam Stedman.'

'Who's he?'

'The waster who first put the whole stupid idea into Jack's head, back in rehab. He was the only one with two good legs, but he was trouble.'

'What happened to him?'

'Doesn't matter now. He got dropped, thank Christ.'

Cauldwell moved on to how they had all met at the Defence Medical Rehabilitation Centre at Headley Court, Surrey, but it was mostly more negative stuff so I let it slide by me. His voice trailed away once he realized I'd zoned out. I saw a couple of men, pissed out of their heads, staggering along, propping each other up. When they saw us they tried to thumb a lift but one lost his balance and they collapsed in a heap.

'So, anyway, Stone, I'm hoping that one way or another Jack and I can get back on better terms.'

Right. So this was set to be the reunion from Hell. On ice.

'I'm relying on you, Stone, to be an emissary. Don't let me down.' He pulled into a petrol station but came to a halt some way from the pumps, took out his phone and sent a text.

'What happens now?'

Before he could answer, a small Toyota SUV cruised past and pulled up just ahead of us.

'Time to meet one of your fellow travellers. Part of the deal I put together.'

The Toyota took off and we followed.

'Where are we going?'

Cauldwell was now concentrating on the vehicle in front as it bounced over the ice. 'I don't know. I'll explain all later. Let's just get there.'

7

'So – who is your deal with, exactly?'

'Oh, they've got an interest in the ice. They're always up there, fiddling around, checking it out . . .' He knew I was expecting more. 'Environmental types.'

'Change of heart for you?'

'Not entirely. They survey the ice, monitoring the melt rate. It's all very high tech – most of it goes straight over my head.' He wafted his hands as if he was trying to dismiss the subject. It wasn't like Cauldwell to own up to ignorance. He used to be the one who always knew better.

'Why on foot?'

'Oh, I don't know, something to do with reading the ice.'

More hand waving. They were barely on the wheel.

'What matters is their expertise. The Arctic's a killer. The icepack can open up and dump you in freezing water. It can pile up and stop you in your tracks. And then there's handling the temperatures. With the sort of expertise I'm laying on, you won't have to worry about that side of things.'

He lapsed into silence. This was Cauldwell all over. He never had much time for detail in the military, just wanted the job done.

I couldn't tell if this was his way of trying to make amends for being a less than perfect father, press-ganging Jack into the army only to have his leg blown off. One thing was certain: with all the negativity coming off him, I wasn't surprised Jack had been giving him a wide berth.

The Toyota turned up a narrow road bordered on each side by faded red or blue wooden buildings. Cauldwell let the wheels spin and the vehicle fishtailed wildly. 'Fucking ice rink.' He got it back into shape, and as we gained a bit of height I looked back over the drab, neat town, with the looming mountains crowded round it. Apart from the houses, everything was either grey or brown, standard municipal and grim, reminiscent of any number of barracks or similar shitholes I'd been in over the years. I almost felt at home.

'Why all the cloak-and-dagger – meeting up in garage forecourts?'

He brushed it off. 'There's all sorts round here, and the people I've done the deal with aren't too popular with some of the other traffic through here right now. There's plenty of interest in what's going on up there, so they keep a low profile. This is a small town.'

'Interest . . . As in oil and gas?' The Owl's terrified face flashed up briefly on the screen inside my head.

Cauldwell's hands were flapping again. 'All kinds of things.'

'But if they're trying to protect the ice, aren't they the good guys?'

'Ah, well, that depends on your point of view.'

His answers were all dismissive. But I wasn't ready to be dismissed, and he knew it. His impatience was starting to show through again.

'Look, this isn't one of those missions that needs three-hundred-and-sixty-degree knowledge. It's just a tab across the ice, OK?'

The building was as nondescript as you could get, a grey wooden box with a steep, gabled roof. As the Toyota approached, a roller-door opened. The vehicle turned in and came to a stop beside a couple of snow-mobiles and the world's supply of expedition gear. Tents, sleeping bags, stoves, airbeds, shovels, all box-fresh. Cauldwell pulled in next to it and the door closed behind us. A knitted yellow yeti hat, accompanied by a matching hipster beard, jumped out of the Toyota and waved.

Cauldwell got out and strode up to their owner, hand extended, but the guy ignored it and locked him in a hug, which Cauldwell tried and failed to evade.

As soon as he could breathe again, Cauldwell introduced us. 'This is Nick Stone, the man who'll be joining you. Nick, meet Rune Vargen.'

8

Close up, Cauldwell's new best friend looked like
something that had fallen off the troll shelf at Toys R
Us. He turned to me with the same grin but didn't do
the hug. He just pumped my hand as he greeted me
with an accent straight out of a yogurt commercial. 'We
are so happy to be your partners on this courageous
venture. Your country must be so proud of what you
are planning to do.'

He glanced down at my legs.

'Stone's here for backup.'

'Ah . . . of course.'

The hint of hesitation told me my presence had
been sprung on him too. But it didn't dampen his
enthusiasm as he herded us towards a steep flight of
stairs. 'Yes. And, let me say, it's a great honour to be
embarking on this adventure. We are privileged to
be considered by Mr Cauldwell to act as your support,
and it's a tribute to the historic friendship between the

peoples of Norway and the, er, *great* nation of, er, Great Britain.'

He was putting on a big show for an audience of two, but Cauldwell seemed to rise to it. He went into G7 Summit mode. 'Yes, absolutely. And we're equally grateful to you for stepping in at such short notice. Without you and your people this expedition would have had to be put on ice . . . er . . . as it were.'

This time his laugh was tentative, and with good reason.

Rune looked confused, then beamed. 'Ah – oh, yes, English joke. Very good! Come, come.'

He shepherded us up the steep wooden stairs to the upper level where there was a small office set-up among a collection of ancient sofas that had been covered with blankets to hide their sins, and to provide a clean enough place to put a sleeping bag.

The work space consisted of a table and chairs, a coffee machine and an open packet of Axa Go'mix, a Norwegian breakfast cereal. A couple of thick, ancient-looking woollen coats hung from hooks by the door.

A big dog-eared poster of what Svalbard looked like in the summer – pretty much the same as it did now, with a bit less snow below the peaks – took up most of the opposite wall, which it shared with a rack containing two well-worn bolt-action hunting rifles. The varnish on their wooden furniture had been worn away years ago. There was another steep set of stairs to a bunk-bed with a blue sleeping bag spilling out of it. Rune followed my gaze and hurriedly reached up to push the bag out of sight. The place resembled a student crash pad.

'This your HQ?'

'No, I use it when I'm up here. I am sorry for the drawn-out way you arrived but I like to keep my distance from everyone here. My work is not understood by many.'

'Cauldwell explained.'

'Coffee, or something stronger?'

'Coffee's fine.'

Rune pulled off his duvet. Without it, he turned into a round-shouldered, skinny-armed forty-something, with a small pot belly that suggested years spent bending over a microscope or a computer screen rather than braving the most extreme weather on the planet. And the big beard fanning out from his chin was now less hipster and more garden gnome.

Nothing about him filled me with confidence. Most brainy people's bodies just provide them with the equipment to get their heads to meetings. But appearances can be misleading at ground level too. Cauldwell might have lost a fortune – and had a blind spot when it came to his boy – but he wasn't a complete dickhead. He wouldn't have let this cartoon Scandinavian anywhere near the expedition if he didn't know his stuff. Rune rubbed his hands together eagerly.

'Would you like to see my presentation?' He gave a nervous chuckle. 'Don't worry, it is only ten slides.'

He apologized that the coffee machine was *kaput*, boiled a saucepan of water and made a couple of mugs of instant, then dug a carton of UHT milk out of an otherwise empty cupboard and put the whole lot in front of us. 'Help yourselves.'

He reached for a lumpy old Sony laptop, the sort that

gamers lugged around in a shopping trolley. 'This won't take long, I promise.'

I didn't hold my breath. Powering that thing up would take time. Its lid had so many stickers on it, from Greenpeace to the Co-op, that they were probably holding the thing together. He flipped it open, and as the screen decided if it wanted to spark up or not, he sorted through a collection of USB sticks on a key ring. Eventually he got the one he was after and married it up with the laptop, which had finally decided to play ball. It must have been friendly, because it didn't even ask for a password.

I've never been much of a PowerPoint fan, and it was all I could do to stay awake as he launched into his spiel. But I did my best, figuring that something might come in useful later. The gist was that while everyone seemed to agree the icepack was shrinking each year because it was getting warmer – the temperature in Longyearbyen was a little higher than it had been the year before – no one knew which chunk of the stuff that covered the six-million-square-mile polar ocean was most prone to erosion. Rune's mission in life was to shed some light on this by planting a series of monitors from the edge of the pack all the way to the Pole.

He snapped the lid shut and gave us another high-wattage grin. 'So you can see that we are the perfect people for you to team up with, yes?'

For a moment I felt like I'd wandered into a tree-huggers' strategy meeting. Cauldwell, I could see, was struggling to pay attention – clearly his mind was elsewhere.

What I still didn't get was why Rune would be so

willing to partner up with Cauldwell's bunch of basket cases.

As soon as it was over, Cauldwell clapped his hands. 'Very good show. Cracking stuff.'

Rune looked delighted and relieved – as if he'd been pitching for a job rather than doing him a big favour – then turned to see if I felt the same.

'Yeah, very interesting, thanks. But I still don't get why you need us along.'

Out of the corner of my eye, I saw Cauldwell purse his lips. He had always hated being quizzed about detail but I didn't give a fuck about that. He gave his answer before Rune could open his mouth. 'Oh, you know, like I explained in the G-Wagen, people like Rune and his group aren't viewed kindly by some so-called experts round here or the energy industry generally. This way, they can do their work undercover – no one's worried about a group skiing to the Pole. Helps smooth the way, good old-fashioned heroism, that sort of thing . . .'

'Yeah, and?' I looked at Rune. Maybe he could come up with something more convincing.

He flapped his arms and glanced around the room for inspiration as Cauldwell cut back in: 'What our Norwegian friend here is too modest to tell you is that his organization is all about the benefit to the environment and to society. That's what motivates him. Call it idealistic, call it whatever, but that's his thing.'

Rune glowed with relief.

'And your organization? What does it consist of?'

'Just me, really. When I need help, I call on our friends.' He nodded eagerly, as if this was going to fill me with confidence, but his eyes kept flicking to Cauldwell. 'I like to keep things light and simple. Not hire people then have to let them go, you know. And smaller overheads is more ecological. Sustainability is the future.'

My thoughts went back to the Owl and his oil-sniffing friend. 'Well, I'm all for saving the planet, what's left of it. So maybe you've got a view about all these oil people up here.'

Rune laughed nervously. 'Well—'

Cauldwell cut across him again: 'Look, we haven't got time to go into all that right now, have we? It's hardly relevant.'

Whatever. I was tempted to keep probing just because it got up Cauldwell's nose, but what mattered to me much more was the expertise Rune was planning to bring with him. Walking to the Pole, as Cauldwell had already warned, wasn't for amateurs – however many legs they had – and having this pot-bellied dwarf along for the ride wasn't going to change that overnight. 'When do I meet the rest of your team?'

9

Rune looked blank.

'You know, the guys who are going to show us the way to the Pole.'

He coughed. 'Yes, yes. They will be flying in very soon. You will like them for sure. Special-forces-trained, with Arctic speciality, and capability for all thinkable situations.'

Cauldwell joined in the nod-fest – though he knew very well that I wasn't going to take Rune's word for it. Practically every chancer on the circuit claimed SF credentials. I didn't give much of a shit what happened to me right now, but if this was going to be done properly – and I'd be herding a group of lads towards the most northerly point on the planet – I'd need some good backup. 'Do you have their CVs or profiles?'

Cauldwell waved away the question. 'Oh, they're top people, don't you worry, Stone. You don't have to check everything. Leave that to me.'

My questions were pissing him off. But what did he expect? He knew well enough that I was a life member of the awkward squad. I wasn't going to take any of this at face value. If the army taught you anything, it was to check everything before any operation, then check it again. But he was determined to shut me down.

'You'll just have to take my word for it, Stone. These people are all first class. I wouldn't be involving them if they weren't. And time is of the essence.'

'Yeah, and remind me why?'

Cauldwell was really exasperated now and part of me was enjoying it. 'Because time is money, isn't it? We need momentum. Get the job done and move on. Right, Rune?'

Once more Rune nodded dutifully. 'And your men are all prepared and ready to go?' he asked me.

Cauldwell butted in again: 'Goodness, yes. All fighting fit and ready for the fray.'

That was an interesting change of attitude. Ten minutes ago Cauldwell had had Jack's mates written off.

To me he said, 'That kit downstairs? All for the trip, hand-picked by Rune's chaps. I've got them the very best of everything they need.'

The Norwegian was nodding rapidly. 'Good, good, because we have to move quickly. The window of opportunity is very narrow.'

Maybe Rune had been railroaded into this and I wasn't the only one looking for answers. 'I don't think speed is going to be one of their assets.'

Once again Cauldwell weighed in: 'Rune just means

the route is only open for a short period. There is an airstrip on the ice but it's only operational for a few weeks.'

Rune agreed.

Fine. Whatever. I didn't want to hang around either.

'To get back to the point – soon as we can, Rune, we'll get you to meet the team. Jack's a first-rate chap.'

Rune stepped away to take a phone call and I shrugged a 'What the fuck?' at Cauldwell.

He glared right back. 'Look, Stone, frankly, it's all a bit of a scramble. This situation only came up forty-eight hours ago, but it solves a lot of problems for everybody. So let's not sound like we're looking any gift horses in the mouth, OK?'

When anyone said 'frankly' to me, I knew they were lying. 'But why all the gloss? If Rune gets the wrong idea about Jack and his mates he could be in for some big surprises and potential fuck-ups.'

'Rune's guides know what to do. They could get a bunch of geriatrics to the Pole if they had to.'

'You've vetted them, have you?'

'Don't be awkward, Stone. Just take it from me, they'll know what they're doing. Let's deal with one thing at a time. Your job is to get Jack on board, then get him to the Pole. I'll worry about the rest.' He sighed, knowing I was almost pissed off enough to bin the whole idea. 'Look, sorry if I'm sounding impatient. Just want to make this work for Jack. I . . . I owe him that, I suppose, after all he's been through. What matters is getting him hooked up with Rune. Leave me out of it as much as you can. The more he gets a sniff that I'm behind it, the more likely he is to cut up rough. But the

42

truth is, he's never had an opportunity like this before. And it's about time he got his own way.'

Was that what Cauldwell really thought? I hoped so, for Jack's sake.

'OK.' I kept my voice low. 'But before I see him, and before you walk me into any more meetings where no one's expecting me, I'm going to need a proper briefing. The full three-sixty.'

Rune finished his call and Cauldwell got to his feet. 'I think that's plenty of information for now. Thank you for your time, Rune. We'll be seeing you very shortly.'

I shook hands with Rune as Cauldwell headed for the door. 'Mate, thanks for that – and can I take your number, in case I need some help?'

'But of course. No problem.' He scribbled it down on a ripped sheet of A4, then waited expectantly for me to return the favour.

'Thanks, Rune. Hope to see you soon.'

10

Back in the Merc, Cauldwell was like a coiled spring so I piled in first. 'If you want someone who doesn't ask questions when questions need to be asked, I'm the wrong man. Rune's clearly got no idea how fit they are.'

'So?'

'*Fighting* fit? Ready for the fray?'

He sighed. 'Look, if these people drop out like the last lot, Jack goes home with nothing and we'll never hear the last of it. He's set his heart on this. And so has his mother, more to the point. Your task is to make sure it all comes together.'

He stared off into the darkness. I was getting the message. Maybe I did have to give Cauldwell the benefit of the doubt. Maybe he really did have his son's best interests at heart.

'He always had this ridiculous idea in his head that he wanted to be an explorer. I blame David Attenborough. And I don't mind admitting I never thought he had it in him. No capacity for endurance

– none whatsoever. He's a good lad, but lacks self-direction. That's why I steered him towards the army – for his own good, so maybe he'd learn some of that. You know what I mean, don't you, Stone?'

Better than he realized. The army could make a man out of almost anyone, but Cauldwell was another matter: a hard bastard for anyone to please. Who'd want to be his son?

As if he'd decided to justify his position, he added, 'In any case, it seemed the natural thing to do.'

To him, maybe. 'And he went along with it?'

'Well . . . he came round in the end.'

And then some bits of him got left in Afghanistan. 'So you blame yourself for what happened next.'

He didn't like that, but I didn't care. If only for their sake, I needed to know as much as possible about what I was getting into. He reddened and his voice went up a few decibels. 'That's not what I'm saying at all. He was a bloody fool to have been where he was at that . . .'

He tailed off. Guilt mixed with anger made a toxic cocktail.

'Anyway, that's all in the past now. Water under the bridge.' He was trying to convince himself as much as me – and failing. 'What matters now is getting this show on the road.'

'So?'

He gave me one of his looks. 'So you're going to meet him – deliver the good news. Coming from you it'll . . . Well, there won't be any baggage, will there?'

'So I've just dropped into Svalbard like his guardian angel?'

'That's the ticket.' He gripped my shoulder. 'Use

your powers of persuasion. You've always had a reputation for getting what you want. I doubt you've lost your touch.'

His capacity for fitting the facts to his opinions never ceased to amaze me. I didn't count family mediation as one of my core skills at the best of times – and this wasn't the best of times by a very long shot. Never mind that he wanted me to mislead Jack about his involvement.

There was now more than a hint of desperation in his eye. He was running out of options. He'd offered me the job. I'd accepted it. So I decided I might as well give it a go.

'Where can I find him?'

'He's staying at the Miners' Refuge, the town's cheapest guesthouse. But you'll find him in the Spitsbergen Bar and Grill. Get down there and give him the facts of life.'

I got out. My breath clouded in front of me in the freezing night air. At least, it called itself night, even if it didn't look like it.

'Oh, and you'll need one of these.' He reached into the glove compartment and pulled out something silky that felt like a tie.

'The Spitsbergen Bar and Grill has a dress code?'

'Very funny, Stone.'

I opened it out: an eye mask.

'So you can get some sleep.'

And he was gone.

11

The Spitsbergen Bar and Grill turned out to be a slightly grander version of Rune's building, in the same flat-pack style – another job lot of Norwegian pine.

As I opened the inner door, a massive shout went up on the far side of the room. A giant TV screen was showing a football match to a group of about forty onlookers. Almost all of them were in the same sort of gear, padded dungarees with zips up the outside of the legs so they could be pulled on and off over boots. I made my way through a fug of sweat, smoke and alcohol so thick I could have sliced it up and had it for dinner with chips.

It was an international set, but more piston than jet. Tough-looking Africans, Asians and Chinese mixed with Scandinavians and, of course, Russians, all in chunky sweaters and fleeces, their heavy-duty work coats on a long row of hooks by the door or thrown over the backs of chairs.

Everyone had a beard. It helped with insulation and, anyway, shaving was a pain in these conditions. There were plenty of signs of cold injuries, hands trussed up in cotton wool, which made lifting a pint a two-fist job. Several had gel pads over their noses and foreheads where they'd caught the wind. They also had the resigned expressions of men who couldn't stop gathering wherever there was a fast buck to be made from dangerous manual labour without a safety net.

Maybe the Owl had been right: this was the twenty-first-century Klondike – oil prospectors, engineers, labourers who pumped the stuff out from under the permafrost or from the freezing oceans, all there in search of the pot of black gold at the end of the rainbow. In 1840s California it was the shovel-sellers who made the big bucks. Here in Svalbard, I didn't need the Owl to tell me it was the lawyers.

I skirted the TV audience – no clean faces there – and burrowed further into the crowd. The football sounds gave way to some forgettable Euro-rap, its pulsing beat almost impossible to distinguish from the hubbub.

A sign hanging above the optics boasted 'The Coolest Bar in the World – Literally!'. In front of it stood a droid in a leather waistcoat, with the drooping build of an off-form sumo wrestler. His solid, bald-headed presence seemed custom-built to deter bad behaviour when tempers frayed, as they always would in a place with too many men, too much alcohol and too little distraction. I hoped it worked, for his sake. He'd kicked the steroids, but looked as if anything more strenuous than lifting a bar-stool might bring on cardiac arrest.

A tall woman with bottle-blonde hair stood behind

the bar, prettier than the clientele deserved, and with an attitude that said they could look but not touch. I settled myself on a vacant stool, shoved my day sack down at my feet and ordered a Diet Coke. Men who didn't drink would have been rarer there than sun-loungers, but she served it without raising an eyebrow. I got a laugh when I asked her to repeat the price, though. No wonder the place was so full of piss-artists: the soft drinks cost way more than the beer.

Jack Cauldwell had changed dramatically since my last sight of him. Partly it was the hair: much thicker and wilder. He was still only in his twenties, but wore the look of someone much older. He wasn't alone in that – I'd seen it before on any number of once fresh faces, after a bit of shot and shell, facing a new set of battles back in so-called civilization. His skin had the colour and texture that too much alcohol or weather can beat into it, but it was hard to tell in that light which was to blame.

He was at a corner table with four bodies. One was mixed race, with a mass of dreadlocks tied at the back; his posture told me he was ex-services but hadn't seen the gym in a while. Another had a shaved scalp and was jiggling a little, not in time to the music, but from nerves or something chemical. The third seemed to enjoy being the centre of attention. Good-looking in an upmarket sort of way, head thrown back, pleased with himself. In fact, he seemed pretty much perfect until he adjusted himself in his chair to get closer to the woman beside him. His right sleeve was empty.

He draped his arm over her shoulders, asserting his right to the only female customer in the place. I didn't blame him. She had short, jet-black hair and, to add to the semi-Goth look, a nose piercing and a small silver ring in her left eyebrow. Their body language suggested they were an item. She sipped her drink and gazed up at him as he held forth.

I tried to picture this crew striding across the ice – and failed. If first impressions were anything to go by, Cauldwell was right: they looked like a bunch of no-hopers. No wonder the sponsors had fled. And no wonder he wanted someone able-bodied in the mix.

Yet they must have had something going for them or they wouldn't have got that far. I had nothing going for me except the need to get away from myself.

12

I planned to sit back and watch for a bit, get the measure of Jack and his mates as they made swift work of their beers, but he soon caught my eye. At first he gave me a hostile what-you-looking-at? glare. When I raised my glass he frowned, working hard to ID me, until the time-and-place part of his brain kicked in and threw him the answer.

He got up and wove through the crowd towards me, one hand on his left thigh. For a one-legged man he was doing all right. As he drew closer, though, I could see that his once shiny blue eyes were now clouded and tired. Age, experience and long-term pain had conspired to make him a lot more like his dad. Just as well he hadn't got anywhere near a shaving mirror in the last couple of days.

'Hey, Jack . . .' I added my name so as not to embarrass him if that part of his memory had taken a knock too.

'I remember you, Stone. Why wouldn't I?' The same

clipped tone as his old man. If he realized it was hostile, he didn't bother dialling it down. 'What the fuck are you doing here?'

'Just getting away for a bit.'

Technically true. But that wasn't how Jack saw it. His eyes narrowed, full of suspicion. 'Well, this is away, all right. About as away as you can get.'

He shook my hand and some of the Sandhurst pedigree showed through his weariness.

'What're you drinking, Jack?'

'I'm good, thanks.'

'Sure?'

'OK, a pint. Thanks.'

I aimed him at the nearest stool and gave the barmaid a wave. She smiled at him as if they were old friends. He seemed not to notice. Maybe the loss of his sponsors – which I wasn't meant to know about – had sucked up all his mental and emotional energy. A straight guy in those parts would have to be seriously distracted not to spend a moment or two checking out any female, let alone an attractive one.

'How long you been up here?'

He shrugged. 'Couple of weeks. You?'

The blonde set his pint in front of him and tried the smile again. She could have had the pick of the entire room. I wondered what he had that the rest of us didn't.

'Arrived this afternoon. Had some fun and games with the landing.'

He took a sip of beer.

I decided to take the plunge. 'I heard about your walk.'

He stiffened. 'From my old man?'

No way round that. 'Yeah.'

'You keep in touch, then?'

I rolled my eyes. 'You know what the Regiment's like.' I wasn't going to say 'a family'. That was bollocks, and he'd know it. 'So how's it going?'

Jack blew out a lungful of air between pursed lips. 'A few ups and downs.'

I admired his gift for understatement. 'Like what?'

'Well, let's see. Ten days ago the fucking sponsors pulled out.'

'Ah.' For the moment I'd pretend this was news to me.

'The old man was probably delighted. He thinks I can't find my own cock with the light on.'

I let it go. I'd already established that we had one thing in common: not being able to shake off his father. Now I caught a glimpse of what was driving him: the years of being a disappointment, of having his boyhood dreams rubbished, of giving in and dancing to the old man's tune until he'd had half a leg blown off.

'Are you in touch?'

He snorted. 'We don't talk. I realized some things after . . .' He paused. 'You get to spend a *lot* of time thinking when you're on your back in a hospital bed. Too fucking much.' He necked half his drink. 'I promised myself that when I got mobile again I was going to put some clear blue water between my father and me. Switch off the comms, pull up the drawbridge. Go my own way. He didn't like it, of course. He can't stop trying to plan my whole fucking life.'

He took another huge swig. 'Me getting blown up

hasn't changed much . . .' His laugh was more of a bark – dry and full of self-loathing.

'He must have taken it badly.'

Wrong move.

'Oh, fuck, yeah. He "took it badly" all right. He was even angrier and more disappointed than he had been about all my other failures. It was like he thought I'd jumped up and down on that fucking IED just to spite him – to punish him for pushing me into the army in the first place.'

I must have looked sceptical because he went up a gear.

'It was all about *him*. Always. He didn't care about *me*. Everything was about how it reflected on *him*.'

His voice was cold, measured, but his eyes blazed with the anger simmering beneath. Not so much no love lost between them as no love there to lose. Suddenly the emptiness in his face solidified into bitterness and self-pity.

'Christ knows he talked enough about the Regiment, like *you* were his fucking family. Well, it may surprise you to hear that he's never been any sort of fucking father figure to *me*.'

I let him run on until he'd burned off some of the excess resentment and I could shift the focus back to the expedition – not easy, bearing in mind that it wasn't going to happen without the old man.

If I had any chance of making this work I needed to get Jack to trust me. I certainly wasn't going to contradict him. In the circumstances, I figured the less I said the better.

'So if you're here with some kind of olive branch

from the old bastard, you know where you can stick it.'

I thought he was going to fuck off, right there and then. But he stayed where he was.

'You got kids?'

He'd opened a door, whether or not he meant to, and I walked through it.

13

'I'm sure you've got a million reasons to hate your father. And you know what? I don't blame you. Parents fuck you up. Mine did. Then my stepdad did too.'

I thought I'd buried all that shit long ago. I was wrong. Just thinking about it, I felt the ache sweep through me like a toxin. At least physical wounds healed . . . I mentally gripped myself. I wasn't about to turn this into a joint therapy session, with me talking about my loss and him talking about his. I just needed to seize the chance to establish some common ground while it was there. 'Look, I never got to find out what sort of dad I might be, but I do know that every parent makes mistakes. Not just yours.'

'*Mistakes?* That's the fucking understatement of the century.'

'But he's not evil. He wants to do right by you. He's got some new sponsors lined up and—'

'I knew it. You—'

'Listen, he asked me to make you an offer. He knows

you won't take it from him. And it's not just about cash. Some good may come out of this at the same time. Fuck who's doing the giving, or why. It's a way for you and your mates to crack on.'

He wasn't remotely interested in what that good work might be. He wasn't even listening. 'So you *are* his messenger boy.'

'If you like. But if you throw all this back in his face, it'd be a great big shame. It's a means to the Pole. To your goal. You going to chuck everything away simply because he's the middleman? Don't pass up this opportunity. Just fucking grab it, Jack. Life is short. Trust me on this.'

He raised his glass again, fighting to control himself. He was getting so angry that if he'd been a cartoon he'd have had fizzy lines coming out of his head.

'Look, Jack, I'm not here to sort out your family problems. And, to tell you the truth, I don't care if you go to the Pole or freeze to death in the fucking car park.'

'All right, all right.' He held up his free hand. 'But to be very, very clear, I do not want any help, any money, any anything from him. Done.'

I shrugged. 'OK. I'll tell him.'

'Thanks, Nick.' His beer hand started to shake. The rim of his glass missed his mouth and collided with his cheek. It wasn't just his old man that had sparked him up. 'I'm . . . I'm s-sorry . . . for kicking off at you, but . . .'

'Mate, no problem.' I downed half my Coke to give us both a break. 'So what happened with your sponsors? Why did they drop out?'

For the first time since he'd come over to see me, he couldn't look me in the eye.

'Why don't you go the public route, do some kind of charity thing – you know, save the planet? Get sponsorship from a bank or one of the corporates. Get your faces in the papers, raising awareness, cash, that sort of thing.'

'No.'

I got the message. It wasn't happening.

'We all decided we're doing this for *us*, Nick, on our own terms. We're not performing monkeys. No hedge fund is going to be able to throw their petty cash our way so they can make themselves look good. Fuck corporate-responsibility funds. No pictures, no publicity, just us, and what we keep in here.' He tapped the side of his head, then the left side of his chest. 'And here.' He glanced across at his team. 'Whatever, you and I both know this bunch are never going be the stars of anyone's corporate PR video.'

So they'd all fallen for the world's biggest lie. For thousands of years the head-shed had fed their troops on a diet of righteousness, courage, rising to the challenge, all that bollocks that we were all so keen to believe. But once in the fight, we soon discovered that we didn't rise like the legendary warriors of the past: we sank into a dark, lonely place where we'd do almost anything just to stay alive. Like all the poor fuckers that came before them, those lads thought they were worthless because of that big fat lie. The big fat lie that would live longer than they did. A fuck of a lot longer. It would still be spreading its poison in a thousand years' time. The next generation in the fight would look at Jack and his mates and see the heroes they'd been told to be. And the next. And the next. How could any of them measure up?

That was what warrior bullshit did. It made good people think they were worthless. I knew: I'd fallen for it long ago. I also knew I didn't want this lot to keep making that mistake. I wanted them to discover that they were no different from anyone else who'd been in the fight.

14

'Fuck the old man, I don't need his help. I've got it in hand. We're going to get there.'

He had a couple of goes at getting his glass back on the bar top. It didn't improve his mood.

'Does he really think I'm going to give up, get a fucking blanket out of the car, wait for him to come along and save the day? Fuck him.'

Another man joined the group at the table. A few years older than the others, he moved carefully, deliberately, as if his vision was letting him down. When he turned, I saw that his face was shiny down one side. It had the all too familiar snail-trail pattern and drooping eyelid of someone who'd got too close to an inferno.

Not far behind him came a feisty-looking red-headed woman in a white roll-neck sweater. Her hair was a riot of thick curls, the kind that made their owner look like some kind of Celtic warrior. She told the others to make room for the new arrival, and they did.

'Why did they pull out, Jack?'

'Healthandfuckingsafety. Jobsworths who came up with a list of "issues and considerations". That's the whole point of the walk – to *overcome* the issues, to give two fingers to the considerations.

'They bundled us along to the Institute of Naval Medicine to get tested, all that shit, to cover their arses. We did all right – well, most of us did, except on the fucking stupid psych stuff.' He pointed at the one with the dreadlocks. 'Rio's still on meds. He's got nothing happening in one arm, and other . . . stuff he's dealing with.'

From where I was standing, they looked like they all were.

'But he's *positive*, you know? Optimistic. He saw the Taliban skin one of his mates alive, for fuck's sake. He does have some issues, but he knew when to play the race card, and they waved him through – grudgingly. They didn't have much choice.'

He pointed at the one with the shaved head. 'Gabriel's lost his leg below the knee, and has a bit of a short fuse. But then, he does come from Glasgow. They said he was "temperamentally unsuited to functioning in a team".'

I couldn't help smiling. I'd been there, got the T-shirt. And not just the one. A big drawer full of them.

'Will over there,' he pointed to the new arrival with the snail-trail face, 'they didn't have a problem with *him*. His Puma was on VHR night duty, and taken down by the Taliban. They dragged him out of the burning cockpit and held him for a few weeks. But he knows how to win over those smartarse types because he sounds like they do.'

I nearly said, *So do you*. Instead, 'But you're OK, right? They didn't have a problem with you?'

'No, but it's all of us or none. That's what being a team *means*. Stupid fuckwits didn't get that.'

'And the other two lovebirds?'

'That's Leila. She's not part of it. Stedman picked her up in Ukraine or somewhere – I think she's just along for the ride. Who knows what he gets up to?'

Who indeed? I glanced across to see Stedman lifting his good arm from Leila's shoulders so he could give some extra muscle to the punchline of a joke he was telling. But he didn't take it away for long. Fuck knew why. There was nowhere else for her to go.

I scanned Stedman's audience. They seemed pretty cheerful for a bunch of people who'd just had the financial rug pulled out from under their feet. Only Will's partner, the red-headed woman, wasn't laughing.

I nodded in her direction. 'What's her role in all this?'

'Jules? She's Will's wife and doesn't have one on the ice. She'll wait here for Will. She's a doctor – used to be with Médecins Sans Frontières, in Afghanistan and Syria. She knows all there is to know about stumps and prosthetics. You name it, she's chopped it off. Or stuck it back on.'

'Handy.'

'Yeah. Or maybe not.'

I waited.

'Well, I've a feeling it was down to her that they failed Stedman. He had a bit of a habit.' Jack pressed a finger to one nostril and sniffed, in case I wasn't fully on receive.

'Had?'

'All right, has.' He bit his upper lip. 'He's not too discreet about it, and I reckon she let them know. I thought I might have to drop him in order to hang onto the sponsors. Then the fuckers pulled the plug anyway.'

'That's tough.'

'She's here because she invited herself, keeping an eye on Will, giving us the benefit of her wisdom, medical and otherwise. Whether we want it or not.'

He let out a long sigh. Saying it all out loud had probably made the situation feel worse, not better. 'And now we're in danger of losing our window.'

15

Now he'd given me chapter and verse on how fucked up everything was, the light came back into his eyes. Either he was a total fantasist, or there was still a chance the trip was greenlit.

'You heard of Barneo? It's the start line. The Russians build an airstrip on the eighty-ninth degree. Literally. It's only there for April because the ice thins out and melts. Miss that window and we really are fucked. The floe has already snapped once. Global warming . . .'

His brow creased. 'We've got to face facts. If we don't make it this year, it's probably never going to happen. The Norwegians are majorly pissed off with the Russian military build-up. They stopped all flights up there for a couple of days last week, after a para division jumped into Barneo.

'There's a strong possibility that there won't be anything taking off from here next year. So we'd get fucked about by the Russians, screwing us for visas to go via some remote airstrip in the Motherland. Or they could close down Barneo altogether for people like us. They've already said they're setting up camp this year primarily for military and science purposes.'

I knew that the 89th degree, commonly known as the 'last degree', was about sixty nautical miles – or sixty-nine regular ones – from the geographic North Pole. But that was as the crow flew. This lot would have to tab further because of the terrain. They'd have to negotiate their way over or around pressure ridges, and open leads – ice fractures exposing the water – and the shifting sea ice that always headed south. It wouldn't be any fun if it went in the direction you were going, would it?

And to make things even more confusing, there were four poles, not just one. The magnetic North Pole was where all compasses pointed to, but it wasn't, in fact, the top of the world. The Arctic Pole was the point in the Arctic Ocean furthest from land. The geo-magnetic North Pole was the one I couldn't be arsed to find out about, but I knew it had something to do with positive and negative fields between the North and South Poles. Then there was True North: Jack's target, the geographic North Pole. Put your finger on top of the world and you'd be touching it.

I glanced back at the table. More jokes. More laughter. I could tell from his body language that Stedman was everything Jack wasn't. He was the loud one, the centre of attention – the one who, if Cauldwell was right, had spurred Jack into pursuing the dream. He was what control freaks hate most: a challenge to their authority.

Jack dredged up a grin. 'Bit of a reunion.'

'Reunion?'

'Well, Stedman's back in.'

'What changed?'

'He's the one who's going to get us moving.' Jack reached for his glass again. 'Like I said, I've got things in hand. I don't need my old man.'

'Stedman's going to get you moving? How?'

The question came out a bit too fast. He turned wary again, and I made a mental note to dial down.

'Because he can.'

I left my next question hanging, unspoken, in the alcoholic haze between us.

He was showing a bit of steel now. 'Let's just say we're back in the game.'

Jack was smarter – and tougher – than his old man realized. Cauldwell's plan had crashed and burned. And the man he most despised appeared to have come to the rescue.

16

My sat phone was vibrating. It was tucked away inside my thermals, along with the passport hanging around my neck and the roll of USD I always kept within reach to buy or bribe my way out of the shit. I didn't need to fish it out and look at the screen: only Cauldwell had the number.

Jack picked up a fresh pint, drained it, and set it back down. Then he slid off his stool. 'I need to piss. See you around, Nick. Thanks for the drink. You can tell the old man when you see him that he can stay out of my life. I'm standing on my own two feet.'

He smirked at the well-worn gag, then turned to disappear into the smoky darkness.

'Good luck, Jack.'

There was nothing else to say.

The match on the TV was over and the audience was surging back towards the bar. I grabbed my day sack and headed into the half-chilled chamber between the inner and outer doors to get at least two bars on my sat phone.

Cauldwell answered before the third ring.

'He's got some new funding, from another source.'

'What? Where from? Who, for Chrissake?'

'Wouldn't say.'

'Well, that's out of the bloody question,' he spluttered. 'The boy's an idiot. Didn't you tell him about Rune? What have you been doing all this time? Playing with yourself?'

I wasn't going to rise to that. The outer doors opened, blasting me with the Arctic night, and a man in a greasy parka barged past.

'He's not an idiot. And he's your son. His first question was about you.'

'And?'

'It's something to do with one of the team. Stedman. He's back on board.'

'*What?*'

'The new source of funding. But I don't know any more than that.'

Cauldwell exploded. '*No – no way!* For fuck's sake. The man's a junkie and a crook. He should be in prison!'

Typical Cauldwell, always ready to condemn.

'This is a complete and utter disaster. They have *got* to go with Rune. You have to make it happen. If they don't, I'll personally see to it that—'

'That what, exactly? We're not in the fucking army now.'

There was a pause while the news sank in.

'I'm very disappointed in you, Stone. You've lost your touch. What's the matter with you? He's not going with anyone else. End of.'

I was about to tell him to fuck off when I realized he'd hung up.

17

I shoved the sat phone away and got ready to leave. As I zipped and hooded up, I turned towards the inner doors to give the team one more look through the squares of glass and to wish them good luck. But I never got to wish anything. The greasy-parka man who had burst in while I was on the phone was looming over Jack's table and certainly not offering to buy a round. They looked like they were doing their best to ignore him.

I pushed my way back through. The volume of the sound system had dropped a couple of decibels. Maybe the staff thought it would calm the punters down. Whatever, it wasn't working. I was too far away to pick up more than the odd word, but I could tell from the rhythms of his speech he was speaking Russian. I could also tell that he was far from happy – and not just because Russians always sounded angry.

He had long, matted black hair, scraped back in a ponytail, and a thick gold ring in his left ear. A dirty-gloved forefinger stabbed the air in front of Stedman's nose and globules of spit caught the light as he shouted into his face. He switched his attack to Leila, who wasn't flapping as much as I would have expected.

Stedman continued to ignore him, which wound him up further. The football fans had filled the space between the bar and the tables and a few were starting to take an interest in the new excitement. His finger stabbing went a bit too far and connected with Leila's shoulder. She reeled back and looked furiously at Stedman, but it was Will with the burn-scarred face who got to his feet.

Jules grabbed his arm and tried to pull him down, but he shook her off. Jack was nowhere to be seen.

The crowd between me and the table was about five deep. Then it parted and I caught a glimpse of something dull and metallic in Ponytail's right hand.

The droid in the leather waistcoat was already out from behind the bar and wading towards them with surprising speed but he still had some way to go. Gabriel was on his feet as well, and Rio with the dreads was about to hit his own personal launch pad.

I dropped my day sack so both my hands were free as the droid aimed for the shrinking space between Ponytail and Jack's crew. I reached down into the dark, a few inches above the blade. Rather than making a show of bringing the Russian's arm up and bending it back for the enjoyment of the growing audience, and probably starting the Third World War, I kept mine straight, elbow locked, gripped his wrist and pressed a thumbnail deep into his flesh.

He turned in surprise and enveloped me in a cloud of weapons-grade vodka and sauerkraut. It catapulted me straight back to Moscow and everything that went with it, like someone putting on the wrong CD. But instead of taking my eye off the ball, I drilled that bit harder.

I heard the knife clatter to the floor, but kept on going as I moved my face closer to his. 'Nice and peaceful. *Staryye druz'ya.*'

He gritted his teeth, but his dentistry still allowed a fair amount of spit to dribble out between them.

It was over in less than a minute. The droid took his other arm and we escorted him to the door. He went quietly, but the look on his face said he wouldn't forget me. And not in a good way.

18

I came back towards the table and picked up the ugly little weapon Ponytail had so carelessly dropped before deciding to leave. Its blade wasn't much bigger than a Stanley knife's, designed to slip easily into a pocket and slice through electrical cables and whatever else got in its way.

I turned my attention to Jack's crew. Even if they'd all been sober they were in no condition to defend themselves with any degree of efficiency, but I didn't need to tell them that.

Gabriel spoke first: 'Where did you learn to handle yourself like that? Basra?' It was broad Jock.

'Nah. Bermondsey.'

They all laughed and I was one of the gang. Will waved me towards a chair.

Leila managed a grateful smile, but it was a struggle. She wasn't amused by Stedman's under-performance. Worse, she was flapping.

Stedman was ignoring us both, trying to listen to

something on his phone. Then Jack appeared, and glared at me. Will came to the rescue. 'Hey, Jack, your mate's a bit handy – why didn't you introduce us?'

He was still giving me the evil eye. The droid shuffled by and gave me a big squeeze on the shoulder, pleased to have order restored. Will pulled Jack down and gave him a rapid update on what he had missed.

Jules beamed her gratitude, presumably for preventing her husband from getting kicked to shit. Then she looked anxiously at Leila, the only one who could enlighten them about the substance of Ponytail's rant. 'So, what was all that about?'

Leila waved at Jules as if she was wafting away a bad smell, but that didn't do it for Will. He seemed much more bothered by the fact that his partner was being dismissed. My guess was that he was a bit of a Boy Scout, who stood up when ungentlemanly behaviour was in sight.

'He don't like to see fellow Ukrainian sitting with foreigners.' She gave a what-can-you-do? shrug. 'He's very drunk.'

Will and Jules seemed convinced by that because they were drunk themselves. I wasn't. My Russian was only one grade above shite but among the words I had picked out from the tirade were *protsent*, meaning percentage, and *konkurentsiya*, competition. Sure, the guy could have been asking where he could get the most kroner for his roubles but, if so, he was taking the exchange rate a bit personally.

Jack was still staring at me, mystified. Maybe he was wondering if this was all part of some scheme of his old man's. He also didn't seem too pleased about his mates welcoming me, but right now there was nothing he could do about it. And since I'd gained entry I decided I might as well stick around and find out where Stedman had got the finance for the trip.

While he was still busy tapping away one-handed at shit on his phone, I watched Leila. Ponytail had spooked her, all right, and her expression suggested that she knew full well what he'd been on about, but when I gave her a questioning look she pretended not to understand.

Eventually Stedman got tired of trying to complete his download and turned to her, giving me an appreciative wink on the way. 'Anything I need to know?'

Leila shook her head.

'Good show.'

He sounded a bit of a Hooray: no end of confidence, not much curiosity – a lethal combination I'd experienced from too many Ruperts down the years. It was a great defence mechanism, enabling them to sail along oblivious to all the shit kicking off around them. Half of me admired it; the other half went ballistic.

He treated me to the world's biggest grin. 'Nice work.'

I put out my left hand in deference to the lack of his right. 'Nick.'

'Stedman. I know, a surname. I've been saddled with it since prep school.'

We shook.

'Ready for the big walk?'

He leaned across the table as if he was about to whisper something, but his volume was turned up high enough for everyone to hear. He jabbed a finger in Jack's direction. 'That one-legged fucker tried to get rid of me. Didn't think I'd cut it – did you?'

His eyes were a touch watery. He was just as pissed as the rest of them, but his extreme indignation was only partly fuelled by alcohol. From where I sat, their once brotherly bond had mutated into a barely repressed rivalry – potentially lethal in a situation where survival would depend on absolute trust and cooperation. I reckoned a pat on the back from Stedman would be a recce for a stabbing.

'You need me now, don't you, Jack? In fact, you can't take a step without me, can you? Two legs, mate! I'm indi-fucking-spensable.'

Jack laughed along, though his brow stayed furrowed. The others were clearly enjoying his discomfort and Stedman was soaking up the attention.

'Wrote me off as a fucking junkie.'

It prompted Jack to wave a finger in protest. 'I never said that.'

'Didn't need to, did you? It was written all over your arsy face.'

Jack groaned and rolled his eyes but let him have his moment.

'So! When do we start?' Stedman was on a roll.

Jack raised both hands, palms upwards. 'Soon as you get the cash. There's a lot of kit we still need to source. And a lot of fuel we need to burn.'

Stedman instantly recovered from his rejection and slapped the table. 'Twenty-four hours, max. No problem. Just leave everything to me.'

Gabriel inserted himself into the exchange, glancing

from Stedman to Jack, then back to Stedman. 'Thought you said it was a done deal.'

Stedman smoothed the air with one flattened hand and rubbed some of the moisture out of his half-pissed eyes. 'Like I said, this time tomorrow. OK?' He patted his breast pocket.

I concentrated on something in the middle distance, willing Gabriel to keep probing.

Stedman stretched himself out in his seat and grinned at Leila, who now smiled back adoringly, as if he was the man who could make everything in her life perfect.

'O-kaay.' Gabriel was not totally satisfied with the answer. He just wanted to get stuck into the trip.

Stedman raised his glass. 'Here's to you.' He emptied what was left in it down his throat. Then he turned back to Leila and planted a fat kiss on her lips.

She blushed. All this time her eyes had been scanning the bar, as if she was expecting Ponytail to reappear, with backup.

'My round.' There was some resistance to this as their residual gratitude bubbled up, but I had a reason to return to the bar.

19

The barmaid stepped towards me and looked surprised when I turned to the droid instead. I gave him my order and nodded at the door where we had deposited our friend Ponytail. 'That guy a regular?'

He shrugged wearily. 'I see him before maybe.'

Not much of an answer.

'How often?'

He jerked a thumb towards Jack's crew. 'Tell your friends to be careful.'

'Of what, exactly?'

'His people you don't want to have problem with.'

'Who are they?'

'From the mine in Barentsburg. They come from Russia, Ukraine. Stay through the summer.' Clearly he was counting the days till winter.

'Good for business, though?'

He snorted. 'For how long who knows? Mines are fucked. Coal nobody wants.' He made a slashing movement with his hand. Then he gripped the edge of the bar and leaned towards me. 'Your friends at the table are nice people. But foolish, eh? They shouldn't be here. They don't want to have problem with his kind. It goes best here when people do their job, then go home.'

Before I could cram in another question he dropped my change into my palm and shuffled off to another customer. I went back to the table.

Stedman jabbed a finger towards me, still speaking to Jack. 'So where does he fit in?'

'I don't. I'm just passing through.'

'Who passes through this arsehole of a place? There's nowhere else to go.'

'I know that now I'm here.'

'So when are you flying out?' Jack's question sounded like an order, or an attempt at one.

'Not sure yet.'

'And where are you getting your head down?' His question suggested that, wherever it was, he was looking forward to me getting out of his way.

'The Radisson.'

'Same as them.' He indicated Stedman and Leila. 'All right for some.'

Leila got up and stared very directly at Stedman. 'I want to go now.'

He didn't react.

'I'm very tired. It's been a long day.'

Stedman pursed his lips. 'You know the way.'

She gave him a venomous look. Evidently she hadn't planned on finding her own way to the hotel, especially after what had just happened.

He rolled his eyes. 'Can't you see? I'm busy here.'

It was obvious that Jack had had his fill of me. Which made it my cue to leave. 'I'll walk you back.'

Leila smiled. Stedman seemed relieved. So did Jack, I guessed for different reasons.

As I got to my feet I offered him my hand and he took it. 'Nick, sorry for getting pissed off at you. It's just the old man – you know.'

We separated and I put on my duvet jacket, zipped up my day sack and threw it over one shoulder.

'And thanks for what you did earlier. Appreciate it.'

I waved away the gratitude and nodded at the others. 'Good luck.'

Leila had also gathered her stuff and we turned for the door. Jack held out his hand once more and we repeated the performance.

There was a thump as Gabriel slammed his half-leg down on the table. His carbon-fibre foot kept his new calf upright as he and Rio started to pour their beers into Gabriel's new drinking jug.

'Good to see you again, Jack. I hope your plans work out.' I meant what I said. He deserved a break. They all did.

We left as Gabriel began sharing the contents of his new beer jug with Rio.

20

It wasn't far – we probably had fifteen minutes to fill en route. Maybe she wasn't the chatty type. I'd find out soon enough.

I pushed open the outer door and we were assaulted by air that was even colder than when I'd landed. 'So Stedman's saved the day.'

She grimaced. 'I guess so.'

'You don't think he'll get the money tomorrow?'

She shook her head. 'Oh, no, not at all. He will.'

'You're worried they won't make it?'

She laughed at the very idea. 'Nothing gets in Stedman's way. He needs challenge like dog needs bone.'

'Why aren't you going to be part of it? It would be a once-in-a-lifetime trip.'

She chortled, like it was the craziest thing she'd ever heard. She was loosening up a bit. 'No way. I go back to London as soon as they leave.'

The wind knifed into us.

'So how did you two meet?'

She smiled. I braced myself for the love story of the century.

'He came to Kiev to close a contract to supply not guns, but kit – body armour, NV goggles. He hired me as interpreter.'

'You've always done that, interpreting?'

She flared her studded nostrils. 'Why not? I am bilingual. I have master's in linguistics from Kiev University.'

Prickly.

'People like you are the reason us Brits are so crap at languages.' The charm offensive wasn't doing it, but I didn't let that stop me. 'And now you're based in London?'

She cheered up. 'London is most wonderful city in the world.'

London: safe haven for the best and brightest in flight from all the world's black spots. Ukraine had recently joined the list. Their loss, our gain.

'The ponytail guy in the bar – he's from Ukraine too? Someone you know?'

'Why would I?' Now she was angry and embarrassed.

Realizing I could tell she was lying, she glanced over her shoulder to check out the street.

'So tell me then. What was the rant about?'

She didn't answer.

'You know "rant"? Angry speech, outburst . . .'

'It was nothing. Just some idiot.'

'He was upset at seeing a Ukrainian beauty sitting with decadent Westerners?'

'I said it was nothing.'

'People don't get knives out for nothing.'

'How should I know?' Her voice went up an octave. 'He was drunk. Who cares?'

'So, nothing to do with money, then. Or percentages. Or competition.'

She peered at me from inside her hood. I could see her thinking: *How much did this guy hear or understand?* 'What are you? A fucking spy?'

'I'm just watching Jack's back.'

She was very agitated now. I was on to something.

'Was it about you, or something to do with Stedman?'

She stopped suddenly and pushed her face so close to mine that I could see the indentations of her nose jewel. 'Who are you? Nobody! You should keep out of other people's fucking businesses.' Her eyes flashed and her face froze and her expression became unreadable. 'I am going to hotel now. Good night.'

She turned a corner.

'Leila . . .'

Nothing.

'Leila?'

'Yes?' Her voice carried back to me through the darkness.

'The hotel's the other way.'

21

My room was hot and stank of stale, recycled air. I shook off my coat and boots and made myself a brew. The sachet of instant coffee might have been left behind by one of the first polar explorers – what had once been granules fell out of the wrapper like a solid lump of toffee.

There was no point in talking to Cauldwell or Jack again. They were big enough and ugly enough to sort themselves out.

I lay down and shut my eyes. Big mistake. I couldn't stop Anna and Nicholai crowding in on me. I opened them, and they were still there. Sleep was off the agenda. Staying awake and doing stuff was the only way I could sometimes keep them at bay.

I was still numb about their death. If I'd described what I was going through to anyone, which I hadn't, I'd have said my brain had flipped a switch inside me in an attempt to put my whole system on standby, and pushed whatever I should be feeling into somewhere safe until I could find the strength to take it out and deal with it.

I'd lost friends before, loved ones, too. Was it possible that there had been so many of them that I'd become immune to grief?

I hadn't gone to see Anna's body in the hospital, or Nicholai's, and I hadn't stood at their gravesides. Maybe I should have. My mantra had always been *Why worry about what you can't change?* For the first time ever, it wasn't doing its job. Some days, I was rooted in the shallows, unable to move, being knocked back repeatedly by a series of massive waves and left breathless and disoriented. Others, my head was just above water, but the undertow could drag me down at any moment. Mostly the waves were up to my waist and it took all my strength simply to walk through them.

I wrenched myself back to the real world. Maybe it wasn't a 'fuck it' after all. Jack could be facing a bit of drama, as well as the others. Stedman didn't add up, and Ponytail's appearance only reinforced the feeling.

Whatever Leila was doing with Stedman in Svalbard *had* to be connected with Ponytail and his *protsent* – or someone else's. And he hadn't run across her by chance: he'd barged into the place and made a beeline for her. What was their history? Maybe there wasn't one. Maybe he was just pissed off with Stedman, and language was all they had in common. That made some kind of sense. Perhaps she really was along for the ride.

But, fuck it, so what? If Stedman took delivery of the funding tomorrow, they'd all get to go on the trip. Only Cauldwell would be pissed off, which wasn't a bad thing.

I turned over and pulled the blankets almost over my head, trying to persuade myself that I'd drift off to sleep and wake up in the morning without being assaulted by any uncomfortable thoughts or dreams or nightmares.

Of course it wasn't happening. I lay on my side, staring at the chrome doorknob to the bathroom, thinking about Jack and his dad and how fucked up they were. But no matter how fucked up Cauldwell appeared to his son, at least he still had a son to worry about, even if he displayed his concern in such a dysfunctional way. Who knew? Maybe I would have gone the same route.

Sleep stayed beyond my reach. I wasn't sure I wanted it. I got up, emptied another solid block of ancient Nescafé into the used mug, put the kettle on, munched the two complimentary ginger nuts as I waited for it to boil, and asked myself a question I'd spent a lifetime trying to avoid: what next?

Cauldwell was pissed off that Rune wasn't going, and even more pissed off that Stedman was – but again, so what? He'd still want to make sure his son came back alive, even if it was only so he could say, 'I told you so.' Tough. Jack wasn't going to allow that.

Steam billowed out of the spout and I spent a couple of minutes prodding the block of instant, a mini-iceberg in the mug, encouraging it to dissolve.

Maybe I was taking too long to get this brew drinkable. Maybe I was trying to give myself a different reason for wanting to make sure Jack would be OK, and that the trip would happen without anyone getting on the wrong end of a Ukrainian cable-cutter. As I sat down on a chair that was pretending to be leather, at a table that was pretending to be wood, I tried to be honest with myself.

Was I trying to fill a void? Was I jumping through Cauldwell's hoops because Jack was his son and I no longer had one?

I wasn't there for the money. I had half a million USD sitting in a Zürich bank account. Millions had fallen into my lap over the last couple of years; it had had nowhere else to go because its previous owner was dead. I'd tried to put the whole lot in trust for Nicholai when I'd split from Anna, but she'd insisted I keep a few quid for myself. Luckily, I'd let her win – the Swiss lawyers said the trust would take years to unravel.

Was I there because Anna wouldn't have wanted me to curl up on the floor and sob into the carpet? If I was to get through this, I had to keep moving. It had to be better to move away from the shit in my head instead of towards it, right?

One thing I did know: I was never going to do drugs or alcohol to avoid it. Avoiding sleep seemed to help. Every time I closed my eyes, I had the same nightmare. I woke up in the morning and my face was wet.

Maybe I'd thrown myself into the land of the midnight sun because sleep there was almost an extreme sport. People who lived in the High North experienced extremes of light and darkness, summer and winter, which produced winners and losers. I told myself that if I could stay awake, I'd be a winner.

So, yeah, that was it.

Maybe.

Keep myself awake and I'd be bombproof.

In truth, all I knew was that thinking about it made me more tired than I'd ever been in my life. Made my eyelids so heavy that I couldn't stop them drooping, and if I wasn't careful, I'd fall into the darkness.

22

I jerked awake, still in the fake leather chair, covered with sweat.

I opened my laptop. I had to do something – *anything* – to snap myself out of it.

Stedman and Jack had developed quite a bond in rehab. Lads with their kind of challenges tended to huddle together and get quite tribal, especially when the rest of the world hadn't a clue how to deal with them. But Jack had dropped Stedman from the expedition. A habit was a pretty basic no-no, and in Stedman's situation it often went with drug dependence, if you didn't get a mental grip. But now his disqualification had been forgotten because he'd found a suitcase full of cash. Had he done it in Ukraine? And did it come with one of those devices that would blow up in Jack's face when he opened it?

Stedman's online presence was next to zero. No Facebook, Twitter or Instagram, which didn't go with his extrovert persona and taste for being at the centre of things. There was no address or registered company listing either. In this day and age that really was being invisible. The only rational explanation was that his profile had been given a good wipe-down by someone who knew what they were doing. So what had made him want to keep his head down?

I tried browsing images. There was the inevitable avalanche of Stedmans from around the world, posing golf club in hand. I was about to bin it in when something caught my eye – a big colour photo of a City type looking serious outside Snaresbrook Crown Court. And beside him, there was Stedman, in full uniform, shaved and groomed, every inch the upright British officer. I hit the link to the *Mail Online*. He'd gone to all that trouble to delete himself, only to end up appearing high on the home page of a tabloid. The Invisible Man had emerged from the shadows into the spotlight. Why?

'*Wounded Hero Stands Up for Accused Brother,*' said the headline. It went on: *Disgraced City trader Christopher Stedman leaves court with decorated war-hero brother Adam . . .*

I read on: *At the trial, Adam Stedman, who lost an arm in Afghanistan, spoke of his younger brother's devoted care for their mother, who died of liver cancer earlier this year . . .*

There he was beside his brother, face to camera, all his medals on display, the empty right sleeve of his tunic folded and pinned. A subtler move would have been to tuck it into his side pocket. But that wouldn't have screamed 'War Hero' as loudly.

Stedman obviously guarded his privacy vigilantly. Stepping into the media glare like that would have been a very big deal. An act of brotherly love and solidarity? I scanned the rest of the story. Christopher, a derivatives trader, had been fucking about playing Masters of the Universe with his fellow traders. He'd narrowly escaped doing time, but the fat fine for his part in the scam meant he wouldn't be going to lunch by helicopter in the near future. Having to pay his own costs should have cleaned him out altogether. Whoever was now bankrolling the expedition, it surely couldn't be him.

I was still awake, so before I wrote off Stedman's brother as the money connection, I searched some more. The trial didn't seem to have dented his lifestyle – he was splashed all over the gossip pages: glitzy parties, gallery openings, racing events and weddings, each time with a different date on his arm. Even his Thameside penthouse was available to view in the 'How to Spend It' section of the *FT*, with a lavish spread featuring a bath supposedly carved out of a lump of rock crystal – and all after the court case. So who was picking up the tab for the disgraced trader's lifestyle now?

I decided to take a closer look at whom he was partying with. Most of them seemed to be over- or under-dressed women. There were eight images of him splashed across *Tatler Online*, usually centre stage, with a babe on each arm – models, heiresses, whatever. There was a handful of posh boys in the frame too, none of whom looked like he'd done a decent day's work in his life. From the helpful captions I made a list and checked them out one by one. Ninety minutes later I had a pretty comprehensive map of his social world.

The common denominator was inherited wealth, much of it probably kept offshore. Not one of them was self-made. Several from the Gulf States, either late teens or twenties, who shipped their blinged-up cars to London for the summer, stayed at the Dorchester, where they could see the motor from their suite, hung out in members' clubs charging a grand for a bottle of Krug, and staggered out at five a.m. to roar up and down the King's Road, winding up the local residents.

The others were mainly Russian expats, sons of oligarchs who had taken flight from Mr Putin. This was very elevated company to hang out and keep up with. They didn't seem the sort who'd organize a whip-round to keep young Christopher in crystal baths.

One who appeared very frequently at Stedman Junior's side was Uri Arkov, a baby-faced twenty-five-year-old. His old man had decamped from Moscow to Cyprus ten years ago, from where he ran an air-freight operation. Among other things, they offered an exclusive door-to-door VIP service promising, for a mere thirty thousand dollars, to deliver your favourite vehicle from your home garage – be it in Dubai, Ibiza or Shanghai – to the London hotel of your choice. A nice gig, if flying motors around the world was your thing. But what caught my attention was the name: Skyship.

I'd seen it on a cargo plane parked up at Longyearbyen airport. They had a forty-strong fleet, so it wasn't such a coincidence. But I hadn't seen any Lamborghini Aventadors doing doughnuts on the permafrost. What else did Skyship carry? Apart from the car thing, the rest of their cargo was listed as 'general freight'.

I finally decided to get my head down. I shut the

laptop, killed the light and got undressed. The room was still too bright. As I reached for the eye mask, I caught sight of something small and flat in the thin strip of light beneath the door.

It didn't say a lot: *6 a.m. Blue VW Transporter. Car park. Jules.*

23

The VW nine-seater's lights were off but a plume of exhaust vapour and the condensation on the inside of the windows showed it was occupied. The note had been for real. I knocked on the passenger window as the wind, now stronger still, attacked my face. A gloved hand swiped a porthole in the condensation and a face peered out briefly. Then the door opened to reveal Jules at the wheel, her red hair covered with her parka hood and its fur ruff.

'Get in.'

I pulled myself into the warmth of the front passenger seat. 'Where's Will?'

'Asleep, at last. I wanted to connect last night, but it was a bit crowded for a discreet chat.'

'I didn't know we needed one.' I was hungry and tired. This had better have a point.

She put the vehicle into gear and moved off.

'Where are we headed?'

'Just somewhere we can talk in a neutral space.'

She'd been watching too many spy films, but I was too fucked to care. I just sat back and enjoyed the heat.

Less than a block in I could see she knew what she was doing: holding the revs low, turning into a skid, letting the engine do the braking. Being a medic in war zones required a whole lot of skills beyond the actual doctoring.

'Does this involve breakfast?'

'There may be something left in there.' She waved me towards a grey alloy Stanley flask in the rear footwell. A bolt-action rifle lay across the seat above it – I hoped it was for the bears. I reached for the flask. It was half empty and what was left was cold.

Her face was etched with worry. She had a lot more on her mind than coffee.

'I need your help.'

The outside went by in a whitish-grey blur.

'You saw what happened last night. Stedman is a fucking liability. He's completely unsuitable. *And* he's trouble.'

I was tempted to ask what it had to do with me, but knew she was probably right, and after my internet trawl I wanted to know more. 'In what way exactly?'

'Every way. Look at him.'

'Can you narrow it down a bit?'

'How about the guy with the knife for a start?'

'Yeah, what was that about?'

'How would I know? It was all in Russian. I only have French and German.'

'Leila say anything to you? On the way to the hotel she claimed he was just some drunken nutter.'

She pulled the hood down so I could get the full force of her glare. *'Really?'*

'Stedman didn't seem that bothered . . .'

'Well, there's our problem in one. The only thing he gives a shit about is Adam Stedman.'

'What does Will think? He know you're here?'

She eased the VW round a corner and turned into a narrow, unlit alley between two buildings. I figured she wasn't going to reach for the rifle so I sat tight.

'So you and Will aren't on the same page about Stedman.'

She gave a humourless smile. 'Will only ever sees the good in people.'

'But Stedman? He seems to have rescued the expedition.'

She gave me an exasperated look. 'Jack dropped him after Alverstoke. Do you know why?'

Alverstoke was the Institute of Naval Medicine, where they'd have been tested for general fitness and resistance to extreme temperatures, among other things – and rigorously. I didn't say that Jack had mentioned a drug habit.

'Because he used blood doping and bronchodilators to pass.'

This sounded a bit more calculated.

'He took some of his own blood and re-injected it immediately before the tests, to increase his oxygen saturation. It's standard practice in athletics and cycling. Bronchodilators are like asthma treatments – they boost your lung capacity – so he scored as much fitter than he actually was. But he overdid it, of course, so his levels were implausibly high.'

'And you found him out?'

She rolled her eyes. 'That and the cocaine. It was obvious. Or it *should* have been. I mean, that's what the monitors are *for*. No one believes me, but my bet is they looked the other way – none of them had the balls to say, because of their . . . because of what the boys had all been through, and what they were trying to do.'

'So you told Jack.'

'I had to. I went over all their readings with a fine-tooth comb. Will was furious. Thought I didn't trust him. It caused quite a rift. In fact, I tend not to trust anyone. Anyway, that's not the point. Stedman's readings were too good to be true so I demanded they do them again. He's physically not up to it, he's a liar, and I was glad he was found out. He could have brought the whole thing down.'

'Must have been a hard decision for Jack.'

'It was out of his hands.'

'How come?'

She took a deep breath. 'Because I told his father.'

That explained a lot.

'Well, I thought Stedman and Jack might find a way of suppressing it. I mean, you can't stop someone going to the Arctic. But when his father weighed in, Jack was fresh out of choices.'

No wonder Jack was so keen to keep his old man away from this.

24

I was starting to get a clearer picture of Jules: tough, professional, by the book, and definitely not one to cross. The sort of person who could be a godsend and a massive pain in the arse at the same time.

'Now he's back, and already there's trouble.'

'What sort of trouble?'

'This! Having rows with people in bars. People with *knives*, for God's sake. He's totally out of control.'

'The row seemed to be with Leila.'

'Yes, well, she's in it up to her neck.'

'In what?'

She shook her head. 'This . . . deal, whatever it is. The money that's magically going to come our way.'

'Why are you telling me all this?'

'You know Jack's father, don't you? Can't you get him to intervene?'

'Jack's his own man.'

A pair of eyes suddenly appeared very close to the bonnet of the minibus, just above head height. She stiffened and braked.

The outline of the reindeer the eyes belonged to emerged out of the darkness. She flashed the main beams and it trotted away. She was in no mood to appreciate the wildlife.

'Come on, Nick, surely you don't expect me to believe you turned up here and bumped into him completely by chance.'

'So you want Stedman out – even though it might jeopardize the trip?'

'Will's not walking to the Pole with that twat. Not if I have anything to do with it.'

'That doesn't seem to be how he sees it.'

She sighed. 'He's so – argh! I have to look after him, OK? If that man goes on this trip, he'll put them all in danger – not least my husband. And this may not mean much to you, but I'd very much like him to come back alive.'

'So tell him not to go.'

'You don't understand. He doesn't care if Stedman is on it or not. He doesn't see what a risk he is – he just wants it to happen. Will *needs* this expedition. His head is in bits, not just his face. He needs it to help him put everything back in some kind of order. He needs to reinvent himself – get past his past. It eats away at him, every single day.

'The expedition is all he's focused on for the last year. He is capable, I know. I've trained with him, with the team, from the start. Not to go would destroy him. It would destroy them all.'

I couldn't see the problem, but that was because I didn't love Will, I supposed. Stedman could get the cash. So what if it turned out to be dodgy and he was on the trip? There were five of them, enough bodies to keep each other going. No matter what bits and pieces they were missing, they still needed to challenge and redefine themselves. I understood that, and could probably have done with a chunk of it myself. 'OK, maybe we can sort things out another way. What do you know about where the cash comes from, and Stedman's plan? What's he said to Will and the others?'

'I don't know.' She seemed pained. 'But whatever the so-called plan is, you're probably too late to do anything about it. Where were you a week ago?'

Thinking about my dead wife and son, and beating myself up because I was still trying to keep their death at a distance.

And in that same instant I realized something.

I'd seen plenty of guys like Will in my time, stuck in a black hole, gripped by depression. Enough of them, for sure, to know that what affected someone physically would also affect them mentally – and whatever affected them mentally would ultimately affect them physically.

When any of the lads had been killed, I'd seen their mates react in a host of different ways. I'd seen them throw themselves into work or family or any number of meaningless activities to make themselves so busy they didn't have time to process the shit. Some made pilgrimages to where their mates had died, built cairns, set up charities. Grief projects. *Was this my job?*

But my numbness – my coldness – wasn't denial or disbelief or any of that psychobabble shit. It was just me, Nick Stone, dealing with things in my own way.

The questions were being asked. My head just wasn't ready yet to take it all in and deal with the fallout.

There were times when I couldn't feel but that didn't mean I didn't care. It was my bubble, like the expedition was theirs. Why wasn't I reacting normally to Anna and Nicholai's deaths? Fuck it, maybe I was. Will was doing it his way. I was doing it mine – the only way I knew.

I clicked back into info-gathering mode. 'How much kit have they already got?'

'The basics – skis, tents, clothing and so on from their original sponsors, which was how they were able to run the pre-trip. But that's all. They've been practising like mad since they got here.'

'What else do they need?'

'They've got the pulks, the stoves, the toolkits, but not enough dehydrated meals or cooking fuel – or, of course, the cash to fly them north.'

That would be a big spend. It would cost more to fly to the start line than a first-class return from London to Sydney.

'What about guides? Who's in charge of navigation?'

She shook her head in despair. 'Because they've been in the fight they think everything else is a piece of piss.' She glared at me in case I was guilty of making the same mistake.

I steered the conversation back to Stedman. 'Do you have any idea what time Stedman's meeting was?'

'Why do you think we're sitting in this thing?' She pointed to the road signs that told us we were heading towards the airport. 'Talk to him, Nick.'

Maybe she was a spy after all.

'OK. I'll do my best to find out what he's up to. The thing is, without Stedman, the expedition is fucked. And the more desperate anyone is for cash, the more problems come with it. But they're big boys, you know.'

She drove the rest of the way in silence, and dropped me by the terminal building.

25

On the other side of the massive glass wall that bordered the runway, and brought some very dull light into the building, an Antonov 74 sat alongside a couple of Russian-made red Mi-8 helis.

The AN-74 had no markings, apart from its identification letters: UIA. So it was Ukrainian, and had to be the air bridge to Barneo. It was the only thing out there that had been built to conquer extreme weather and survive every kind of dodgy landing strip – and one of the check-in desks boasted a board with a picture of the 74 landing on ice, with 'BARNEO' plastered all over it. The wide-diameter, twin-engine pods mounted on top of its wings had earned it the nickname Cheburashka, after a big-eared Soviet-era cartoon mouse that was still popular back east.

A few heavily padded and hooded ground crew were moving about on the apron, and one of the aircraft, in Arktikol livery, was being fuelled. There was no sign of Stedman inside the hall, just a life-size statue of a bear. It dominated the vast open space, in case anyone had forgotten that a few of them were wandering about outside.

The place was deserted, except for a cleaner working his way methodically across the glossy floor with a scissor-mop, trapping cups, food trays and other shit. The café hadn't opened but I spotted a coffee machine opposite the freight desk. Since there was nothing to eat I pressed the milk and sugar options to add some excitement. The result was warm and brown but any resemblance to coffee ended right there.

A woman in a parka with the world's biggest ruff round her hood appeared behind the freight desk, pulled off a pair of padded gloves and cupped her hands over her mouth to warm them. I approached the counter. She surveyed me through narrowed eyes, then turned away.

'Morning. Seen a man with one arm around here?'

She turned back. Her eyes narrowed further and she treated me to the sort of look you'd give someone who asked if you'd seen a man with one arm in a deserted airport, prior to calling security.

No answer.

'Do you speak English?'

'Of course.'

Russian: just my luck.

'Do Skyship make regular flights into Svalbard?'

Again she acted as if she hadn't heard me. Years of stonewalling unwelcome questions – or any questions at all – combined with the cruel wind whipping off the airfield had frozen her features into a permanent expression of contempt. It was all too familiar from my previous dealings with Russian officialdom. The only upside of Anna's death should have been that I would never again have to deal with people like that. Now they seemed to be everywhere I went.

'Sometimes.'

Helpful.

I felt my life ebbing away. Stedman was probably long gone.

Then she jutted her chin. 'Phone.'

'Phone?'

'Your friend.'

'I don't have his number.'

'*At* phone.' She gave her hands another blow and pointed to my left. 'By toilet.'

A breakthrough. She must be only half Russian.

'Thanks.'

A couple of minibuses pulled up outside and disgorged a group of excited and well-insulated Japanese hikers. They were unfeasibly energetic for that time of the morning. Perhaps this was the trip of a lifetime. Anyway, I made use of them as I didn't want to spook Stedman if he caught sight of me. As they headed towards Departures, I jinked to the right so they were between me and the toilets.

Sure enough, there was a row of payphones, just like the nice lady had said. An endangered species in most places, they must still have been in fashion in Svalbard because the mobile signal was shit. Stedman was hunched over a receiver.

I held my position behind the gaggle of Japanese and watched. Even at this distance and out of earshot I could tell the call wasn't going well. He talked rapidly, nodding for emphasis. Then he held the receiver away from his face, frowned at it in dismay, and slammed it down on the cradle. I saw his shoulders sag as he leaned his forehead against the transparent Perspex hood.

His deflation didn't last long. He felt in his pocket and pulled out a fistful of change, some of which fell to the floor as he tried to put it on the shelf beside the phone. It was painful to watch.

He counted to three, pinched a couple of coins between the thumb and forefinger that were wrapped round the receiver, fed them into the slot and dialled. Then he waited a full minute.

No answer.

He repeated the procedure. After about forty-five seconds he spoke rapidly but in more measured tones, then listened, then dropped the phone back onto its cradle. He looked utterly defeated now, a far cry from the man who'd held court in the bar a few short hours ago. Was that the end of the money?

'Hey, look who we got here!'

I felt a hand clamp onto my shoulder.

At first I didn't register the face beaming down at me out of a thick, home-knitted balaclava.

It was the Owl. Fucking great timing.

'Hey.' I tried to say it quietly. Maybe that would bring his volume down a few decibels.

It didn't.

'So, headed out on your voyage to the top of the world?'

He didn't wait for an answer – he was too busy beckoning to another man. 'Hey, Bern, it's the crazy Brit I told you about. The guy who's hikin' to the goddamn Pole!'

His voice was so loud the Japanese turned and stared. We shook hands, or rather brushed them, due to the thickness of the gloves.

Bern didn't show the enthusiasm the Owl seemed to be expecting.

'On foot, for Chrissakes! Who does that?'

Bern was younger than the Owl, in the same stiff, new-bought kit – another corporate suit a long way out of his comfort zone. Swathed in a huge Russian tank-commander-style fur hat and balaclava he looked comically sinister, like a kid whose mother had sent him to a fancy-dress party as a terrorist but didn't want him to catch cold.

A few metres away Munnelly, the oil-sniffer, was with several other men who seemed a lot more at home. None of them was talking. They kept very still, maybe conserving energy, or just bored with all that Midwestern jumpy up and down stuff, which the Owl seemed unable to control.

I heard the clatter of a twin-rotor heli. A red Chinook was on its finals outside in the gloom, rotors feathered a few metres off the ice. The men around Munnelly came alive and picked up their bags.

The Owl muttered to himself and patted his pockets as if they were being invaded by bees. 'Shit, shit.'

I peered over his shoulder. Stedman was still at the phone booth, trying to make another call. 'You OK, mate?'

'My glove. I lost it. And I don't want these guys to know. It's, like, your basic safety procedure, ain't it? And they're gonna think, well . . .'

Another day, another panic attack.

'I'm no good at this. I shoulda stayed at my desk.'

Munnelly was giving him a weary look, like an RSM zeroing in on a thumbprint on a recruit's toecap. If the Owl took his hand out of his pocket for more than ten seconds out there he'd get frostbite – a very short step to the loss of his fingers.

I pulled out my spares. 'I always carry an extra pair.'

'My friend, you're a true English gentleman.' He was almost tearful.

'That's the first time I've ever been called that.' I jutted my chin in the direction of the Chinook. 'That yours?'

'Sure thing. *Adios, amigo*. And thanks a million.' He saluted and scuttled off to catch up with the others.

The Japanese had gone too. And so had Stedman.

26

I spotted him on a bench, hunched over his mobile, waving it around, trying to capture a signal. I walked up to him and held out my sat phone. 'Try this. By the window. But go steady on the minutes. They're expensive.'

His face was taut and blotched, and the whites of his eyes were bloodshot, a far cry from last night's King of Smug. 'Why are you here?'

I waved in the direction of the heli desk where the Japanese ice tourists had clustered. 'I was seeing about a trip round the island, but everything's booked up.'

His face was blank. His mind was on other things. 'I've got to get to Barentsburg.'

The mining settlement, run by the Russians. 'What's there?'

He didn't answer, just gazed out onto the apron, where the Arktikol Mil was parked up.

'You catching a heli?'

'They only take company personnel. I'll have to go by road.'

'There isn't one.'

He swung round. '*What?* How the *fuck* do you get anywhere in this shithole?'

He was in a massive flap and I'd just made it a few degrees worse. 'Snowmobile. It's fifty-five, sixty Ks from here. You could do it in about three hours.'

As well as having the means to talk, spend or bribe my way out of trouble, I'd always taken the trouble to find out where I could run to wherever I was fucking about. Around here, Barentsburg was all there was.

'Yeah, very funny.' He pointed at his stump with his remaining index finger.

Last night he'd been the hero of the hour, his babe looking on adoringly. Seven hours on, he had shrivelled. The air had seeped out of him.

'Couldn't Jack or one of the others help you out?'

He grimaced. 'Shit, no.'

Then he saw his answer had come out too fast, like whatever he was doing was something he didn't want them to know about. 'It's just . . . someone I've got to meet. He was supposed to be here but . . .'

'Right.' I left the silence for him to fill, not moving but not questioning either.

'Look, stay out of it, OK? Go and have your joy ride.'

'Whatever.' I shrugged and pocketed the phone, then stepped away. I knew his kind all too well. I'd served under men like him. Full of confidence until the shit met the fan. He'd come to his senses soon – and later on decide he'd taken control once more.

'Wait – wait a sec. It's Nick, isn't it?'

I turned.

'You're going sightseeing?'

'That was the plan.'

'Right.'

Meek wasn't a word I would have associated with Stedman but he had almost morphed into little-boy-lost. Probably a strategy he deployed with Leila when he wasn't ignoring her.

'Look, I can't handle a snowmobile myself. But I could hang on.'

I stared at him blankly.

'It's just – I've got to see this guy. He was supposed to RV with me here but he couldn't make it. It's just a meet – half an hour, if that.'

'This connected with you bailing out the trip?'

'Yeah.'

'You got the money to hire a snowmobile?'

Another sheepish look. 'Not immediately, no.'

So he was begging now.

'Don't you need Leila to interpret?'

'No – his English is fine.'

But Stedman didn't look as if fluency of conversation was the most important thing on his mind. He was bent over in his chair, his arm folded, but not in pain – not physical pain, anyway.

'I have to meet him. If we don't have the money, we don't go. That's it, the end.'

He sat up, but only to slump into the chair and pull at the material that should have been covering an arm. 'Look at me! I can't even ride a fucking snowmobile.'

He looked up and I was sure tears were forming. He took a series of sharp breaths to fight them back. 'I have to get there, Nick. I need this trip. I need to do something for *me*. I need to show myself I'm not some fucked-up cripple. You know, you get it – everyone loves us "heroes", but in five years' time they won't give a shit. I'll just be some fucker with a blue badge on his windscreen.'

His attempts to hold back the tears stopped working and he used his palm to wipe them away. 'I need to know different, Nick. I need to . . .'

He was getting too worked up to find the words. He didn't need to. I understood. I did know. I did get it. This lot weren't the first I'd come across with bits missing. It wasn't just the physical damage they had to deal with – that could be gripped and managed – it was the mental side of things that could fuck people up even more, if it wasn't properly addressed.

This was the start of Stedman's blue-badge life, and it needed to be lived as positively as his old one. He needed to prove to himself and the rest of the world that he was still the same person. Otherwise he'd just be held together by a couple of medal ribbons and a bunch of war stories that no one gave a shit about.

I got that, and even if I wouldn't trust him to post a letter, there was a big difference between want and need – Jack, Stedman and Will had the need.

'OK, you're on.'

'There is one other thing . . .'

I waited as he wiped away the final tears.

'Jack can't know about this.' He held up his damp hand. 'Or the meeting. None of them can . . .'

27

There weren't any car-rental desks at the airport. Why would there be? But snowmobiles were easy to rent – as long as you were nice to Sven, whose Portakabin was just outside the terminal building. He had the monopoly.

'That one?' I pointed at the biggest, meanest machine. It had a seat-jack fitted, so I could take a passenger.

Sven nodded approvingly. His name badge was trying hard to give his business the mega-corporate feel, but failing. The same went for the oil-covered dungarees and equally oil-stained parka, which didn't quite protect his once white shirt and tie. '*Ja!* The Yamaha Nytro XTX. Liquid-fuelled triple with one-oh-four-nine cc four-stroke. The suspension's got thirty-five to forty centimetres of travel but with two up will bottom out if you take any big bumps. Where you guys headed?'

'Barentsburg.'

Doubt flickered across his features, but he wasn't about to talk himself out of some business. 'Well, it's pretty smooth all the way if you just follow the sat nav. Barentsburg is the first pre-set. You guys know how to use it?'

It wasn't just the machine we needed. Helmets and full kit were part of the deal. Our gear wasn't nearly thick enough to withstand the core temperatures, let alone the wind chill.

'You have your own guns, yes?' He made it sound like asking if we had hats. 'You must have weapons. In fact, you are forbidden to go without them.'

That was very clear from the rifle-shaped plastic containers that were fitted to the side of each snow-mobile, like a modern-day cowboy's saddle holster for a Winchester to fight off all those Comanches.

'It's the law. Some problems with bears. We have about five hundred here on Spitsbergen.'

Sven selected a pair of Mauser bolt-actions from the array of rifles and flare guns in a steel cabinet behind his desk. He held out the weapons. 'Ah . . . sorry . . .' He was embarrassed.

'Don't be!' Stedman grabbed the nearest Mauser and showed us how he would aim it, pressing the butt plate into his shoulder and balancing it on his chest. Then he started to laugh and handed it to me.

The weapon had no magazine, so I opened the bolt to check the chamber. 'Sven, how about a flare gun for my mate here? We can scare them first, yeah? It'll be a shame to drop one if we don't have to.'

Sven turned back to the rack. 'Sure, no problem. You need one for emergencies anyway. You have met bears before?'

'A few years ago, but once is enough, yeah?'

'I only like to tell people who know what they're doing to use flares – otherwise the bear gets too close. It is best for people who do not know bear to just shoot and be safe.' He handed me something like a toy pistol, bright red with a black handgrip.

'Well, at least we won't lose it in the snow.'

Then he held out a bubble-wrapped six-pack of flares the size of a shotgun cartridge. 'Each one lasts for about eight seconds, and can be seen for over thirty kilometres. We don't want to lose you out there.'

We each pulled on an all-in-one red cold-weather jumpsuit over our own kit. Stedman refused our offers of help, so I used the time he took to load up the ten-round mag. That was all I needed. If it took more ammo than that to sort out a bear, we really would have fucked up and the bear deserved to eat us.

Stedman finished off kitting up as I broke the flare gun like a twelve-bore, pushed home a cartridge and closed the barrel. 'Here, loaded and made ready.' I pointed to the right-hand side of the weapon. 'Safety's on.'

Stedman shoved the thing into his left chest pocket for easy access. He zipped up and gave it a pat. 'Dressed for bear, eh?'

He was clearly enjoying the process. I supposed it was like the good old days, which was why I'd done it. But he shouldn't have got too pleased with himself – he'd been a bit hasty zipping up. 'The rest of the flares . . .'

His face reddened from the neck up. He picked up the bubblewrap and put it into his right-hand breast pocket.

114

Sven finished off the paperwork and checked to see if he had a signal for the card machine.

'You guys have insurance?'

I looked at Stedman. I knew the answer and so did Sven.

'You must pay deposit for rescue. In case we have to come and get you.'

Another six hundred kroner – plus a hundred a day for the bolt-action and twenty a day for the flare gun.

Sven took my plain black card, with nothing more than a SIM embedded on the front and a magnetic strip on the back, and gave both it and me the once-over.

'It's OK. It'll work.'

It did look a bit dodgy, but when you had a few bob and didn't want too many people to know where you were and what you were spending your cash on, it helped that there were still banks that valued privacy as much as I did.

'You want two or three days?' Sven almost licked his lips at the thought.

'Just one.'

His face fell as he prodded his tablet, but he wasn't giving up easily. 'Snow is due later. Better you stay over.'

'It's OK. We're coming straight back.' Stedman seemed to have recovered some of his legendary confidence. 'Only need to be there half an hour, max.'

Sven sighed. He wasn't convinced, and neither was I.

28

I could feel my sat phone vibrating again as I slid the Mauser sling over my shoulder. I wasn't in the mood for another earful, so left it in my pocket until it buzzed again, short and sharp. A message or a text. Much better: waffle wasn't on the agenda.

It was a text: *Mission critical U ABSOLUTELY must get Jack on board ASAFP. Whatever it takes.*

The question was: whose mission was he talking about? While Stedman was putting on his helmet, I called Cauldwell back. 'Why the panic? Something changed?'

'I mean it, Stone. Whatever it takes. Jack *has* to go with Rune.'

'Why? As long as they get there, why flap about who's paying?'

He didn't answer immediately. This was becoming a bit of a habit.

'I don't have time to explain and you don't need to know. Just get Jack on board with Rune. Today. It *has* to be today.'

Both money trees sounded equally dodgy to me. Stedman's because he was Stedman, and Cauldwell's because it had everything to do with him and what he had promised – or was getting out of the deal. I decided to go with Stedman and see what came of it. Convincing Jack wouldn't be any easier, but I'd cross that bridge when I came to it.

'I got things to do now. I'll call tomorrow.'

There was no hesitation from him now: 'No. I leave for Oslo today. The weather is closing in. It has to be today. You need to convince Jack *now*.'

I glanced at Stedman in case he'd overheard the screeching, but he was busy sorting his kit. 'I'll call tomorrow.' I powered down before he had a chance to answer.

The sky was bright and clear with no sign yet of the weather Sven and Cauldwell had warned me about. The helmets had tinted visors – the snow was blinding.

Stedman was getting impatient. 'Can we get going now?' He adjusted his helmet and dropped the visor.

I took his loose sleeve and tucked it into a pocket. 'We'll leave as soon as you tell me who we're meeting and why. If you're not in the mood to share, you crack on.'

Stedman went into used-car-salesman mode. 'Look, I'd love to explain, but I can't. Not yet, anyway. They want it kept quiet. There's one last detail I need to sort, and then we're in business.'

I began to unzip, willing Stedman to tell me before I got the padding off. It would be a serious pain putting it back on again. I was going to take him whatever, but it would be good to know more. Knowledge was power.

'You'll get *your* money no matter what. I can arrange that when we get back . . .'

I peeled the outer layer off one shoulder.

'OK, OK. It's – it's something I need to do for my brother. I do him a favour, we get the cash and we're good to go.'

'Christopher? The one you went to court for?'

'How the fuck—'

'I do my homework. What "something"?'

Stedman took a breath and prepared to explain. 'He has these . . . There are some people he works with. They ship stuff all over. Mining machinery, industrial diamond core bits, that sort of thing. I gather they use them for exploring new seams or something. I'm not exactly an expert.' He laughed nervously. 'Anyhow, the Russians can't access them that easily, because of the embargoes and whatnot over Ukraine, but Chris can, so I fixed something up with Leila's contacts.' He gripped my shoulder. 'Listen, it's OK – a little low-level sanction busting inside the arsehole of the world. Every fucker's at it.' Some of his trademark bravado was creeping back. I didn't fancy being on the receiving end of too much more.

'Skyship – they part of this?'

He hesitated, then: 'Yeah. I was supposed to make the handover at Longyearbyen, only for some reason the shipment got put straight on a heli for Barentsburg.'

I stayed focused on him while I absorbed this, waiting for more.

'Their guy should have contacted me to complete the formalities.'

'And the ponytail last night?'

'That's just some shit with Leila – some twat who has a thing for her. Ukrainians . . .' He grimaced, then his expression changed. 'The walk. It's all I care about. You get that, don't you?'

I eased myself onto the snowmobile and checked that the sat nav was ready to take us to Barentsburg. It was attached to the handlebars and powered like it would be on a motorbike. But this device didn't have Delia or James explaining what road you were on and when to turn. It worked on longs and lats and gave a bearing to your destination, just like a boat's navigation system. All I had to do was keep in the same direction as the arrow on the extremely boring grey-scale display, and if I had to deviate because of the surface conditions it would get me back on track.

The triple made a rich, thudding growl at idle, which turned into a rasping whine when I opened it up. Stedman slotted himself on behind and I put it into gear. The controls felt vague and imprecise through the thick mittens. I took off slowly so we could both get used to it. Without two arms, he'd have his work cut out to stay on.

29

Early on, the hard-packed base was scored with tracks, but they soon petered out. Then all that was left was white stuff stretching into the far distance until it met the sky. A picture-postcard scene – as long as you were admiring it from the comfort of an armchair. It looked so good because strong winds had blasted the snow smooth and given much of it an icy crust. I wasn't looking forward to getting one myself. The quicker we got there the better.

Sat nav pointed me towards some high ground like a broken molar. Once we'd rounded it, I locked onto the tail of another snowmobile that seemed to be headed in the same direction. It was going a lot faster, probably because there was only one rider aboard, and soon disappeared.

I kept our skis in its compacted track, so was able to get some speed up. I could feel the wind pushing against me. The microscopic gap between my hood and my helmet was enough to allow an icy blast to attack the top of my head. I couldn't be arsed to stop, just tilted it forwards and rolled my eyes upwards so I could still see where the fuck we were going.

It didn't last long. Stedman hit me repeatedly on the shoulder and shouted what I presumed was 'Stop!'

As soon as he could, he jumped off the machine, swinging his arm about to generate some heat.

'Fuck that!'

I spotted the problem immediately. He hadn't managed to completely fasten his outerwear. Keeping the engine ticking over, because now wasn't the time to have it fail, I jumped off, made sure everything was zipped up and pulled tight, and sorted out my hood. Fuck knows how this lot were going to get on if they succeeded in funding the trip. There weren't going to be enough arms and legs to go round.

We headed west across the Longyearbyen Glacier then up over the Fadalsbakken Hill. It was just a load of white shit to me, but sat nav kept me briefed at the bottom of the screen.

Crossing the Grondalen River presented no challenge: it was caked with layers of winter ice and snow, and indistinguishable from its surroundings. We made our way up a steep incline as the dark grey cloud blotted out the sun. With two up, it was quite a workout for the snowmobile. Neither of us attempted to speak over the steady thrum of the engine – there were limits to how much I could take of Stedman's waffle, anyway.

More cloud rolled in from the east and a big twin-rotor heli – a Chinook, probably – thundered through the shit that kept gathering above us.

We completed the steepest part of the climb and I

gave the machine as much power as I dared whenever the way ahead seemed smooth enough, but there were patches where holes had opened up or hard clumps of ice lay just beneath the surface, big enough to snag one of the skis and send us over. Stedman kept a steady grip on me, but he was constrained by how much he could brace himself, so I did my best not to throw the thing around.

The wind had got up and was whipping the top layer of snow into a mist that shrouded our knees, obscured the surface and masked any obstacles. I dropped our speed as we reached the apex and kicked on to what appeared to be a straight downhill run.

It should have been a piece of piss. Stedman shifted on his perch behind me as I steered to avoid the one rock I could clearly see and the rear track stepped out. I corrected it but Stedman had swung back the other way at the same moment. We started fishtailing and rocking. It was all I could do to stop doing a ninety straight into the rocks on our left. I held it, but the right ski started to lift. Both of us leaned the other way. It wasn't enough. The machine bucked and our world turned upside-down.

We landed in the snow. That should have been the end of it, but it was just the beginning. The surface was icy smooth and the incline enough to send us tobogganing down the slope. I'd stopped rolling and was on my front, facing forwards, powerless to stop.

Something slammed into my foot and spun me sideways. Stedman, also out of control, sliding on his back, his arm flapping at the air. But that wasn't our biggest problem. The snowmobile was catching us up fast, on its flank, propped up by one ski, doing a slow-motion pirouette.

I reached out, grabbed one of his calves with both hands, managed to roll onto my side and curled my legs. I spotted a shallow dip to our left and steered us towards it. There was a strong chance of the hardware following us and fucking us up big-time, but it was a risk worth taking.

We must have hit twenty, maybe thirty Ks an hour on our arses, Gore-Tex rasping against the ice. He was still yelling and trying to break free, but I held his leg firm. We rolled, one over the other, until we ground to a halt, throwing up a cloud of ice dust, which obscured my view of the slope behind us. The whereabouts of the snowmobile was all I cared about. A second later it rolled over and crashed to a halt about two metres away.

I picked myself up and shook off the snow before it could make its way into any gaps in my clothing. Stedman hadn't stopped yelling, which wasn't going to get us anywhere. I screamed back at him to shut the fuck up, but at least he was conscious. After a few moments, he levered himself onto his knees, managed to shake off his mitten and pull off his helmet. 'Fucking fuck!' Off came the balaclava as well. Toys out of the pram.

The wind and snow were kicking up more strongly with every passing second, so I had to yell at him at top volume. 'Put your kit back on. It's done.' I picked up his balaclava and yanked it down over his eyes and ears. 'Honking won't change a thing. So get your act together or you'll lose your other arm. And your stupid fucking head as well.'

There was nothing for him to punch, apart from me, but that didn't stop him lashing out into thin air – until he must have realized how ridiculous he looked. He tucked his hand beneath his armpit, leaned forwards and lowered his voice to a croak. 'What a *fucking* fuck-up . . .'

I left him to sort out his own fucking fuck-up and stumbled and slid back to the snowmobile. It had lost a headlamp and one of its skis was bent. The control-panel housing had also come adrift and the sat nav was a little confused, but the motor was still idling. I checked that it was out of gear, then heaved it upright. It hadn't hit a wall or a tree or an oncoming vehicle, so it was pretty much intact – and these things were built for this kind of shit.

The cover was still on the holster, undamaged, but I still couldn't help myself and unclipped its lid to check the weapon was still there. Inspect, don't expect and all that?

Weapons were part of every soldier's routine, twenty-four/seven, and we had a strange relationship with them. We protected them more carefully than the people we loved, and kept them cleaner than we did ourselves. We had to be in control of them at all times. We never left them unattended, and in the battle-space, they were never more than an arm's length away. But as soon as the shit hit the fan, they simply became a tool. If they worked, we kept them; if they didn't, we binned them and reached for another.

There was a loud pop from behind me and one of Sven's fireworks arced through the gloom to my right. I tightened my grip on the butt and pulled the weapon free from its holster, keeping eyes on the direction the flare was heading. And there it was: a big, white, fantastic-looking monster – but too close for comfort. The bear had stopped maybe thirty metres away, nose in the air, smelling us out, wondering what we tasted like, and if it was worth the effort to come and see.

I rested the bolt-action on the snowmobile, not looking down the iron sight yet, just at the bear. I'd never seen one so close. He reared up like a prize-fighter and gave us both a look that said, 'Yeah, I know. I'm fucking amazing.' As the flare died he turned slowly away and headed for the high ground in search of a less challenging snack.

Stedman had ejected the cartridge but was every bit as captivated as I had been. It didn't stop the soldier in him reloading though.

'Our lucky day, Nick.'

I had to agree with him on that. But that was as close to a bear as I wanted to get.

He heaved himself up, replaced his crash helmet and slapped off some of the ice particles that had gathered on his legs and arm as he moved back towards me.

'What's his name? The guy you're going to meet.'

'Khorek.'

'That's not a name.'

He glared at me. 'What d'you mean?'

'It's Russian for "ferret".'

'Don't be ridiculous.' He hesitated. 'How d'you know that?'

From Nicholai's book, about Khorek the naughty ferret who wouldn't brush his teeth. They all fall out in the night – a nice story for kids. It was sitting in a box in the apartment, with the other parts of me that weren't here.

'So it's a nickname. They've all got these long fucking Russian names.'

'That still doesn't tell me who he is.'

He shrugged. 'One of Leila's cousins. He's on maintenance or something.'

He slipped over and landed on his arse. This time he didn't swear. I helped him up.

He waved his stump. All meek now. 'Look, I really appreciate this, OK?'

'Sort your glove out and let's crack on.'

'Whatever you're thinking, it's all completely OK. Just a neat way round the sanctions. No one cares.'

Whatever.

We got back on the machine and headed into the great white void.

30

Barentsburg
Latitude: 78.0648 North
Longitude: 14.2335 East

The first we saw of the place was a charred, semi-derelict building at the top of a slope, though how anything could burn in that cold it was hard to imagine. The soot-blackened walls contrasted starkly with the fluffy white drifts that had collected against them.

We crested the hill and the settlement materialized through the gloom below us. I didn't slow now. A kilometre-high wall of nimbostratus had cut out much of the remaining light and was preparing to take another massive dump.

Either side of our route down to the cluster of buildings on the shore were slag heaps, white-coated but unmistakable by their angular shape: shards of scrap metal, bits of decommissioned equipment from the mine, massive rusted wheels that had once sat on high steel platforms to lift and lower miners through the shafts.

A towering chimney chucked out a steady plume of smoke, pockmarking its surroundings with grime. A few of the houses had evidently been abandoned long since, wooden skeletons crushed by the weight of snow from above and the shifting foundations beneath.

Then, as if a sudden splash of colour had been beamed in, *Star Trek* style, we came to a gleaming red steel, one-storey structure, the sort no modern industrial estate could live without, with two equally shiny red GAZ-71s sitting on the spotless concrete outside it.

The Russian Army all-purpose machines were mounted on tank tracks, with a forward cab and a big deck at the back that could be adapted to carry troops or lug loads. They weren't fast, but could travel over anything, including ice, deep snow or water. These had had their rear platforms converted to carry a massive foam tank and fire hose. Maybe they were a present from Putin to brighten up the town's favourite family destination.

The colour fest didn't go on for long. More empty buildings were sinking on their stilts further down the slope, and behind them a row of concrete barracks that looked like part of a Soviet gulag.

In fact the whole town looked like a penal colony, and might as well have been one. Even its welcome sign, in Cyrillic, was pitted with rust and decay. All I knew, from checking out my places to run to, was that it was a freak of history. The Russians had mined there since the early 1920s, before the archipelago had come under Norwegian sovereignty. Keeping hold of it had appealed to them more for strategic reasons than profit, and it was still administered through state-owned Arktikol. From our vantage point, it was no more than a haphazard huddle of buildings ripe for closure.

We dropped our speed and coasted into town like Eskimo versions of Clint Eastwood. Some kids pulling a homemade sledge waved at us, until a man with a cigarette stuck in the side of his mouth barked at them through a window and they scattered.

We passed what looked like a clinic, daubed with a red cross and murals of Red Square and the Mr Whippy domes of St Basil's Cathedral, then a sports centre complete with peeling Soviet-era posters showing the cream of Russian youth reaching for the red socialist sky. A game of volleyball inside was its only sign of life.

There was none of the bling of modern Russia, just the crumbling substrata of the old Soviet Union, which were never far below the surface of Putin's utopian dream. How handy it was for him to have a foothold already established in a NATO outpost.

The imaginatively named Barentsburg Hotel looked more like a prison, a brutal concrete monolith with small, slit-shaped windows that would probably have been listed if it had been built in the UK. It glowered over the jumble of surrounding buildings, some of which had tried to cheer themselves up with paintings of the bumper Siberian wheat harvest of 1963.

The jewel in its crown, at the centre of what passed for the town square, frowning down from a corrugated grey stone column resembling a giant radiator, was a bust of Lenin. The Arctic blast had chomped away at the face of the long-dead leader – an enduring reminder that if anyone was going to inherit the earth, it was probably the weather. This was the USSR's graveyard, and in a few decades' time the whole settlement might well have slid into the sea.

We came to a stop beside an ancient blue Russian-made UAZ-452 four-wheel-drive minibus, with chains round its tyres, in front of the hotel steps. It was abnormally pristine in contrast to the grubby building behind. Everything else had a permanent coating of dirt and frost.

We dismounted and gave our legs a shake in an attempt to get some life back into them. I hefted the bolt-action's sling over my shoulder, helped Stedman remove his helmet and we went up the steps.

'He said to wait in the lobby and they'd fetch him.'

'Why not call him?'

'They said just wait.'

'They?'

'His people. The ones I was on the phone to at the airport.'

We went through two sets of glass doors and into the deserted foyer. It was straight out of *The Shining*: worn wooden walls, flooring that creaked and no one at the desk. Our only welcome was the blast of dry heat, and the glimmer of brightness from a family of Russian dolls in a glass display case.

I suddenly pictured Anna giggling with delight as she held up the set she'd bought me when we'd first moved in together – all her nation's leaders from Lenin through to Medvedev. She'd hidden Putin, pretending they hadn't dared include him.

A couple of old, duveted men had sauntered up to the parked snowmobile and now stood beside it, smoking. Stedman glared at them through the window.

'Just curious. It's a small town.'

He shook his head at his own paranoia.

'You're here now, Stedman. Just do what you have to do, yeah?'

He nodded, but I could feel the tension coming off him in waves.

After a few seconds a pale, round-faced teenager – it was hard to tell which gender under the parka and hood – appeared from a side door and stared at us.

'We . . . are . . . here . . . for . . . Khorek.' Stedman was from the speak-slowly-and-loudly-and-they'll-understand school of international communication.

The kid looked blank, hesitated a moment, did a U-turn and exited without a word.

'That went well.'

He ignored me.

Through a glass door I saw what might be the dining room, if greasy spoons could be called such.

'Come on, let's get something to eat. He'll find us. It's not like there's anywhere else to go, is it?'

31

He didn't want to move but I steered him through and grabbed a table by the window. After a minute a waitress appeared, or maybe the cook; her apron was grubby and she had a hair net. Maybe she was both.

I asked for a menu in Russian.

Stedman was wrong-footed. 'I didn't know you spoke—'

'You didn't ask.'

The waitress replied in English, without even a flicker of a smile. 'No menu. Pork.'

'Two porks, then.' I gave her a grin, which did nothing to warm her spirits. 'Please . . .'

She pointed at the bolt-action, which I'd put on the floor. 'In foyer. Behind desk.'

As I returned and pulled back my chair, the foyer filled with the sound of surprisingly cheerful men. Stedman looked round and, for a moment, I entertained myself by imagining that the mine management would appear *en masse*, thank him effusively for securing their drills, and the deal would be done with a kiss and a cuddle. But the group exited through the main doors and a few seconds later I heard the UAZ chunter into life.

We sat and waited. The pork was a long time coming. 'So, how did you lose it?'

He glanced at what was left of his arm, as if he was still surprised it wasn't there. 'Helmand. On patrol. Our Husky took three RPGs in one go and brewed up. I was about ten metres away, about to get on board, and took a big piece of the blast. But you know when events just take over, and you don't feel anything? My three lads were still in the wagon.'

The waitress reappeared carrying a tray with a plate of black bread and two large bowls of what looked like stew. 'You want beer?'

I leaped in before Stedman had the chance to order some Dutch courage. 'Two Cokes, please.' I nodded at him, not wanting to break the flow. It was getting difficult for him.

'I managed to drag the two in the rear seats out. They were badly burned, still on fire but breathing. Young Jez, the driver, couldn't move. His legs were fucked, so I had to go in and get him. But the flames . . . I couldn't . . .' He paused. 'I thought I was going to be OK – it was just, you know, trauma in the arm, secondary missiles in my chest and a load of second degree. But infection set in while I was in hospital back in the UK. The bacteria got into the wound and that was it, necrosis.'

She returned with two small glasses of what had once been fizzy Fanta.

Stedman shifted in his seat and took two deep gulps before continuing. 'So the arm had to go and the lung was fucked, but I was the lucky one. None of the rest made it. Shit, the eldest was only twenty-three.'

It had probably made him all the more determined to go for it and fuck the consequences, crashing into things, hoping his WTF bravado would somehow see him through.

He peered down at the bowl of whatever it was. 'I'm not very hungry.'

'Can't blame you for that, but the fillet steak is off, and who knows how long this is going to take?'

It was hot and greasy and I didn't give a shit. The ride, the fall and the cold had burned every free calorie.

We'd just got started when two men appeared, one tall and slim, the other chunky and squat. The slim one had designer trackies under a black parka and a sweatshirt with a Love Moschino logo. He was wearing a TAG Heuer Aquaracer, which he presumably slipped off and put in a velvet case before he went on his mining shift. He didn't look like a Khorek. His face was broad and bearded, and even under the layers I could see that he'd done some work to keep in shape.

The squat one, on the other hand, hadn't seen the inside of a gym in his life. He hung back while Watch Man glided to our table and helped himself to a chair. The only sound in the room came from beside the door: rapid wheezy breaths suggesting that the Chunk was in the grip of early-onset emphysema.

Stedman spoke first. This was his gig after all, and I had some stew to demolish. 'Khorek?'

It was only now I realized he'd never set eyes on the guy before.

There was a beat before our new best mate answered. 'Who is this?' His watch glittered as he flicked a hand my way.

'This is Nick. My driver.' He indicated his lack of a second arm. 'You're Khorek?'

'We see him when I want to see him.' Watch Man sucked his teeth. 'Go ahead. Eat.'

He looked towards the kitchen and the waitress burst through the swing doors and scuttled across, like George Clooney had just walked in. Watch Man quashed her excitement with a bark. '*Vodka dlya nashikh posetiteley.*' Vodka for our visitors.

I held up a finger. 'Another Coke for me.'

Watch Man's brow furrowed.

'*Ya na lekarstva.* I'm on medication.'

He didn't seem too offended by my abstinence. His manner was remote but focused. Stedman eyed him cautiously. I'd met Russian police who behaved more like gangsters and Russian gangsters who behaved more like police, so just because Watch Man presented himself like a small-town pimp didn't mean he wasn't a hot-shot mining engineer. Another sidekick came in and joined the Chunk. He was a bigger model, half man, half bear, in a thick coat and enormous work boots that dribbled slush all over the floor.

Watch Man peered at Stedman and frowned. It was what Russians did, even at weddings. 'You and Khorek, family?'

Stedman shot me an anxious glance. 'No – my . . . he's my girlfriend's cousin. I mean, we're engaged, sort of.'

Watch Man nodded. 'Ah, so *like* family.'

Stedman's face was reddening. I could practically see the blood pulsing round it. He blinked rapidly and avoided my gaze. Watch Man reached into his parka, pulled out a state-of-the-art iridium sat phone that made mine look steam-powered and presented it to us to admire. Then he bent over it and punched in a number.

The waitress arrived with a bottle of vodka, two shot glasses and a tumbler of flat orange. Stedman downed his shot without so much as a *Nostrovya*, like he needed it badly. Watch Man muttered, '*Pyat minut*,' into his phone, then killed the call and got to his feet.

Five minutes till what?

'OK, we go.'

'Go where?'

'Khorek.'

On the way out I headed for my Mauser, but Watch Man waved me away from it. 'Is OK. No bears.'

What was happening in Stedman's head now he knew the weapon was staying at the hotel wasn't clear. The cogs were turning but they weren't meshing. Then, without any warning, he came to a halt. He stood, legs apart, his one hand on his hip and raised his voice again, like an exasperated headmaster. 'I want to see Khorek here. *Right here*. That was the arrangement. At the hotel.'

I was also concerned that the weapon wasn't coming with us. It was always good to have protection from everything, including bears, but this time, not even old habits were enough to stop me leaving. The objective of this fuck-about was to get to Khorek and collect the money. If the bolt-action made Watch Man nervous about taking us, I'd leave it. This still didn't feel right, but then again, what had these last two days?

Stedman's speech made no impact on Watch Man. 'We go to him. He expects you.'

Stedman flushed. He had no power to make anyone do anything. Maybe it had dawned on him what a twat he was being. But it hadn't. He swallowed, straightened up and pulled himself together, like he was preparing to lead his men over the top.

Watch Man was waiting.

I gripped Stedman's elbow and pushed him forward. 'Don't be a dickhead. Let's go.'

The cloud cover had turned a dark cobalt blue and a sharper, more persistent gale was advancing on us from the north. Watch Man, Chunk and Half Bear walked three abreast, slowly, despite the cold, like they'd been studying *Reservoir Dogs*. The two who were looking at our snowmobile remained in position, oblivious of the cold. I glimpsed the UAZ minibus moving tentatively away from us before turning a corner and disappearing completely.

We crossed the square, went down some steps and followed a path towards a long, low building set apart from the rest. Further to the east, the rotors of two or three helicopters were visible above the rooftops.

We turned sharp left down a less-trampled path of ice between two empty, partly demolished corrugated-iron sheds. Watch Man knocked sharply on a metal door. It was unlocked from inside and opened with a ferocious shriek. We stepped into a decaying concrete room lit by a single paraffin lamp. If this was Khorek's place, he needed to pay much more attention to *Homes & Gardens*.

32

The room was freezing cold and windowless. On the rusted steel desk was an ancient laptop, lid closed. The man in the metal chair behind it had a face so thin and ferret-like there was no need for an introduction.

Khorek stared blankly at us. His eyes bulged, maybe from spending a lot of time underground. They were also moist and red-rimmed, and his face was swollen, red and blotchy. Some of that could have been put down to bad diet and a lack of grooming but, in spite of the cold, sweat beads were hatching around the tufts of receding hair on his forehead. He had been fucked up, but he wasn't flapping.

Whatever I might have been expecting, this wasn't it. Khorek's gaze shifted to Watch Man, who stepped up to the desk and looked down at him. No question who was in charge here.

So that was problem number one. The man we had come to see was not *the* man. Problem number two was the third man in the room, who must have been keeping Khorek company while we were getting pork down us. He grinned when he recognized me: Ponytail, whom I'd persuaded to fuck off out of the bar last night. If only I'd known, I could have brought back his little knife for him.

The door was closed behind me, leaving just the five of us in the room.

Problem number three was on a metal table against the wall, the two-metre-square reinforced-plywood crate with Skyship labelling. The seals had been broken and the lid prised off. So that bit of Stedman's story checked out: the shipment had gone through to Barentsburg, and maybe the sight of it gave him a last vestige of hope that he was going to get his cash.

The crate had been partly unpacked. The grey plastic bundles that lay stacked beside it didn't look much like they contained drill bits. They looked a lot more like shrink-wrapped bricks. Heroin or cocaine, it didn't matter to me what they contained: it was their shape that meant trouble.

I took a step towards them to get a better look but Ponytail moved out from behind Khorek clutching a brand-new blade in his fist. It was perfectly clean and I wanted it to stay that way. I stepped back.

Stedman sparked up: 'Well, I see you got the shipment.' But he was talking to Khorek, who was the monkey, not the organ grinder.

I pointed to Watch Man. 'He's your man now.'

'Can we get on with the transfer?'

His instruction had no impact. No one moved or spoke. He waved his good arm at the product stacked on the table. 'We had a deal, for fuck's sake. Let's close it.'

Watch Man wiped a hand over his beard. 'Barentsburg is small place, poor place. Life here very hard. We help each other. When we don't, is trouble.' He looked down at the Ferret. 'Too small for competition.'

Khorek's grasp of English might not have been up there with Watch Man's but he was catching the drift.

I was too. Things had just gone downhill fast. Watch Man was the go-to guy. And Khorek had been stupid enough to try to muscle in on his business. The gear in Stedman's container, coming via his brother's rich friends, might be an improvement on what Watch Man was hawking. If his regular supply came through Russia or Ukraine it had probably been cut with all manner of adulterants along the way, not to mention a blast of hairspray to stop the inferior-quality bricks crumbling. Still, Watch Man had the trade sewn up. You didn't simply turn up and set out your stall. Not if you wanted to see the spring, whenever that was. I was beginning to regret leaving the Mauser behind.

Beyoncé started singing 'Halo' very loudly from Watch Man's mobile. From the look of things, it was the closest he was ever going to get to one.

He turned away, phone to ear and spare hand covering it, Japanese style. I watched Khorek's eyes dart between Stedman and Watch Man. He was even more out of his depth than my one-armed passenger. The two deserved each other – chancers who thought they could make a fast buck without thinking through the consequences. Anyone with two brain cells wouldn't set up a burger stall without finding out who dominated the local pitches – unless he wanted to see the thing going up in flames. I knew that for a fact. My stepdad had had just the one when he'd taken the fast-food industry by storm outside Millwall football ground.

This was going to spiral down into a pile of shit if nothing was done. One of us needed to try to smooth over the cracks if we wanted to get out of there in one piece.

Watch Man finished the call. His head jerked up. 'In Barentsburg, we don't want trouble with foreigners. Trouble bring Norwegian government policemen and more problems. Mining business right now very bad, mine maybe sold. We want to keep our jobs if that happen. So, no trouble with foreigners.'

A gleam of stupidity or hope, I couldn't work out which, had found its way into Stedman's head.

'Well, we don't want any trouble either. I just need the money and we'll be out of here.'

The brightness in his voice didn't match the hollow look in his eyes.

Watch Man gazed at him with a mixture of amusement and pity. He hadn't lured Stedman all the way to Barentsburg so he could pay for something he had already stolen, or to tell him the merger of their two business empires had hit the buffers.

Stedman's desperation bubbled up now. 'I want my money or—'

Fuck knows how he would have finished the sentence, but Watch Man's finger on his chest cut him short. 'No, I want *my* money. *I* want money so there is no trouble.'

Stedman's mouth opened but nothing came out. He needed to do this more often, so he could get into the habit of saying the third thing that came into his head instead of the first.

Watch Man turned back to Khorek, who was somehow still defiant. 'Khorek very good family man, very loyal to family. Even now he not help us.' He leaned forward, flipped open Khorek's laptop and started to tap away at the keyboard. He glanced up at Stedman, his eyes gleaming in the glow of the screen. 'But I think you help instead . . .'

He tapped the lid. 'This tell me Khorek has number to send. And you, Stedman, you also give ID code to finish transfer.'

An Ethernet cable snaked out and disappeared through a hole in the wall. I guessed it would continue along the street to wherever it could grab a connection. Watch Man had it all worked out, and he was about to read Stedman his horoscope.

'So, now you make Khorek give number and you give number. You transfer money to me, then no trouble for you, for Khorek. No trouble for no one.'

Stedman stepped forward and slammed his hand down on the surface of the table, like he was showing a full house. I pulled him back. He didn't understand the world he had just walked into. It was one I constantly – and mostly unsuccessfully – tried to avoid.

'Don't you get it? The deal isn't going to happen. Lesson learned. Do what he says and let's get out of here. If we can.'

'No.'

Watch Man started to mutter as he got busy again

with his index fingers. 'You people stupid, so stupid. Why you people . . .' His voice tailed off as he found what he needed and turned the screen towards us. The soundtrack and the Skype image juddered, but its message was clear. Leila's face was streaked with tears and mascara. The shadows in the background suggested there were two of them with her and the wallpaper behind them was familiar. They were in the Radisson. She cried out as someone grabbed her neck and pushed her closer to the camera.

'Stedman . . . you there? Please . . . you . . . Khorek, you must pay them or . . . Help me, Stedman, please you must . . . Khorek . . .'

It was a pitiful sight but the one family member in the room was unmoved. I glanced at Khorek.

'She nothing to me. She *ublyudok . . . shlak.'*

My Russian definitely stretched to 'bastard' and 'slag'.

They were the first words we had heard from Ferret. He made a fist with the thumb thrust between the index and second finger, which roughly translated as *You're getting nothing from me.* Then he slammed his fist hard on the metal desk so the noise reverberated around the room.

Watch Man was clued up, but had he planned for this? He didn't keep me waiting for an answer. He hit Khorek with a wide swing of an open hand that was nearly the size of the laptop. Khorek went down with a scream, along with the computer. Watch Man's boot immediately made contact with the body, and didn't stop there. All I could see from our side of the desk was an eerie kaleidoscope of shadow and light. Ponytail

144

watched the drama, unmoved. I got the impression that he'd seen this episode before.

I ran out of time to think of a way out as Watch Man left Khorek to his latest helping of pain and headed towards us.

33

I swung my eyes towards Stedman. The zipped pocket on the left side of his chest suddenly became my whole world.

I charged towards him at ramming speed. Words were superfluous: he would have had to understand what I wanted, and then do what I wanted, and there wasn't a nanosecond to spare.

I crashed into him and carried on going until he hit the wall. I knew there would be noise and movement behind me, but I didn't hear it because I didn't need to. I had no control of what was happening there, only of what was in front of me.

'*What the fuck?*'

I pushed my left shoulder into his right one, keeping him pinned. My eyes burned into that zip. Then I took half a step back, ripped it open with one hand, reached inside with the other and grasped the flare gun's pistol grip. In the same fluid motion I collapsed to the floor and twisted around, pushing back the safety with my thumb, and fired into what was getting far too close.

The room exploded with blindingly bright light and smoke. Watch Man dropped to the ground, the burning ball of magnesium embedded in his calf.

I kicked away Stedman, who had fallen on top of me as Watch Man loosed off a succession of rapid-fire shrieks. He convulsed on the floor, burning his fingers as he tried to tear the mini-inferno out of his flesh before it could eat its way inside him.

'Flare! Another flare!'

Ponytail wasn't taking any chances. He had overturned the desk and got himself behind it. Now he started to push it forwards, like a battering ram, to get to me.

'Flare! Another flare! Fucking flare!'

All I got was the bubblewrap thrown at me. I tossed him the pistol. 'Load the fucker!'

The desk was scraping its way closer. I leaped over it, and Ponytail, aiming for the paraffin lamp that had just toppled to the ground. I grabbed it, turned back to Ponytail and brought it down on the top of his skull. The glass smashed and my weapon of choice clattered to the floor.

I kicked into his head as hard and quickly as I could to keep him down. The flare died but Watch Man continued to scream. My nostrils filled with the acrid reek of wet, burning flesh.

I heard more screams from behind me but they were Stedman's. He was on his feet and passing me.

He kicked into Khorek, punching as best he could with one good arm.

We had done what we needed, gained the initiative.

'Let's go. Come on!'

Stedman delivered another two kicks into his target. 'Go! *Go!*'

He wasn't listening. I had to pull at his empty sleeve. 'Fuck's sake, come on!'

'Leila . . . !'

'Nothing we can do here.'

I pulled him off Khorek and dragged him towards the door. It gave a creak, as if someone was on his way through but hesitating. I turned back to Stedman. 'The pistol, hit the door! Hit it!'

'Fuck! Fuck!' He gestured to the other side of the desk. It was still on the floor, along with the bubblewrap.

I let go of him and pointed at Ponytail. 'Keep that fucker down!'

As Stedman got busy with his boots again, I hurled myself back over the desk, grabbed the cartridge bubblewrap, lasered in on my objective and loaded.

The door opened enough for Half Bear to squeeze through it. I fired, but he reacted too sharply and jerked back outside. The flare ricocheted off the wall and back into the room. In moments the whole place was ablaze again with light, smoke, screams, and the hiss of burning magnesium. The fiery ball burned its way into the floor and ignited the spilled paraffin. Ponytail tried to douse the flames on his jacket and head. It wasn't happening.

Reloading the weapon, I went for the door. Stedman would follow. Who wouldn't, out of a burning room? I fired into the icy pathway either side of the dilapidated metal sheds, then reloaded with the last cartridge and headed out into the cold and the bubble of bright white light.

A fresh load of snow had started dumping itself from the sky and my boots crushed through it onto the ice below. I kept the weapon up, in the aim, ready for Half Bear.

For all I knew, the entire population could come out in a big show of solidarity with Watch Man and we'd be on our way down a mineshaft if we didn't get a move on. But, with luck, they'd be just like anyone else, knowing what was in their best interests – to keep their distance from anything that sounded like a drama. Either way, I didn't aim to hang about long enough to find out. We had to get away from the immediate area, and out of the town. As soon as I got us clear of the corrugated-iron sheds, I set off towards the snowmobile.

Stedman did his best to keep up. Thank fuck it was only an arm he'd lost. We didn't have all night.

I reached the steps by the harbour and had to wait. Stedman was wheezing and flagging. I sucked in ice-cold gulps of air that hurt as they hit my lungs. 'Get a fucking move on!'

'Don't leave me.'

'Shut the fuck up and run.'

We headed into the square. I checked behind us. People were starting to gather as they came out of the buildings surrounding Lenin.

It was pointless firing a warning shot. These fuckers had hunting rifles above their fireplaces. Besides, I might need the last cartridge to get us out of any real shit.

I patted my breast pocket to check the snowmobile keys. They were still there. But the snowmobile wasn't.

The UAZ minibus was, though, ticking over and ready to roll. I started towards it, preparing myself to grip the driver and drag him out onto the ice, get Stedman into the fucking thing, and move. It didn't matter where to. It would only be used for shuttling people around the town to the mine complex and down to the docks. Anywhere beyond that, it would be fucked. But so what? We needed to get the fuck away from this mob, and Stedman wasn't up to it.

'The van, come on!'

The group behind us shouted and started to close in. On our left, another three had emerged from what looked like a garage. A group of bodies appeared on the hotel steps and headed for the UAZ.

'Oh, fuck . . .' Stedman sank onto his knees.

'Get up!'

The group on the steps was much the largest, but they weren't showing any interest in us. Several had laptop cases and were bidding each other loud fare-wells. A delegation of some sort? I didn't give a fuck who they were: the flare-gun would soon move them out of our way.

And then, in their midst, a familiar face turned my way.

34

It was the Owl.

Standing alongside him was Munnelly. Both men stared at me, the crowd in the mid-distance, and Stedman lagging behind me by three or four metres. He was clearly in shit-state.

The bodies had got to about three hundred metres away and showed no signs of stopping. I made out the odd angry shout. It must have been obvious to the two Americans that something was wrong.

Munnelly took it all in, then glanced at me quizzically.

The Owl had a smile on his face that was straight out of the fast-food guide to customer care.

I beamed back at him. 'Mate – am I glad to see you. I remember you mentioning this place. We had some time to kill and . . . Anyway, our vehicle got stolen so we went looking for it. Just wait a minute. Don't go away.'

I turned and ran back to Stedman, grabbed hold of

him as if I was offering much-needed help. 'Shut the fuck up and get in the van.'

He coughed. 'Nick, I'm sorry, my lung, it's fucked. I'm fucked.'

I ignored him. 'Get to the van, and get in.'

All that other shit was for another day.

I half dragged him to the door and let him make his own way aboard. Then I ran back to the steps. Munnelly kept his eyes on the mob but the Owl came down to meet me. 'Shit, you had your vehicle stolen?'

'Yeah.' I checked behind me. Stedman was inside the van. 'We tried finding it. I don't know what we did or said, but we must have pissed somebody off.'

He was still wearing his greeter's grin but Munnelly had had enough. He moved down a couple of steps until we were eyeball to eyeball. 'What do you want? Why is he already in the vehicle?'

I kept it simple, this time. 'We have no transport. We need your help. All we want is a ride back.'

Munnelly turned on his heel. As he walked past me, he managed to barge into my shoulder, just to make a point, then made a beeline for the front seat. The Owl followed briskly, and so did I.

The driver was now flapping big-time. He didn't want to piss off his mates outside. So Munnelly made the decision for him. 'Get this motherfucker moving!' He poked the guy in the shoulder to emphasize each word.

The driver did exactly as he was told. He cranked it into gear and we started to trundle down the hill.

The Owl took Stedman's hand and shook. 'I'm Sam. You are?'

'Stedman.'

The smile stayed fixed as we moved down the road. The mini-mob stayed where they were, watching.

'Stedman? Cool name.'

35

Thirty minutes later, I watched the cluster of grey shapes that made up Barentsburg drop away beneath us, then get swallowed by a thick shelf of cloud. I turned away from the bubble window on the side of the Chinook's fuselage.

Stedman was slumped next to me on the nylon-webbing seat that ran the length of the hold. Bathed in the gentle red glow of the aircraft's night lighting, he stared sightlessly at the alloy decking beneath our feet.

At least his breathing was getting back to normal. He'd been hit by secondary missile fragments in Afghan, the shit that's scattered by a high-explosive detonation. Metal, wood, rock, you name it. Anything in the close area of the blast fragmentizes and sprays out as far as it can at high velocity, like thousands of miniature bullets. Some had entered his chest cavity and a lung. It was a fucker, but his injuries appeared to have one good side effect: after a period of strong exertion, he wasn't his normal gobby self. Since we'd come aboard, he'd been doing what I told him to do, which was to shut up.

I knew he was flapping about Leila, but there was nothing we could do about that until we got back to Longyearbyen. I could have got hold of Jack or another member of the team via their hotel, and asked them to help her, but to me it boiled down to a simple numbers game. Three bodies – Stedman, Leila, and me – were already in the shit. Shoving into it another five, who had nothing to do with this drama, made no sense whatsoever. They would have no idea what might be waiting for them at the Radisson.

It was tough shit for her, but if you tried to fuck about with other people's money and power, then tough shit happened. Stedman would have to learn to live with it. If Leila had made it through whatever they'd done to her, I reckoned she'd already be on a flight, and looking to trade Stedman in for a more reliable model.

My main concern was what exactly we had left back there in Barentsburg, and would it be following us? I had to assume it would. Watch Man, with his anger-management issues, wounded leg and wounded pride, would need to show us who was boss. And Khorek, plus whatever and whoever he represented, would be just as pissed off. The rest of the team were connected to this shit by pure association; the only option open to me, Stedman and the rest of them was very simple. We all had to make as much distance as we could from Svalbard, and fast.

There might still be a chance that the team could go north if Jack would climb down from his high horse, take Cauldwell's offer and let Rune on board with his guides. But Stedman and I would have to totally detach ourselves from the team.

It would make Jules happy if Stedman was gone, and to make sure he didn't want to stick with me to avoid whatever might be coming our way, I could convince him he could still complete an ice walk, but in Antarctica, on his own.

Stedman came out of his trance. The timing was so perfect I wondered if he'd been reading my thoughts. 'I've been a twat. I know I have, OK? But we have to get to Leila. She needs help.'

'Wait out and shut up. We'll sort her out as soon as we get there. There's nothing we can do right now. But, remember, you've got to stand by for bad news. It might be too late. Just keep a grip of yourself. We still have a job to do when we land.'

Stedman didn't acknowledge, just resumed his deck-staring pose.

Munnelly was sitting forward, just behind the pilots, talking shit into a headset. Across the deck from us on the opposite length of seating was the Owl, both hands firmly gripping the seat's aluminium tubing, preparing himself for an instant crash.

I had to shout over the roar of the rotors. 'Thanks for the lift.'

He gave me a knowing shrug and turned up his fast-food grin to full sizzle.

I wasn't too sure if he had bought the stolen-snowmobile story. It was hard to tell behind that smile. Munnelly hadn't believed a word, but who gave a fuck? We were out of the immediate danger area and that was all that mattered for now.

The Owl shook his head pityingly, but I couldn't make out what he was saying over the noise. I unbuckled and crossed the deck to sit next to him.

'I said, Russians. Whaddaya expect? Consider it a favour returned.'

I wanted to friend up even more with him because he might come in handy if things got out of control in Longyearbyen.

'You strike any deals back there?'

He sighed, as if the idea was ridiculous. 'Just a fishing expedition mostly. See what they got.' He leaned closer. 'Plus, the Russian Mafia are in there, using it as a front for God knows what. Fact.'

I tried to seem convincingly surprised. 'What?'

'Anyway, Putin's never going to give up his toehold in a NATO country just like that. Why would he?' He smirked and leaned even closer. 'Besides, we got other fish to fry.' He changed his tune. 'Your North Pole buddy OK there? Looks kinda green.'

'He's fine, just not good in helicopters. Much better on ice.'

The Owl gave one of his trademark smiles that didn't really tell me if he'd got the joke or not. 'Say, how did he . . . ?' He made a chopping movement against his arm.

'Left it in a wood-chipper.'

The Owl's eyes bulged. There was a second while he computed it. 'For real?'

I shrugged. 'Yup, but he bullshits about it. Says it was bitten off by a shark.'

The Owl roared with laughter and I liked to think Munnelly would have joined in if he could have heard it over the din. 'Ah, Nick, you Brits crack me up.'

I sensed that nothing else was going to be said of any value on the bonding front. The Owl was gripping either side of his seat even harder.

'Listen, I'd better go back to my mate. Keep him company before he pukes up everywhere.' I grabbed a couple of sick bags and crossed to Stedman. I shoved a bag at his face. 'Take it.'

He did as he was told, but gave me a sideways look. 'You saved my life.'

'Forget it. If I'd stopped to think about it I'd probably have left you behind.'

He wasn't sure I was joking, and neither was I. But the long face was starting to irritate me even more.

He turned to the bubble window, and disappeared into his own world of agony and defeat. I'd met survivors like him who'd become reckless – their near-death experience gave them delusions of immortality. And that, along with the memory of his dead mates, probably made him all the more determined to go for it and fuck the consequences – crashing into things, hoping his WTF bravado would somehow see him through.

I couldn't help having some sympathy for him. At least he was trying to make something happen. But that didn't mean I felt I could rely on him. He might not even learn the blindingly obvious lessons from what we'd just been through.

I sat back and caught Munnelly studying us. He wanted us out of his Chinook, and never to see us again.

It was only when we'd debussed that I wondered how the Owl knew my name.

36

Longyearbyen
Latitude: 78.2232 North
Longitude: 15.6267 East

We stood to the side of an old warehouse three build-ings down from the Radisson, in the lee of a long line of industrial-sized wheelie-bins. Even though I had Sven's padded outer gear on and there was total cloud cover, the wind bit into me. It didn't help that I was totally fucked and in need of sleep.

Cauldwell's mobile bounced me to voicemail so I closed down.

I passed the sat phone to Stedman and got my gloved hands under my armpits, which I knew would help a little, and started to stamp my feet on the ice, which I knew never did.

He made yet another call, this time to the lobby. I'd binned his mobile as soon as we landed. Had Leila given Watch Man or Khorek his number? Did they know how to locate it? It didn't matter now – but the downside was that he didn't know any of the team's numbers. Why should he? That was the SIM card's job.

'No, I won't leave a message. I'll call her mobile.'

I shook my head, and not just because of the chill. He'd already left five messages for Leila. He had to expect the worst, and we now had two reasons to get out of town, the island, the whole archipelago, as soon as. She was clearly connected to Stedman, and Stedman was connected to the rest of the team. And, whether I liked it or not, to me.

He cancelled the call and was about to hit redial. I unfolded my arms so I could rip the thing away from him and power down. Batteries died very quickly in this kind of weather.

'Bin the calls, mate. If she hasn't answered yet, it isn't happening. You, me – we'll be getting out of here on the first flight. It doesn't matter where it's going, we need to be on it. You then go your own way, but for fuck's sake keep your head down. No gobbing off. If she's dead, you'll be found sooner or later, but you deny everything and say you saw the body and just panicked, OK?'

He nodded, but I didn't care what he said if the police eventually caught up with him. I would be long gone. I just needed him to have something in his head that sounded plausible so it would be easy for me to get him off Spitsbergen as quickly and as smoothly as possible. It killed two birds with one stone: it not only gave me some time to get detached from this shit, but also he would have no way of involving the rest of the team.

I was staying with him until we'd got to the airport

and got tickets to make sure he didn't have the chance to do any more damage than he had already. I certainly didn't want him getting wobbly and going to the police – or, even worse, trying to solve a situation that he had no information about and very little capability of sorting out even if he did.

'But what if she's still alive, Nick? What if they still have her? She could still be in the room—'

'What can you do? Burst in and use your one-armed superpowers to save her from the nasty men?'

I understood his concern, of course, but I was starting to get impatient. If Leila was alive, great. If she wasn't, we weren't about to magic her back.

'Get a grip. Last time you had to get a move on, you couldn't even run up the stairs. You tried to make contact and you got nothing. So now you need – *we* need – to get the fuck away from here. We need distance before we try for a taxi to the airport. We then wait for the fucking thing to open.'

I emerged from the cover of the bins and started towards the back of the building, away from the hotel. But Stedman wasn't following. I turned back. It didn't matter what he thought about the situation, or what he wanted out of it, because he was coming with me.

'No, *no* . . . Nick, listen. My passport . . . it's in the room . . .'

I pushed him up against the wall. He kept perfectly still as I unzipped the outer gear and checked.

He wasn't lying.

'Fuck's sake. *Switch on.*'

From the far end of the line came a loud crash, and the noise got louder still as the bins cannoned into each other like falling dominoes. The one nearest us toppled over completely.

Fight or flight? It was a simple decision. We turned and ran. But not from Watch Man and his crew – from a fucking great bear, and we kept running. Neither of us wanted to become a substitute for its normal morning croissants.

As we turned the corner onto the main drag I started to see the funny side. I shouted back to Stedman, if only to get him moving quicker. 'It must have liked the smell of you yesterday. You should be flattered.'

We slowed when we were within reach of the Radisson's entrance.

'Got your key card?'

He nodded.

'OK, this is the plan. Do what I say when I say it. Or I hand you straight back to the bear.'

37

Leila was heading for the taxi rank, dragging a well-worn black plastic suitcase behind her. She had spruced herself up since the Skype call. But a change of clothes and a fresh layer of make-up hadn't done much to cover the bruising.

Stedman stretched out his arm, but the love-fest looked like it was going to be short-lived.

'Babe, thank God, I've been—'

'Don't come near me, *asshole*!'

'Babe, please keep it down. Listen, I can—'

She did quieten down. She leaned as close to Stedman's face as she had to mine last night. 'I don't want to listen. Not to you. Not ever again.'

Stedman was too concerned with his own self-justification to sense what had changed and what now had to happen. 'I'm not the arsehole. Check out your shit-for-brains cousin. He forgot to tell you someone's already got the place sewn up. All this shit is his fucking fault. We could have been killed back there.'

They could sort this on their own time. Or not. I moved alongside them. 'Where are they? You know?'

She treated me to the same death stare she'd given Stedman. Then her eyes filled. She was becoming human again.

So was he. 'Babe, you all right?'

After being completely wrapped up in his own defensive position, Stedman had finally noticed the marks and discovered he really was an arsehole.

'What did they do to you?'

'What do you *think*?' She fought it, but the tears started to fall.

Stedman wrapped his arms around her and Leila hugged him back. No matter how pissed off she was with him, she couldn't resist the comfort.

I made eye contact. 'There're no flights yet – it's too early. We need to get off the street. Let's all go to my room.'

As I turned and made for the revolving door, two Toyota SUVs with flashing yellow roof lights and blue bear decals on virtually every panel sped past and disappeared down the service road.

Jules chose that moment to emerge from the hotel, talking animatedly into her mobile. She killed the call when she caught sight of the two of them embracing. Her eyes widened at the sight of Leila's bruises, then the mess Khorek's floor had made of Sven's onesie. Her mouth did too – until she made the very sensible decision not to ask any questions. She gestured at Stedman. 'I've been trying to find him. The rest of them are out training. Gabriel's got problems with his prosthetic.'

She studied the pair once more. I didn't see much in the way of sympathy.

Two foghorns blasted from somewhere along the service road. She turned back to me, unaffected by the noise. They'd been here too long. 'Did he make the deal? They need to know what's happening.'

'Gabriel OK?' One of us would give her the bad news soon, but she'd have to earn it.

She swung instantly into doctor speak. 'The socket on his prosthetic isn't a great match, so he gets chafing. The chafing makes his stump swell. Most of the time, he puts up with it. That's the problem with all of them. They won't let on they're in pain until it fells them. They think their own sheer bloody-mindedness is going to keep everything moving. I—'

'Yeah, he's in pain. Can it be sorted later?'

There wasn't time for the full BUPA-funded consultation. All I needed to know was that he wasn't lying there with blood spurting all over the shop.

'Well, yes, but I want to see for myself. If they're going to—'

'Where are they training?'

'Just outside town. I'm on my way there now. The weather is closing in and they could do with the experience. If, of course, they *are* going. Did he make the deal?'

'Good. I need to see Jack. Will you take us, once this lot's sorted? Won't be long.'

It had better not be. My thoughts were still very much focused on Watch Man. Jules sensed the worst and turned to Leila: maybe she could get some sense out of her. There was no way she was about to say anything useful to Stedman.

'Leila, do you know if—'

'Fuck off,' Leila spat, before Jules could finish.

Stedman made a last futile attempt at a kiss. Maybe it was to soothe her, maybe it was an attempt at making up. Either way, it wasn't welcome.

'Fuck off, all of you. I'm done here. I'm going home.'

Stedman tried to hold onto her but she shrugged off his hand.

Jules realized that this particular patient was going downhill fast. 'What's happening, Nick? Tell me! Look at the state of her. I'm getting *really* concerned. Are the team going?'

'He fucked up. The deal didn't happen. Wait here.'

I left Jules at the top of the steps and grabbed Stedman by his empty sleeve. 'Mate, she's not interested. Let her go. It's safer for her. Remember, we've still got a problem.'

I loosened my grip and moved away, back to Jules, as Leila's cab left the rank.

Jules was visibly upset, and that probably didn't happen often. But she couldn't give a fuck about these two. 'What are we going to do now? They'll be heartbroken. All this time, waiting, hoping . . .' She dug around for her mobile.

I jumped in before she could fuck the situation up even more. 'Wait, not yet. It might not be over. I may have a way of getting the trip back on line – without Stedman.'

She wasn't convinced.

'Jules, just hold the call. Give me a minute to sort him out and then I'll explain. I'll meet you in the lobby. They – you – need to know what's going on, because it could affect you all. I'm not bullshitting, it's serious, but there could be some good news here.'

It wasn't met with the smile of relief I was hoping for.

'No Stedman?'

Still nothing.

'See you in a minute, yeah?' I twisted the mobile out of her hand and bounced down the steps. I needed to get this fucker under control first.

Jules turned back to the lobby. The expression on her face said she was trying to work out precisely what to say to me about ripping her mobile out of her hand. She didn't seem able to find the words yet. But she would. That was what doctors did.

I tugged at Stedman's empty sleeve once more. 'Let's move. Nothing's changed. We've still got to get out. Grab your passport and check out. Anything that doesn't fit in a carry-on, just leave in your room.'

We reached the door.

'If the room is fucked up, sort it the best you can.'

We filed into the lobby and I led him straight to the lifts. 'I'll meet you down here in fifteen, ready to move.'

Jules was waiting by Reception. I gave her the mobile back. It was the closest I could come to a peace-offering. She still didn't smile.

'Right, here's what happened. But when you explain to them, do not exaggerate, and at the same time don't understate. OK?'

'Don't patronize me. Just tell me, for God's sake.'

Fair one. It *was* patronizing. But some people couldn't stop themselves corrupting information they'd been given to pass on. I should have been making the call myself but I didn't have time.

We walked to the side of the lift shaft and I explained everything: why the deal hadn't happened, why Leila's face was fucked up, why the team might be in danger, and why Stedman and I were now leaving the island.

Jules took in everything, hanging onto the glimmer of hope I gave her that the trip could still be on.

'OK, Nick. Give me a couple of seconds.' She sucked it all in and composed herself. 'So, what now?'

'Make the call. I've got to make one myself. And tuck yourself into a corner, out of plain view, in case the Barentsburg crew come looking for me and Stedman . . . and maybe make a connection with you from last night.'

38

I sat by the window in my room to get a signal on the
sat phone, and cut away from Cauldwell's mobile as it
went into message mode for the second time since I'd
been in the hotel.

I fished the bit of paper with Rune's sat phone
number out of my neck wallet and checked every car
that pulled up outside as I dialled.

The yogurt-commercial voice clicked in so quickly it
took me a moment to ping that it wasn't a recorded
message. I heard the wind blasting his handset. 'Mate,
Nick Stone.'

'Ah, thank the goodness. I've been desperate to
speak with you. I should have taken your number. I
can't get hold of Mr Cauldwell.'

'No problem, we got each other now. Listen, can we
meet at your place?'

'Not possible, sadly. We are in Barneo. Mr Cauldwell
said you come yesterday. Where is the delay?'

'No worries.' I tried to sound upbeat. 'The team are almost ready to join you.'

Rune gave me the Scandi version of a laugh. At least I'd made someone happy today.

'Thank you. We cannot go from here without you guys. Is there a problem? Can I help?'

'No, mate, it's all good. All sorted.'

'You must come, soon as you can. We cannot move without.'

I couldn't see why. But whatever it was that the team was supposed to be able to supply, this show needed to get on the road. 'Great. How do they get there? You have the tickets? You need names, that sort of thing?'

There was an awkward pause. Then: 'I thought Mr Cauldwell had organized . . . Sorry, I . . . A little confused. You need to buy them there. Maybe Mr Cauldwell can help. But is very important you hurry – we have a short window. The weather comes up from south. If flights cannot see the runway, there is no flying. I told Mr Cauldwell, he needs to get every-one here *very* soon.'

'What about kit? We haven't—'

'Nick, everything you need is here. Mr Cauldwell asked us to freight everything with us. You come with clothes, boots. You all need spare bindings, do not forget. On the ice, there are no ski stores.' It must have been an ice-people joke. He liked that one.

'OK, got it. I have two things for you. One, I'm drop-ping out.'

Rune went up an octave. 'But, Nick, we need you. That's what Mr Cauldwell brought you in for. You got to—'

'Mate, listen to me.' I gave him a second to come back down. 'Make sure the team think I'm now sponsoring the trip. It's the only way I'm going to get them on board.'

Rune just wanted the team there. 'Sure, Nick, whatever we need to do, right? That father–son problem they have. We can help smooth that over.'

'I'll confirm our ETA in the next—'

'I must know in two hours.'

'OK.'

'Also, please, no mention of what I'm about, or Armancore. Mr Cauldwell wouldn't like that. Please remember.'

I closed down the call, picked up my day sack and went back down to the lobby. Jules, mobile in hand, was scanning the area, doing what I'd asked her to do.

She jumped to her feet. Impatience was taking over. But I wasn't there to answer questions, I was there to get things done. 'You talk to Jack?'

She shook her head. 'Just Will.'

'How did he take it?'

She looked at me like I'd landed from outer space. 'How do you think? And how would you expect all of them to take it? Come on, for God's sake, Nick.'

I was going to have to grip her. 'Listen, this situation is nothing to do with me. I'm still here, and I'm trying to rectify the fucking problem. So just take a breath. Please.'

She got it. She took a breath. 'Will . . . of course he's worried. He's worried about the trip, he's worried about the situation we're in, but he's more worried about me.'

I'd already thought about that. 'It's not a problem. You can fly out this morning with me and Stedman. Once you're off the island, he can calm down.'

She wasn't mollified. 'But Will? The team? I don't want to just—'

I held up my hand. 'They'll have to move quickly. There's no time for more practice – they need to get out there and do it.'

Her face lit up. 'Nick, that's so good to hear. But—'

I put up a hand. 'Stop. I'll explain it all soon. The kit's already at Barneo. It's all there, waiting for them. I'll go and get Stedman. You need to call Will again, tell him they should pack their personal kit, boots and spare bindings for a move today.'

The on switch had been thrown in the bit of her head that was marked *Action*. 'On it. I'll bring the minibus to the front and wait.' She was already hitting the mobile keys with her thumb.

'Jules?'

She looked up. Her expression said she was back in the operating theatre.

'Be careful. Outside. Be aware. OK?'

She nodded, but her eyes had gone back to the keys.

'Make sure they remember the bindings. There are no ski stores where they're going.'

She didn't smile. It was almost like she'd heard it before.

I headed for the lift, but spotted Stedman at the desk, checking out. I sat by the front window and waited for him, watching for the VW to roll up and to make sure nobody wanted to fuck around with it out there in the cold.

Stedman joined me, gripping a heavy North Face bag. 'You got your passport?' I wasn't going to let him put us through the same pantomime all over again.

He couldn't tap his pockets to emphasize the point because his hand was full of hold-all. 'Yeah. Really.'

'The room?'

His face clouded. 'The room is a bit . . . fucked up. There's no blood. We're in good shape.'

'What about the rest of your clothes, and hers? She leave any?'

He shook his head. 'Leila tends to hang onto everything she can lay her hands on. Except men, obviously. My clothes are in laundry bags. I dumped them in the service area.'

He didn't bother to conceal how pleased he was with himself. At last he'd done something right.

Jules arrived outside and took up the middle third of the taxi rank, making it very clear she wasn't moving for anyone.

It was probably the last time I was going to be alone with Stedman. 'Remember, you're in the shit with these people. You're in the shit with everyone, for that matter. Let's just sort this out and then you can put some distance between yourself and whatever might be coming your way.'

I stood up, grabbed my day sack and checked the set-up outside one more time. 'Let's go.'

We pushed our way through the revolving doors and down the steps. I shoved Stedman into the back of the VW, behind the passenger seat. He was pressed up against Jules's medical bag, but at least he was out of the way.

I climbed in beside her as she put the minibus in gear. 'You get hold of Will?'

She was paying more attention to the indicator and the rear-view than to me. 'They're packing.' She swung the wheel and put her foot down.

39

I kept an eye on Stedman in my wing mirror. He was staring aimlessly again, the side of his forehead pressed against the glass behind me. His head rocked from side to side as the VW pulled away. He was shutting up, like I'd asked him to, but not because he was being compliant.

I talked to him over my shoulder, but didn't look back. It was a habit I was trying to break. 'Mate, you've got to get past all this shit. She's still breathing, you're still breathing, so you're both still winning. You've got to keep thinking that, OK?'

He didn't even blink.

Jules glanced away from the road. 'Is it really going to happen?'

'If Jack will let it. And if he's not too fucked up by their fond farewell.' I tilted my head in the direction of her best mate in the back, who was still busy staring out of the window at nothing. 'Him stepping away is good for you and the team, right?'

She gave me a don't-fuck-with-me look, then swapped it for something softer now that she was daring to believe Will might actually get what he needed. 'Look, I'm not sure how you came to be here, but . . . I've seen a lot of loss, Nick. A *lot*. And I know two things. One, we all feel responsible for what happens to our loved ones, even in a war. And two, talking's better than silence. We have to mourn. We have to take the internal experience of grief and express it outside ourselves. If you hold it in indefinitely, there will be consequences.

'It's a military thing, Nick, to grieve without properly mourning. But I guess you don't need me to tell you that.'

She glanced in the rear-view. Even though she was in lecture mode, she was taking my warning seriously.

'Instead of being encouraged to express their grief outwardly, and come to terms with bad things they're not necessarily responsible for, soldiers are told, "Get a grip," and "Crack on." Really helpful stuff like that. They often end up grieving deep within themselves, in isolation, instead of mourning outside. They can't find a way to get past the pain and move on.'

I nodded away politely, so she knew I was appreciating the fact that she was sharing her hard-won knowledge. But she didn't know that I *was* responsible. Too fucking responsible. And holding it in was what I did, what I had always done. I was good at it. I had no choice.

The help she was trying to give was for people in the real world, not fuck-ups like me, who spent their life doing the dull, dangerous, mind-destroying shit the squeaky-clean people who called it home wouldn't want on their hands. If I hadn't kept a grip on the shit that had been buzzing around in my head since I was sixteen, I wasn't too sure how I would express it. And I really didn't want to find out.

40

Visibility was deteriorating – the cloud cover felt like a low ceiling we'd bang our heads on if we didn't stay in a crouch.

Jules hustled the VW across the snow like a pro.

'Nice.'

She gave me a withering glare.

'It was meant to be a compliment.'

'The family farm in Devon . . . My father shoved me in the driving seat of our battered Defender as soon as I could reach the pedals. I was a bit of an expert on mud and grass and everything slippery long before I got anywhere near tarmac.'

She gestured back at Stedman, who was curled up now, sparked out, like a kid after too much fun at Alton Towers.

The team were clustered round a couple of snow-mobiles, strapping their kit onto pulks, homemade wooden sledges hitched to the back with climbing rope. I'd seen a lot of those things – they were the locals' favourite DIY project. A big sheet of plywood, a curved plastic nose, a fistful of bungees to strap stuff on and, bingo, you'd turned your snowmo into a minibus.

The ridge that dominated the skyline whenever the sun came out reached up into the cloud behind them.

I twisted around and gave Stedman a prod. He shook himself awake, eyes widening, and glanced around, probably hoping it had all been a bad dream.

Jack started towards us before she brought the wagon to a halt, like those few steps would make all the difference to the time it was going to take to grip Stedman. Well, that was what Jack's face was telling me. I thought I might as well let the two of them get that all over and done with before convincing Jack I had the answer to their problem.

I didn't spot too many hopeful expressions around the place as the three of us got out, and it wasn't because of the weather. I kept a few steps behind Stedman so he had room to do some explaining. Jules heaved her medical bag out of the nine-seater and made for the snowmobiles. Gabriel positioned himself on one of the vehicle's seats, ready for her to take a look at his stump.

Jack studied the snow between his boots, kicking it into a small hummock as Stedman stammered out his confession.

'I . . . I – I'm sorry, Jack. I . . . should have told you about . . . the money. The deal. Where Leila was in all this . . . But I knew how important it was to you . . . to me . . . fuck it, to all of us . . .'

The others had stopped what they were doing and listened in. A few very long seconds passed after

Stedman had stumbled to a halt with a final couple of sorrys. None of them moved or spoke.

Without any warning, Jack jumped forward and rammed his forehead into Stedman's face. He lost his balance and slipped over in the snow, then bent down, hands glued to his skull as he took the pain that always followed a badly planted head-butt.

Everyone stood rooted to the spot except Jack, who finally got himself upright, turned and walked away.

Stedman was still down in the snow, nose leaking. Jules rushed over, but the cold would probably stop the bleeding just as well as anything she could do for him.

I moved to where Jack had retreated. Hands on hips, breathing hard, he turned away as I got nearer.

I put a firm hand on his shoulder. 'You have to get out of here, Jack. All of you.'

'Just fuck right off.'

Even Jack probably hadn't seen this side of himself before. The sum total of his anger and frustration about trying and failing to make this thing happen had erupted in that one moment. Maybe he blamed himself for letting Stedman back in, for listening to him, letting the fucker get his hopes up – and, worst of all, for trusting him.

I gripped him, hard. 'Mate, you've got to listen. I can get you all out of this shit and up north. Really.'

He tried to step away but I held on. He didn't want to listen just yet: he'd been badly let down by Stedman, his comrade, his friend, and was still stuck in his trough of self-pity. The bond between them wasn't going to disappear into thin Arctic air. That was what was making the pain inside his head worse than the pain outside – but he had to get over it, and quickly. All that was for another day, when they could face each other across the studio floor in their own private version of *The Jeremy Kyle Show*.

'Mate, chances are, what happened in Barentsburg won't stay in Barentsburg.'

Jack's head was spinning, both physically and mentally. He'd left a crimson starburst on the face of one of his best mates, and he suddenly didn't know which way was up. He didn't know who the fuck to trust. And the fact that his dad had never left him any options had probably prevented him thinking them through in the first place.

'Jack, you've got three choices. You stay here, and try to get the trip back on line yourself – at the same time looking over your shoulder. Or you bin it now and leave with Stedman.' I paused, to let all this sink in. 'Or you go north on my cheque book, no interference from your dad. I've got the guides, the kit and the money.'

There was still no reaction. He needed more time.

I tightened my grip on him.

'Jack, you have to make a decision. Not just for yourself but the others. They need this trip and they need to put some distance between themselves and last night's fuck-up. Right now, you're nothing, big on intentions but with no capability. I'm the fucking capability, so you need to pull your finger out and make a decision, *any* decision.'

He finally raised his eyes to mine. There was no light in them, and that had nothing to do with the cloud cover. 'Like I said, Nick, fuck off.'

I raised my hands and stepped away. He wasn't in the mood to listen.

I started back towards the VW. If Jack couldn't make a decision and keep his team safe, then someone had to.

Gabriel was still on the saddle of the snowmobile with Jules. As she swabbed away at his red and swollen stump, he didn't try to camouflage the pain. Stedman leaned back on the bonnet, a fistful of cotton wool pressed to his nose.

Rio and Will were strapping the last of their kit on the homemade trailers. I shouted over to them to get things moving. 'Lads, you know what's happening. No matter which way, we have to be off the island ASAP. Come over to the wagon. We need to sort this shit out.'

I pointed towards the murk crawling down the mountains behind them. 'That's coming in fast.'

Jack snapped out of it. 'No, stop! Nick, please . . . I'm sorry.'

I kept walking. I didn't want to play hard to get, but he was going to have to work harder than that.

'Wait!'

I took a couple more steps, then let him catch up.

He waved a hand. 'OK, OK. I'm a bit . . . fucked up. I'm sorry.' He took a man-sized breath. 'What do you have, exactly?'

'The same deal your dad had. But I've taken it over. You get two guides and a garden gnome thrown in for luck.'

He looked puzzled but knew it wasn't the time to ask. 'Who are they?'

'Environmentalists. They plant devices all along the route that measure the ice melt.'

'What do they want with us?'

'Mate, you need each other. There's a lot of energy companies up there and people like the Gnome barging in with all their save-the-planet initiatives could jeopardize their cash flow big-time. So they need to slip into a last-degree ski expedition to hood prying eyes, and you need the guides – plus three full sets of arms and legs.'

I looked around at the rest of the team and gave them my best shit-eating grin. 'Let's face it, you need a few more of *them* around here, don't you?'

I still wasn't convinced by the line Cauldwell and Rune had shot me. But so what? It was a means to an end. And it worked. Jack's face creased and I got something approaching a laugh out of him.

'If this turns out to be my father, Nick . . .'

'It was your father – but now it isn't. He's history. I'm paying for everything.'

Jack's expression dialled back to 'concerned'. I couldn't blame him. Mine would have too. Did I have a Stedman-like deal up my sleeve, and were they about to get fucked over once more?

'It's my money, Jack. Really. Mate, I'm loaded. I don't know what to do with the stuff. I *want* to pay. You lot getting to that Pole matters just as much to me as it does to you.' I fell silent for a moment because I'd realized that the words coming out of my mouth were true. 'I get it. I understand. So shut up and let's get sorted. It's cold out here.'

'Yeah . . . What the fuck are we doing?' Jack had re-engaged with the real world.

'Exactly right. More bits will be snapping off that

Barneo ice floe as we speak. Get your team sorted and off to the airport, soon as you can. Jules can take Gabriel back, and drop me and Stedman in town. We'll cab it to the airport to sort out the flights. I think Jules may come with us, but she and Will can work that out.'

His smile – proud but still uncertain – was the one he had used the first time I'd seen him as a zit-faced teenager in the Lines. 'Sounds good.'

'Course it does. I'll call the Gnome and tell him we're on our way.'

41

Compared with yesterday, the terminal building was like a zoo – rammed with overheated people in duvet jackets with day sacks on their backs, wheeling trolley bags with even more North Face hold-alls heaped on top of them. The public-address system waffled on, doing its best to compete with the constant rustle of nylon ski pants and murmurs of apology as passengers bumped into each other.

I glanced at the departures board as we walked in, on the off chance it might contain some vaguely useful information. Where there should have been departure times, the LED display showed nothing but red.

Stedman was busy checking out the crowd and Will's mobile for any sign of Leila. We needed to split the tasks. I pointed to the service desk, which was heaving, just like the check-ins. 'Get three tickets to anywhere. I'll come and pay as soon as I've sorted Barneo out. It doesn't matter if we're all going together or to different places, just get three of us out today. I'll meet you over there.' I pointed to the desk with the AN-74 imagery.

But Stedman wasn't listening. He was still checking the crowds and the mobile screen for Leila.

'Mate, switch on. Lots to do.'

He started to push his way through the throng.

The Barneo desk was the only deserted one. The woman sitting behind it had buried herself in a glossy *Hello!* type magazine – she probably thought it would stop people like us trying to talk to her. She looked extremely bored with whatever she wasn't quite reading. She glanced up as we approached and I recognized her from yesterday. She had pointed me towards Stedman and the phone boxes. Now, with all her outer jackets off, I could see a name badge.

'Hello there, Synne. Is there a flight to Barneo today?' I couldn't tell if she recognized me. Why should she? It was an airport. She saw thousands of faces every week.

She gazed at me, her face broadcasting 'Why would I be sitting here if there weren't any flights?'

Finally, I got a 'Yes.' Then she had second thoughts. 'The weather coming in from the south. Maybe it will delay flights. I do not know.'

She didn't really care either way. It was just another day at the office. And whatever we had to offer wasn't going to compete with Brangelina.

'Is there any way of knowing? Can we check? Can we get some tickets?'

Her eyes dropped reluctantly to her screen and she tapped a few keys. 'Is possible. But it won't be taking off for three, maybe four hours. There's more freight to be loaded.'

I didn't need to know the ins and outs of what was going.

'I want to buy four tickets, open return.'

An operation like this was never going to be set like a normal commercial airline. The weather was a huge factor, as was cramming in as many passengers and as much cargo as possible, to maximize profit. And they didn't even need to know how to spell 'schedule'. Barneo didn't exactly have a holding pattern above it.

'Are you with an expedition?'

'Yes – not me, there's a group coming soon. But there's been a big mess-up.' I went into babbling mode. 'Three of them, the guides, are already on the ice. But the rest of them are still here. I don't know what's happened. All the kit's already been freighted up there so we don't have to worry about extra weight on the aircraft – all they'll have is what they can carry with them. There's just four of them, four seats, please.'

She tapped away as I babbled. I couldn't tell from her expression whether she was onside or still didn't give a shit. It was pointless getting worked up. I had no control over this phase. I just had to let her get on with it.

I was sweating up, thanks to Sven's over-padding, so I started to unzip and peel it off.

She finally found what she needed on the screen. 'It's mostly freight on today's flight. They would have to put on extra seating. Is short notice, but we can get you on. There will be an extra charge.'

No surprises there. I stayed in begging mode. 'They

need to join the rest of the team, or they're going to lose their window. Could you do it for me, please?'

She didn't answer, but her fingers were dancing a flamenco across the keyboard. She looked up as Stedman joined me. 'Oh, you found him. Very good.'

'Nick, there are no flights. The weather . . .' He was talking to me but his eyes were pretty much everywhere else. 'Nothing coming in, so nothing going out. No one knows when that will change. It's shit.'

I turned back to Synne. 'Excuse me.'

'OK, it can be done.' The excitement of it all showed in her face, and I guessed I was about to find out why. 'In all . . . three hundred and forty-eight thousand dollars.'

Stedman froze halfway through trying to fight his arm out of its sleeve. '*What?* For a two-and-a-half-hour flight?'

'You want to take the train instead?' She pursed her lips. 'That price includes up to three days' use of the ice-camp facilities and your helicopter flight back from the Pole. You are the expedition, no?'

It was like it was Stedman's own personal savings. 'Yes, but – really?'

Synne gave him a what-the-hell-are-you-on? look. 'Extra seating will also have to be put on the aircraft. And it's the last year the service will operate from here. I think they do not care if you fly or not.'

I dipped into my neck wallet as Stedman managed to shake off his sleeve. I caught Synne's half-smile. It told me that I was only a step away from some middle-aged American tourist digging into a bum-bag.

Stedman was still preoccupied with the Barneo

logistics. 'Really? That's going to happen? They're going to cut loose from Norway?'

'Yes. Next year, all from Russia.'

I held out my card. 'The team will give you the details you need when they get here.'

She took the card and inspected it suspiciously, checking the back for identification having studied the front for embossed numbers and found none. Her eyes narrowed.

'It will work.' I pointed at the reader. 'It'll give you a number to ring.' I got back to Stedman and made sure I had his attention. 'You sure there are no flights out? We can't get out anywhere?'

'Nothing.'

'And nobody's got any idea of when we can?'

'Nothing's going to happen until the weather lifts. Even if it gets better down south and they can take off – they'll just follow the storm. It's heading north. Nobody knows anything. What are we going to do, Nick?'

'I'll think on it. Listen – I've got to go and square things with Sven. You sort out the rest of the team when they arrive, get their passport details, anything that's needed. Get them on the manifest. But try and keep an eye on what's going on with the flights, yeah? Keep switched on, mate.'

'Excuse me but . . . ?' Synne's voice, from behind me.

She held out a phone. Claudia Nangel, my incredibly correct, well-spoken relationship manager, would be at the other end. She was on call twenty-four/seven for any big transactions. I'd never met her, but she was like a long-lost old-school maiden aunt who was short on cuddles but always there to help. I pictured her gazing out of her window at some shimmering Swiss lake as she talked to her customers at all hours of the day and night.

I confirmed the sum and answered three security questions, the answers to which didn't always spring to mind when she asked them. Then I had to dredge up some random digits from my number code, and that was even worse. I knew her voice-recognition software would be checking simultaneously for a match against my previous conversations with her. The call ended, with a very Teutonic 'Thank you very much, Herr Stone. Goodbye.'

I handed back the receiver to Synne as her machine whined a confirmed sale and spewed paper.

I shouldered my day sack, tucked the onesies under my arm and reached the exit just as Jack and the lads tumbled in, encased in duvets and beanies, lugging backpacks full of cold-weather kit.

I stopped long enough for a warp-speed info dump. 'I've got seats, return. Stedman's waiting for you at the Barneo desk. There are no flights going south, so I don't know when we're getting out but I'm working on it.'

Jules had been working on it too. 'I could go with Will and wait at Barneo, couldn't I?'

It sounded good to me: one less body to think about, and Gabriel needed all the help she could give. I waved her in the direction of Synne and her card reader. 'Let's see if we can get another seat. Have you still got the minibus?'

'I dropped it off at the rental place.'

'No problem. I'll be back in a couple of minutes to pay.'

I headed for Sven, and thought about renting another van. If Stedman and I had to stay here until the weather lifted, it would be better if Jules went with the team. I could see a couple of rough nights ahead of us stuck in the back of a van with a pissed-off bear banging on the doors. I didn't want to stay in town, and I wasn't going to use a hotel. If they had any sense, Watch Man and crew would be checking for us – especially if they knew there were no flights out. We could stay in the airport, but it would probably be empty soon, exposing us even more, or we might get thrown out at night-time. Stedman and I could take a van, drive to the outskirts, and have some cold nights, but it didn't really matter. It was all about keeping out of the way until we could get a flight out of here. No one in their right mind stayed in a metal box in these conditions, and that was what I wanted everyone to keep thinking while me and Stedman wrapped up warm.

42

I piled into Sven's Portakabin with his gear held out in front of me and a smile radiant enough to melt the ice cap. 'Morning, mate.'

He smiled right back – but his smile faded when he discovered I didn't have the Mauser or the helmets. He checked over my shoulder, hoping to spot a Yamaha Nytro XTX liquid-fuelled triple with 1049cc four-stroke through the frosted windows.

'Don't bother. We had a drama.' I kept it smiley as I dropped the kit on the counter, then fed him the same lie I'd fed the Owl.

'At the end, they gave us a lift back in their helicopter. Otherwise we would have been fucked. We didn't know what to do. Were there police in the town? Were *they* the ones who were pissed off with us? Was the snowmobile stolen? We didn't know. We were too busy shitting ourselves. They had rifles.'

Sven had had enough of my waffle super-bomb. 'Please, I understand. But immediately I have to call the police here, and then there is the insurance form. And I have to take an excess from your card. There's very much to do.'

He seemed more pissed off about all the paperwork than he was about the losses. He started pulling out drawer after drawer beneath the counter.

I wasn't going to stand there signing forms in triplicate all day, and I certainly wasn't going to be interviewed by the local police. 'Listen, mate, how about I sort this out for you right now?'

'Yes, but we have to, er . . .' He pulled out a thick wad of papers and put them on the desk.

Enough was enough. 'Mate, I'll pay for a brand-new Yamaha right now. I'll be happy, you'll be happy, and your insurance company will be over the fucking moon. How much are they?'

'A hundred and forty thousand kroner. The taxes . . .'

'Mate, it's all right. That's about seventeen thousand US dollars. So let's say eighteen thousand, and that'll include the helmets, the weapon, everything. What do you say? However you play it with your insurers is up to you. I don't want anything to do with it. I can't hang around.' I handed him the magic card and stood by for the call from Claudia.

He snapped it in, not quite sure what kind of scam he was getting involved in. He dialled the number and handed me his phone.

She asked me to tell her when I'd last used the card, and for how much. Really? I'd spoken to her about fifteen minutes ago. But rules were rules, I supposed. She told me with total indifference that the account was nearly dry, and I assured her that I was aware of that, and all was good. I just had a couple of expenses I needed to cover, which probably added up to less than the amount they spent on mineral water for their office each month. And they still had the boy's trust fund cash in their vaults, so I wasn't about to drive them out of business.

Sven was all smiles again as soon as his machine started to whir and paper spilled out of its mouth. It still felt like imaginary money to me, but all those zeroes had clearly made his day. It seemed like a good moment to ask him a favour. 'Sven, mate, can I keep the padded gear?' I'd decided it might come in handy. Stedman and I were going to spend a couple of nights out in the cold, keeping out of sight, out of mind.

Sven didn't seem to have a problem with that. He was still too busy admiring the merchant's copy of our transaction. And, anyway, what the fuck did he care? I'd paid for them a hundred times over.

I did my best to cram them into my day sack as I walked past the row of snowmobiles where our Yamaha wasn't parked. But there was too much duvet. It reminded me of a badly packed Boy Scout's ruck-sack. A kettle and a tin mug hanging off the back, and I would have looked the part.

43

It was impossible to miss Rio and Gabriel at their high table, beers in hand, as I passed the massive picture windows of the terminal building. They lifted their glasses as I got nearer. Clearly everyone had got their tickets.

I waved and headed towards the entrance and that blast of hot air I was about to receive. There were two people ahead of me who, I assumed, were doing exactly the same thing. Then they stopped and half turned, their faces visible under their heavy parkas. It took only a split second to read their minds. I might have thought I was going to enter the terminal, but Ponytail and Half Bear had other plans.

I spun on my heel.

There was no way I was going to let them reach the team. They had tickets and they had a way out.

I broke into a run. I sprinted across the icy road, away from the terminal, trying hard not to fall. I headed towards the low, steel, industrial-type building that housed the municipal snow ploughs, and ran along the side of it, looking for the next turn so I could get out of their line of sight.

Those two weren't going to be as fast as me. They were carrying some lard. But losing them wasn't the plan. If they lost me they might go back to the terminal, and everything would go to rat-shit.

The end of the building was maybe ten metres away. My boots crunched into the thick virgin snow, leaving signs that even a blind man could follow. Exactly what I wanted.

I turned the corner, getting out of their sight. It opened up into a parking area with heavy trucks, some with trailers, all coated with snow.

I wove my way between the vehicles, out of their sight, but they'd be able to follow the tracks. I was starting to sweat under my own padding but, thank fuck, I didn't have Sven's gear on as well. The ice-cold air burned my throat as I gulped oxygen, eyes scanning for somewhere to stand and fight – and, hopefully, something to fight with.

I moved between two large trucks. Either they hadn't been used for a long time or there'd been a big dump of snow. The snow was getting deep and it was starting to slow me down.

Hanging off the sides of the flatbed to my right were the buckle ends of the thick white ratchet straps that were used to keep freight on the flatbeds from moving. I dropped to my knees and unhooked a strap from under the flatbed. There was a metre-length of nylon webbing with a D hook on one end and a lump of dull, pitted stainless-steel ratchet on the other. Wrapping the webbing round my glove so the ratchet was secured above the web of my hand, I moved back towards the front of the truck, retracing my tracks. I waited, facing away from the end of the truck so my condensation wouldn't be blowing into their line of sight.

My ears strained to hear the crunch of snow and the heavy breathing getting closer. I sucked in oxygen and readied myself.

I could hear the breathing; I could hear the crunching.

As soon as it got to the end, I turned and slammed the ratchet down into the face of whoever it was. He dropped and I waited for the next one. He didn't appear.

I checked round the corner, to see Half Bear on the ground. I needed to stop him getting up. One punch from him and I wouldn't get up again.

As I moved back to him, I heard the crunch of snow behind me, then laboured breathing. I turned to see Ponytail coming at me fast. They'd split up. He slammed into me, taking me down into the snow next to Half Bear, who was now recovering. My day sack dug into the snow like an anchor, making it hard to move.

I tried to bring the ratchet up onto the side of Ponytail's hooded head.

It just hit his shoulder as he came down at me, with no result at all. I kicked and bucked. I tried to bite his face as he got on top of me, but that soon stopped as he brought his heavy head down hard onto the top of mine. My brain went white and pain screamed deep into my head. My nose filled with snot and my eyes streamed as they tried to protect themselves from whatever was coming next.

I was losing it. I was losing control. I fought the pain, knowing that if I succumbed, they wouldn't give me time to recover. Ever.

I was trying to move my body, as if that would keep me awake and alive. The whiteout in my head turned to starbursts in front of my eyes. My brain tried to work out what the fuck was going on.

There were shouts above me. I thought I could recognize them but I didn't really care. My head wouldn't let me. And then there were more shouts, bodies above me.

Ponytail thudded into the snow next to me. I didn't know what was happening but I knew I had to get away. I started to crawl but I couldn't get far. I was too fucked. I turned back and saw Rio. He was punching with his one fist, and kicking into Ponytail's head. Anywhere he could get it in. At least, I thought it was him. I could see a dark face.

I knew the other voice. Gabriel looked over, sitting astride Half Bear, piling in with his fists to his head, into his face, ramming and ramming, making sure those gloves did the worst business they could.

I thought I shouted to Rio, 'Here – take, take!' as I tried to throw the buckle to him.

He saw it anyway. He grabbed the webbing and rained the ratchet down onto Ponytail's hood.

I forced myself to recover. Grabbing a handful of snow, I rubbed it over my face.

Gabriel had done what he needed to do. He sat astride Half Bear, fighting for breath, his fists resting on a chest that wasn't moving at all.

I sat up as Rio stopped hitting Ponytail. His head was battered.

Gabriel pulled off his glove with his teeth and checked Half Bear's carotid on his neck. 'You OK, Nick?'

'Yeah, give me a minute.'

Gabriel put his glove back on. 'This fucker's clock has stopped.'

Rio did the same with Ponytail. 'He's still breathing.'

Gabriel found it difficult to get back onto his one leg but finally managed it. 'Not for long.' He shuffled the two or so metres to Rio and picked up the webbing strap. He looked over at me. 'Nick, pull this fucker's head up.'

It was a two-man job to lift the drug dealer's head and clear the parka away to expose his neck and face. There wasn't too much blood flowing: the ratchet had been going onto the beanie and the hood. Most of his ponytail had been burned away. The dressings on his burns had come away with the beating and me pulling off the hood and the beanie. The side of his face looked like he'd just had a chemical peel.

Gabriel threw the webbing around his neck and got his real foot against the back of Ponytail's neck, and pulled so hard he fell back onto his arse, but he kept his leg straight to maintain the tug-of-war against the neck.

Rio grabbed what was left of Ponytail's hair to pull his head and neck the opposite way. There was no kicking, no fighting from Ponytail. Within two minutes he was gone.

Gabriel let go of the strap and fell back into the snow. He muttered, between deep breaths, 'Bunch of cunts.'

Rio fell to his knees. He gathered up Ponytail's

beanie and some of the bloodstained snow and shoved it into his hood.

I struggled out of my day sack straps as my head started to get back to where it should have been. 'Thanks. How the fuck did you know?'

Gabriel lay flat on his back, staring at the sky. 'Rio went to get a beer in for you – thanks for the tickets and all that. Then I saw these two ne'er-do-wells.'

Rio finished scooping up the bloodied snow and pulled Ponytail's hood back over him. He did it up with the snow inside.

Gabriel started to get himself upright. 'I recognized that fucker. And then you saw them and did a runner.'

Rio came over to Gabriel and held out his hand to help him up. 'We know why you did that, Nick. It's us thanking you.'

I pushed myself up on my feet and brushed off as much snow as I could before it started to make its way inside my jacket and melt. I would have a headache and a bit of a bump, but that would be covered up by my beanie.

'Lads, we've got to dump these two – just long enough for us to get the fuck out of here, at least.'

Gabriel giggled at Rio. 'Let's get on with it then – and get the fuck out, eh?'

The truck I'd got the strap from was closest and the wind had formed a berm of snow from the ground up onto the side of the cab, then up and over the side of the flatbed. Underneath was effectively a snow-cave. I pointed. 'Let's get them under there, cover them up, and hope the storm covers our tracks when it arrives.'

I got my day sack on and grabbed Half Bear's wrists,

ready to pull. 'I'll get them under there, you two cover them up – otherwise we're going to be here all fucking day. In this line of work, you need two arms and two legs on one body.'

Gabriel was already gathering up the snow that Half Bear had leaked into and let out a laugh. Rio joined in as they headed towards the truck.

44

We tramped back towards the terminal, cleaning ourselves up as far as we could. Gabriel's stump was
hurting again. He took a blister pack of codeine out of
his pocket.

'Mate, I could do with a couple of those.'

He popped two and passed me the rest of the twelve.
'Don't take them all at once.'

Rio slapped him on the back as he dry-swallowed
and he had a brief choking fit.

'You bastard!'

'Don't worry, I wouldn't kill you. It's your round.'

Rio pushed at Gabriel with his arm, as if to clear him
out of the way so he could talk to me. 'That fucker's so
tight – if you shoved a lump of coal up his arse, you'd
have a diamond in no time.' He switched from giggles
to serious. I hadn't seen him do that yet. 'Is there anything we need to know?'

'No. It's all good. All sorted.'

And it was. Except that although we'd done enough

to prevent Ponytail and Half Bear from being found until we were well away from there, Watch Man wouldn't meet the news of their sudden disappearance by assuming the lads had suddenly decided to nip off for a few days on a Caribbean beach without telling anyone. And, besides, he hadn't struck me as the forgiving kind.

At the very least, the team coming back might be a problem, but they'd cross that bridge when they came to it. What mattered now was now. I gave it to them straight. 'Lads, you need to keep this from everyone else, OK? No one needs to know.'

They both looked at me as if I were mad.

'I know, but it just needs to be said. You definitely saw no one else with them?'

'No one.' Gabriel played insulted. 'We might be short of a few other things, but we've still got our eyes and our brain cells.'

We got the welcome blast of hot air as we went through the automatic glass doors. Rio and Gabriel peeled off to the bar. I went in search of the rest of the team, making sure my beanie covered the lump on my head. I found them with coffee and buns, scrunched around a table that was far too small for them and their gear, right under an arrivals and departures board that told anyone who could be bothered to look that there were no arrivals or departures.

Jack jumped to his feet. 'Nick, Jules has a ticket and we want to say thank you so much for—'

'Mate, save it . . .' I picked up a half-eaten ham and cheese roll from under their pile of used paper plates '. . . for when we're all at Barneo.' The smile was pretty much glued to my face. Maybe I'd find a way of making it more than skin-deep somewhere along the line. 'There's a change of plan. Me and Stedman are coming too. There are still no flights and it's too dangerous here for us two.'

Jules unhooked herself from Will and got to her feet, like she was going to make a speech.

I raised a hand. 'It's no drama. He's going to stay with you and me at the ice camp, Jules, while this lot go and play Captain Scott.'

Jack laughed, but it wasn't full voltage.

Jules was in there first. 'Captain Scott? Maybe Adam can follow the example of Captain Oates.'

This time no one laughed. Which I reckon suited Jules just fine. I didn't think she'd meant it as a joke.

I grabbed Stedman's attention and pointed at the Barneo desk. 'We'd better go and check.'

Jack didn't move a muscle as Stedman stood. Then he offered him his hand. They shook as I shoved what was left of the roll down my neck. Bygones weren't yet bygones, but loyalty was clearly top of his list of priorities rather than blind stupidity. I hoped he was right.

'Nice.' He couldn't hold back his joy at the latest reunion, unlike Jules. But fuck it: Stedman was staying with us, so we could control him.

Jack turned towards the bar. 'I'll go and tell Rio and Gabriel.'

'OK. All meet back here.' I moved away with Stedman, knowing that wasn't going to happen. The other two would stay at the bar and buy another drink to celebrate whatever they could think of.

Stedman checked his mobile again as we fought our way across the concourse.

We stepped over a couple of groups who were sitting on the floor, leaning against their trolleys and bags, getting into sandwiches and cans of Coke.

Stedman kept scanning the crowd.

'Mate, you've got to stop.'

Stedman knew it but just couldn't help himself. 'There were a couple of flights out this morning, and she was early enough to catch one, but . . . I've left messages, texts, WhatsApps . . . I just want to know she's safe . . .'

He was about to start flapping again.

'Mate, if you can't see her and her phone's turned off, there's not a lot you can do, is there? Chances are, you're right, she got away. We've got other things here to sort out.' I yanked his sleeve, not for the first time that day.

He nodded, but still glanced left and right as we walked. 'You and Jack – you're back to best mates, then? I thought Jack had had enough of you?'

Stedman shook his head. 'We're really close.'

I checked out his squashed nose and thought, Yeah, you don't get much closer than a head-butt.

'Always will be. No matter what. We came back from Bastion on the same medevac. Had next-door beds at Selly Oak. He must have said this to you because he tells everyone. He reckons it was me who made him believe he could get out there and do this.'

'Once you've shared a bedpan, you've bonded. I get it.'

Stedman stopped in the midst of the chaos of bags and people. There was more than a hint of the old swagger. 'No, you don't, Nick. There's more to it than that.' He gave me a no-fucking-about look, the first I'd ever seen from him. His default expressions were self-pity, sad or pissed off.

'No matter how much I fuck up, he *will* forgive and forget. And you know what? I'd do the same for him. That's what no one understands.'

He watched my face and waited for me to nod back. I did. Maybe Cauldwell had it wrong. Maybe this lad wasn't the devil incarnate, the bastard who'd persuaded his son to overreach himself.

The mobile vibrated in his hand and all his Christmases had come at once.

'Leila? . . . Yes!' Nodding like the Duracell Bunny, he lifted the mobile so I could read the WhatsApp: *Now fuck off and die.*

I carried on walking. 'Let's see if my best friend Synne can fall under your spell too – and help you play bedpans at latitude eighty-nine. Then I'll get something to eat. That roll made me even more hungry.'

45

Floating platforms of ice dotted the coal-black ocean below us as we lifted from the archipelago, but we were soon lost in clouds as we gained height for the two-and-a-half-hour journey north.

The team and I weren't alone aboard the twin-jet Antonov Cheburashka. A group of Chinese tourists in extra-thick Day-Glo pink and lime-green padded suits bounced around like pairs of Teletubbies on each side of the aisle.

I was surrounded by a TV crew. In the window seat next to me, a pretty Chinese woman, the presenter, perhaps, with a big expensive fur hat covering her short, pudding-basin haircut stroked the make-up case on her lap, like it was a cat.

Her two crew were in the seats just in front. They carried their kit with them as hand luggage, and had clearly seen it, done it, bought the 'I Was At the North Pole' T-shirt. They'd pulled on eyeshades and sparked out as soon as they were seated. These boys were definitely too cool for school, and wanted us to know it. The woman smiled at me politely. I hoped she'd follow their example and get her head down.

At the bargain price of just another eighty-two thousand dollars, the airline had managed to scrape together another three seats, and bolt them into the Antonov. Almost half of the cabin had been stripped to make room for cargo, most of which seemed to be drums of fuel on pallets and the fluorescent crew bags.

I'd called Rune to give him the good news that there were extra bodies coming. He didn't sound fazed, just went straight into geek mode about kit – or the lack of it. He used the word 'challenge' more than once.

I told him not to worry. Three of us would be staying at Barneo.

At least the heating was working on the aircraft. I took my duvet off and shoved it under the seat in front. Soon, I hoped, I'd get comfortable, join the TV crew and get my head down.

It wasn't to be. I got a tap on my right shoulder from a hysterical Rio, who should have been strapped in across the aisle and a row behind. Gabriel was in the window seat, pumping his arm like a piston and doing the eyebrow workout as he gestured towards my neighbour. I wasn't sure if he was trying to tell me he wanted to have sex with her, or that I should be trying to.

Will and Jules were fast asleep in front of them. Will was leaning against the window blind and Jules had wrapped herself around his arm. They were using their jackets as pillows.

Jack and Stedman sat together two rows ahead of

me, the other side of the TV crew, doing exactly the same – left ears pushed back against the headrests, eyelids clamped shut, mouths open and dribbling. They looked like not very grown-up versions of Tweedledum and Tweedledee, but I couldn't help feeling a twinge of envy. Sleep and alcohol seemed to have dimmed their nightmares.

The Antonov's crew, in practical green overalls, were busy sorting out the brew trolley and stocking it with sandwich packs. I decided to get a couple of Gabriel's codeine down me with a mug of tea.

I pulled a glossy magazine from the net in front of me. A picture of the word 'BARNEO' stretched across the cover boasted it had been carved out of ice with a chainsaw – like the Hollywood sign, only cooler. Inside there were pictures of happy people standing on the ice, skiing on the ice, an Antonov landing on the ice, along with a bunch of information about how the ice camp had been set up and why.

The first tourist flights to the North Pole or near it had been made in 2000. The camp was opened every year by the Russian Geographical Society's Expedition Centre. They seemed to be aiming for something between EuroDisney and *Ice Road Truckers*. The rides ranged from extreme tourism – like skiing to the Pole – to tamer helicopter trips or just messing around for a few days within reach of a hairdryer. Some mad fuckers dived under the ice or signed up for a bit of freefall.

The scientific function of the Barneo ice camp had been established in 2006. It was organized by researchers from the Institute of Oceanology at the Russian

Academy of Sciences, the State Oceanographic Institute, and the Arctic and Antarctic Research Institute.

Early each year, their helicopter crews circled for days, searching for a suitable ice floe, at least two metres thick, capable of supporting the enterprise. Fuel had been para-dropped ahead of time, so the helis' range could be extended. The advance party, essential equipment and technology, tents, fuel and food were airlifted to the location they'd selected, and there they waited for the heavy drop to crack on with phase one.

Bulldozers were rigged like armoured vehicles, then thrown out of the back of an Ilyushin with four massive military cargo parachutes deployed, and sometimes a set of rockets with proximity switches that initiated just before they landed to soften the impact. They weren't fucking about – the Ilyushin was the largest transport aircraft on the planet. The Chechen Airborne would have jumped out of them last week, along with their vehicles.

The bulldozers took about a week to scrape out a 1200-metre airstrip, which was then sprayed with seawater to harden it. Our favourite Cheburashka flew in the rest of the gear and crew to set up the Barneo fun park – and to dismantle it no more than four weeks later, before the ice broke up again.

The magazine was packed with nice smiley pictures of happy campers, but somehow missed out the bit about the Chechen paras. No surprises there. Those people were selling the dream. Just not my dream – even though the standard-issue Arctic socks and woolly hat had now been replaced by a whole heap of Gucci kit. But it was a whole lot better than waiting for a flight out of Longyearbyen before an even more pissed-off bunch of Barentsburg locals caught up with me.

The magazine was as expansive about the research conducted at Barneo as it was economical about the paratroopers. The ice camp was currently sited above the Lomonosov Ridge, where the Pacific started to get excited about meeting the Atlantic. It was a blank space on the scientific map of the world, one of those places that was very difficult to get to, vital to the study of the process of the Pacific Mass's distribution – or, to put it another way, the climatic system of the northern hemisphere.

Needless to say, no scientist trying to forecast climate change could afford to do without it. There were a couple of graphs showing how much of the sea ice had melted over the past ten years. The ice limit was now considerably further north than the average in any previous period.

Russia planting flags and sending its military to the area, and everyone else complaining while doing the same themselves, made total sense to me. As the cap retreated to the top of the world, it exposed the ocean and its goodies – a potential treasure trove of hydrocarbons and biological, mineral and transportation resources.

Where would the undersea oil and gas pipelines go? Who would control the all-year shipping lanes? The North-west Passage – the sea route connecting the Pacific and the Atlantic – was becoming more navigable by the day, now that the ice was disappearing. The sea route saved about four thousand cargo miles because tankers and container-ships from China, Japan and even the west coast of the USA didn't have to go through the Panama Canal. Canada had already laid claim to the route by rebranding it the 'Canadian North-west Passage', and demanded that all shipping should report in before they could use it.

The heating was going for it big-time, and my eyelids were starting to droop, but I still needed to get my head around Rune and his eco-thing. That side of things was making less sense to me, not more. For starters, if the Barneo initiative was all about saving the world, why was he so nervous about anyone knowing what he was up to?

46

Barneo ice camp
Latitude: 89.15 North
Longitude: 87.0041 East

I was woken by the general hubbub. My head was back, my mouth wide open. The dribble down the side of my chin told me I must have been snoring. Worse, I had missed the brew and sandwiches, my head hurt and the lump under my beanie felt as big as a football.

My neighbour gave me no indication of how badly my snores had disturbed her flight. She was too busy checking herself in the mirror on the lid of her make-up case.

I peered past her. A brilliantly blue sky collided with a blindingly white blanket of snow. Two clusters of tiny dots stood about a kilometre apart in the distance, one maybe twice the size of the other. As we got nearer, the smaller cluster became a scattering of large hoop-framed red or blue tents. Two Hip helicopters sat on the airstrip, which was surrounded by a square berm of ice to afford it some protection from the wind.

Four snowmobiles sped towards us and came alongside as the stairs and ramp began to lower. Everyone was busy getting their gear on, but I was more interested in the bodies on the snowmobiles.

Everyone outside wore protective glasses or goggles, which made identifying them a challenge. If Rune was out there, he'd have to reassess his grasp of English when this lot waddled down the gangway. They certainly didn't fit Cauldwell's description. 'Fighting fit, ready for the fray' they weren't – but, fuck it, they were here now, a reassuring distance from Barentsburg and its less welcoming inhabitants.

The team were concentrating as hard as I was on zipping up, finding gloves – or, in the case of Stedman and Rio, glove – and giving their sun-gigs a quick wipe as we shuffled towards the exit. The Chinese Day-Glo crew were covered in Bergan designer wear, Oakley super gold or silver-faced ski goggles and neoprene face masks. Their Baffin boots, Canadian made and capable of keeping your feet from freezing in $-100°$ centigrade, made mine look like hand-me-downs.

I was the last to get to the steps. I'd let the Chinese presenter catch up with her sidekicks so she could waffle away to them without having to shout past me. Not that she'd thanked me for it.

In spite of the sunlight, it was colder there than in Longyearbyen, so at least Cauldwell had been right about one thing. Jack and the team had moved to where their packs were being unloaded on the runway. Rune stood alongside them in his bright red coat, wild hair bursting out of his neck warmer and beanie. I couldn't read his expression at this distance.

The Chinese Day-Glo troupe were still blocking my way, shrieking about the cold, trying to take photos as they went. Watching them discover they couldn't operate their smartphones with their gloves on brought me as close to laughter as I'd managed to get in a while.

Rune waved at me as I carried on down the steps, pulling down his sun-gigs just in case I thought he was a madman.

We shook through gloved hands. He was smiling, but pirate smiling: it wasn't real. 'Nick, is so good that you made it. The weather down south, we thought that—'

We had more important things to talk about than the weather. 'What? You turning into a Brit?'

It took him a second or two to realize it was a joke. He gave a strangulated chuckle.

'Mate, don't forget I'm funding this now. Jack's dad, Armancore, what you're up to, whoever, whatever, I don't care. I just need to get these lads to the Pole. It means everything to them.'

He gave me a serious nod. 'We will try. Believe me, it also means much to us.'

We shifted to the rear of the aircraft, where everyone was retrieving their kit from a pile. The Chinese tourists had been herded there as well. The film crew rigged themselves up and began filming as the front-of-house, complete with immaculate make-up, explained their great adventure to camera. Either that or she was describing Rune's outfit to the folks at home.

'Jack, this is Rune. He and his guides are going to get the team there.'

Jack was in as good a mood as I'd ever seen him. 'Rune, how can we begin to thank you?'

The Norwegian grinned, but he was still nervous. He'd obviously watched them doing the Ryanair-lads-on-the-piss waddle down the stairs and hoped they weren't his responsibility. 'We are very privileged to be assisting you on your great venture. It is Nick who we both should be thanking.' He couldn't help but gaze down at where Jack's leg used to be.

Rio jumped in and flapped his stump, like the vestigial wing on a flightless bird. 'It's amazing what you can do with one of these. Watch this.'

He wedged his day sack into his armpit and clamped it with the stump, stood to attention, and saluted.

Rune nodded politely. Maybe in Norway people with disabilities didn't take the piss out of themselves. Maybe Norwegians in general didn't take the piss out of themselves.

His next surprise came from Gabriel, who gave him a hug. 'No problem, wee man. You probably weren't expecting a bunch of extras from *Mad Max*, but we're OK as long as we get to glue the right bits and pieces onto ourselves.' Another big hug.

Rune took a gulp of air as Gabriel let him go. 'Er, no problem . . .' His relief at being set free was clear to see. 'You British! You make fun of everything. But for the next part we must be serious.'

'Sure, whatever, boss.' Rio stood to attention and saluted him again, to the riotous applause of everyone, except Will. Jules was busy rubbing weapons-grade sunblock onto his grafts, like she was about to send his ten-year-old self to his first day at summer camp.

The Chinese tourists headed for the tents, unable to contain their excitement at being there and on film. As they slipped and slithered their way over the ice they made my lot look practically Olympic.

One of the ground crew approached. 'Lady and gentlemen. Please, the far right tent. Please.'

Rune had other plans. 'Nick, can you stay back for a while? I have something important we must talk about.'

I let the rest of them get ahead, narrowly avoiding a collision with the Chinese presenter as she made a bee-line for me. Rune turned towards his snowmobile and beckoned me to follow.

'Hello, I am Biyu Feng from CCTV International.'

Her English was impressive, and so was her smile – as it would have to be if you presented on China's international news channel. It wasn't just the BBC and CNN getting their shit screened in hotels and living rooms around the planet.

'I'm here for important travel documentary about new trend for Arctic tourism from China. You and your friends, you are on holiday?'

'Sort of.' I turned away from their camera. I didn't think they were shooting, but I didn't want to risk it.

She gave me a look that suggested the most important thing in her life was to find out what 'sort of' meant. It was pointless fucking her off as she would poke her nose in even more. Besides, what had we to hide? We could only be up there on the ice for one reason.

'I'm with a group of British ex-military amputees.

217

They lost their limbs in Afghanistan, and they're going to walk to the Pole, unsupported.'

She didn't reply, but it wasn't because she couldn't understand me, unless my accent was worse than I'd thought. Maybe it was context.

'"Unsupported" means going with what they can carry or drag. It's not just a physical challenge, it's a journey of another kind – an emotional journey. A spiritual journey, maybe.'

She had understood every word from the start.

'Wow. That is impressive. Excuse me one minute.'

Rune beckoned me frantically as she went into a huddle with her technicians. He was a bag of nerves. 'What did she want?'

'Why? Is it a problem?'

He lowered his voice. 'Very important we don't talk about what I am doing here on Barneo. Nothing about the monitors. We are here purely to assist you on your expedition. Nothing else. Very important. We are your guides. Nothing to trouble the Russians.'

He waved towards where the rest of them were disappearing into the camp.

'Yup, I get it. I've told her what my lot are going to do. That's it. There's no point avoiding that shit – it only makes things worse.'

But it wasn't just her he was worried about.

'Mate, what the fuck is wrong?'

'It's that here, now, there is a . . .' He jammed his lips together and made a pressing motion with his hands.

'A clampdown?'

'Any excuse they are using, the military, to prevent movement.'

'What? You mean the Chechens? That their camp is about a K away?'

He nodded, checking the area for eavesdroppers.

'And Norway being pissed off with them being here?'

He nodded again. 'They closed down the flights last week.'

'Yeah, I know.'

'But it isn't just about the Russians landing here. Some Alpha Group guys from Directorate A of the FSB Special Purpose Centre – they flew into Longyearbyen under cover as part of the training.'

Those lads were Russia's SF and shit hot. Infiltration wouldn't be that hard, given Russian influence here. Perhaps they'd been tasked to recce the airport so they'd be able to destroy the capability of aircraft taking off if things escalated and the war of words ended. In other words, a covert attack on an airport that belonged to a NATO country.

'This is bad, Nick, very bad. It's how they started in Crimea, and look what happened. Norway had no choice but to retaliate with a show of strength.'

'So the Russians are retaliating against the retaliation with a show of strength of their own?'

He moved closer, so his mouth was only inches from my ear. 'A Swedish meteorological team tried to come through here two days ago. They were arrested and accused of espionage. Now everybody has to be personally approved by the military, and you guys were not on the advance manifest for this flight, so . . .'

'Well, we're here now. You met them? They difficult?'

The reporter glided back up. 'We would very much like to film you if—'

Rune cut in: 'Absolutely not. Please leave us. We are in discussion.'

Clearly Rune didn't operate at his sparkling best when he was agitated. I gave her an apologetic shrug as she shrank away.

I had more than the Russians on my mind. 'You get hold of Cauldwell?'

'No, I am very worried . . .'

I wasn't too fussed. All that mattered now was the trip. We were on the ice, almost spitting distance from the Pole, and Cauldwell wasn't. 'Not a problem. But this Chechen thing could be.'

'Yes. I am concerned because—'

'Come on then, we need to sort this shit out.' There was no way we could be on the back foot. There was common ground to work with: suffering ex-military and Afghanistan were two things the Chechens would have very strong views about. I just hoped they were positive.

I jumped on the back of Rune's snowmobile and we headed to the ice camp.

47

We roared across to a blue hooped tent on the far right of the cluster that was big enough to drive a vehicle into. Outside it sat what, from a distance, had looked like a Viking amphibious armoured all-terrain vehicle. One of ours. But as we got closer, I saw it was a white-camouflaged MOSV, a Russian tracked vehicle for bouncing across snow and swimming through swamps.

It was essentially two metal boxes linked by a bar so the thing could bend, and judging by the rutted highway leading to the second camp, it had been back and forth between the two on a regular basis since it was dropped last week.

A thermometer dangled on para cord outside the entrance to the tent, pirouetting in the wind. Rune grabbed it as we went past. 'Minus twenty-one. Hmm. Warmer than it should be.'

Inside, I banged the ice off my boots as he opened the alloy door set into a solid half-moon frame.

The small porch area was gloomy, but I could still

see the wind-chill-factor calculation card on each wall, below a small white marker board warning everyone that the wind speed was now 16 k.p.h.

I had never really understood how to work that stuff out, so kept one fact in my head: exposed flesh froze in sixty seconds or less at −9° centigrade in a 40 k.p.h. wind. But all I really needed to remember was to keep well covered.

We took off our jackets, gloves and hats and hung them next to a row of military green parkas and white Gore-Tex outers. Russian murmurs filtered through from beyond the next half-moon wall that led into the main part of the tent.

'I explained who the team are.' Rune treated me to a blast of garlic breath as he whispered into my ear. 'I am not sure if telling him they were ex-military was helpful at all.'

I pushed through the door into a wall of heat far stronger than the one at Longyearbyen's terminal entrance. I heard the low, almost comforting hiss of aviation fuel being forced under pressure into what looked like a hi-tech log burner. The room smelt of helicopters.

At the far end, maybe twenty metres away, there were two men in uniform. Light-grey fold-down plastic tables were stacked behind them, with chairs to match. They sat the other side of one of the two that had been unstacked, like a couple of court officials waiting to pass judgement. Which, in a way, I supposed they were.

They didn't look up as we entered: they were poring over a pile of familiar maroon passports.

We carried on towards them, aiming at the table alongside theirs. A water-boiler took pride of place on it, surrounded by blue plastic mugs and an assortment of brew kits, biscuits, jams and bread, but I wasn't expecting an invitation any time soon.

We were still a few steps away when Rune began his introductions. He tried to sound calm, but I could almost hear his knees knocking.

'Sir, this is Mr Stone, the—'

The older official lifted his hand, inviting Rune to shut up while he finished checking what were certainly their passports. I unzipped my jacket, dug in my neck wallet for mine and passed it to the younger one.

From their bearing, I could tell they were officers. They were dressed in faded brown down inner jackets. Beneath those I saw partly unzipped fleeces and *telnyashka*s, the Russian paratroopers' blue and white striped T-shirt. Their faces were impossible to read, and not just because both were forested with the kind of beards that seemed intent on invading their noses and eyes. Both had dark skin and thick curly hair. They were Chechens, and that meant they were war-hardened. The West might have sharpened its skills in Iraq and Afghanistan, but these lads had been fighting non-stop for at least twenty years on their own doorstep. The first Chechen War saw the Russian Federation fight against forces who wanted an independent state. It was a relentlessly bloody conflict. During the winter months, the urban warfare was likened to the defence of Stalingrad in 1942–3. Estimates put Russian casualties at around fourteen thousand. There were no casualty figures for the rebels, but civilian dead and injured were estimated at around a hundred thousand.

The first Gulf War didn't solve the problem that had triggered it, and the first Chechen war didn't either – so Part Two wasn't long in coming. That took about ten years, and the casualty figures on all sides were even higher. Putin then installed an ex-rebel fighter as Chechnya's puppet president and thought that had sorted everything in the oil-rich region.

The older of the two had enough grey in his foliage to have fought in both conflicts, and I was sure the pair would be doing their bit against the insurgency that had now sprung up. All was far from good after the second Chechen war, thanks to the rise of Islamic fundamentalism. Jihad was declared on the north Caucasus, and fighters from the Middle East and North Africa were now blowing things up alongside ISIL and all the other extremist groups devoted to the cause of an independent state, the Caucasus Emirate.

Killing jihadis was one of the reasons Russia had been bombing the shit out of Syria. The whole country was behind that campaign because they'd had enough of jihadis fucking around at home. They didn't want any more. The Russian TV weather forecasters, in their tight pencil skirts and big hair, used to spend quality time checking out Syria and reporting the likely level of visibility for their bombers.

The senior officer finally looked up from the passport he had been studying, and now neatly replaced on his pile. The younger one continued to interrogate mine.

'So, you are UK military?'

'Sir, ex-military. Wounded men . . .' I'd already

decided to play the Afghan card. The Russians knew all about the Muj skinning their mates alive. '. . . casualties of the war in Afghanistan. They suffered—'

I was cut halfway through my pitch by the same hand gesture as my opened passport was handed across to him. 'You have been to Moscow?'

'I lived there for a while. My wife is . . . She was Russian.'

I waited for a reaction to 'was', but didn't even get a raised eyebrow. Maybe it got lost in translation. Whatever, it prevented me having to dwell on it.

The veteran checked every page, forensically examining the dates of my visa stamps.

'And you? You are *povrezhdennyy*?'

I had to rack my brain on that one. I was pretty sure it meant 'defective' or 'faulty'. 'No, sir. I am not wounded. I am here to help them recover.'

I tapped the side of my head, because the bruise on the front of it wouldn't have enjoyed the attention. 'We all know it is not just the body that can experience pain. This is a chance for these men to—'

'Why have your team arrived here with no notice?' His eyes drilled into mine. 'We require forty-eight hours' notice of arrivals to Barneo. Like your guides.'

The young officer grabbed their mugs and went for a refill.

'But we—'

Rune tried to jump in but I didn't have any control of what he was about to say so went first: 'These men are traumatized because of what they have gone through. Every day they are trying to overcome their demons, their nightmares.'

225

I touched the side of my head once more. 'This is the greatest challenge they have ever attempted. They doubt that they are still men. They doubt that they are still able to triumph. I wasn't even sure they would be able to come here, to the ice camp. It took time, and only today did they make their brave decision. Our country does not treat our veterans as it should. These men feel that they have been left on the scrapheap. Now they have found the courage to face their fears, as comrades, as brothers . . .'

Another black coffee was placed carefully in front of him.

I hoped he was still in listening mode, not side-tracked by the strong brew he was sipping. The younger one, I didn't worry about: he showed no sign of speaking English. 'These men have come a very long way, physically and mentally, and now they want to take those last few steps to the Pole. They want, they need, they *deserve* to recover their dignity.'

He placed the mug gently back on the table and ran a hand across his forehead. 'That is a very strong word. That is why we are here, we Russians, we also want – no, *deserve* – our dignity to be returned. In the West, you see this as annexation, the state becoming too strong, its people too aggressive, so you must bite back. But why are we always seen as the aggressor?'

He was right, of course. Russia as a source of military concern was back in fashion. But I wasn't there to discuss the rebirth of the Cold War. I was there to get the lads out into the real cold. I kept my mouth shut as he started to flick through the passports again. I wanted him to look more carefully at the photographs and see the faces of men who had once, not so long ago, been young, vigorous and optimistic before they had suffered traumatic injury, like so many of his own brothers in arms.

Rune kept shifting his weight from one foot to the other. He was not a relaxing presence. We all ignored him.

The older officer came to my passport and didn't bother to open it. He used it to point at me instead.

'These men, do you know if they will make it to the Pole? My *kapitan* says some have legs missing.'

'Yes. They do – and others have lost an arm.'

He frowned. 'What if one – maybe two, maybe more – has to be rescued? Who will pay for the helicopter? Do they have insurance?'

Again, I answered before Rune had a chance to. 'Sir, they cannot afford such insurance. But I can. I will cover any costs. It is as important to me that these men achieve their goal as it is to them.'

If a heli had to come and get us out of the shit, I'd just hope they didn't have a ticket inspector on board. I was fast running out of cash and Barneo wasn't about to offer a disabled discount.

He regarded me impassively, but made me feel like he was staring into the depths of my fucked-up soul. After what was probably only a few seconds the beard twitched, a small clearing opened in the forest and a thin smile appeared.

Ha, maybe telling the truth did sometimes work.

He waffled away to his *kapitan*, who picked up the team's passports and exited.

'Let us hope we all regain our dignity.' He passed mine to me across the table.

I picked it up and slid it back into the wallet.

'You will need to leave as soon as possible. The ice here has snapped twice since we landed. Barneo will maybe close early this year. If so, they will come and find you.'

'Thank you.'

He sat back and focused his full attention on the coffee.

48

We crossed paths with the *kapitan* as we crunched over the ice.

He gave a nod. I couldn't tell if it was a smiley one beneath his hood, mask and glasses.

'I do hope your team meets with success.'

So he was fluent in English, after all. There was definitely a big fat grin hiding under there.

The entrance to the mess tent was identical to the last one, but the get-rid-of-the-ice-from-your-boots-and-hang-up-your-coat area was packed with jackets, gloves and sun-gigs.

As soon as we pushed through the inner door, we were hit by a welcome blast of heat and a barrage of noise. Chinese, Russian and English fought it out with the music blasting from the kitchen area at the far end. The tables were rammed with people eating off blue plastic plates. Our crew were about midway down.

There were two new faces.

'The guides?'

'*Ja*. Good men.' Rune was back in a happy place. 'Hal and Jan.'

We greeted them as we passed. Jules was still giving them back their passports. None of them seemed remotely concerned that the Russian military had removed them for inspection. They had found their way to a happy place too. Maybe one of these days I'd ask them the way.

The serving area was plastered with signs in every language except Swahili, instructing us to use the hand sanitizer before touching the plates, mugs or cutlery. I leaned across Rune and immediately obeyed. Vomiting and diarrhoea were the last things anyone wanted up here – although the music now spewing out of a cook's iPad came a close second. Despite Anna's best efforts to persuade me otherwise, I still hated Russian folk.

The menu offered a choice of reindeer stew or reindeer stew. Alongside it were trays of what looked like shrink-wrapped blocks of lard. Rune eyed them with extreme distaste. '*Salo*, pig fat. They call it a delicacy. Whatever you do, don't touch it.'

He leaned in and helped himself to several blocks of the stuff.

I ladled some stew onto my plate and decided to save the pig fat for another day. Hal and Jan joined us for a refill. Their mugs weren't empty, but it gave them the opportunity to check in with Rune. He confirmed that all was good with the Chechens.

'Nick was very helpful.'

I shook hands with them both and was rewarded with the smallest nice-to-meet-you nods. As Hal refreshed his hot chocolate and two Chinese women helped themselves to seconds of *salo*, Jan took care of business. 'We must leave as soon as we can. I told them they need to sort out their kit and be ready to move as soon as we do. We have no time.'

Rune couldn't have agreed more. I wasn't sure if it was because Jan had repeated what he had just said, or because he was scared of them. They certainly didn't feel like a team.

I reckoned they were in their mid-thirties and miserable fuckers. They weren't chalk and cheese, but there was a distinct difference between them. Jan was the smaller of the two, about a head shorter than me, and most definitely from that part of the world. Like Munnelly, he had the Inuit look, but unlike him, his facial hair began and ended with a sparse goatee and moustache, which were still struggling to get beyond the bum-fluff stage. Hal was Viking stock, with a thick, dark brown beard that looked like a porcupine's quills, and I only came up to his chin.

I didn't mind getting blanked by these two. I wasn't looking for any more new best mates. I already had a nice bunch of walking wounded, and as long as the Norwegians got the team to the Pole, so what? I didn't need nice. I needed the job done.

Rune was still agreeing with everything they said as we moved back to the table. It wasn't a good sign.

Everyone was in high spirits, especially Jack. 'Nick! Hal and Jan are ex-FSK.' He beamed at them. 'Nick is ex-SAS.'

The FSK had grown out of the Resistance during the Nazi occupation of Norway during the Second World War, and distinguished themselves by knocking out

Germany's atomic facilities. Since then they'd been doing quite a bit. The Balkans, Afghanistan, anti-terror operations, and a convincing imitation of Alpha Group by producing target packs for key Russian communications, transport and power grids, if it ever kicked off east of the border.

Jack grinned at me, like a drinks-party host, encouraging me to start a conversation.

I had a more important mission: to get the stew down my neck. I also popped a couple of codeine. Everyone else was throwing back pills like they were going out of style. No one gave me a second glance, apart from Rio, who caught my eye and half winked.

Still munching stew, I shifted my attention to Jan. 'Were you part of K-Bar?' Task Force K-Bar was the first major ground deployment into Afghanistan. Norway had been one of the seven participating nations.

The Norwegian dipped his head – just the once.

The team waited for more but he and Hal carried on eating. Instead of elaborating, Hal turned to Jack. 'So, you all OK to walk, yes? We will leave soon.' Small-talk obviously wasn't their thing. Good.

All the team were up for it big-time, except perhaps Will. Jules was making all the enthusiastic noises. He nodded slowly and left it at that.

Biyu Feng lunged in our direction with the brightest of smiles. She really wasn't giving up without a fight.

Her eyes darted from one of us to the next, desperate to make earnest contact with the whole group. 'Your story is amazing and our viewers would be humbled and at the same time energized if we could share it. You must be so proud of yourselves – that you can show the world what people like you are capable of.'

Rune and his not-really-mates turned their backs and were mumbling away in Norwegian. Then Hal and Jan abruptly stood up and left Rune to give her the good news. 'No. We will be leaving here *very* soon, and—'

'Please, sir, let me finish.' Biyu was almost wetting herself with anxiety. She was in full love-bomb mode – the media always were when they were trying to get people onside. The double whammy for her was having such a wide range of missing bits on offer. She'd already prepared her acceptance speech for the Emmy Awards. 'Can we film you putting on your new arms and legs while you tell us your story? It's best for us to show that you are very, very brave disabled people to take on such danger.'

It was a couple of beats before Jules realized she was serious. 'One, they don't call themselves disabled. They're wounded ex-servicemen. And two, putting on prosthetics is an intimate thing for them, like getting dressed. They won't want to be filmed.'

'Then how will our viewers know they are – disfigured?'

As Jules bristled, Gabriel stood up and grinned. 'I'll show you anything you want to see, darlin'. . .'

His hand was hovering dangerously close to his flies. Jules zeroed in and dragged him back into his chair.

'You can film me putting my leg on, OK? But it would be a private thing. And then I'll give you an interview.'

Rio waved what was left of his arm at Biyu. 'And me. My story is *much* bigger than his.'

Rune pushed back his chair and attempted to get the team back into the real world. 'We are leaving *very* soon. In maybe three hours. So we had better get everything sorted out.'

Stedman got up too. 'Rune, I'm back on the team.' He didn't know whether to look me straight in the eye, or avoid it completely. He ended up falling between all the available stools. 'I'm coming to the Pole.'

Jules didn't bother to stand but had the same statement to make. 'Me too. I've come this far with Will so why not the whole way?'

She held a hand out to clasp her husband's. I'd never seen a man look so relieved.

Rune shot me a glance. He was concerned but, fuck it, why not? They were both here, and I wasn't going to stand in their way if the rest of the team wanted them to stick around.

49

All the brand-new kit had to be unloaded from wooden packing containers before being laid out and allocated. There would have been more chiefs than Indians if everybody had got involved in this part, so Gabriel and Rio were left in one of the smaller white admin tents to crack on. It made sense. They could get interviewed while they sorted everything out in front of the camera, and Gabriel strapped his lump of plastic to himself.

I pushed my way through the internal door with two brews for them after passing the team's red plastic pulks, stacked up outside on the ice, along with a dozen or so five-litre cans of cooking fuel.

I got an enthusiastic welcome from Rio but not so from Gabriel. He already had his leg off and was sitting on the floor, preoccupied with testing burners. These were very simple, a red aluminium fuel canister attached to a pressure pump, and a line to a regular-looking gas-ring burner and cooking-pot arms. Gabriel was busy pumping away to make sure there was enough pressure to force the fuel into the burner before it could be lit. They couldn't assume they worked just because they were shiny – and it would be no good moaning to the manufacturer via sat phone if they were out on the ice and the things didn't function.

In neat lines, exactly as I would have expected of ex-military, Rio and Gabriel had arranged individual layouts of kit for each team member. Sleeping bag, airbed, roll mat. On top of each sleeping bag there were two stainless-steel flasks and a one-litre Nalgene bottle. The Nalgenes weren't to drink out of: the wide-rimmed plastic containers were to piss in at night. Once you'd crawled into a sleeping bag you didn't want to have to crawl out again.

There were also rations: brew kits, soups, biscuits and, most importantly, a blue plastic mug and an alloy spoon with an extra-long stem so it could be pushed all the way into the foil sachets of food. The vast majority was dehydrated cereals or porridge for the morning, and meat and rice or rice and meat for the day's last hot meal. Each kit layout also had a mountain of chocolate bars and bags of nuts for munchie stops during the day.

The team kit was a separate pile, awaiting distribution. There was a brown shovel that would be used to build a wall to protect them from the wind while they were trying to have a shit. Every tent also had a blue shovel, which would be used to pile snow to keep the thing getting blown away and also for cooking, and there were ice saws, rolls of para cord, matches, toilet paper, cooking pots, hand brushes, knives, screwdrivers, and all the other bits and pieces that would be needed for travelling unsupported.

I put Rio's brew on the seat of a plastic chair as he threw a tube of sunscreen onto each pile of kit.

With both Jules and Stedman now on the trip, there shouldn't have been enough kit. But there were seven piles in the line.

'Rio, mate, where's the extra kit come from?'

'Rune – he's been blagging it off the expedition lads. You know, the ones looking after the Chinese.'

'He's thought of everything, hasn't he?'

Rio was in agreement. 'Yep, but fuck it. We're so close I'd still go in shorts and fucking flip-flops!'

I looked down at Gabriel to see if he was laughing at the joke, too, as he closed down one of the burners, just as Rio threw one of the tubes directly at him.

'Don't worry about that miserable fucker.'

Another tube flew Gabriel's way.

'Oi, shithead, we'll get there, mate. All right?'

I placed Gabriel's brew beside him on the floor.

'No bother. Not coming back if I don't.'

He said it so quietly I almost thought I'd imagined it.

'What the fuck does that mean, you mumbling midget?'

He let out a sigh and pulled open a seam of Gore-Tex to produce a creased photo: two boys and a woman, lined up for the camera, grinning. 'First you get the wounded hero's big welcome home. The whole street wants to buy you a pint and that. Then, when you've been pissed for a week, what the fuck else do you do? Sit around, watch the footie, get pissed again?' He shook his head. 'Had a bit of a disagreement with my old lady and she threw me out. She doesn't want me around the kids, "unsettling" them.'

He put the photo back. 'Anyhow the judge says I'm not allowed back in the house, so she won't be waiting with the red carpet out.'

I didn't say anything. I'd heard it all before and not just from lads who'd been fucked up like him. It wasn't that long ago I'd read about an ex-para who'd suddenly snapped and stabbed his two toddlers. And he *knew* he had a problem, had actually tried to get help. I tried to force the image of small, dead children out of my head. I'd had enough of that shit.

'Fuck knows if they'll ever care their daddy got to the Pole. But you got to try – leave behind something positive. Maybe they'll get it when they're older.'

The comment hung in the air.

He looked up and frowned. 'You got kids?'

He'd let me in a little. I owed him. 'Yeah, I did. He died. Long story.'

The permanent hard-man expression thawed a little, as if he was changing channels. 'Fuck. I'm sorry, man.'

I realized he was looking past me. Rio was standing there, embarrassed.

As if by way of changing the subject, he started working off his left glove. I hadn't noticed the state of his hand before. He had just two fingers and they seemed to be fixed in a semi-permanent hook, so just getting the glove off was a challenge in itself. Something so small, which we all took for granted. He held it up and waggled his fingers. 'Got a bit of movement there, see?'

Gabriel rolled his eyes. It was party-trick time. 'Fuck off back to Jamaica.'

'Brixton. I'm more fucking British than you.' He

waggled the fingers again. The arm, however, hung semi-limp. Most of the muscle had been destroyed.

'Wait – get this, yeah? First six months there was nothing happening. No signal. They kept operating, kept going with the physio, twelve hundred and fifty-five hours. I kept track. Nothing. I told them to cut the fucking thing off and give me a new one, but exactly two years to the day after the injury, I felt this twitch.'

Gabriel rolled his eyes even more now. He'd heard this one way too many times.

'So fucking what?'

'So fucking . . . I know what you're up to. A bit of rumpy-stumpy with the exotic east, eh?' He mimicked getting his flies open and a very bad Jock accent. 'I'll show you anything you want to see, darling.'

I wasn't too sure if Gabriel was more pissed off that his plan had been exposed – not that he'd been that subtle about it – or that he'd had to listen to his country's identity being annihilated:

'But she doesn't want some fucking cowboy electrician, does she? She wants a real soldier. That's me, mate, infantry – not some fucking helicopter fuse-box repair man.'

Rio had him biting now and wasn't giving up. 'I've got another twitch somewhere else. And if Miss China plays her cards right, I'll let her do a lot more than just make it twitch. A bit of horizontal *Lapp* dancing, eh, get it?'

The last of the sunscreen got thrown at Gabriel and they both burst out laughing as the TV crew pushed their way into the tent.

Rio was right on it and started to walk towards her.

'Biyu! Brilliant, right on time. Come on, let's talk about why I'm here.'

Gabriel was too slow, trying to get up with one leg and a stump.

I left them to it, and headed to get a brew.

50

A couple of bodies were washing up at the back of the mess tent. Jules and Will were at the table where we'd left them an hour ago, and it didn't look good. He had his head in his hands and she had her arms around him, rocking him back and forth. The Russian folk singer was still going strong on the iPad, but it wasn't his fault.

'I'm sorry I'm sorry I'm sorry . . .'

'Sssh . . .' Jules kissed the top of his head and glanced up at me, her face a mixture of anxiety and sadness. 'It only happens . . . Usually it's in his sleep. But this . . .'

A new mantra clicked in: 'I didn't help them. I could have, and I didn't, could have and I didn't . . .'

She stroked his hair, trying to comfort him, like a mother soothing her child. 'I know, babe, I know. I'll come with you. I'll be there for you. I'll help you . . . We all will . . .'

I held up five digits and pointed towards the door.

She nodded immediately. 'Will, darling, I'll just be a few minutes. I need to tell Jack and the team I'm coming too. Nick's right here.'

He muttered a stream of apologies as I took her place. He didn't need to. I got straight into it. 'Mate, don't say sorry. You've got nothing to say sorry for.'

He shook his head, like an automaton. 'Nick, look at the state of me. I'll hold the team back. I'll—'

'No, mate. You won't. No more than the rest of us. Me included. I'll come with you on the ice.'

He looked up. His cheeks and the palms of his hands were wet with tears.

I leaned forward so our faces were only inches apart. I wanted it to be confidential, because it was. 'A month ago, I lost my son and my wife. I should have been able to save them. But I couldn't . . . So I've got a better idea of what's going on in your head than even your wife does. That's why I know how important it is to get out there – achieving, fighting against something that's bigger than you, stronger than you, and doesn't give a fuck about you or your problems, not only fighting it but winning . . . That's why I know you need to get out there. Not for Jules. Not for the team. But for *you*, mate. Just *you*.'

He let his hands drop into his lap.

I gave him a moment to absorb the message. And took a moment myself to wonder where all this wisdom was coming from.

'Listen, Will, you can't bring your crew back any more than I can bring back my family. You can't dwell on the what-ifs and if-onlys. Sometimes there really isn't anything you could have done differently. You didn't plan for your crew to die. It happened.

'We do the best we can with whatever we know at the time. And when we know better, we do better. We don't have complete control . . . and so shit happens.'

I saw a glimmer of hope surfacing through his pain. 'You've got over it so quickly. That's what I need, Nick.'

'I haven't got over it. I've just parked it. Believe me, there are no rules for this shit. No SOPs. What you feel is what you feel. Look, the death of your mates changes your life for ever. Not because things will never be good again, but because *you* will never be the same as you were before. Do something positive with that knowledge, mate. Help the others. Help me. Help yourself. You've lost your crew. I've lost my family. We've all lost bits of ourselves. In our own different ways, we're *both* grieving.

'So let's both get out there and conquer the shit in our heads. We owe it to the people we've lost. We owe it to each other. We owe it to ourselves. Jules will help you. But you'll have to help her too. And I'll need you to help me.'

He filled his lungs and let the air out slowly through pursed lips. 'I don't think—'

I gripped his shoulder. 'Don't think, mate, for fuck's sake. Just *do*.' I got up and headed for the boiler. I needed to get him back into the real world so he could get his face cleaned up and crack on. I was feeling very pleased with myself for conjuring up such an emotional pitch, but then had to admit that the reason it was so good and heartfelt was because it was true.

I kicked off our new routine by doing something I should have done hours ago. I reached for the iPad and shut up the folk singer. It was the only therapy I needed. I felt better immediately.

I waved a blue mug. 'Will, mate! You take sugar?'

51

The whole team had assembled on the far side of the berm that protected the camp. We were finally moving. Sort of: the team were still climbing into their skis and harnesses.

Jan and Hal stood motionless at the front of the struggling line-up. Like them, I had my hood up and stood with my back to the wind. I'd clipped my harness to the bungee/rope combo that yoked me to my pulk. Skis on and poles in hand, I felt myself grinning like an idiot under my neoprene face mask at the multi-coloured Gore-Tex gang-fuck unfolding in front of me. I started to freeze, but at least it sorted out the pain in my head.

Jan and Hal's expressions seemed much the same with their masks and goggles in place as they had without them. They couldn't see the funny side of this at all. They were going to start moving at the top of the hour, come what may.

Rune, on the other hand, was making warm, cuddly

and encouraging noises to all and sundry. His harness was attached to his pulk, but lying on the ice alongside his skis and poles.

I waved him over and did my best to make myself heard through my face protector. 'Mate, just leave 'em to it. They'll soon sort themselves out. No problem.'

'Do you think they'll be able to make it?'

I was beginning to wonder whether he ever expected anything to turn out OK.

'No drama. They just need a little longer, that's all.'

I couldn't tell if he was convinced. All I could see was my own reflection in his goggles, looking back at me. He nodded as Hal shouted the two-minute warning.

No matter who was or wasn't ready, the guides were setting off. It had to be that way, or the group would take even longer to get where they needed to be. It was up to each team member to make sure they were ready to move on time. We had seven days of distance and nine days of food ahead of us, so we had to get on with it.

'Rune!'

He turned.

'Maybe ask them to give four minutes' warning during the munchie stops.'

Rune ran to his pulk because he, too, was under the two-minute rule. I couldn't be arsed to talk directly with the guides: they clearly wanted fuck-all to do with us.

At the top of the hour precisely they set off north. I stayed where I was, intending to bring up the rear. The two Norwegians pulled longer fibre-glass pulks. They were carrying not only the safety kit to drag someone out of the sea if they fell through the ice, but also, I presumed, the monitors.

I could see the Chechen camp now, definitely twice the size of Barneo and bristling with communications masts. Wagons moved about purposefully. Whatever they were up to, we were heading in the opposite direction.

Rio and Gabriel were closest to me, and finally ready. They'd spent the last hour bickering. From what I could gather, Biyu had got her interview. Gabriel being filmed putting on his leg had gone better than expected, because Rio had joined in, and that had really pissed Gabriel off. If you believed Rio's version of events, Biyu absorbed everything he said with fascination and wonder, then got her kit off for a bout of rumpy-stumpy.

'Fuck me, it doesn't get better than this! The North Pole, *and* a shag! Living the dream, mate. Living the dream.'

The team started to shake out into a line. Jules and Will were immediately ahead of me. Inside each of our pulks was a large red nylon bag with extra chunky zip so it could be unfastened with gloves on. It contained all our kit, apart from the airbeds. Inflating them at the end of the day was hard, time-consuming work, so we'd half filled them and strapped them on top of the load.

I was also carrying one of the three partly constructed but folded tents on top of my pulk. It would be a pain in the arse fucking about with poles and holes in the freezing cold, especially if we had a drama and had to get someone out of the wind and into a sleeping bag at warp speed.

I'd positioned the waistband of my harness low on my hips so it could take the weight of the pulk as I slid one ski in front of the other. Dragging it felt a bit like trying to take a big dog for a walk when it just wanted to lie down. Every step demanded a firm tug on the reins, but I soon developed some kind of rhythm. It took me back to the times I'd played snow soldiers in Norway.

When the going was smooth the skis moved silkily across the surface of the ice, but as soon as it got bumpy we slowed to a crawl. We had to remind ourselves that the most important thing was to stick together and not let ourselves get strung out over a couple of hundred metres. If that happened with individuals who were already under pressure, they'd start to get isolated and grind to a halt – or, just as bad, they'd try to speed up, get themselves more fucked up, and string out the team even more.

After about ten minutes I started to heat up – but not too much. The trick was to keep warm without over-heating. If you started to sweat you'd get wet and then you'd get cold and if you were losing your core body heat you were fucked because the next thing that happened was that you died.

We weren't built to exist so far north. Human beings are homoeothermic: our bodies try to maintain a constant temperature, irrespective of their ambience. The skin, fat, muscle and limbs act as a buffer zone between our hot inner core and the outside world, protecting the brain and other vital organs in the skull, chest and abdomen as far as possible from catastrophic changes in temperature.

The maintenance of internal body heat is the most significant factor in determining survival. Even in extreme conditions, your core temperature will seldom vary more than two degrees either way. If it does, you're history.

As it burns fuel, your body generates energy and heat. When you start to shiver, it's telling you that you're losing heat faster than you're replacing it. The shivering reflex exercises a whole load of muscles, increasing heat production by burning more fuel, but it can't work miracles.

A thermostat sited in the nerve tissue at the base of the brain controls the production and dissipation of heat, and monitors all your bits to maintain a constant temperature. When hypothermia kicks in, the thermostat instructs heat to be drawn from the extremities to the core. Your hands and feet start to stiffen.

As the core temperature drops, the body also draws heat from the head. Circulation slows. The brain no longer gets the oxygen and sugar it needs. You stop shivering, and you stop worrying too. You feel a kind of crazy exhilaration. You're about to be set free.

But the truth is, you're dying.

You're dying, and you couldn't care less. Your only hope to stop that happening is to add heat from an external source – dry clothes, a fire, hot drinks, another body.

I pulled my hood back and shared my *Star Wars* look

– black fleece balaclava topped off with a black beanie, goggles and mask – with the world. Then I unzipped the vents under my arms to regulate what was going on inside my Gore-Tex outer shell. All I had on beneath it was a base layer of merino wool long johns and long-sleeved shirt. As far as I was concerned, a thin wool layer was still the best way of wicking away leakage while maintaining warmth. It certainly seemed to work for sheep.

Wool was a hygroscopic insulator, so could soak up a fair amount of moisture without feeling wet. The crimp in its fibres created tiny air pockets, unlike cotton in which each strand lay flat – hence the old saying: 'In the hills, cotton kills.'

The downside to wearing less than I probably would have on a winter's day in England was that if you weren't moving you were freezing.

Every member of the team had now found their own rhythm, and was overcoming whatever fuckabout they had to deal with. I had some of my own. Number one was the condensation that had built up inside my goggles and instantly turned to ice. I had to turn my head every which way until I found a sliver of clear lens to check where I was going.

My face mask also grew a thick layer of ice, making it more difficult to breathe, and my nostrils filled with congealed moisture. I tried to blame the kit that Rune had begged and borrowed. But it was my problem and I needed to sort it out. After all, teams of lads were doing pretty much the same thing up here not long ago in polo-neck jumpers, waxed jackets and strips of canvas wrapped around their boots and they'd survived long enough to become First World War cannon-fodder.

There was nothing I could do about any of it for now. It would have to wait. Personal shit wasn't allowed to slow or stop the line once it had kicked into gear.

52

The caravan club continued to pull its way north until the smaller guide, Jan, held up his poles and crossed them over his head. It was time for our first break. Every hour from now we would pause for a ten-minute munchie stop to drip-feed the eight thousand calories we were each going to need every day. We had covered maybe just under a nautical mile. The line had strung out – Gabriel and Jack were a little slower than the rest. Jan and Hal had no such excuse: they were simply covering the ground too quickly.

The team made a little extra effort to close up before stopping completely. That probably wouldn't be happening by the end of the day.

The routine was simple: stop, back to the wind, poles down, zip up vents, hood up, and take out your duvet jacket from the front of the pulk bag, for easy access, and get it on over your harness, then zip up again so that as little heat as possible was lost.

Just before I completely zipped up my duvet, I pulled

off my goggles and shoved them inside my jacket, pulling both the Gore-Tex and duvet hood over most of my face to keep the sun's UV from bouncing off the ice and fucking up my eyes. Snow blindness wasn't permanent, but it was really painful. I'd learned that lesson the hard way all those years ago in Norway.

I ripped off my neoprene mask and gave it a good beating against my leg to break off the ice while I closed each nostril in turn to clear all the shit that was up them. I could hear the same sounds coming from the rest of the team.

The munchie bags for each day were also at the front of the pulk's bags, along with the two one-litre steel flasks filled with hot water. The munchies were the high-calorie items on the individual kit piles like chocolate and nuts. We had unpacked the chocolate from its wrapping, broken it down into bite-sized pieces, and shoved them into daily bags so our gloves could stay on during the breaks. We kept our skis on, too, ready to be on the move again in ten minutes.

I pulled out my bag and drink, and got ready to get stuck into a cube of *salo*. I thought I'd give it a go, seeing as the fat was nothing but calories. I'd got half a dozen of them from the cooks and cut them up.

Will and Jules were still standing, just as the rest of the team were. That was another thing that would change as the day went on. Will was shoving a glove full of nuts down his neck as Jules poured him some water. His head was up and moving, everything he looked at reflected in his gold-filmed goggles lenses with a couple of days' growth underneath that had started to gather the first bits of ice. He gazed in awe at the

252

empty white wilderness in front of him. We were on our own now: nothing between us and the Pole. All there was to see in any direction was a world of snow-covered ice, criss-crossed with pressure ridges, no points of reference, just white ice and brilliantly blue sky. All very nice, but a killer if your body didn't generate heat.

I tried my first cube as Jack was getting his Gore-Tex bottoms open to have a piss. He was taking so long to get past his base layer I hoped he wasn't desperate.

It might have been cold up there, but it was as easy to dehydrate in the Arctic as it was in the Sahara. A body could lose as much as four litres a day through the nose and mouth, like some panting dog. If you didn't force yourself to take fluids you were fucked. But that wasn't as simple as it sounded, because one of the strange things the body did in extreme cold was not tell you when you were thirsty. On top of that, it wanted to urinate more. It closed down peripheral blood vessels so it could concentrate on maintaining its core temperature. As blood flowed round a smaller system, the body thought it was holding onto too much fluid and wanted to piss it out. Normally water loss would make the blood saltier, so you felt thirsty and replaced the lost fluid, but in cold regions the salt landed up on the ice with the urine, along with potassium, both of which should have stayed to keep the nervous system and muscles cracking on. That was why, on a munchie stop, we drank, whether we felt like it or not.

The *salo* was frozen, so I had to crunch into the meaty-tasting fat and suck on it, like an ice-lolly.

'Hey, Will. No Costas here, mate, eh?'

I got some water down me to prepare for another *salo* cube and secretly wished there was a large cappuccino waiting for me at the next stop. I also hoped I'd closed my eyes enough to protect them from the UV that was bouncing off the ice.

'You know what, Nick? That's partly what I'm trying to get away from.' Will handed back the flask cup to Jules. 'One of the worst things about the whole recovery business is that it infantilizes you. You start behaving like a kid again because everybody wants to do things for you.'

Jules nodded slowly in agreement as she refilled the cup and handed it back to him.

'After a while, Nick, it does your head in – not that my head isn't already a bit . . .' He pointed at his temple and twirled his index finger. It was hard to know to what extent he was joking.

'I'm fucking terrified of all that space out there and it's all your fault, Nick.'

There was a smile but he meant it.

'What's there to be frightened of?'

'Except freezing to death.'

I held up my last *salo* cube for this stop. 'This might kill you, though.'

Jules pushed up the last centimetre of zip on his duvet, then turned to me. 'Be serious for a minute, Nick. Don't you *ever*—'

'Nope.'

Her face softened. 'Your wife and child – Will told me.'

'Well, you understand, then. It's not like I'm going to escape and get off this planet alive, is it?'

Her eyes widened. 'I guess that makes you just as

much a casualty as this lot, then, in a way.' She studied me levelly. 'You're not as bombproof as you look, you know.'

I didn't like the implications of that. But she was in her comfort zone, telling people what was what.

'You'll have to face it sooner or later or you'll suffer, like Will. Maybe that's why you decided to come along at the last minute, or maybe it wasn't. Maybe you just wanted an excuse, and sharing with Will was the excuse you needed.'

Half of me wanted to tell her to keep the fuck out of my business, but the other half said maybe she had a point. She waved at her husband, who was still sucking in the emptiness.

'Ask Will and he'd say he thinks he's just the luckiest man in the world to have survived relatively intact. But every night, when he finally goes to sleep, he dreams the same dream.'

'Yeah, but he's here, with you, with us.'

'Everyone can always take a step back, Nick.'

This time I didn't respond. Just took it in. For all her mother-hen bossiness, she knew what she was talking about, which was something, and she wasn't demanding a response.

'And don't worry – I won't tell anyone you're human. Your secret's safe with me.'

Salvation came from the head of the line. 'Four minutes! Four minutes!'

The command was shouted down the line.

I wasn't too worried about having every munchie stop becoming a therapy session. We'd all be too fucked to talk soon.

53

I packed the rest of my munchies and my flask, then waited until the very last second before stuffing my duvet away.

Ahead of me Gabriel was trying to push off, but having trouble staying on his skis. 'Shite!'

Rio was still having a one-armed fight with his duvet and laughing at the spectacle as Jack, packed and ready, skied a couple of metres and held out a pole. 'Come on, Braveheart. Rise up and be a nation. We don't want to freeze our bollocks off before we've even started.'

I dug out my goggles while the rest of the team enjoyed the show. I bit into the fingers of my right glove, pulled out my hand and rubbed like a madman at the semi-melted ice coating the inside of the lens. Just breathing on it was no use: condensation froze instantly, and made the situation worse. I hoped I could soak up the damp with my merino wool inner before it refroze. Half a lens was better than none.

One more wipe and I got them back on my face. With luck, my body heat would keep the bits I'd cleared from icing over again. I smacked my face mask on my leg a couple more times and rigged it up.

Up front, Jan and Hal were ready to move off again. They leaned forward on their poles, twisting around to check what was happening behind them. I shoved my duvet away and assumed a similar position – hood up, vented up, back to the wind, ready to launch.

They started moving at what was probably the four-minute mark precisely, and so did I. But not everyone was following. Will and Jules were set: there was no fucking about from her. She should have been on the team from the start.

Stedman and Jack were sorted too, but were still busy helping Rio and Gabriel. Gabriel was now upright, and taking the piss out of Rio because he couldn't grip the zip well enough to do it up. Jack was doing it for him, but having only three working arms between them complicated the process.

Rune reached them seconds before they finally got their shit together. 'Please, we need to get moving – if you're stuck in one place for too long out here, you die. We must move.'

We all knew we had to keep moving, but Rune was obsessed.

I got my mouth close to his ear, or at least the Gore-Tex over it. 'Mate, it's not a problem. Look at them taking the piss. It's all good. They've trained together. They're working together, like they're still in the army. They're helping each other. They'll soon sort themselves out, you'll see. Right now you need to grip those two . . .'

I pointed at Hal and Jan. They were way out in front and pulling further ahead. 'Their job is to show us where to go and to help the team get there. It's not to show us how fast they can move and fuck the rest of us. The team have a lot to contend with – not only the cold.'

He said nothing, just looked uncomfortable.

'Mate, if you don't tell them, I will.'

He waggled a fat gloved finger at me. 'Well, you can try . . .'

'They're your people, aren't they? You need to grip 'em.'

'They are not mine.' He went silent for a moment. I guessed he was sucking his teeth under his face mask. 'They are Mr Cauldwell's men. They are from Armancore. There was a last-minute change, not long before Mr Cauldwell told me you were arriving. Everything changed, I do not know why. You must ask Mr Cauldwell to explain these things.'

He paused, as the team made their way slowly by, heads down, hoods still back for a few minutes more. I couldn't see Rune's face, so I couldn't tell whether the discomfort in his tone was simply to do with being pissed off or if he was frightened. That wasn't my problem right now, but I'd need to keep an eye on our Scandi mates in case it became so.

'So how come those two don't give a fuck and Cauldwell gets to order you about?'

He shrugged. 'I got into debt. Armancore bailed me out. There's not much money in the campaign for the environment.'

'So what does Armancore get for its money?'

'Data.'

'About the ice?'

'The ice, the seabed. That's all my area.'

'So you're now an oil prospector?'

'Each party wants to get it before the other. That is why we need to move as fast as possible, to plant the sensors before the ice melts.'

'The Norwegians want to be first?'

He paused to get his breath back. Talking in these conditions was a challenge. 'Not exactly.'

'So who? Exactly.'

'Armancore's interests are with the Russians.'

'So we aren't providing cover for you to wage some eco war but to do something that might spark off a real one?'

'Nick, I have no choice.' Rune was flapping enough to start his own wind farm. 'Please believe me, *no* choice . . .'

'So why all the sneaky-beaky shit at Barneo? The Chechens would have waved you through, probably rolled out the red carpet for you. Why do you need us lot?'

'I have no idea, Nick. What I have told you is all I know. I am sorry, but . . . Mr Cauldwell, he explained he knew of a way I could get onto the ice without anyone understanding the reason, and I had no choice. I am sorry.'

I felt better that I had an even bigger reason to dislike the guides. Just like Quisling, the Norwegian leader who'd collaborated with Hitler in the Second World War, they had crossed over to the darker side.

The front of the line was getting further away by the

minute. I pointed a pole towards the two Quislings. 'Mate, you will be if you don't get those two to slow down.'

Rune moved off towards them, digging in his poles like he was competing in the Winter Olympics.

'Rune!'

He stopped and twisted his top half back towards me.

'The team must not know about this. Those two fuckers up front? They mustn't know you told me. And definitely not Cauldwell. Got it?'

He nodded and moved off. I might have been imagining it, but there now seemed to be a bit of a spring in his step. And why not? He should have been over the moon, because he didn't want anyone to know what he'd been getting up to.

Fuck it, so what? had always been my default position, because whatever shit I was in usually only affected me. But not now, not for the next seven days. I needed Rune to keep his mouth shut so the team could get on with what they were there for.

I also needed to have a think about this. And there was no better place on earth to do that than here. The world's three dominant religions came from the desert for one very simple reason: there's fuck-all else to do in it.

I pulled down my hood, ventilated my jacket, tilted my head so I could see through a gap in the ice inside my goggles, and took my place at the end of the line.

54

Our ninth munchie stop felt like a lifetime ago, apart from the ever-present taste of *salo*, the gift that went on giving. The team were slowing. We really should have ended the first day at our seventh munchie stop, but the Quislings just kept on going, like they had an urgent dinner date ten miles ahead. I was going to have to grip them both tomorrow if it happened again.

On the plus side of covering more distance, I'd finally got a half-decent view through my goggles. Only a third of the left-hand lens was frozen; the rest was just covered with ice crazing so I felt like I was walking through a snowstorm rather than doing it under a clear blue sky.

The sun had circled around us, rising and dipping as if it was bouncing off the horizon in very slow motion, like one of the early computer games I'd played in the Tidworth pubs as an eighteen-year-old squaddie. The light gave us no idea of the time, and it was easy to lose all sense of not only where we were in the day but also which direction we were heading. The feeling of disorientation wasn't helped by the landscape: there still wasn't one – just a vast, barren field of white stretching to each horizon.

The only variation was a slight crust on the ice field ahead of us, which started to grow in size as we got closer. If anyone was flagging, no one was prepared to admit or show it. But that was how it was for these people: they had been trained to crack on, and then lived it.

By the fourth munchie stop everyone had made the extra effort to close up, but only with their buddy. It came instinctively: it was all about helping your mates. Rio and Gabriel had spent most of the breaks on the verge of punching, helping or laughing at each other, as they munched, drank and zipped up. Stedman and Jack had more of a bromance going on. They'd left the head-butting behind them, and were now simply pleased to be there for each other. I couldn't work out why Jules was so concerned about Will. She was by far the fittest and most able of us all, and if Will had problems she could probably just zip him into his pulk bag and drag the fucker to the Pole by herself.

The most important thing for all of them was the mission, the task, the job, whatever anybody wanted to call it. Everything they did individually was for the benefit of the team, and the team existed only to complete the mission. This shit was easy once you understood that.

The theory had it that the physical side was always filled with pain. Looking ahead of me at the line, and at the amount of plastic they had to use between them just to function, was a prime example.

As for the other three, fuck you, Norway. *Nul points*. Whatever you're really up to, just get us all to the Pole.

55

Up ahead the Quislings stopped, but the message they shouted back told us it wasn't permanent. 'No stop . . . No stop.'

They checked their sat nav and moved another five hundred metres, then stopped again. Jan crossed his poles, and this time both men removed their harnesses. It was the end of the day's tab. They'd pushed the pace without really bothering to check that we were in tow behind them. But everyone had stuck together regardless. It had been painful for some but a good day's tab for all.

Tomorrow, however, looked like it was going to be a fucker. A pressure ridge – where two floes collided – loomed about a mile away. It looked as if the gods had taken a very big can of squirty cream and blasted a long, messy line of it across the ice.

At this distance it was impossible to tell, but they could be at least five metres high and forty wide – which meant a long day for people dragging weight with fewer than the usual number of limbs between them.

This time the whole team bunched up as one. We knew what we had to do. There were three three-bag tents. The Quislings and Rune had one. The bromancers shared the second with Rio and Gabriel. Four in a three-bag tent wasn't as bad as it sounded. More bodies equalled more heat. The third tent, strapped down on top of my pulk, was for Will and us two remaining hangers-on.

The Quislings had taken their time deciding where to stop, but siting the tents wasn't a precise science. The tents obeyed the same rule as our bodies did out there: if they were static, it was back to the wind. Beyond that, the only how-to trick was to put the thing up as quickly as you could, then jump inside. There would be no singing songs or reliving the day's japes around the campfire. It was too cold.

I dropped my poles and harness onto the ice and unfastened my bindings before hooding and zipping up. I took the mask off, cleared my nose for what I hoped would be the last time that day and dug about inside my goggles, then grabbed the tent off my pulk. Walking felt strange after being on skis all day: I felt like a toddler trying to find his feet.

The tents had been partly assembled before we left Barneo. The fibre-glass poles had been threaded through the sleeves of the outer shell and the sleeping compartment attached to the inside. To pack the tent away, the poles simply had to be broken in half so the material could be folded and wrapped.

All we had to do now was reverse the process. I

threw the thing onto the ice and knelt to undo the bungees. Jules and Will joined me. They'd done the training together, so probably had a routine.

'What you want me to do?' Jules was on top of her game, as usual. The bungees came off and were placed inside the pulk bag. They'd be lost to the ice overnight even if the wind didn't blow them away so, like everything else, they had to be zipped up, secured or worn. 'Will normally sorts out the inside and I deal with the outside.'

'Then I'll dig the trench and set up the burners.' That sounded good to me: digging to keep warm, then hot soup to finish the job.

The Quislings' tent was already up on the far side of Jack's – fuck everyone else.

We fitted the poles together with gloved hands and all three of us lifted the dome-shaped tent, its sleeping compartment hanging perfectly in place under the top sheet, and turned its back to the wind before plonking it on the ice. The performance going on next to us was more Billy Smart's Big Top than Arctic explorer. Rune still seemed concerned, but he needn't have. The lads knew what they were doing – it just took longer.

A series of low, rumbling thuds, like distant cannon fire, stopped us all in our tracks. We scanned the surrounding area as if there were something to see.

Jack was the first to spark up. 'Oi, Rio! The Taliban are still after you.'

'Yeah, funny. But what the fuck?'

Rune did his mother-hen dance around us once again. 'Just a couple of ice masses coming together. You'll get used to it.'

While Jules held the tent in place, Will and I anchored it with our six skis and poles. We didn't need pegs – they would just have given us more weight to drag – and this way, we also knew that our kit was secure. Five minutes later it sat there, like a Burger King party hat.

The three of us got our tent bags out of our pulks and dumped them on the ice, along with our flasks, at the entrance to the tent. They contained our sleeping bags and personal bits, along with the evening's food and drink. Waffle at this point was a waste of energy, and wouldn't get anything sorted more swiftly. It could wait until we were warming our hands on that first Cup-A-Soup.

Will unzipped the front flap, climbed inside and took off his boots before crawling in deeper. It was like living in a desert: if you brought sand into the house you'd get a good slapping, and rightly so. But at least sand could be swept away. Ice in the sleeping compartment was a complete no-no. It would melt with your body heat and soak your kit. You got more than a slapping for that.

The sleeping compartment took up the rear two-thirds of the interior. It also had a zip door that we'd close when we got our heads down. Once we were tucked up inside, there would be no reason to leave, unless we needed a dump.

The porch, the space between it and the entrance, which would be used for keeping stuff out of the rain in the UK, would be our cooking area. I grabbed our blue alloy shovel and extended the shaft. As Jules lobbed the tent bags through to Will, I dropped to my knees and marked out a two-foot by five-foot rectangle. Then I began to dig.

Having a big trench in the ice made life a lot easier. It meant we had somewhere to sit and get our boots on and off, for starters, and somewhere safe to cook and make brews, because we wouldn't be rolling around and bumping into each other. And the heap of surplus ice I was producing, shovelled to the front of the porch area, would supply our cooking water.

Apart from anything else, digging kept me warm. I'd learned a basic rule of Arctic survival long ago: if volunteers are needed for a job that requires physical effort, always put up your hand.

Will finished blowing up the first Therm-A-Rest, straightened his back and reached for the next while I kept digging and Jules fished the burners and pots out of the pulks.

'Nick, get a move on!'

I pulled a roll mat and the inflated Therm-A-Rest Will had just been working on and shifted my arse onto them, then swung my legs into the nearly completed trench.

Jules poked her head through the flap. 'Come on, Will, put some puff into it! That's my bed you're making!' She gave him the world's biggest grin.

I leaned out as she passed the cooking kit through to me and I caught a glimpse of the other two tents. The Quislings' was already zipped up tight, and so were their pulks, but Rune was still outside, putting the finishing touches on the windbreak for the toilet area. He'd volunteered to dig it for the whole trip, either to regain his eco credentials or to spend less time with his Norwegian mates.

Billy Smart's Big Top was not far behind us. Jack and

Stedman were still wrestling their group's tent bags off the pulks.

Jules had one more job to do. I handed her the shovel and she zipped up the flap from the outside, leaving me and Will completely enclosed. We felt warmer immediately.

I grabbed the cooking board – a three-foot-by-two plywood sheet with bungees attached – and man-handled it into place as Jules methodically tugged out the hem of the tent. Soon, all I could hear was the scrape of the shovel as she weighed it down with ice.

All good. It would help prevent the wind pushing its way into our mobile hotel suite, and improve our chances of the fucking thing not blowing away during the night.

56

Jules kept shovelling and Will kept blowing lungfuls of air into Therm-A-Rest number three.

I'd positioned the cooking board across from me, the other side of the trench, so it acted like a table, and shoved ice underneath until it was level. Now I secured the canisters on top with the bungees. They would be refilled every morning after breakfast from the five-litre fuel cans that were loaded onto the pulks.

With the burners sitting safely upright, I got busy with the pressure pump, releasing a small amount of fuel into one of the reservoirs and igniting it. Lighters didn't always work in these conditions, and if Swan Vestas had been good enough for Shackleton, they were good enough for me.

I waited until my small ball of flame had heated up the metal of the burner before I released the pressure pump. There was a reassuring hiss and a burst of heat from the first ring. I shook each of our flasks, checking for leftover liquid, and poured some, about an inch, into the larger of the two pots before lifting it onto the burner.

Melting chunks of ice took for ever, so kick-starting the process with water was always a bonus. In any case, I couldn't have put the ice straight into a hot pan. It would have burned like milk.

Once I had the second burner up and running I poured what was left in the flasks into the smaller pot, and added a couple of scoops from the larger one. The system was simple: the ice from the trench was our water supply, the larger pot was our immersion heater, and the smaller pot was the tap.

I opened the small vent in the top sheet above the cooker board to let out as much of the vapour as possible. At no time would we allow the pots to boil. Steam condensed and almost immediately turned to ice. There was already enough of that stuff around and the trick was to keep it outside the tent.

Will had sorted out the sleeping compartment. Roll mats down, Therm-A-Rests on top, and sleeping bags pulled out of their bags. I asked him to throw me the mugs, and tonight's and tomorrow morning's food.

The very first thing we needed to get down us was the Cup-A-Soups, two each, then we'd move on to the meat and rice. Then biscuits and tea with enough sugar in it to frighten up a *Daily Mail* headline.

And that wouldn't be the end of the night's work for the burners. We had to melt more ice to fill the flasks with water to heat in the morning to make breakfast quicker, then needed to melt even more ice when we woke up to refill the flasks so we could set off with two litres each. Even though ice melted quicker than snow, the whole performance would take about three hours. The upside was that it meant three hours' worth of heat finding its way into the sleeping compartment.

Jules unzipped the entrance flap from the outside, crawled through, eased her feet into the trench next to me, then zipped it back up again with the same care that she'd have used to stitch a wound. If you pushed and pulled these things, like a demented gorilla, and they bust, that was everyone inside fucked for the duration.

She slid the blue shovel into the water-supply pile, pulled down her hood and removed her goggles, then leaned towards me. I realized she wanted the hiss of the burners to cover her whisper. 'Would it be all right if Will cooked?'

That wasn't a problem for me. I leaned back into the sleeping compartment. 'Mate, do you want to do your Jamie Oliver impression tonight? I'll sort the flasks last thing.'

His reply couldn't have been more upbeat. 'I'd love to. And don't worry about the flasks. I'll do the lot.'

Jules started undoing her boots as I got my goggles back on and zipped everything up.

'Right. I'm going to put Rune's facilities to the test.' It was the first time today that my goggles had been clear, and they gave me an amazing view. The wind was on a mission to peel the top layer off the ice and it hung in there at knee height like mist, making the three tightly fastened tents look like they were floating in a desert of white. Now and again there was a murmur of appreciation from inside them as the Cup-A-Soup found its target and condensation billowed from the vents before being whipped away into the endlessly clear blue sky.

I shook the ice off my pulk bag, kitted myself up with toilet roll and dump bags, and crunched my way across to Rune's brand-new toilet. What I saw when I got there was not the Inuit version of a pub urinal. He hadn't just thrown up one ice wall, he'd constructed three in a metre-high open square. He'd fashioned a dumping monument.

It seemed a pity not to spend as much time there as he'd taken to build it, but browsing the colour supplement and cracking the crossword weren't on the agenda. This might be a mundane event in the real world but when skin froze in minutes it was a major deal. So you pissed onto the snow then unzipped and pulled down your Gore-Tex trousers, long johns and whatever so you could bend and fill the bag as quickly as possible.

You couldn't just shit on the ice and blame it on the bears because they didn't bother tabbing this far, even when there was at least a week's food heading north. And we didn't need Rune to tell us that there would be mountains of shit and Tesco's toilet paper all over the Arctic unless we bagged every dump – and the misfires too – and took it back to Barneo. At least it would be frozen when we got it back to the pulks, so we didn't have to drag the smell as well as the weight.

But I didn't have to meet that challenge right now. Irrespective of what I'd said to Jules and Will, I wasn't out there for a dump. I was hoping to make that part of my morning routine, because a munchie stop wasn't long enough.

I turned and slowed so the crunch of my footsteps

wasn't so loud and aimed for the Quislings' and Rune's pulks. I wanted to take a closer look at the monitors.

It would have been a waste of time trying to be subtle about the next bit. It wasn't as if I could wait until it was dark. The thin blanket of ice fell away as I unzipped the first bag. Inside, I found a thin aluminium case, maybe a metre long, which wasn't part of any standard Arctic kit I could think of.

I carefully undid the two retaining clips and lifted the hinged lid to reveal nine lumps of stainless steel that looked like blinged-up RPG warheads. They lay in a neat row, slotted into their custom-moulded polystyrene packing. The tenth was missing.

Maybe they needed nine. Maybe they'd already started inserting them into the ice. I guessed I'd find out soon enough. Right now, at least I knew they existed. Before zipping up again I spotted a familiar shape in a nylon-padded bag. It wasn't difficult to feel the hard steel of a long-barrelled revolver, probably a .44, even through my gloves.

I left everything exactly as I'd found it, and as I started to retrace my steps to the Cup-A-Soup, the pulk bag had already grown a new coating of frost.

I had to assume that both the Quislings would be carrying, not just one. They might claim they were playing 'better safe than sorry' on the bear front, but if that was the case, why hadn't they told us where the weapons were? During my soldiers-on-ice days we used to run a tripwire around the tents – basically a couple of ring-pull personal alarm devices attached to a ski pole and a length of para cord doubling as a perimeter fence. The theory was that the bear would trip the cord and trigger the alarm. Then it was all hands on deck with the flare guns and assault rifles. Maybe the Quislings also had them tucked away for a rainy day, and didn't want us to know that either.

Stedman emerged as I passed Billy's Big Top, waved at my toilet roll, then spotted my empty bag. 'No luck?'

'Need to get into a routine.'

Stedman didn't dwell on it. He broke into a run towards the monument.

57

Will was busy shovelling ice into the immersion heater but stopped long enough to pass me a mug of chicken soup as I took my place beside him. 'So, Nick, what'll it be? Lobster in its own shell drizzled with a citrus *jus*, and T-bone steak with lashings of sauce Béarnaise and chunky sweet-potato fries?'

'Not tonight, Chef.' I flattened the palm of my hand and raised it to nose height. 'I'm up to here with Surf 'n' Turf. Haven't you got something with rice?'

The soup had been chilling while I was outside. I emptied the mug in a few gulps and handed it back for a refill, then pulled off my boots and climbed through into the sleeping compartment.

Jules was all sorted and comfy in the back of it, digging her long spoon into a food pouch. Her bottom half was cocooned in her bag, her top half in her duvet. Two sets of gloves, hats, masks and vapour-barrier socks were pegged out to dry on a length of para cord attached to the top of the dome. The burners would do

276

their stuff on them for now, and with luck our body heat would finish the job overnight.

A loud yell came from the next tent, which I assumed was aimed at Stedman. 'Stay out there, you dirty fucker.'

Will grinned as he leaned back and handed me my second Cup-A-Soup – minestrone this time, and much hotter.

The shouts, laughter and abuse carried on at top volume for a few seconds more, and we joined in without having a clue what it was about.

I sat on top of my sleeping bag, took a few sips of the new taste sensation and began to sort myself out. I shrugged off my outer shell, replaced it with the duvet jacket and shoved the Gore-Tex top and bottoms into my tent bag, which would soon become my pillow. I peeled off both pairs of thick socks, leaving the dump bags I'd first covered my feet with on display. Jules took one look and her eyebrows disappeared under her fringe. I didn't bother to explain. They were a whole lot less high-tech than the super-comfy vapour barriers that she and Will had on display, but worked just as effectively.

If ice melted inside our boots we were in trouble. Not only would it soak our socks, but also the inner lining of our boots. Not surprisingly, there was always a lot of effort to make sure that no ice entered a boot, simply by doing the thing up correctly. But sweat was also the enemy because it made the inside of the boot just as wet if unchecked. If wet, the layer of insulation around our feet would stop working, and they would freeze. A VB prevented the moisture from migrating and so kept the inside of the boot dry and warm. In extreme cold, some people put on a thin pair of socks, then added my version of a vapour barrier because they thought it was more comfortable. I could never be arsed because it meant having to dry them out each night.

The inside of the first dump bag was so wet that it really didn't want to part company with my skin. When I finally persuaded them to separate, I was left with a set of toes, a sole and a heel like a bag of pickled walnuts. But they were still a long way from freezing.

Once I'd checked for blisters, Jules threw me some Johnson's Baby Powder. I squirted a small cloud into my first sock, gave it a shake and put it back on. Then I shoved my foot into my sleeping bag and repeated the process.

I folded the VBs and pushed then into my duvet pocket to keep today's sweat nice and warm for tomorrow. Then all I had to do was hang up my mask, gloves and headgear. Jules glanced at the lump on my hairline but said nothing.

Will removed my now empty minestrone mug and handed me my main course. 'Tea's on the way.'

I took the steaming pouch. The spoon was already dug in and ready for action.

'You have about four minutes.'

I gripped the top of the pouch and gave the contents a stir. These packs took a lot of water to reconstitute, which was great for the food and great for us. The downside was that once it was all mixed in, it took another ten minutes for the food to be ready to eat.

As Will got busy with the burners again, I leaned

close enough to Jules for her to know what flavour my soups had been. 'Why have you gone soft over Stedman? I thought you were going to jump up and down when he said he was coming?'

Her forehead creased. 'I can't take this away from him, not now he's so close.'

I couldn't wait any longer for my food, even though it meant I was going to have to live with the crunchy bits.

Jules lay back, resting her head on her tent bag, and for a minute or two it looked like her VBs were the things that interested her most in the world.

'Are you going to check Gabriel's leg? See if the others are OK?'

She rocked her head from side to side. 'They're big lads. If they need me, they'll shout. This is all about them doing it for themselves. You know that. They don't want – or need – me to turn into their mother.'

I finished the rice and meat and tried not to get too excited by the prospect of meat and rice tomorrow. I swapped the empty packet for a brew. It was warm inside the tent now and the hiss of the burners sounded even more comforting because of it. It certainly seemed to be working for Jules. She'd just closed her eyes and gave no sign of being in a hurry to open them again.

I leaned back on my tent bag and rested the tea on my chest. Will had spooned in so much sugar it was starting to coat my nasal membranes. I took the opportunity of doing something else I'd not done lately. I let my mind wander back through the events of the day.

I'd spent far too much time being angry with Cauldwell, the Quislings, Russians, Rune – in fact, everything and anyone to do with this trip, apart from Jules and the team. But it was worth it because a good honk was always satisfying to get out of the way.

Once happy that I had had a go at everyone that needed it, I started to think about why I was there.

Telling Rune to keep quiet about whatever was happening behind the scenes, I wasn't just thinking about the team making it to the Pole. But it had been worth it, because I'd come to the conclusion that I really did need it as much as Will did, as much as they all did. I was as determined as they were that nothing should stand in our way – not even a .44 Magnum.

If there came a time when the team needed to know what Rune and the Quislings were really up to, so be it. But until then, rattling the bars on that particular cage wouldn't achieve anything. We were here, we were moving, and before the week was out we'd be close enough to the Pole not just to spit at it but also to piss on it.

Our real mission, our task, whatever people wanted to call it, was much bigger than that, of course, but there would be no stopping Jack and Will, Gabriel and Rio once they had had the most northerly piss anyone could have. And it looked like even Stedman was on the road to redemption.

As for me, only time would tell.

Keeping my eyes closed, I lifted my head just enough to take a sip of my far-from-sugar-free brew, and thought how good it was to be there.

58

I woke up to the sound of the outer shell being brushed free of ice, and pulled off the eye mask that Cauldwell had given me. At least he'd come good about something. Some people didn't like constant exposure to daylight as it messed up their sleep rhythms and made them feel knackered. I still couldn't make up my mind if I was one of them or not, so it was always good to hedge my bets. But at least with constant daylight I could see what I was doing all the time and avoided having torchlight burning into my eyes as other people sorted themselves out.

The condensation generated by the three of us during the night had created a frozen crust on the fabric above our heads. The crust that overhung the trench had a thicker layer from last night's brew fest, which had continued, on and off, until we finally fell asleep. That was the stuff Will was brushing away. Sensibly enough, he didn't want to work at the cooking board in a rainstorm once he'd sparked up the burners.

I checked my watch. It was just after 06.00, time to start brushing and brewing. The Quislings would start skiing at exactly ten, which gave us four hours – more than enough time to sort ourselves out, eat and drink, and, just as important, have a dump, before packing up the tents, throwing on our harnesses and being in position for the four-minute warning. Fuck 'em.

I looked to my right to see Jules checking on Will's progress. She'd obviously been thinking similar thoughts. He now sat on the edge of the trench, duveted up, with his back to us, giving his full attention to the immersion heater. I hoped both pots were full. I was in the mood for a king-size brew.

Will turned and grinned. 'Morning.'

He'd been reading my mind.

I was glad he found the cooking board therapeutic. Prepping food and cooking meals for us wouldn't immediately wipe out Will's failure to drag his mates out of the aircraft, but every journey really did start with a single step.

As a young squaddie, I'd not even heard of PTSD. It was explained to me, a revelation, after the Gulf War, and until then, anyone exhibiting the symptoms was seen as trying to pull a fast one – cooking up a case for a medical discharge and the pension that went with it.

When young men in my infantry battalion had tried to commit suicide – by taking drugs, cutting their wrists, or drinking cleaning fluid – they were punished, not offered a helping hand. They were banged up in the guardroom, not taken to the medical centre. Even men who simply broke down and cried for no apparent reason were dismissed as wankers. After all, we were rough, tough soldiers and they were just jelly-heads who couldn't hack it.

Since the post-9/11 wars, PTSD has been recognized for what it is. People like Will weren't jelly-heads, they were casualties of war, just as much as any of the four in Billy Smart's Big Top and a host of others I'd spent time with. They just needed a little understanding and a whole lot of respect. I wished I'd known that all those years ago. Watching Will make the first brew of the day, I felt like an arsehole all over again.

I cut away long enough to check that the head- and hand-gear hanging above us was dry enough to put on without too much grief. It was – and it would get even drier once the burners generated some heat. Until then, all we could do was talk a load of bollocks while we waited for that first brew and some biscuits, as you did when everyone was in a good mood.

I produced my Nalgene bottle from my bag like a rabbit out of a hat. 'Will, check this out. Half full. Beat that.'

Will threw me the remaining Jammie Dodgers from last night's pack in return. No problems there: I liked the frozen strawberry. It was like sucking a boiled sweet.

He dragged his bag over to retrieve his night's work – like mine, a half-full bottle.

I turned to Jules and gave my Nalgene a shake. The urine fizzed like 7Up.

'Lightweights, the pair of you.'

With a ham actor's flourish, she produced a purple Shewee – and a Nalgene full to the top.

She'd won last night's star prize. I had no option but

to present her with the Jammie Dodgers. Well, four of them, anyway. I kept the one I'd already licked.

Will handed each of us his signature brew – a mug of tea so sweet you could have stood your spoon in it. I dunked my remaining biscuit as the morning's routine began. It would be exactly the same as last night's, but in reverse order.

It wasn't long before he held out the breakfast pouches, full of stodgy, porridge stuff poured over dried apricots. Fantastic. I'd always been a fan of ration-pack food. Even before joining the army I'd been a huge fan of instant mash, boiled sausages and powdered eggs. Maybe it had to do with being brought up on school dinners, then vouchers from the council for more free meals during the holidays, delivered by Meals on Wheels.

Rune's monument began to beckon as the second brew was heading my way. I put it to one side while I unzipped my bag and got dressed.

The wind had died down since last night and the pulks were now just mounds of pulk-shaped ice, and the snow had climbed halfway up the outer sheet of each tent. Only half a pole or ski was left exposed. Now I knew why I'd slept so well, and hadn't even heard Will or Jules filling their Nalgenes. The extra insulation had made the tent warmer.

I crunched my way across virgin ice. I was the first out that morning.

The other two tents also had their burners going. Condensation seeped out of their vents and now hung around a bit to see what would happen next.

Billy's Big Top was bubbling with the usual mix of

laughter, piss-takes and bollocking. I bent down to pick up the frozen hood of an outer shell jacket, which had been left outside the entrance before unzipping its flap, then saw what it contained and left it well alone. I couldn't help laughing as I kicked it away so I could unzip.

I stepped inside and got into the trench next to Jack, and was offered the usual greetings, which ranged from 'Morning' to 'What the fuck do you want?'

As if they didn't know.

The other three were half in, half out of their sleeping bags and in different stages of undress. They were sorting out what was left of their bodies, drinking tea and sharing a pack of ginger nuts to get their calorie count up.

Gabriel was busy dressing his stump. It was in much worse condition than it had been in Longyearbyen, but that was only to be expected. Like Jules had said, they were big lads. Back in the day, they were used to being wet, cold and hungry, and having far more confidence than was sometimes healthy. And that was a good place to be.

He dabbed on a final coat of what smelt like antiseptic, covered it with several layers of stump-shaped dressing and wrapped it in zinc oxide tape. After he'd finished, he let loose a volley of undecipherable Jock swear words. At first I thought he was describing the pain, but then he poked a finger into Stedman's chest. 'Go on, tell him, you dirty fucker.'

Stedman was very proud of himself. 'It was windy, Nick, you know that. It was cold. I had a lot of layers on, and only one hand. What do these fuckers expect?'

'You're right, mate. I certainly wasn't about to help.'

'Nor me!' Still shaking his head, Jack offered me a sip of his brew.

Rio was sorting out two blisters, one on each heel, with a couple of Compeed plasters: little cushions of heaven. 'Hey, Nick, you know we did fourteen nauticals yesterday? That's about twenty-five K. One fuck-off tab, eh?'

He pointed down at his feet. 'Can't wait to tell Biyu about these things. Maybe we'll name our first child Compeed . . .'

Jack gave a snort of laughter. 'Aren't there already enough of your kids contaminating the planet?'

The other two were quick to agree that Rio should keep his dick in his underwear at all times. It had been a long night in Billy Smart's Big Top.

I left them to it.

I heard Norwegian mumblings over the hiss of burners in the Quislings' tent on my way past. Their pulks hadn't been touched. I thought about the .44 again.

I emptied my Nalgene bottle as soon as I arrived at Rune's monument. Then I ran through the sequence that Stedman hadn't quite mastered last night. As I held open my bag and squatted in the middle of the square, the ice shuddered beneath my feet. A nanosecond later it rumbled and shook, like the Arctic was breaking apart.

There was a shout from Rio inside the Big Top. 'Fuck's sake, Nick! You got curry in your rat-packs, or what?'

59

Rune was out and screeching like a hen with a fox in the coop. I had to agree with him. Those weren't the low rumbles of yesterday that sounded like distant cannon fire. This was less like ice coming together and more like ice breaking apart.

I grabbed my long johns and trousers and pulled them up together as quickly as I could. Rune hollered the other side of the wall for everyone to get out of their tents. 'Get dressed! Get packed!'

There was another ominous growl and I had to put all my energy into staying upright.

'Get out! Get out! Pack everything up – quick! Quick!'

I emerged from the monument to find bodies in disarray, some out on the ice, some still in their tents. Some had duvets on. Random items flew out of doorways. People stumbled as they pulled their kit on.

Gabriel was perched on a pulk, trying to sort out his Gore-Tex trousers. Rio was doing his best to help him, and to help himself. Shagging Biyu wasn't so important now. Jack emerged from the tent flap and threw Gabriel his leg.

Rune bounced around, trying to help the other members of Billy's Big Top to get their duvets on and sort themselves out. 'Please hurry, please get dressed. Get the sleeping bags in the pulks first. Then take the tents down.'

'Rune, what on earth is happening?' Jules, trying to make sense of the chaos, was the loudest of them all.

He ran back to her. 'The ice is breaking! Get everything packed – we're going to need it!'

The Quislings seemed to be in no rush. They came out of their tent like it was any other morning. They weren't packing up. They stood there, ears cocked, close together, but it wasn't panic that united them. Something darker was happening. They knew what that sound was.

They exchanged a few words, low and close. Whatever it was, they agreed with each other.

Now they moved with urgency. The small one went straight back into the tent. The other lifted the RPG bling box out of his pulk and thrust it through the flap.

I ran towards our tent. Jules and Will were both there now, cramming kit into any available bag. I uncovered the poles and skis and placed them next to the pulks.

Rune's yells became more strident. Losing an entire expedition wouldn't look great on his CV. I caught a glimpse inside the Quislings' tent as he rushed this way and that. The box was nowhere in sight, but the small one was shovelling snow and ice back into their trench. Outside, the other fucker was retrieving their pistol bags out of each of the pulks.

Fuck it. My priority had to be the kit. If we were getting screwed over by these two, we'd need it to stay alive.

I grabbed Rune's arm as he rushed past me. 'Mate, you've got to stop. Sort out your own kit. The team gets it. We know what we're doing. We understand.'

He switched direction but then stood stock still as he heard the same thing I did. The others stopped what they were doing.

From the other side of the ridge came a slight murmur, which grew into a thrum and finally a clatter of rotors.

The emergency pick-up. Time for the team to get out their disabled discount cards.

60

The heli broke low over the crest. It was small and blue and white. Non-military. Large yellow pontoons for water landings.

This wasn't any pick-up.

It rattled straight over us, then hurtled past, low enough for us to see it was packed with bodies. It flared about twenty metres from the camp and prepared to land, the downdraught blasting us with a storm of ice shards.

I'd spread-eagled myself over the tent and most of the poles to stop them being blown away. Jules and Will were on top of their pulks, hanging onto our sleeping bags and anything else that needed to be pinned down. Rune had thrown himself across mine. Billy's Big Top crew hadn't been so lucky. There weren't enough limbs to go round. Part of their tent hadn't been collapsed, and was caught in the gale. It tumbled away into the distance like a massive empty carrier-bag.

Four incomers stepped out of the cloud of snow and ice. They sported a dazzling array of different-coloured duvets, masks and goggles. But they had one thing in common. They had assault rifles – and they were up and in the shoulder.

There wasn't anything we could do. We had no weapons. We had nowhere to run. Even those of us who could still run.

The heli took off again as soon as it had dropped its cargo, and the ice cloud began to settle.

Weapons . . .

I lifted my head and scanned the surrounding area.

The Quislings were nowhere to be seen. Nothing was coming out of their tent. Its poles were still up; last night's ice mound was still keeping everything anchored.

Three of the incoming duvets advanced purposefully towards it. Yellow and Green in the lead. Red two paces behind. Another one lingered behind, face obscured by dark blue goggles and a black face mask.

'Get down! Stay down! Do not move!'

The shouts were both male and female. Their accent was American, as were their M4 assault rifles. Tactical butts, fully extended, carried in the shoulder, left glove on the forward handle, no guard on the trigger so they could operate them with their gloved right.

Yellow, Green and Red moved relentlessly onwards. No hesitation, just forward movement, weapons up, bearing down on their target.

The heli orbited above them. Still no hesitation. No concern about fire coming back their way.

It was a long time since I'd seen such total intent.

Red wore a day sack with an umbilical cord snaking out of it. He or she was staring into the glass sphere connected to the end of it. I knew what it was. First the weapons, now this. Without a doubt, these were military.

They were a couple of strides from their target. Their body language said it all. They weren't just on the offensive. They were planning an execution.

Rune looked up at the two who were now covering us, trying to make contact. 'We're not doing anything illegal. We are—'

'Rune, shut the fuck up. If they were going to kill us, they'd have done it by now. Don't make them change their minds.' I flicked my head round as Yellow and Green came to a halt and fired a series of rapid shots through the Gore-Tex top sheet.

Their next moves were just as methodical. Yellow stood, weapon in the shoulder, while Green dragged out the Quislings' bodies. Then he went back inside, dropped to his knees, and got to work with a shovel. It wasn't long before the bling box followed them out onto the ice. Only this time there was no trail of blood.

They didn't bother to look inside the sleeping compartment. They'd known what they were there for, and they'd found it. Mission accomplished.

The two covering us didn't react.

Rune shivered. Either he was still flapping, or his core temperature had dropped. But we hadn't been out that long, and had our warm kit on.

The Quislings lay on the ice outside their tent, like a couple of seal cubs that had been clubbed and dragged. Green plunged a knife into the top sheet and started ripping the material apart. Yellow put down his weapon and stepped back to join Red, who was in the middle of a staccato radio exchange. It had to be with the helicopter. The five-seater Enstrom was still orbiting above us.

Green was in the guts of the tent and throwing the contents of the sleeping compartment onto the ice.

So they hadn't finished after all.

61

Green's frenzy had exposed the whole area where the tent had stood. Kit was strewn all over the ice, like a bomb had gone off.

Red was still barking at the heli, peering skywards now, as if that was going to help, and holding out the glass sphere. Yellow looked into it, grabbed the shovel and went to work. He knelt down and swung into the ice, lobbing chunks into the air. It wasn't long before it jarred on something. Moments later the sunlight glinted off the tenth RPG bling.

The Quislings must have planned to dig them in each night under cover of the tent. Now I knew why they'd added those two extra munchie stops yesterday, then had to fuck about with their sat nav before pitching camp. For whatever reason, the 'monitors' had to be inserted at precise locations along the route.

Rune was still keeping his mouth shut, along with

the rest of us. At last he'd seen the light. If somebody was pointing a weapon at you, and you didn't do what they said, you didn't need to be ex-military to work out the probable consequences.

I watched as Yellow carried the RPG bling away from the tent area. There was no ceremony about it: he just placed it in the box with the rest of them and closed it down.

So, what next? And, more importantly still, what about us? Clearly they had a plan – if they hadn't, we would now be lying beside the seal pups. Whatever it was, we were all still breathing. At least for now.

Red snapped on the radio yet again, and all three of them moved towards us. So did the two who were covering.

I could hear Red's voice now. A woman's, from one of the Southern states, and she was telling the heli to come on in. It was now our turn. She barked out the deal: 'If you have a weapon on you, say so now.'

She waited a couple of seconds.

'If you do what we say, all of you will be safe. Do not talk to each other. Do not do *anything* unless we tell you. If you resist, if we see a weapon, we *will* retaliate. We *will* take action.'

That was good enough for me. Crystal clear. I stayed belly-down as they ran their gloves over us, and plasti-cuffed our wrists behind our backs.

They didn't take my neck wallet, but they must have seen the para cord around my neck. It made me feel that I had won a very small battle, and the importance of very small battles should never be underestimated. Hanging onto my passport and cash gave me some hope. Maybe they'd let me keep it because there was fuck-all to do with it up here.

Yellow's eyes were hidden behind mirrored goggle lenses, but he was undoubtedly the boss. He checked out our team one by one, pushing up their chin, pulling up their goggles so he could check each face, then releasing them. One or two sets didn't reseat themselves, and could be manoeuvred back into place only with difficulty, by the rubbing of a head against a pulk.

Soon it was my turn. Head lifted, goggles yanked away, face registered. Then they were slammed back painfully onto the bridge of my nose and I had to perform the same contortions to get them back into position.

The heli came in to land and blew up another storm. Yellow jabbed a gloved finger at the team members he wanted to lift first. Rio and Gabriel were the pick of the bunch, but Gabriel wasn't having any of it. He arched his back. 'I can't walk, mate. Let me get my fucking leg on. I *cannot* walk.'

Yellow didn't acknowledge him but turned and muttered something to one of his sidekicks, then gestured towards Will, Jules and Stedman. They were hauled to their feet and herded into the maelstrom of snow and ice by Red and Green. The heli took off, kept low, banked and headed straight back, keeping really low, towards the ridge. It disappeared over the crest, and so did the sound of its rotors.

But the rumble coming from wherever it was heading still hung in the air.

62

Rio and Gabriel had their plasticuffs cut away so that Rio could help Gabriel sort his shit out. Yellow sent one of his team over to retrieve a sleeping bag that had snagged on one of the Quislings' boots, then threw it over Gabriel's leg to keep it warm. He was rewarded with a thank-you in a weird Jock accent he'd probably never heard before.

It was the most polite I'd heard Gabriel be, but he knew the score. Smile. Be nice when people point guns at you. There's fuck-all that can be done about it, so keep everyone happy and onside.

It had definitely been an execution. They'd known who they wanted, without a shadow of doubt. The tenth 'monitor' had been buried, so I presumed it had been activated, and that was how they'd worked out exactly where their target would be.

That must have been why Red was talking to the heli. They'd have had a location device onboard, and in her day sack I'd seen the bit of kit used by the Marine

Corps to bring in air support. A screen inside the sphere relayed the imagery on the pilot's target-acquisition screen, so the two were in synch. A few shovelfuls of snow and ice weren't going to stop the ground team knowing exactly where to dig.

We were still in the shit – perhaps not up to our necks, like the seal pups had been, but all we could do was wait, do as we were told, and see what the next phase brought.

The low rumble that had sent Rune into a spin still filled the air and the ice continued to tremble beneath us as the heli returned.

It was Rio, Gabriel and Jack's turn to be dragged off their pulks and herded into the ice twister kicked up by the downdraught. I couldn't tell if they were flapping behind their masks and goggles.

Moments later the heli lifted off again, and disappeared back over the ridge. Which left Rune and me, watched over by Yellow. I gave the Norwegian a kick when our guard was still out of earshot. 'Keep it shut. Not a word.'

Yellow came closer, but only to dump the trophy cabinet at the end of our pulk. After that, he ignored us. I could see the reflection of the pressure ridge in his mirrored lenses. Icicles dangled from the breathing holes in his face mask.

He reached into his hood and fucked about with something at the back of his head. The Velcro of his face mask came undone and he took it off. He tilted his head to clear his nostrils into the snow, and I recognized his skin, as brown as a grizzly bear, and the hedge of beard that constituted his first line of defence.

I didn't know what to think, apart from betting that the Owl wasn't out on the ice shooting people. It had been pretty clear from the word go that this shit was likely to be Munnelly's territory. Munnelly: cut him and he bled oil.

I took a very deep breath. I had no control, and until that changed, I had to go with whatever they decided – which I now knew meant whatever Munnelly had in mind.

He fixed his gaze on the ridge again, and I could see the heli in his goggles, cresting the ridge, then heard the whine of its rotors.

He pulled Rune to his feet without a word, then grabbed my arms, wrenched them back and made me lever myself up. He gave us both a shove as the Enstrom landed.

Red emerged from the ice cloud and took over the task of getting us aboard. Munnelly stayed behind us.

The rear compartment of the heli was empty. There was room for three, but no seats: a cargo area. There were two seats in front, one of which was occupied by the pilot. He didn't give us so much as a backward glance. He had his own stuff to do.

The air was thick with snow and ice. Munnelly materialized from its midst, shoved the trophy cabinet in alongside us for Red to sit on, then climbed into the spare seat up front. As soon as he was aboard, the pilot opened the throttle, pulled back on the collective, and we lifted off.

The first thing I thought was: This is warm.

As we climbed, I noticed a small screen attached to the centre console, a bit like a sat nav stuck to a car's windscreen. It looked out of place, unlike standard factory kit.

The front of the aircraft bristled with antennae, which all seemed to have been attached at different angles. The sat nav device had to be the monitors' locator.

As we passed low over the pressure ridge and I caught my first glimpse of the terrain beyond, Rune and I discovered exactly what the rumbling was all about.

63

The icebreaker was seventy or eighty metres long and looked at first glance like an old factory ship, but without the gantry, the nets and all the other fishing gear at the back. Instead, above deck level, there was a platform with a big H painted on it.

Steel steps led three or four metres down to the main deck, which took up about three-quarters of the ship's surface area. It was probably where all the fish or crabs used to go before they were cut up and put into tins.

Up front, just short of the bow, was the bridge tower. It had three levels. The top one was solid glass with bridge wings, balcony-like protrusions that stuck out on each side like bats' ears. As we got closer, I could see that the windows on the lower two levels were frosted.

The deck space was taken up by ISO shipping containers with antennae of all shapes and sizes. The name on the bow was *Lisandro*. There were no flags flying, no numbers, no indication of where *Lisandro* was registered, or to whom. But much of the structure was

sheathed in battleship-grey ice that would have obliter-
ated any identification markings anyway. The only
things that had retained any hint of colour were the
four orange fibre-glass lifeboat capsules, two on each
side of the deck, suspended on steel derricks. They would
have been an add-on since *Lisandro*'s fishing days.

The helicopter rattled past the bridge, coming in on
finals, flared, and finally settled its skids on the platform. The rotors were still turning; the pilot was still
doing his stuff. No one moved in the back. No way was
I doing anything unless I was told to. There was a body
in the back with an M4 on her lap and not even the
ghost of a smile on her face.

Munnelly jumped out, came round to the side of the
heli and pulled open the rear door. There was a rush of
cold wind. Red lifted her arse off the trophy cabinet;
Munnelly grabbed a handle and pulled it out. He didn't
give us even a look of recognition.

The rotors were still turning. The pilot carried on
doing his checks as casually as if he'd just landed at
Ascot with a group of race-goers.

We still weren't told to move. I could feel my wrists
chafing against the plasticuffs and my hands starting
to swell, but I didn't protest. I stared down at my boots,
playing the grey man.

We finally took a couple of kicks into our legs from
Red – nothing malicious, simply a message to get going.
I wanted to obey. I just wanted to make sure I didn't
slip. A four-metre fall could fuck you up big-time if
your hands were cuffed behind your back. And if I was
going to get out of there, I'd need to keep myself fully
intact and functioning.

I shuffled my arse to the edge of the aircraft, swung out my legs and planted my feet on the platform. I scanned the surrounding area as three duvet-clad bodies climbed on board the heli. Apart from the landing pad, the deck was all on one level.

I could feel the vibration from *Lisandro*'s engines through the deck, and the ice groaned and rumbled as the ship continued to cut a path through it, leaving a ribbon of open sea behind it. The five or six crew on deck didn't bother to glance at us as we walked past.

The ISO shipping containers were brand new. So were the power cables that ran across the deck and fed into the new wooden cloakrooms fixed to their entrances, a bit like the ones in Barneo, where people could get their kit off. Close up, the mass of antennae and dishes sprouting from their roofs was like a tangle of weeds that had sprung up randomly, each fighting for its own space.

The heli relaunched and headed back over the pressure ridge, probably to clean up the mess that had been made on the ice.

A body emerged from one of the containers, and through its open door, I saw some kind of mobile office or command centre. It looked like a geeks' convention in there. The people inside were wearing sweatshirts, metal-framed glasses and designer stubble, and seemed to have a whole heap of technology at their disposal.

64

We were shepherded past the ISO containers, on towards the bow and then through a door in the base of the bridge tower. Even before we'd crossed the bulkhead, I was mugged by the heat and the loud thrum of the engines.

Red pulled off her goggles the moment we were inside, then pulled off ours without bothering to remove our hoods first. What did I care? It was warm down there – that was all that mattered.

'Down. Move it.'

We were bundled onto a wide steel stairway and taken deeper into the bowels of the ship. Everything about its interior was harsh and utilitarian. Years and years of red and white gloss paint covered every surface. Each of the huge rectangular bulkhead doors had four big lever handles to make sure that if water dared to force entry it wasn't going anywhere.

We clanked along a narrow passageway with bare strip lighting and foam-padded pipework overhead.

Health and safety instructions were plastered everywhere. The smell of oil and diesel exhaust caught in the soft tissue at the back of my throat.

The further we went, the more worn the paint became, the more the walls were streaked with orange rust marks. The engines hummed in my ears and vibrated under my boots, and the closer we came to the sharp end of the ship, the louder the crunch as it carved its way through the ice.

A forward bulkhead door was wrenched open, and we stepped into an empty space lit by ultra-bright strips. It was about three metres wide at the threshold, then narrowed. I noticed a couple of coiled ropes where it came to a point, their tails disappearing through a couple of holes in the deck. We were in the cable locker, right at the front.

I could feel the bow rise, ride over the next ridge of solid ice, and crash down through it. And I could also feel the gentle right-hand curve that the vessel was making.

The walls and ceiling of this compartment were dark red, and so was the thick industrial linoleum under our boots. I hoped it wasn't to camouflage the blood.

The bulkhead door slammed shut behind us, and one of the levers slid its locks into place with a loud metallic clunk.

Rune lost no time in invading my personal space. 'Nick, I know—'

'*Shut it!*' I shook him off with my shoulder and got eye to eye. 'Shut the fuck up.'

I scanned the place for any indication of CCTV,

microphones, anything that meant someone was watching or listening to anything potentially more interesting than the creaks and groans and rasps of steel grinding through the Arctic pack. All I saw was a speaker, probably a Tannoy.

Then I thought, Fuck it, I've done nothing, the team have done nothing – except to be mad enough to try to ski to the North Pole. I'd been a dickhead for listening to Cauldwell in the first place. We'd left Half Bear and Ponytail under a truck. But that had nothing to do with this.

I moved my mouth closer to Rune's ear. 'What? What is it?' Then I turned my head so he could do the same into mine.

'I know this ship. The *Lisandro*. It's an American exploration vessel. Scientific.'

We started to play mouth to ear.

'So what's it doing ferrying an execution squad? What's that about?'

'I don't know, Nick. But the ice must be getting so thin. This ship shouldn't be able to get this far north so early in the year.'

I moved my head so I could get a good look at his face to reassure myself that he and I still lived on the same planet. 'What are you on about? Mate, I think you'd better stop thinking about death of the ice and all your eco-warrior shit right now, and start thinking about *our* deaths – that's you, me, the team. Didn't you see what happened back there? You think we're plasti-cuffed and locked in here because they don't want us to hurt ourselves, to get our fingers caught in the doors? What the fuck do you think's going on?'

Rune looked dazed, like a kid who's just been told that Father Christmas doesn't really exist. His duvet rustled as he tried to adjust his hands behind him. Maybe his years on the eco picket lines had warped his sense of reality. Perhaps they had once persuaded him of his own ability to influence a situation – even one like this. Not any more, though. He was taking shorter and more hesitant breaths. He was flapping big-time.

'Rune, slow down. Calm. Tell me what this boat does.' I thought he was about to cry. 'Deep breath. What does this boat do?'

I shoved my ear back to his mouth, so he didn't even have to think about moving.

'It tries to locate oil fields by seismic blasting . . . compressed air detonations close to the seabed . . . They reveal the location of oil fields maybe thousands of square miles across. It does *terrible* damage to the ecology of the ocean. The sound they produce underwater is approximately four times that of a jet engine. It can stun and damage the navigational senses of sea life for hundreds of kilometres around. It's killing—'

I stepped away before he started to cry. Tears of distress, tears of rage, whatever. 'That's enough, mate. Now's not the time.' I had to take a few deep breaths myself to get my head around this. 'OK, so tell me about your so-called monitors. They're not about the ice getting fucked up, are they? They're not saving the world. I'm guessing they do exactly the same shit as this ship does.'

I let that sink in, but I didn't give him long.

'Rune, you have to understand that now is not the

time to worry about a shoal of cod getting home in time for tea. The monitors – are they looking for oil? Looking for gas? What are they looking for? They're fuck-all to do with the ice, aren't they?'

Rune had started to shake his head, not bothering to hide the tremor in his voice, but still trying to hold back the tears. 'Nick, you have to believe me. I only found out last night what they were about. These things . . . they send signals. They work their way through the ice floes, they penetrate the seabed. And yes. They're doing the same thing as this ship's doing.'

'Rune, you must have known something was wrong from the start. But you still did it anyway.'

'Cauldwell made me. I had to do as he asked. I had no choice. My debts, I couldn't . . . I told myself it was the lesser of two evils.'

'Know what, Rune? I don't care – all that's history.'

But I was just as guilty of self-deception as he was.

'Nick, they are Russian monitors. They are so sophisticated, so advanced, it makes this ship look like something out of the days of sail. I'm sorry, Nick. I'm *so* sorry . . .'

He couldn't control his tears now. They were soaking the front of his duvet. There was no way he could wipe his face; he had to let them fall.

'I'm so sorry. If I had known this was going to happen, I would have told you. Last night, I would—'

I cut him off. 'It wouldn't have changed anything. And, besides, it's not your fault, it's mine. I should have warned the team about this shit as soon as it started to go wrong.'

I let him get on with his crying. So all this shit really

was about the RPG bling, and the Americans wanting to stop the technology doing its job at source because they wanted to win this war. Because they wanted to win every war – but, then, didn't all sides? They wanted to stop them being used, but they also wanted to get possession of them – find out how the things worked, probably reverse engineer.

All the sweatshirted techies in the ISO containers must have been involved. As soon as they pinged one in action, they were on it. There was no way they were going back empty-handed. But so what? It was done. They'd got what they wanted. All I cared about right now was what was going to happen to us. And where was the rest of the team?

I leaned against one of the red steel bulkheads and suddenly felt incredibly, numbingly tired. I slid down to the deck and just sat there, losing myself among the vessel's vibrations as it pushed forwards, rising and dipping and continuing to carve its way through the ice.

I told myself I might as well rest as much as I could in the warm. Who knew how long we'd be there? Who knew what was going to happen next?

Behind my back, my hands were swelling, with the restriction of blood, and they were overheating inside my gloves. I tried to flex them, but part of me welcomed the pain.

I watched Rune pacing up and down, his hands tied behind his back. He no longer tried to control his sobs, and his head jerked up and down each time he drew a breath.

After five or ten minutes of this, I heard the lever

slam on the other side of the bulkhead door, and it was thrown open.

There were three bodies on the other side of it, and the only one to step through was Munnelly. He pointed at me, and jerked his thumb. 'Stand up.'

65

I started to lever myself off the floor, turning and shifting onto my knees, then slowly pushing myself up the wall.

Rune wanted Munnelly's attention. 'Please . . .' His face was blotchy and wet with tears, snot and saliva.

Munnelly waved a dismissive hand. 'Shut *up*.'

It really wasn't Rune's day.

'But I'm—'

Munnelly sighed. 'I know who you are. Go over there, in the corner – *now*.' His tone was crisp, but not overly threatening. It was more like he was sending a kid to the naughty step.

Rune finally got the message. Now it was my turn.

'You, you stand there too.'

He made sure I was complying, then pushed the door shut.

I joined Rune at the sharp end. The noise there was outrageous. I felt for a moment like they were using my head to beat a path through the ice pack instead of the bow.

We both turned as Munnelly rotated the drop-down handle that controlled the internal latch, then turned to face us. He seemed distracted, but I didn't think that would make much difference to us. We were still plasti-cuffed. And he was the boss.

He looked down at his boots, tapped some ice off the toes, and looked up again. His eyes bored into Rune. *'You . . .'*

The icebreaker lurched, then settled, and lurched again. The hull must have been massively insulated, but the squeal of tortured metal echoed in my head. We must have hit another pressure ridge.

Munnelly realized that unless we were going to shout our way through this interrogation, it was going nowhere. He beckoned us forward, but not so far that I could charge into him.

'Tell me how Cauldwell got you onto the ice. What did he say about the two men he sent with you?' He gave a dismissive wave. 'And about the cylinders? I want you to tell me everything. Don't lie to me. Just take a breath, know that I need to know, and tell me. Now.'

Rune's voice went up an octave. He babbled the same stuff he'd told me. That he was forced into it because his business had gone bust, that he was in debt big-time. Cauldwell had told him these men were going to come along and dig some monitors into the ice. Rune was the front for it, so it looked eco. That was all he knew.

Munnelly leaned against the door, one hand in his pocket, the other stroking his beard. His attention didn't seem to be on either of us. He glanced down at the floor, tapped a boot occasionally, like he'd spotted another tiresome speck of ice he needed to shake off.

Rune stopped and sniffed, trying to sort out the snot pouring from his nose. His beard glistened with it. At least he'd stopped crying.

Munnelly stayed where he was, head down, dipping his toecap in and out of the puddle of water from his boot ice. It was impossible to know what was going on in there. I couldn't see his face, just the top of his head.

'But you do know more than that, don't you? You do.'

It was difficult to hear what he was saying over the background noise now. His voice was low and slow.

It took a second or two for Rune to process the question.

'I promise I know nothing – nothing more. Please, I—'

Munnelly raised his head, then a weary hand. 'Stop. You knew what Cauldwell was doing. You knew what those so-called monitors were capable of doing. You knew where those two men came from. You knew. Yet you still carried on, didn't you? You don't come out of this with an ounce of dignity. You're supposed to be fighting the good fight. Devoting your life to getting in the way of people like me. Where the fuck are your principles? Where's your belief? You're nothing but a husk of a man, held together by fake principles and a handful of dollars. You knew a lot more, and still you didn't refuse. Shame on you.'

Munnelly found his toecaps a lot more interesting than us again. He shook his head slowly with almost headmasterly disappointment. I had to agree with him. Rune was a nice man, but the world was full of nice men. He'd folded really quickly for cash and an easy way out of the shit. That didn't make him bad, just weak. But the fact was, the strong would always prey on the weak.

Munnelly snapped upright and looked directly at Rune. I had a clear view of his face for the first time. The disappointment was genuine: he looked betrayed.

'You may be on the wrong side of this war, but at least the people I'm fighting against, they have conviction, and that I have to admire. So I guess that means I do not admire you.'

Rune was shot to bits. He slouched beside me, head down, sobbing openly again.

Munnelly turned to me. 'And as for your story, Nick. Let's see if you've got any dignity. Let's see if you believe what you're fighting for.'

He folded his arms, and waited.

I shrugged. 'I'm not fighting for anything. I'm not fighting against anything. I was asked to come and look after a team of ex-military amputees. To help them make it to the North Pole.'

I mimicked his tone. Low, disappointed.

Munnelly pursed his lips. 'But, Nick, you know it's more complicated than that, don't you?' He massaged his temples with his fingertips, deep in thought. 'Help me with this one, Nick. I'm here, like the rest of us on board this ship, trying to do my job. Trying to make sure that America, the West, whatever you want to call it, gets a fair share of what's under here.'

He tapped the flooring with the toe of his boot. 'There's a war going on down there, right beneath us. We both know that. And it's getting messier and bloodier by the day. But I try to do it in a way that means it doesn't escalate. None of us wants it to get completely out of control, do we? Neither side wants a full-scale war – real people getting hurt, killed.'

I guessed he counted the Quislings as not real people. I had to agree on that one.

'It's not good if one side starts to get the upper hand, in this quiet but grubby war we're engaged in. The other side has got to make sure that doesn't happen. As long as we both come out about fifty-fifty, everybody gets their share of whatever is buried beneath us. Digging mass graves is never the answer. I've got a role to play in stopping that happening. And you have as well, Nick.'

I nodded slowly. 'I've been learning more about this shit every day. But I didn't come here to do the digging. I came up here to help the team. I guess I made the wrong call when I decided not to share with them what I was learning. All they want to do is get their dignity back, to try to feel as good as they used to. To be back on top of their game. And you know what? They were all right until that Enstrom appeared.' I paused. 'Where are they? They OK?'

He dug his right hand into his yellow duvet for a packet of lozenges. He took one out and peeled it. The ritual got his full attention. 'Don't worry about them. I really wish they'd made it to the Pole, that it hadn't turned out like this. But let's not kid ourselves. You used them. And now we have a situation here. You've made our lives – and theirs – very, very difficult.'

He sucked so hard on his lozenge that I thought he was going to swallow his tongue.

'We both know we're fighting a covert war here, Nick. But you and Cauldwell, what you've done is brought some real people into it and put them in a *very* precarious position. And that could be dangerous for all of us. I'll be honest with you. I'm not yet sure how we can deal with it.'

Something else seemed to fly into his head. He stared at me, jaw working overtime. 'Do you know what I find so . . . wrong? No, not wrong, more . . . despicable. That someone could put their son in danger like that. His own son. And you let it happen.'

He balled the lozenge wrapper and flicked it towards us.

'So this is what I want to know, Nick. When did Cauldwell get you involved with Armancore? What other work has Cauldwell been doing for Armancore? These are very simple questions, Nick. Think. Who are Cauldwell's contacts, in Armancore and in Russia – and anywhere else? I need to know these things, Nick. And you need to tell me.'

Genuine disgust was etched on his face as he carried on sucking, and it had nothing to do with the lozenge. The irony of what he called the 'situation' wasn't lost on me. Having spent a lifetime in the shit, I was now about to have to take the pain for someone else's dishonesty. Fuck it, I didn't care. However much I'd tried to convince myself that my world could be divided up into neat packages of good or bad, light or dark, white or black, most of it was still lost in shades of grey.

'Look, Mr Munnelly – it is Munnelly, isn't it? I know nothing. Really. I was called in by Cauldwell to help with the team. Encourage them. Protect them. Look after them. And that's all. You'll have to ask him.'

Munnelly screwed up his face, ran a hand over his beard again, and finally crunched into the sweet. 'We tried that.' He let the statement sink in for a second or so. 'Nick, think about your own safety – but, more importantly, think about the team's safety. I will find out what you know – one way or another.'

I tried to keep it calm and monotone. 'Munnelly—'

His hand shot up, palm outwards. 'Enough. I know you're no choirboy, Nick. The Good Samaritan act doesn't wash with me. We had each other's measure on the flight in, didn't we? I saw the look in your eyes. You saw the same in mine. I know all about your SF background with Cauldwell. I know that you live in Moscow. And I'm talking Moscow, Russia, not Moscow, Idaho. Russia, Nick. Ring any bells?

'The rest of the dots are pretty easily joined. If you're not going to help me, you're not going to help yourself. And, worse still, you're not going to help the team. We are at war here. Make no mistake about it. And you need to help me stop this thing escalating. Do you understand me?'

He turned his back on me.

His hand was about halfway towards the door handle when there was a deafening metallic boom. The whole supposedly watertight compartment shook. It was like our car had just been rammed by a truck. Even the bulkheads got whiplash. All three of us were thrown to the deck. The strip lights went out. A split second later, emergency lamps glowed red from the walls.

The air filled with klaxons.

I lay on my side, tucked in my chin and raised my knees as close as I could to my chest, in case there was another bang immediately.

Then I raised my head and rolled onto my knees. Munnelly was clutching his left temple. The shunt must have thrown him against the bulkhead door. He'd taken a hit. He wasn't getting up as quickly as I was.

I yelled at Rune. He was still on lying on his side.

The Tannoy made soothing noises from somewhere above us. The voice was so calm it could only have been a recording. It ordered the crew to shut down the engines and go to emergency stations.

I got to my feet at the same time that Rune did, and realized that the ship had stopped. I reached the door, turned my back to it, and lifted the latch. Munnelly was still down, trying to recover. Blood was seeping through his fingers as he clutched the side of his head.

Rune looked at the man in yellow as if he was an experiment that had gone badly wrong for no discernible reason. He'd stopped leaking tears; now his expression was unreadable.

'Rune, get outside!'

He pushed his way past me and I followed. I used my back to close the door and slammed down one of the levers on the outside of the bulkhead with my elbow.

'What happened?'

'Fuck what happened. We need to find the team.'

But first I needed to find something that would get us out of the plasticuffs.

66

The vessel gave another massive shudder.

I sprinted down the narrow passageway, retracing the route we'd taken on the way in. Rune was somewhere behind me. I didn't bother checking. He had all his arms and legs, he could get on with it. The team couldn't.

I came to a junction and heard shouts around the corner. The passageway filled with a flurry of commands and running feet.

'The cable locker. He's in there with two of them. Go!'

I waited to take them on.

'Roger that.'

Day sack. Miss Kentucky.

I stayed where I was and waited for her to take a pace around the corner towards us and be in dead ground from the rest of them. I was fresh out of options.

The moment she appeared, I closed my eyes and slammed the top of my skull hard into her face. I didn't know where it landed, but there were starbursts behind my eyes.

She went down. I stayed standing, just about, screwing up my face in pain. My eyes streamed and my nose filled with snot. If you were going to head-butt somebody, you really had to go for it. Male or female. No half measures. The downside was, it hurt.

The boat's Tannoy kept right on going, with its looped sequence of monotone pre-recorded instructions. Everything was under control. The red lights glowed. It could have been happening in my head, for all I knew. But it wasn't.

I turned to Rune, my eyes still smarting. 'Kick her coat open – fucking get on with it!'

She was starting to move. Her legs flexed then straightened, trying to regain some form of control.

I knelt down, my shin planted across her neck.

'Rune, feel down her belt – maybe her trouser pocket . . . We need a knife. Get on with it . . .'

You were only as sharp as your knife. This lot were very sharp indeed, except when they ran around blind corners, and in environments like this they would all carry something like a Leatherman. Something that could grip and twist and cut would be part of who they were.

Rune was on his knees, on the deck, leaning back, hands scrabbling awkwardly inside her duvet.

'Try her pockets.'

And there it was, clipped in her right-hand pocket, an all-steel, military-looking Gerber Paraframe.

Rune was still feeling his way. 'That's it, Rune – that's a knife.'

His fingers fumbled until it opened, and he grasped it in his hand. The blade made short work of the tough plastic.

I felt movement under my shin as Rune cut me free. She was starting to recover.

'Get her back to the bow.'

He grabbed hold of her legs and started to drag her down the way we'd come. As he did so, her duvet rose up towards her chest to expose a 9mm SIG in a black matt polymer holster too, and two spare mags.

She was about a head taller and probably a third heavier than Rune. The ship lurched again and we were all thrown against the bulkhead. It didn't help that he was still in panic mode. I snatched the weapon and tucked it into my duvet jacket with the spare magazines.

'Drop her. Leave her. Go and wait at the door.'

I started dragging her myself. I wanted to get her inside the cable-locker room before she recovered enough to fight or raise the alarm. The Tannoy kept feeding calm, collected instructions about what kit went where.

It was all geeky. 'The G-Set 104, the D minus-6 kit . . .'

We got to the door. I dropped her legs and she groaned.

I bore down on her. 'My team. Where are they?' I gave her a kick, mostly to remind her of who was top dog now.

Whatever, I wasn't getting answers.

I couldn't tell if it was down to pain or resistance. Either way, it didn't really matter. We were well out of time. I got up, threw the latch, pushed open the door and stepped back. Inside, Munnelly was still bleeding, still on his knees.

I stabbed a finger at him. 'You, move back. Into the room.'

Then I gave her another kick. 'You, inside. Get inside.'

She started a semi-crawl, taking her time.

'Rune, fucking get her in there. Push her. Stay this side of the door.'

I focused on Munnelly as Rune bent down in front of me and tried to force her in.

'Where's everyone else? Where's the team?'

The dead eyes were back. He looked at me like he had on the plane and shook his head. 'Haven't you done enough damage?'

The ship lurched another few degrees and a yell echoed down the passageway. I lost my balance and hit a bulkhead. Munnelly thrust his hand down onto the floor to brace himself. He wasn't so groggy now. He was a picture of defiance. He wasn't going to give me anything.

And neither was she.

Fuck it. I shoved Rune out of the way, grabbed her belt and the scruff of her duvet and launched her bodily over the dwarf bulkhead. Then I slammed the door and spun the deadlocks back into position.

67

They had to be at the front of the boat like we had been, but in the bridge tower or one of the admin levels below it. The holds that would have been full of rotting cod or dead whales in the old days were too big to keep prisoners securely. And the ISO containers on the main deck were more to do with work than containment.

I checked the junction again where I'd dropped Miss Kentucky. There was movement, way down the passageway, near the bottom of the steel stairway we'd descended from the deck. Activity, but no shouting: people had control and were getting on with it. They would have rehearsed abandon-ship drills almost every day of their lives.

The Tannoy continued to dole out its bland monotone instructions. Then, above it, I heard a command: everyone move up to the top deck.

Rune and I pulled open doors and more doors.

'Will! Stedman! Jules!'

No reply.

The red emergency lights gave us cover, made us just another bunch of bodies rushing around. Then, behind us, I heard, 'Oi – *oi!*'

I spun round. Gabriel and Rio were at the junction. I ran back, feeling the world's biggest grin spread across my face. 'Thank fuck we found you!'

'Nah, mate. *We* found *you.*'

The rest of them barrelled round the corner. Jules was beaming too. 'Found you! We've been looking everywhere. What happened?'

'Don't know. And I'm not staying long enough to ask. We need to get off this thing.'

I turned left again, heading for the main stairway. I didn't need to check they were behind me. They'd get there. I had my reasons. I hoped that by the time everyone caught up I'd have had an idea.

I ran up the steps and lay on the gantry at the top, next to the open door. Normally it would have been closed, like on any ship, let alone something out there. I stuck my head out and looked left down to the deck. I saw maybe twenty bodies, hustling to launch the two orange lifeboat capsules this side of the icebreaker. Three bodies ran out of an ISO container carrying kit. One was clutching a thin aluminium box, maybe a metre long.

I could feel the ship listing.

The helicopter was back on the landing pad, still free of the supporting struts that would secure its rotors and hold it to the deck when it wasn't in use. It must have been prepared to take off again after its last sortie.

I legged it back down to the rest of the team. 'They're

abandoning ship.' I didn't waste time registering their reactions: they'd probably worked it out for themselves.

I caught Will's eye. 'Mate, the heli. Can you fly an Enstrom? Stupid question. Course you can . . .'

But his face fell. It was like I'd asked him to fire up an Apollo space rocket. I didn't get an answer.

'You can sort it, can't you?' I knew he could physically, but his challenge was mental.

'. . . well, I suppose . . .'

'Not good enough. The answer has to be yes. I need you to get this lot off safely.' I grabbed him by the shoulders. 'Here's how it is. Remember when your Puma brewed up, and the other lads didn't make it? Remember what that did to you, how badly it hurt when you could no longer do a fucking thing about it? Well, here's your second chance. This one *is* in your hands. So get switched on. Do your stuff, yeah?'

His face remained blank.

I kept staring at him, in laser mode, excluding everybody else, but kept my voice low. 'Mate, they need you to get that thing airborne. You can take care of everybody. I can't do it. Only you can.'

The ship gave another lurch, and we all gripped whatever we could. 'Will, the answer's got to be yes, and it's got to be now. You *know* you can do it.'

Jules stepped in. Put her hand on his shoulder. 'He *can* do it.' She had eye-to-eye with her husband. For a moment, they were in their own little world.

I let them get on with it and turned to the others. 'Right, here's the deal. Will's going to fly. Jules goes up front with him. Gabriel, Rio and Rune in the back.'

Rio sparked up. 'Hold up, mate, what about you lot? We're a team, right, stick together?'

I shook my head. 'We've got to be sensible about this. Room for five, right? You've both got kids. These two fuckers,' I jabbed a finger at Jack and Stedman, 'they've got each other, and me, I've got fuck-all. It's simple maths, mate. Get in the aircraft and fuck off.'

I pointed at Rune. 'And you're going, because you know the whole story. You need to tell the people who matter what's happened, and why. Do you understand?'

The rest of the team looked confused. 'Later on. Rune, do you understand?'

He'd gone white as the sheet ice that surrounded us. 'Nick, surely they will have sent an SOS? Help will be coming, right?'

'Don't count on it. You were in that room a minute ago with Munnelly. Do not assume anything. That goes for all of us. Do not assume anything. Just take the aircraft, get out of the area and get on the radio. There'll be emergency kit on board. Try and get to Barneo – anywhere, as long as it's not here. *Go!*'

Gabriel wasn't happy. 'Yeah, but we've got to get past—'

'That's your job.' I pulled out the SIG and the two mags, and gave them to him. 'The doorways to the ISO containers – as you look at the helicopter, they're to the right. Get round the left-hand side. Get Will in the aircraft, get the thing started and *get going.*'

He took the pistol, and started to take command. 'Rio, get Will and Jules upstairs. Let's go.'

I was expecting a wisecrack, but Rio swung straight

into action. He shepherded Will and Jules ahead of him.

Jules stopped, turned three steps up and caught my eye, but I shook my head. 'There's no time for that. It doesn't matter. You can do all that shit over coffee and sticky buns. Just get him on that aircraft – get him flying.'

I watched them reach the top of the stairway and turn right, round the front of the bridge tower, to avoid anyone working the ISO containers and the boats.

Then I turned to Jack and Stedman. 'OK, let's get off this fucking thing.'

68

When your options were zero, it was always easy to decide what to do.

'Listen in. This side is going under first. We have to go round to the other safety capsules. If they're loading them, we need to grab anything we can use to get off this thing. Or we just sit here and wait to drown. Or get wet and cold and then drown.'

They grinned, as you do when everything's turned to rat-shit and you've got a few bits missing.

'We've got to stay clear of those ISO containers. Fuck knows how those guys are going to react.'

I raced up to the main deck, stopped just short of the exit and cocked an ear. The Tannoy fell silent and I could hear the bulkheads creak and complain, the shouts of the bodies pouring out of the containers laden with gizmos. I had no idea what they were carrying, but it had to be very important for them to risk their own lives to save it.

I turned back. The other two were negotiating the

steps as fast as they could. Stedman had a grip on Jack and was hauling him up.

'Lads, give me two minutes. If I'm not back in two, crack on.'

I didn't wait for a reply. I pushed past them and ran along the passageway. There was no way I was going to leave those two in the cable locker. They deserved a fighting chance, same as the rest of us. Navies that were kicking the shit out of each other one minute would pick up survivors the next. We weren't at war just yet.

I reached the bulkhead door and slammed the latch over. Even though the whole superstructure was moaning and groaning like it was in its death throes, they couldn't have missed the clunk. They were cautious opening up, but this was their choice. I wasn't going to do it and risk losing a fight.

I turned and ran again, sweat gathering under my duvet. Jack and Stedman were still at the top of the stairway, looking out and down.

Jack had news when I reached them. 'We heard two shots.'

We lay on the landing with our heads stuck out over the threshold. Sweat was pouring down the side of my face. In seconds, it would have frozen.

The heli started up. Stedman clapped a hand on my shoulder. 'You hear that?'

'I may be fucked, but I'm not deaf, and we gotta get moving too.'

I checked quickly down below, to make sure Munnelly wasn't about to launch himself on us, then stood up, slipped out of the door and right, towards the bow. I sensed rather than saw the increasing panic on the deck behind me.

I didn't need to check that the other two were with me. I could hear them curse as the ship yawed and tilted. We now had an uphill climb along the front of the bridge tower.

I heard the roar of the heli's rotors.

The Enstrom flew past, then turned back on itself as Jules spotted us. Will kept the thing in a hover less than ten metres away. His face was a picture of absolute concentration. This was his life's mission. This was his time.

Jules was in the seat next to him. I could see her shouting, then gesticulating wildly towards the port side of the icebreaker, the side we were heading for.

It had now lifted high enough to make the ice pack no longer visible. All I could see was sky.

I waved back at her, trying to fuck them off. They'd done their bit. There was nothing else they could do. We were fucked if we went higher. The heli turned away, and we saw the other three in the back, faces to the window, expressionless, as the Enstrom headed south.

'Let's go. Up to the bridge!'

Having one option was better than having none. They turned and followed.

I retraced our journey around the base of the bridge tower. The crew had stopped saving their kit and started saving themselves. Bodies were clambering aboard the lifeboats. I saw Munnelly, standing between the water and the ISO containers, shouting orders to the last. There was no sign of the woman, but I was sure she was up on deck somewhere.

Back inside the superstructure, I scrambled from one step to the next, heading what used to be upwards and was now quite a lot sideways. Behind me, Jack was flagging. His plastic leg seemed to have stopped obeying orders. Stedman braced himself against the bulkhead and held out his good arm, letting Jack grab it and lever himself up.

I reached the top and had to stop. I'd been expecting drama but the bridge was empty. It was also warm. I could smell the coffee, because most of it was no longer in the pot.

Radar screens glowed, and every other piece of machinery within reach was flashing or bleeping loudly, telling the icebreaker what it already knew: it was in the shit.

The wipers kept scraping across the front and rear windows because nobody had told them not to. The last few bodies on the main deck had disappeared inside the lifeboats and hatches were being slammed shut. They knew it wasn't going to take long.

I headed left, through the door onto the bridge wing. I was moving downhill. This fucking thing was going to reach the point of no return very, very soon. I shouted back over my shoulder. 'Come on, *come on.*' As if that was going to help. As if they needed any incentive.

Jack and Stedman clambered onto the bridge.

They slid out onto the wing. The icepack was maybe twenty metres below us. The *Lisandro* heaved and rolled, and this time it didn't stop. There was a deafening series of shrieks, cracks, bangs and groans. Any second now the vessel was going to come out with a white flag.

I grabbed hold of Jack, the nearest body, and dragged him closer to me. 'You ready?'

There was no time for him to answer. The side of the bridge wing was almost a horizontal platform beneath our feet. There was a massive explosion somewhere below us and the platform plunged downwards like a broken lift.

I kept a hand on Jack, and he had hold of Stedman. I could hear the water rushing up, and the ice rupturing and splintering and sending up a glittering but impenetrable cloud.

We couldn't see what we were about to jump into. We just jumped. The hand gripping didn't last more than a second.

69

I was in freefall.

Still no imagery below me. A blurred glimpse of a lifeboat in my peripheral vision, caught under the side of the breaker's hull, in the process of being sucked into dark water.

I braced myself for landing. I just didn't know what I'd be landing in. I heard screams and yet more explosions of ice, one of which was right beneath my feet as I hit the ground.

The cloud was thinning and settling but the ice pack was trembling. Huge chunks of the stuff were being thrown up behind me. My ears were filled with the sound of rushing water. I spun round and faced the channel. The breaker's bow was now completely submerged and its stern had reared up towards the sky. It was howling and whimpering like a caged animal. Or maybe that was the ice around me. A lead opened up barely a metre from where I was standing, lengthened and widened.

I scrambled and slid away as best I could. Not looking up, or sideways, just down, running, staggering, slipping, crawling, running again – anything to make distance. The ice moved around me. I stopped and turned back, in time to see what remained of the *Lisandro* finally surrender and vanish into the dark water. All that was left was maybe a half-dozen survivors, thrashing and screaming, but sound and movement doesn't last long in the Arctic Ocean.

A couple of safety capsules still bobbed around in the channel, but they were crushed and mangled, semi-submerged. I stared at the bodies alongside them, trying to identify duvets.

'Jack! Stedman! Jack! *Jack!*'

The wind had picked up. It gave the cold even more of a sting, but had carried the remains of the ice and snow cloud away. The air was clear and the blue sky returned.

'Jack! Stedman!'

I heard a cry from behind me.

Jack was about twenty metres away, dragging his false leg behind him. He stopped and dropped onto his good knee. He wasn't trying to lever himself upright, though. He seemed to be trying to get down onto his belt buckle. He was shouting down into the ice.

When I reached him, I saw why.

He was lying next to a lead.

Stedman was floundering in the water beneath him. He managed to thrust his good arm into the air. Jack grabbed it. Stedman thrashed his legs, trying to gain enough momentum to lever himself onto the ice.

Jack grabbed a fistful of sodden duvet with his other hand.

Stedman was fighting for breath. The shock was sucking everything out of his lungs.

I threw myself down next to Jack. 'Breathe! Breathe!'

I added my hands to Jack's. We heaved together and beached Stedman on the ice. We both knew what we needed to do. Jack was totally focused. He knew his best mate would die if we didn't do something quickly.

'It's OK, we're here.' His voice was extraordinarily calm. 'We're going to get you sorted.'

'You get his kit off.' I unzipped my duvet, pulled it off and trapped it with my foot so we didn't lose it to the wind. Then I ripped off my Gore-Tex jacket and handed him my woollen base layer. 'Get both layers on him.'

The cold gripped me like a vice. My core heat was still up there, but it wouldn't be for long if I didn't sort myself out. I replaced my Gore-Tex jacket, dropped my arse onto the ice, pulled off my boots and unzipped the sides of my trousers so we could exchange our base layers.

When I got to my feet again, exposing myself to the wind, I was shivering within seconds. I handed Jack the long johns and pulled up the zip on the Gore-Tex trousers. It was easier said than done – my fingers were so cold they felt like they were about to drop off.

Jack had already transferred my base-layer top and duvet onto Stedman, hood up, and was now pulling off his boots and Gore-Tex trousers. It was my turn to talk while Jack concentrated on replacing his mate's insulation. 'Mate, keep breathing.'

Stedman's teeth were about to shake themselves loose, but I kept my voice as calm and emotionless as possible. 'Not long now. We're going to get you warm, and get you moved. We're going to get you out of the wind.'

He tugged off Stedman's long johns while I peeled off my outer socks and threw them over. I removed my second layer too, along with my vapour barrier, and swapped them over, so I now had my last remaining pair of dry socks inside the VB.

Jack remained incredibly calm, methodical, and totally focused. He shoved Stedman's hand into the pocket of my jacket, giving him a constant stream of encouragement. 'It's all right, mate. It's all right. Yes, that's good. Toasty, eh? We're going to get you out of here, soon as . . .'

I wrung out his base layers as best I could with hands that were freezing fast. The rest of my body wasn't far behind. I could almost feel the heat leaking from my core. I had to get a move on.

I undid my jacket again and pulled on Stedman's very clammy woollens, long johns, socks and boots, which had already started to freeze on the inside. Then I zipped everything up and started swinging my arms and stamping my feet to warm up the pockets of air in the way that Stedman was no longer capable of doing.

I crouched down again as soon as I could. 'Mate, I'm going to get you up now. Jack, give me a hand. One, two, and three . . .'

I didn't wait for any acknowledgement. I wrapped my arms around his trunk, hauled him upright and hoisted him onto my shoulder, knowing that if I didn't get moving, I'd be joining him. I could feel him shivering big-time.

I began to walk as fast as I could, swinging my body vigorously left and right to generate heat. I squinted through the ultraviolet bouncing off the ice, searching for somewhere – anywhere – we could find shelter.

I could hear the steady crunch of Jack's boots behind me. The only other sounds were our laboured breathing and the whistle of the wind.

Shards of ice as jagged as broken glass were strewn across our path. A hundred ahead lay the first of a series of what looked like baby pressure ridges. They were unlike any I'd come across. Maybe they'd been created by the movement of the *Lisandro*.

I soon found a mini version of Rune's monument – a hollow in the ice with walls about a metre high on each side of it. I eased Stedman off my shoulders and manoeuvred him inside. 'We're out of the wind, mate. Not long now . . .'

Jack lay prone on the ice to act as insulation so I could put Stedman on top of a body before I went out to gather further building material. Exaggerating every movement to generate heat, I excavated every slab of ice I could get my hands on and carried them back to the hollow.

There was a chance the crew of the breaker had sent out a general risk SOS, but I thought it unlikely. The Chechens would have been the quickest to respond, and very happy to take possession of all the shiny kit the geeks had been playing with on the *Lisandro*. Maybe they'd sent an internal mayday call to the US Navy, but I had no idea how far away they might be.

All I knew for sure was that the heli had taken off successfully, so that was where I placed my hope. But our first priority remained the simplest of all: to live long enough to be rescued. After I'd heaved the last block of our ramshackle igloo into place, I got down on my knees and crawled into the cave.

I knew that the heat I'd generated would soon dissipate, but I needed to transfer as much of it as possible to Stedman.

70

We couldn't afford to waste a single therm of body heat now. Whichever of us was wearing the dry duvet would lie on the ice, the bottom layer of the Stedman sandwich. Jack and I swapped places – and duvets – as soon as the top man couldn't take the cold any more. Who knew how long we'd be there? Whether help or another drama appeared on the near horizon, I didn't care. As long as it was something.

The wind found its way through every gap in the roof of my igloo, no matter how small, and blasted us with needles of ice. The sound it made was as eerie as our solitude – like a big unfriendly giant blowing across the neck of a bottle.

Jack's body was starting to shake. We'd both had better days out.

As our next changeover approached, Jack said he was going to have a piss.

'Don't, mate. Think of all that steam and liquid leaving you, leaving us.' I tried to take his mind off it.

'I'll tell you the best way I've found to keep the cold at bay . . .'

He wasn't biting.

'Never fails . . .'

From under his hood came a muffled 'What's that, then?'

'Dream, mate. Dream. Just think to yourself that this will all be over soon. This time tomorrow you're going to be in a hot bath with a huge mug of coffee and a fat sticky bun. This time tomorrow we'll all be laughing about this shit. This time tomorrow—'

'Nick . . .'

'Yup?'

'It's my turn with the duvet.'

We swapped places. Now I lay on top, wrapping my arms around Stedman, tucking his head into the space between my neck and my shoulder.

Maybe an hour later, the situation was getting out of control.

Jack and I were still muttering words of encouragement, making stupid, irrelevant jokes, but we were all shivering convulsively. My hands were numb, frozen and searingly painful.

As my core temperature continued to drop, I was starting to feel light-headed. And I wasn't the only one.

Stedman had been mumbling from time to time. Now he was getting increasingly incoherent. It wasn't a good sign. His central thermostat had gone into melt-down, sucking the heat from the head, leaching the oxygen and sugar from his brain.

Hypothermia was coming in fast – with the real danger that he didn't know it was happening. One of the first things it did was take away your will to help yourself. You stopped shivering. You stopped worrying. You were dying, and you couldn't give a shit. Your pulse would become irregular. Drowsiness would give way to semi-consciousness, then a little further along the line, unconsciousness. The only stop after that was getting dead.

Jack was now back on top of the sandwich, and sensed it. He gripped into Stedman even more. 'Mate . . . it's . . . OK. We're here. We're . . . here . . .'

Stedman shouted, and thrashed about. Jack kept holding him as I brought my arms up and hugged him into me.

I looked up at Jack, as we sandwiched Stedman between us, and blamed myself. I should have told the team everything; should have given them the option of pulling out.

Stedman made a noise that was half sigh, half cough, and then a low groan.

Jack lowered his mouth to Stedman's ear. 'Remember Catterick? Pretending to be . . . airline pilots . . . fuck's sake. 'Member? We would have . . . pulled it off . . . if their husbands . . . hadn't turned up.'

He somehow managed a snort of laughter, even though his best mate was about to die and there wasn't a thing he could do about it.

'Running down . . . high street . . . trying . . . get away . . .'

Stedman reached out for Jack's face, brushed the underside of his chin with the tips of his gloved fingers.

Jack's hand grasped Stedman's.

'Tell you what . . . If they'd . . . caught us . . . would have been us . . . fucked.'

I thought I heard Stedman giggle, but maybe I was imagining it. Then his body went still.

I craned my neck to one side. Jack's eyes were closed, his hand holding Stedman's against the side of his face.

I gave him a minute with his friend, but we had to get moving. 'Mate, you know we have to sort ourselves out now, don't you?'

His eyes remained closed, but he gave a couple of nods. He did know. Of course he did. He finally rolled off Stedman's body and lay beside me.

I took off my glove, put my frozen middle and forefinger into my mouth to try to warm them up, then touched Stedman's neck, trying to find his carotid pulse. I could feel nothing. His skin was as cold as mine. But we needed to be sure.

Jack was still grasping his hand.

'Jack, mate,' I kept my voice low, 'can you check his breath?'

He gave a reluctant nod. He knew what we had to do, but it didn't make it any easier. His lids flickered open. He pulled back his hood, lowered his face mask and gradually raised his head until his right eyeball and a patch of cheek were a couple of millimetres away from Stedman's nose and mouth.

He seemed to stay in that position for ever.

When he finally sank back onto the ice I saw tears welling in his eyes.

'He's gone.'

I gave him another thirty seconds, then eased Stedman off me and rolled him onto his back. Jack pushed himself up onto his knees. I retrieved my duvet, then unzipped Stedman's Gore-Tex jacket and handed it to him. Even a tiny bit more warmth was all we needed to give us a bit of hope. I recovered my boots and dry socks and rearranged the vapour barrier. It would take a while for my feet to warm up again, but they would once we got going.

Jack was on his arse, watching me. That was all I wanted him to do. The tears were starting to freeze on his cheeks. The more layers we had on, the more air would be trapped, and that was what would save us. The outer-shell trousers and base layers came next. I handed him the merino top, and kept the long johns for myself.

Jack rearranged his clothing in slow motion. I was about to say, 'Get moving, get some heat,' but thought better of it.

His speech was still slurred, but less so now.

'Know what, Nick? Stedman . . . totally turned everything around for me. We did that for each other . . . I suppose. When I got out of . . . Headley Court, I wasn't all there . . . I was even worse mentally . . . right on the edge. Stedman was the same . . . We were both fucked. My old man was making it worse for me . . . He took against Stedman . . . Don't know why. Stedman could be a twat . . . You know that . . . But at the end of the day he was just . . . Stedman . . . wasn't he?'

Then it all came out in a rush. He'd felt worthless. He'd had enough. He'd been literally on the way to the railway bridge when Stedman had managed to talk him out of it. They'd made a deal to say fuck it to everyone. A pact to depend on each other.

'Because no one else really gives a fuck . . . do they, Nick? Does *anyone* give a fuck?'

He zipped up the Gore-Tex jacket halfway, then stopped.

'Look, Nick . . . I know you and Jules . . . my dad . . . Everyone sees him, *saw* him, as a fuck-up. And they weren't completely wrong . . . But I'm only here because of him.'

Fresh tears began to tumble as he stared at the near naked body beside me. 'And *he*'s only here because of me. So . . . where does that leave us?'

I glanced down too. Stedman's skin was colourless. His body had already started to shrink in the extreme cold.

Then I looked up again, and got some eye to eye. 'It's all about life now, Jack. And if we don't get some action going, we're going to be joining him.'

'Action?' Jack wasn't convinced. 'What action?'

For the first time, he sounded defeated. I needed to reset him. 'We need to think about fluids, mate, hot fluids. We can't eat snow.' He knew this shit, but that wasn't the point. He needed something to concentrate on. 'You waste crucial body heat melting it in your mouth, and it cools the body from the inside. Chills the vital organs in the body core. So, our first task is to get one of those fucked-up survival boats closer to the ice, see what's in them. Then we can start thinking about what to do with it.'

I zipped up the Gore-Tex trousers and couldn't wait to get my body moving to generate a bit of heat.

'Mate, we've got to leave him now. We've got to get moving, or we'll both be joining him.'

He didn't move a muscle.

I was about to grab him and give him a good shake while dragging him out onto the ice when we both heard the unmistakable sounds of tracked vehicles.

Jack lit up like someone had just recharged his batteries. He was set to race out of the cave.

Now I had to make him stay exactly where he was. I held on to him, just in case. 'Let's see who they are first.'

71

I knelt just inside the entrance to the igloo. The wind whipped needles of ice into my face as soon as I leaned out, so I had to squint.

A white skin had started to form on the canal carved out by the *Lisandro* – almost enough to camouflage the darkness of the water but not enough to hide the horror of what had happened there. Yellow and red lifejackets were dotted about at random, frozen in place, some framing a head and shoulders, others a rigid, out-stretched arm.

The only craft in sight were two wrecked survival capsules, both semi-submerged. Bodies were still aboard, stiff as mummies, some clinging on for what must once have seemed dear life. I spotted a couple of brightly coloured duvet jackets on our side of the channel. Their owners had somehow managed to claw their way onto the ice. They probably shouldn't have bothered. If they'd stayed in the water, it would have taken them less time to die.

Dark, angular shapes were heading towards us, exhaust stacks doing their bit to widen the hole in the ozone layer. I could tell they were Russian from the clinking sound of their tracks. Five of them. The last vehicle was dragging what looked like a load of mangled wreckage behind it.

Jack joined me, kneeling too, not moving as they drew closer. We recognized the Russian equivalents of the Viking – and the significance of the tangled remains of a steel cockpit and rotor blades bringing up the rear.

Jack's head dropped.

'Mate, we don't yet know anything for sure. And there may be other survivors out there, like us, trying to stay out of the wind. Let's see if any of them break cover. Then we'll check out the Russians' reaction. It'll only take a little while longer.'

We reversed into our shelter. The wagons passed no more than fifty metres away from us, heading towards the channel, tracks clinking. Once the sound had died, I crawled out again.

The front two vehicles bristled with antennae and satellite dishes. They wanted the gizmos. I studied the heli as closely as I could. I didn't see any scorch marks. It hadn't gone up in flames. The yellow pontoons were heavily buckled. Two rotor blades were lashed to the roof beside them. One had worked itself loose and its tip was bouncing across the ice.

Jack moved alongside me again, his chest heaving. It had nothing to do with the cold.

'Mate, let's wait. Let's just . . . wait.'

I didn't need to draw him pictures. We both knew

that if any survivors did front up, they might get dropped.

The lead wagons stopped a few metres short of the channel. The last one seemed to be trying to get as close to the edge of the pack as it could without toppling in, then veered to the right, exposing the heli to the sea. Bodies in standard white Arctic kit clambered out of all five vehicles, some with weapons.

The first thing they did was check the dead on the ice. There was lots of shouting and gesticulating. One figure pointed towards what was left of the survival capsules.

I saw the biggest puff of smoke yet spew out of the lead vehicle's exhaust stack and heard the engine rev. The top turret opened and a head emerged. The vehicle crept forwards. These things were amphibious, but they wouldn't want to get swamped by their own bow wave. It tipped into the water and made its way to the nearest capsule. No grateful survivors jumped out to thank their saviours.

Jack shivered. 'Nick, what next?'

'We wait.'

I watched as the Russians dragged the casualties out of the craft and tossed them overboard. Half a dozen squaddies clustered around the wreckage of the heli, pushing, pulling, shifting it half a metre at a time. It didn't take them long to give it the same treatment.

I had a last look around to see if anybody was breaking cover. Either there were no survivors, or they were being as cautious as we were.

I motioned Jack back into the igloo. Both of us were shivering big-time. I had to lay it on the line. 'We've got to give ourselves up, mate. There's no other option. If we stay here, we're dead. I don't think anyone else is coming.'

'But the boat – it must have sent . . .'

'I don't think so.' And now wasn't the time to explain that if the Americans *were* coming, we might be in even more danger.

'No, we have to go now. Otherwise, we've got twenty-four hours, thirty-six at best, before we're history. The heli didn't make it. We're getting no help from anywhere else.'

Jack nodded slowly. He was really starting to suffer.

'Your leg OK?'

He nodded again, but I could see that he was thinking the same as I was: maybe they'd have a medic under one of those smokestacks.

We clambered out and started walking. His leg was really hurting him. I hoped that the movement would get some blood running around that stump.

I gripped his arm. 'Stick to the truth, OK? Tell them exactly what happened. Tell them why you're here. Tell them what you know.' I started waving my arms.

'Over here! Help, help, *help!*'

I'd stick to the truth, too. Well, Jack's truth, anyway.

72

They didn't hear us at first. Their engines drowned out our shouts. We were sixty metres away when a couple of squaddies finally turned and saw us.

I ran towards them, like the most grateful survivor on earth – or that's how I hoped it looked. I pulled down my face mask and pushed back my hood. The cold immediately rushed in to attack my bare skin, but I didn't want to be confused with an incoming threat. And if it all went wrong, at least I was heading towards the rounds rather than running away.

We kept moving forwards.

Four weapons were eased off their slings and into four pairs of hands.

I kept going, faster and faster, waving and yelling, incredibly happy to see them.

Jack was a few paces behind, doing much the same.

Weapons were still in hand, not in the shoulder.

I got to within about five metres of them, then checked behind me. Jack was still trying to keep up, but he was lagging. I was all smiles and gratitude. 'Thank you! English! Does anybody speak English? My friend, he's in pain. His leg . . .'

I pointed down at my own. Two of the squaddies advanced, but not to help me – to grab and search. I had no problems with that.

I felt my zips being pulled down, my Velcro fasteners being ripped open. Mitten-clad hands probed and tested every angle and crevice, checking for a weapon.

Jack moved closer, hands up, waiting for his turn.

They removed my passport and neck wallet and showed no intention of wanting to return them. I didn't give a shit. Anywhere else on the planet, that would have been a problem. But not here, not now. I read it as a sign that they were going to keep us alive. At least for now.

One of the squaddies searching Jack gave a shout. I turned round to see him pointing at the prosthetic leg beneath the Gore-Tex.

'My friend, he's in pain. Much pain!' I mimed much pain. 'My friend Jack – he has no leg. Much, much pain . . .'

As I worked on the sympathy vote, I saw out of the corner of my eye the last of the rotors being sent to join the icebreaker. The pontoons would be staying where they were. They wouldn't sink.

The second of the wrecked survival boats had been tied up alongside the floating wagon, and bits and pieces of kit were being loaded aboard. The rest of the bodies had already been hauled out and tipped into the sea.

They didn't seem that keen to have an audience.

Almost immediately we were turned away and guided – not manhandled – to the rear of the wagon that had been dragging the heli. A gust of hot air hit us as the door was thrown open and we were motioned inside.

We were not alone.

Gabriel was seated on one of the benches that ran along the side of the vehicle and Rio was on the floor, sorting out his Jock mate's stump with a dressing from one of the vehicle's trauma packs. Both had lacerations on their faces. They were in shit state. The windburn on Gabriel's nose and forehead was starting to bubble up into a rash of little blisters. Rio's lips were severely cracked. Jack and I probably weren't in mint condition either.

Cracked lips or not, it didn't stop us grinning from ear to ear. The fact was, we were in a large aluminium insulated box, they had large insulated mugs in their hands, and whatever they contained, it was steaming. We climbed in and the door was closed behind us.

One of our escorts swung himself up into the cab in front of us, and started gobbing off. It wasn't the first sign of madness: I could see a wire twirling between the dash and his head. He was reporting in to the boss, who must have been on the floating wagon because this guy kept looking out towards the channel, where the last of the geeks' shiny stuff was being transferred into Russian hands.

I looked down to get eye-to-eye with Rio as he offered me his brew. I didn't even need to ask the question.

He shook his head. 'No, mate. Gone.' He gestured over his shoulder to where the last bits of the Enstrom had just been chucked into the water. 'Burial at sea.'

We were all silent for a moment. Gabriel concentrated hard on his dressing.

'Stedman?'

'Same. The cold fucked him.'

Gabriel reached out to Jack, took his arm and gripped it. 'I'm sorry.'

I took a gulp of Rio's brew. It was coffee, powdered milk, lots of sugar. I could feel it travel down my throat and into my stomach, creating much-needed warmth as it went. I took another. Jack did the same from Gabriel's brew.

'So?'

Gabriel focused two hundred per cent on the process of removing Jack's carbon-fibre leg. He still didn't look up. 'We were sorting the rotor restraints when a couple of guys tried to stop us. I had to drop one. The other suddenly decided he didn't need to get involved. We climbed onboard. Will was a star. He got the aircraft up, gave you lot the warning and headed south for Barneo. Then, at around the fifteen K mark . . .'

He paused. When he continued, his voice was huskier. 'The explosion at the stern of the boat, it must have fucked the engine. We were losing height. Will fought it. As soon as the thing started to malfunction, the freewheeling unit should have cut in, so he could auto-rotate and land. But it didn't.

'Will . . . somehow kept it stable. And as we came in, he tried to flare, but something happened and the tail hit first and we crashed. Fucking nightmare. Jules . . .'

He tailed off again, and Jack gripped his shoulder.

'She . . . died instantly. So did Will. Rune lasted

another twenty minutes. Long enough to say sorry about three hundred times. We'd have been dead within a day if we'd stayed out in the open. We had nowhere to go, nowhere to hide. Then the Russians turned up. Like you, we had to take our chances with these lads.

'But Will. What a star.'

He wasn't wrong there.

No one spoke.

The silence was broken by Jack's gasp when Gabriel finally managed to liberate his stump from the socket of his prosthesis, and unwrap it. I only needed one glance to know that Jack was a fucking star, too. The last ten centimetres of it was like a plate of chopped liver.

73

As I finished Rio's brew I looked round for the BV. Every military vehicle had a boiling vessel, a steel kettle to heat up water, and this one was no exception. Beside it was a jar of coffee with a bright yellow label, the powdered milk, and a can of sugar.

I took both mugs, and as I started to fill them, I glanced through the porthole that separated us from the front cab. On the dash was a GPS screen. I tried to focus on the glow, tried to read the latitude and longitude, and find out where exactly all this shit had happened.

'Nick?' Gabriel finished unrolling a bandage. 'What about you three?'

I shared the broad detail. It was all they needed. And, however much of a dickhead he'd been before the trip, Stedman was Jack's best mate. Chapter and verse wouldn't help him either.

We lost ourselves in the healing ritual of creams and dressings. Even the Russian version of zinc-oxide tape smelt reassuringly the same. Two freshly covered amputated legs were now enjoying the warming air, and some of the tension was seeping out of four sets of shoulder muscles. The engines of those vehicles were kept running constantly out there, in case they didn't restart. It was fantastic. My face was starting to sting, and I knew that my fingers and toes soon would as well, when they began the journey back to life.

I pushed the valve at the base of the BV and released steaming water into the mugs while the rest watched the squaddies moving about on the ice in their massive insulated boots. 'There'll be no sign of anything within the hour. Just like the Americans at our camp. There'll be fuck-all left – I'd bet the farm on it. Any idea what happened to the ship?'

I took a sip of the first brew and handed it to Gabriel to pass around.

'The engine went up. Fuck knows, the list is endless.'

Gabriel was pissed off with himself. 'That's when all the damage was done. I should have checked the air-frame, just a quick look, but with those guys coming up, trying to keep everyone back . . .' He shook his head. 'Will was on it. We were motoring. I just didn't have time to check.'

'It's not your fault.' And it wasn't. It was mine.

Rio passed the brew back to me once it had gone full circle, then turned his head to check what was happening on the water.

'That wagon's coming back. It's been out there for ever, checking those lifeboats. See all that kit they dragged on board?'

The amphibian clawed its way back onto the ice. A white-covered body jumped out of the front passenger seat when it came to a stop beside us. He was wearing a neoprene face mask, but the way he was ordering people about said 'Rupert' to me without a doubt. He started towards us.

'Lads, whatever happens, we just tell them the truth, yeah?'

Gabriel and Rio shot me a collective *What the fuck?*

'Not that. The truth about the trip. Who you are, why you're here. We aren't part of all this shit, all right? That's all you've got to say.'

Jack looked across to me, steam rising from his hair, as it probably was from mine. 'What? Nothing about what?'

The door opened and the white-clad officer climbed in, swinging a small bin-liner. He sat down on Gabriel's bench and handed it to him. I could now see that it had some lumpy bits at the bottom.

Gabriel looked inside as the officer took off his head-gear. Gabriel grinned and displayed the contents – bars and bars of Alenka chocolate. It was one of the few luxuries that were shared around – though not with everybody – during the Soviet era, and still a Russian favourite. Gabriel continued the tradition. 'Great – thank you.'

I handed a bar to the officer, whom I now recognized as the *kapitan* who'd dealt with our passports in Barneo. He didn't acknowledge the connection but nodded his thanks, and admired it with the eager anticipation of a seven-year-old. Myth had it that the doll-like girl on the wrapper was Stalin's grandchild. It was open at each end, like a sleeve. Even after all these years, tradition demanded that it should be removed intact, with appropriate reverence.

In their haste, Gabriel, Rio and Jack simply ripped Stalin's granddaughter in half, and our compartment was soon filled with a sweet vanilla smell. Even bad chocolate tasted good at such times – and this wasn't bad at all.

The *kapitan* turned down a drink from a mug that was now chocolate-rimmed, and I thanked him again.

He gave a curt nod. 'No problem.'

The door opened and a squaddie handed him something. When it closed again, his expression was a whole lot sterner. 'One of your group is . . . unaccounted for.'

No one answered. Rio was finishing off his chocolate bar. Jack was adjusting his leg. He'd inserted the bandaged stump into the socket. Gabriel was doing the same.

I took a big gulp of coffee in case it turned out to be my last. 'He's dead. Hypothermia. He's in a shelter about a hundred and fifty away – just follow our tracks. You'll want the body, won't you?'

'Yes, I will.' Then he broke off a chunk of Alenka and spent longer than was necessary enjoying its taste. 'I'm very conflicted. I'm not sure if I should feel sorry for you and your group. Or if I wish I was about to make you disappear.'

He held up his hand, palm outwards, when he saw that I was about to reply.

'But the truth is that whatever happens to you now is out of my hands. I'm a soldier. I respect you as soldiers. I respect you all for your courage and

358

determination. I hope that I have as much of both if I'm ever wounded.'

He leaned across, opened the door again and let in the cold, engine noise and clinking of tracks as he shouted a series of commands. Three squaddies arrived at the double and lined up outside.

'If you really are who you say you are, I'm sorry. This war should not be for your eyes. You are . . .'

He searched for the right words. I had them for him. Munnelly had already put them there for me. 'We're just real people in a very precarious position.'

He smiled, but it soon faded. 'Yes, thank you.' He pointed at Jack, Rio, Gabriel and their injuries. 'I hope I'm not wrong. I want to be right.' The *kapitan* nodded a gracious farewell and headed out into the snow, where he waved an arm to indicate the general area of the igloo and issued another string of commands.

Without exchanging a word, we got the rest of the chocolate down our necks and into our pockets as fast as we could. None of us knew when we were going to get fed next. If at all.

Rio got more brews on the go as the vehicle picked up revs, and more squaddies piled into our front cab. Seconds later, we were on the move.

Two dull explosions kicked off about a hundred metres behind us as the driver paralleled the *Lisandro*'s channel. I looked through a porthole to see water pluming into the blue sky, along with the wreckage of the two survival capsules. It wasn't long before they followed everything else to the bottom of the Arctic Ocean.

Rio thrust the mugs back into our hands, full to the

brim with hot coffee. Lumps of powdered milk floated on top. There was no time to get fancy. We just wanted to get food and liquid down us before whatever happened happened.

After maybe five hundred metres we stopped.

We all pressed our faces to the nearest portholes as an antenna the size of a flag-pole emerged from the thin ice in the centre of the channel. Others, stubbier, followed. The Empire State Building was erupting from the bottom of the ocean.

Next came a massive jet-black cylinder, covered with anti-sonar pads, the latest stealth technology. It pushed its way up into the sky, blocking the sun.

Bodies began to swarm out of a top hatch. As they did so, Rio said what we were all thinking: 'Fuck me. No need for a list, then, eh?'

74

Russian submarines had always seemed a lot fatter to me than Western ones. As we walked up the gangway, I could see that this Dolgorukiy class was no exception. The deck was two or three metres above the waterline, the width of a football pitch and the length of several more.

Those monsters rarely came up for air in the outside world. They didn't enjoy the exposure – which suggested that the body in the peaked cap I could see at the top of the conning tower was pretty sure the Americans weren't heading our way. I hoped he was right. Sinking the ship was an act of war, and I didn't want to be caught up in the middle of it.

Gabriel and Jack were finding it hard to negotiate the slope. Rio and I stopped and gave them a helping hand.

Two divers stood by at the top of the gangway with dry-bags and fins. They weren't there especially for us, though. We weren't honoured guests. It was a standard operating procedure in case someone fell into the sea.

There was an arch in front of the conning tower, and we were handed a brush to knock the ice off our boots, then ushered through it. I went first, and immediately felt the heat. I also felt the all-pervading calm, which submarines need. And because this was a nuclear-attack boat, there was no smell of diesel. After the icebreaker, this thing was a seven-star Hilton.

Two of the crew helped steady Jack as he stumbled down the last couple of rungs of the ladder. I blamed the cheap rubber flip-flops we'd had to put on whichever of our feet still had toes before being allowed to come aboard. It was like being invited onto an oligarch's plaything – which in a way I supposed this was.

I'd kept my socks on, though, and would keep my boots close to hand at all times now. The others did the same. But it still took me back to my time on a British frigate in the Mediterranean, wearing trainers on duty for the first time in my military career. I'd thought it was great – you didn't have to be able to see your face in the toecaps. That Type 21 vessel would have been built in the seventies. This was one of the new generation of attack boats I'd seen on the news in Moscow every week – another part of the process of restoring pride to the Motherland.

Jack rested against the ladder. Now it was Gabriel's turn to attempt the flip-flop challenge. We were in something like a highly polished service corridor or an efficiently run office: hardly a whisper, apart from the movement of bodies, the odd blip, and unhurried, businesslike intercom messages.

Tellingly, the place was filled with white light. It must have been daytime in the real world.

The high-tech in the control centre put NASA to shame. The crew studied their consoles, not remotely interested in what was being brought aboard. We were just cargo to be taken somewhere. They already knew all they needed to know. Everything was so intimate on a boat: they'd have been told exactly what was going on here, and why.

They all wore tracksuits and trainers. Uniforms were for the return to port, the parade on deck, the whole navy thing to make their supreme leader happy and their mums proud. At sea, it was all about the balance of life, and the expertise of the personnel. The stakes were too high to play it any other way. When it came down to it, the boat and its crew existed for only one reason: to take the world's most sophisticated weapons systems for regular swims, undetected before they launched and destroyed half the planet.

These Dolgorukiy-class subs were multipurpose. As well as torpedoes and all the traditional stuff, they carried a whole range of state-of-the-art killing machinery. News reports constantly displayed two dozen tubes full of Cruise missiles, ready to be unleashed at any moment, and cohorts of Russian politicians saying how wonderful it was that they were once more major players on the world stage.

The official ceremony raising the Russian Navy colours on this new class of submarine had taken place in 2013. The Russian deputy prime minister had gone on TV and announced, 'Tremble, bourgeoisie! You're done with!'

Anna had laughed like a drain, but the PM had had a point.

These craft had come a long, long way since the *Kursk*, which had sunk to the bottom of the sea when a torpedo exploded on board in 2000. Twenty-three of the crew survived the blast, but then made what the media called the ultimate sacrifice. In other words, they died slowly and painfully of hypothermia and asphyxiation because the Russian head-shed were too proud to accept any outside help.

Anna had always maintained that there was more to it than just an unhappy accident. An American sub had been in the area when the *Kursk* went down.

We were led away by a couple of crew members so young they could barely grow bum-fluff. Their skin was dull and zitty after however long it was they had been deprived of natural light. They weren't overly friendly, but they weren't pointing pistols at us, and that was the main thing.

We passed along a narrow passageway lined with pipes sending water here, electricity there, then another with nothing much at all, until we came to a compartment the size of a walk-in closet. Piles of blankets were stacked in one corner. The door was locked behind us, but I didn't mind. We were dry; we were comfortable; we were warm. Fantastic.

The door opened again and brought more good news – four white plastic vacuum flasks, mugs, and a couple of plates piled high with something like pitta bread. The fact was, no matter who you were or where you came from, military all around the world didn't have any problem translating 'We're cold and hungry.'

It was almost a common language.

Jack gave a very gracious thank-you. The young guys nodded and closed us down once more.

Gabriel had already taken his leg off. Now he unscrewed the nearest flask. 'Soup. Great.'

He passed around the mugs. I dipped my pitta into mint pea soup. The igloo seemed to belong to a different world.

I was about to get Jack's attention and launch into: 'See? I told you. *This time tomorrow we'll all be laughing about this shit.*' But I thought better of it: that was meant to be for the three of us.

Rio opted for a chocolate appetizer. He kept his voice as low as the boat's gentle electric hum. 'Where the fuck now?'

The intercom made a series of announcements, which seemed to be met with a flurry of calm, measured and efficient activity in the passageway outside. I felt the nose tilt into the beginnings of a dive.

'Where now?' Jack looked darkly at Rio. 'There's your answer. Onwards and downwards.'

My soup and pitta were finished. I held up my Alenka bar. 'We're warm, we've been fed, which is a lot better than we were a couple of hours ago. Everything after that is a bonus.'

Jack thought about it and gave me a hint of a smile. 'Men wanted for hazardous journey.' His accent was pure Eton. '"Low wages, bitter cold, long hours of complete darkness, safe return doubtful. Honour and recognition in event of success."'

Rio didn't have a clue. 'What the fuck you on about?'

'Shackleton. His recruitment ad in *The Times*.'

Rio nodded. His face may have been covered with soup and chocolate, but he knew something about it. 'Yeah, but all that lot got back safe, didn't they?'

Jack didn't want to pursue the Shackleton theme. He had something else on his mind. 'What was it you didn't want to talk about in the wagon, Nick? What were you three on about?'

Gabriel waited for my answer, but Rio jumped straight in. 'We should tell him. No harm in it now, is there?'

I placed Stalin's granddaughter carefully on my blanket. At least she was still smiling at me.

As I unwrapped the silver foil, I ran through where Stedman's cash had been supposed to come from, why the deal had gone wrong, and why Ponytail and Half Bear had got dead at the airport.

'What? You three killed them, at the fucking airport? What happens when we get back?'

The other two exchanged a smile and slowly shook their heads.

Jack clicked. 'Ah, yeah. Doesn't really matter now, does it?'

I decided I couldn't face the chocolate, and put it down beside my duvet-jacket pillow. 'There's something else you all need to know. The reason we're here, the reason the others aren't . . . It's my fault. I knew what was happening but I didn't tell you, didn't give you the option to back out.'

They all stopped eating and drinking and stared at me as I told them I'd lied about the Cauldwell connection, that I'd known something was going on at Barneo, but was really just thinking of myself, that I'd come to realize I wanted this trip as much as any of them. And I told them that, when we were on the ice, I'd become pretty sure I knew what the Quislings were doing, what Rune was up to with the so-called monitors.

I explained what Munnelly had told me, and what was actually happening up there – and why Russian submarines were torpedoing American research vessels.

And, finally, I told them that I was sorry. I'd fucked up big-time.

There was no reaction as they thought about it and took everything in.

Gabriel was the first to spark up. 'So? What the fuck? I would have done the same.' He looked around. 'We all would have, no?'

Jack nodded vigorously. 'I would *so* have done the same.'

Rio agreed. 'Yeah, count me in. And it's not every day you get to help kick off the Third World War.'

Jack lay down, and we all took his cue. We started to pull the covers over us as we tried not to think about what might be happening up above us in the real world.

Rio must have had a thought about the substance of his joke and summed up the situation: 'Shit.'

I lay with my head on my duvet, covered with two soft nylon blankets, not sure how I felt about their reaction. Maybe they really would have done the same as me, but that didn't make me feel completely at ease. I felt like I should have been made to feel shit, feel some of that guilt I'd talked Will out of.

75

I woke to the sounds of the intercom dishing out a string of monotone instructions, but that wasn't what had broken my sleep. I could feel motion. We were still moving forwards, but now we were also moving up.

The others stirred, responding to the same sensation.

Gabriel was sitting bolt upright, trying to listen to the announcement, as if he could interpret. 'For fuck's sake, man. Is that Russian, or has the guy burned his tongue?'

'You really complaining about his accent, you oatmeal savage?' Rio pushed his way up onto his arse and mimicked talking into a mic. 'Hello, Pot . . . Hello, Pot, do you read me? Kettle calling . . .'

Jack checked his watch. 'Shit, it's been over sixteen hours.'

It was then I realized we'd gone to red light. It was dark o'clock in the real world above us.

He levered himself up. 'Where do you think we are?'

'The Northern Fleet is based in Severomorsk. I guess we could have come that far south. These things can shift.'

I heard muffled voices outside the door. It swung open to reveal the return of the bum-fluff crew. The bad news was, they hadn't brought food.

They beckoned us. 'Come, come.'

Behind them were a couple of not-so-young, not-so-slight guys, presumably detailed to ensure we did as we were told.

This shit had just got serious.

I picked my half-melted Alenka bar off the floor, shoved it down my neck, pulled on my duvet and helped Jack sort out his leg. Rio was doing the same for Gabriel. Nobody said a word. We didn't need to. The boat had levelled off. We all knew we were entering a new phase, and we were all thinking the same thing. Rio's refrain: What the fuck now?

The lads hurried us up, which they hadn't done sixteen hours ago. We were soon shuffling our way back towards the ladder into the conning-tower arch. At the top, we were told to put on our boots.

Another game-changer? Had the effort to keep us alive after all that we had seen and touched now been dumped – like everything else – at the bottom of the Arctic Ocean?

One of the crew opened the hatch. A diver was waiting for us.

We might have red light down here, but it was light out there, even though the sky above us was a dull, dark grey. We were still well within the Arctic Circle.

It was clearly a good thing we were still breathing,

but the effort it had taken for this boat to get us to wherever we were now wasn't because of some brotherhood of the sea. There was a plan. And the problem with other people's plans was that they hardly ever turned out to be the best ones.

As I came out onto the deck in front of the conning tower, the water was choppy; whitecaps crested the waves. I could hear them bouncing against the hull below us.

The diver gripped me to keep me steady, and helped me as I sorted out my feet. It seemed we weren't about to be thrown overboard. I tugged up my hood and pulled the cord as tightly as I could around my face.

I could now see that platforms of ice dotted the black ocean.

Then I saw a small mass of white light. Maybe three or four Ks away. It was always difficult to judge distance at sea. Well, it was for me, anyway. But I was definitely not imagining it.

Jack was next out. I grabbed him and helped him, made sure he hung onto the rail.

'What do you think, Nick?'

'I think we're not in the Motherland. Otherwise why not just park up normally? But we're definitely south. The ice is floating, not solid. And the weather: shit. That's what we left, mate – shit weather coming up from the south. The Russians have islands in the Arctic as well. They've got archipelagos. Maybe they can't park up at them. I don't know.'

Rio was next out and needed extra help to make sure his good arm was secure. Jack did his hood up for him as he held on with his arm. 'I hope that fucking scabby Jock gets up here next. I want him to suffer.'

His eyes narrowed and I followed his gaze. In the gloom, I could see the dark shape of a boat manoeuvring between the ice floes at high speed. It was coming towards us.

Rio turned to me, making sure I could see his face. 'Mate, what Gabriel said before, about you thinking you fucked up? Really, all of us would have done the same. Whatever happens next, fuck it.'

The boat was alongside us in seconds, a big RIB with three Yamaha 75s on the back, and a white but battered and grimy fibre-glass cover as an improvised wheel-house. It wasn't military. I didn't know if that was a good thing or a bad thing. But if it meant we were about to get on land, it was good for only two reasons worth thinking about. Because it meant we had a chance to escape and make distance.

There were three people onboard, and they threw out ropes to the divers, who lashed the RIB to the boat, then lowered their gangway onto the smaller area of exposed decking at the rear.

The divers pointed downwards. It was time for us to go. I went first as the RIB swayed in the swell. As I reached the bottom, I was grabbed to steady me, then pushed onboard. I sat on the fibre-glass bench at the front by the bow.

Above me, at the top of the conning tower, stood the same small collection of men who'd watched us board the previous day. They were busy scanning the sea with binos. Their body language said they wanted out of there fast.

The rest of the team gradually assembled, and we huddled at the front of the cubby as the RIB moved off at a speed that could only have been achieved by somebody who knew where they were going and what they were doing.

The bow bounced up and smacked down on each wave. All we could do was accept the hard landing, try to stabilize ourselves, then brace ourselves for the next.

At first, I didn't give a fuck. I doubted any of us did. We were all looking through the old, scratched, frosted Perspex windows, at the ribbon of white light along the coastline starting to grow, and then at the shapes of buildings as they emerged: harsh, angular industrial structures.

And then, higher up, we could see bigger buildings. Apartment blocks? Somehow it made me feel better. There was habitation.

I could see Rio checking out the decay along the jagged, rocky coastline – hundreds of metres of rusted, collapsing conveyor belts that led from the buildings towards the sea. He was muttering to himself, 'Where the fuck are we?'

Gabriel turned to him and gave a shrug. It was then that I spotted a ceremonial plinth, with a head at the top, looking towards the sea.

It could only be Lenin.

'Fuck,' I muttered. 'I know.'

76

Barentsburg
Latitude: 78.0820 North
Longitude: 14.1867 East

We weren't in military hands any more, or at least not overtly, that was for sure. This island belonged to a NATO country. Not that that had meant much to the submariners behind us, or to the Russian special forces who had been covertly recceing Longyearbyen airport.

So who were the RIB crew if they weren't military? Police? No. The Russians wouldn't just hand us over to the police. We'd seen too much. We could say too much. Maybe part of their intelligence service. I guessed we'd find out sooner or later who wanted us in Barentsburg, and why.

We obviously weren't heading for the harbour – I could see its rectangular concrete breakwaters off to the right, jutting out of the sea. We were heading to the left, away from the lights, towards a stretch of beach towered over by some massive rocks. The closer we got, the higher they became.

I could see the waves breaking on them with an endless sequence of big white explosions. Sixty or seventy metres from the beach, the RIB slowed suddenly, the engine just ticking over as the cox manoeuvred us in the swell.

There was a reception committee on the shoreline, standing by the silhouette of a vehicle. By the time we were twenty out, I could see that four bodies were waiting for us. The cox gave it some revs, then cut the engines altogether. He lifted the props and locked them horizontal as we coasted in. The vehicle now came clearly into view: the blue UAZ four-wheel-drive minibus.

The shore crew were careful not to get their boots wet. They waited as the RIB rode a wave in and beached itself, like a killer whale going for a seal, then grabbed the bow line and pulled it onto the shingle as the water receded.

We were ushered almost silently off the front of the RIB and onto the shingle. Rio turned back and grabbed hold of Gabriel to make sure that when he came down he didn't fuck his stump up any more than he had already.

There may have been a dull, grey light, but the lack of voices at first and now the low mumblings made it feel as if we were fucking about in the middle of the night. Maybe it was.

Two of the reception committee made sure we weren't going anywhere as the other two pushed the

RIB back into the sea. The crew paddled out far enough to be able to lower and reactivate the outboards, then vanished into the gloom.

All four bodies corralled and herded us towards the minibus.

Jack closed up on me. 'Where are we? How do you know?'

'Barentsburg. Me and Stedman?'

I could see what the other two were thinking because it had crossed my mind as well. Payback time for the two bodies at the airport . . . 'Lads, we're about to find out.'

We were shoved into the back of the UAZ.

A fifth guy was already in the wagon, at the wheel. I recognized him. He'd ferried me and Stedman to the heli with the Owl and Munnelly. He did a double-take, then turned his full attention to the windscreen. He clearly didn't want anything to do with whatever shit was happening behind him.

The minibus answered one question for me: the dashboard clock showed 03.30.

I sat back. It didn't do much to help our situation, but it felt good to be aware of something.

Rio gave me a nod. They all knew not to talk, just to comply, whatever the five wanted us to do. It wasn't rocket science. They were worker bees, doing what they'd been ordered to do. If we resisted, they'd fight back. They had to make sure we were delivered.

The tyre-chains clattered on the ice as we lurched up the track, away from the beach and onto the high ground.

The vehicle slid off to the side a couple of times, the

driver correcting with aggressive hand turns and lots of revs. Instead of going right and into the built-up area where Lenin lived, we went left into the land of industrial decay, past the rusting mine wheels and the other relics of happier times. Even the snow was grey in this part of town, and everything was covered with it – the derelict tin buildings, the sunken wooden structures, and the featureless blocks that might have been airlifted in from East Berlin on a slow day.

Eventually we shuddered to a halt outside one, a particularly badly stained concrete monstrosity with regimented lines of very small windows barred with rusted mesh. When I'd first seen these buildings, they'd reminded me of a Soviet gulag. I was right: we were going to jail. There were no lights outside, or peeping through the mesh.

A low but still surprisingly high-tech electronic buzz released the main door as we debussed. It swung open far enough for another man mountain to appear. Part beer-gut, part padded coat, he beckoned us in. We were herded up the gulag steps and through the entrance, where another four equally gargantuan escorts were waiting.

It was the stench that hit me first: very strong disinfectant, then tobacco smoke so sweet and strong you could taste as well as smell it and, finally, musty undertones of decay. The concrete walls and floor of the interior glistened with streams and puddles of rancid water. Oily reflections of a single forty-watt ceiling bulb bounced along the corridor that ran away to our left. A once forbidding steel-barred gate now hung limply from a single hinge. We passed the gate and the cells along the corridor, all of which were empty.

The place had probably seen a lot of business in its heyday, dishing out good old-fashioned Soviet punishment for murder and mayhem, for being drunk in charge of a mine shaft, or for tearing the wrapper off an Alenka bar the wrong way. But now, like the rest of the town, it was the province of the living dead.

There might have been electricity, but there was no heat. I didn't know if that was a good or bad sign. At least the chill kept the smell under some kind of control. Beer-gut pointed to the cell at the end of the corridor and we filed in.

I could make out two sets of ancient steel bunkbeds in the gloom, one on each side of what the estate agent's particulars would have described as a window, secured by wire mesh, and a bucket in the middle of the floor. As soon as we were in, the slam of the door and the buzz of its electromagnetic lock told us we weren't going anywhere fast.

The first thing we checked was the blanket pile. One each. No pillows. The mattresses were pitted and piss-stained, no covers, just rectangular lumps of crumbling foam. It was a far cry from our plush Dolgorukiy-class cruise ship.

Gabriel swung his good leg onto the end of the right-hand bunk and reached up to press the mesh. 'Nope. What now?' The cell was so small he didn't have to raise his voice.

Rio had draped a blanket over his shoulders. 'Keep warm, mate. That's what.'

Gabriel hopped back down, and I threw one over to

him. 'Well, at least we're still moving. And we know where we are.'

Rio climbed onto the opposite top bunk, and Gabriel slid into the one beneath. 'And at least we're on firm ground. Thank fuck for that.'

I took the other top bunk, and fell straight through. There was next to no support. Then I heard movement outside, and the buzz of the lock. The door opened with a tired metallic rattle, which continued for a couple of seconds after it had come to a standstill.

Beer-gut stood at the threshold with two of the still fully padded escorts. They were clearly as cold as we were. He had a very small torch in his very large paw. It threw out just enough light to identify our faces, but that was all he needed. It was mine he was after.

The escorts dragged me to my feet and out of the cell, and told me without words that they'd fill me in if they had to. My request to take a blanket with me went unheeded. I might regret that if I was dragged away to some new place.

I was moved along with a bit of help from a dig between my shoulder blades. We went back along the corridor, past the steel gate that could no longer stand to attention, and left, leaving the main entrance behind us.

Not far beyond the turn was what looked like the guardroom. The bunkbeds there boasted vintage horsehair mattresses and pillows positioned so that all of them could watch the ancient box TV. It was balanced on top of a fridge, which had been parked on a flaking metal desk with a lifetime's supply of brew rings.

A random selection of electric convector heaters, hold-alls and washbags made it clear that this place hadn't been used for a while. The faded calendar on the wall featured two women, with big 1980s hair, who were concentrating hard on showing each other a good time.

Just past the guardroom door was the mains cabinet, the size of a double wardrobe. Once upon a time it would have been secure, but now it was as resigned to its fate as the steel gate. The rusted interior looked as if a family-sized pot of spaghetti had been thrown into it and left to congeal, but a new set of wires bound with insulation tape had been introduced to the chaos, probably to get the locks and lights working so we could all enjoy our stay.

Immediately after we had passed the cabinet, Beer-gut shoved me against the wall and held me there while the escorts disappeared through the next door on my right. The first emerged almost immediately, gripping a pair of legs partly covered with a torn and flapping green parka. As he backed out further I could see a pair of plasticuffed hands, a torso and then a battered and very dead face as the second escort appeared, his hands bunched beneath Cauldwell's armpits.

I was rammed against the wall as the two escorts moved Cauldwell past me to the main door. It buzzed open to reveal the waiting UAZ.

I had seen what they wanted me to, and nodded at Beer-gut to let him know I'd got the message. A couple of metres or so of rust stains and puddles, then I was pushed through the next thin steel door into another rank and gloom-filled room. This wasn't a cell. This was the gulag's version of a conference room, but it still had only one naked forty-watt bulb dangling from the middle of the ceiling. It cast just enough light for me to make out vaguely human shapes in the shadows at the rear.

I was guided towards a Formica-topped trestle table, which had been set up about three-quarters of the way in. It was probably the newest thing in the building. The shapes became more distinct the further we went, and the one that stepped forward needed no introduction. I was guided to a wooden, classroom-style chair, but not yet encouraged to sit.

The Owl picked up its twin, on his side of the table, and dragged it round so he could station himself a couple of feet away.

I didn't know what to expect, but got the biggest and best fast-food welcome ever. 'Hiya, Nick. How are ya?'

Then he sat down, made himself comfortable and invited me to do the same.

77

He'd come forward on his own. The other two bodies were still way back in the shadows – Americans, Russians, whoever the fuck they were.

The Owl's appearance put another whole layer of shit on the situation. Yet at the same time it was strangely comforting to see a familiar face. He was his normal goofy smiley self, like he was thanking me for ordering the extra-large, and did I want big fries and a litre of Coke with that? To start with, he simply sat there, looking me up and down. 'Jeez, you've been in the wars, Mister, and no mistake.'

I'd been all wrong about the guy. I'd been taken in by the cartoon version he'd sold of himself. I'd had him down as the collegiate dumb-ass, but he wasn't. It had been confidence that gave him that smile and that cosiness.

Two large white china mugs appeared out of the gloom and were left steaming on the table top. I didn't move. Impassive and unworried was the look I was aiming for. It had never been hard to achieve, because that was the way I always felt when I was in this kind of drama. But I was normally the only one in the shit. This time I had others to think of.

The Owl was concerned that I wasn't touching my brew. 'Nick, please, take a hot one.' He leaned across and picked up the nearest, turned the handle of the other towards me and eased it across.

I took it, and nodded my thanks.

'Hey, no problem. I've got to tell you, it's no home-store brand here, my friend.' He raised his mug in a toast. We both took a sip of very thick, sweet hot chocolate. It was more like a pudding than a drink. I wondered how many of Stalin's granddaughters it had taken to frighten these up.

'Pretty good, huh? Am I right?' He beamed at me as I tried to take bigger sips, wishing I had asbestos lips. The Owl managed a couple of slurps.

I kept the hot chocolate between my hands, wanting to keep control of it in case it was taken away from me as part of some power trip, some interrogation technique that might be gathering momentum just around the corner.

'The seating plan on the inbound flight – you, next to me . . .' The Owl blew across the surface of his brew.

'That was on purpose, wasn't it? You knew all along.'

I was on the receiving end of a few more kilowatts of Greeter's Grin. Then he returned his mug to the table and looked me straight in the eye. It was confession time. 'You got me, Nick. I was interested in what you might know, what you might say, what you might feel – all that kinda thing.' He shrugged. 'I'm sorry.'

'But you really do hate flying?'

He placed his hands between his thighs, and hunched his shoulders, probably to keep warm. His face was a picture of anxious concern as he leaned towards me. 'Do I fucking hate flying! Sweet Jesus . . . bouncing up, bouncing down, up and down, up and down.' He released his hands and gave me a double thumbs-up. 'I've got to thank you for your help. That breathing thing, it really helps. I'm sure going to use that trick again.'

I kept my focus on the liquid Alenka. 'Well, you might have your weaknesses, but you're no backroom boy, are you?'

His hands went back between his legs. 'Oh, but I am, Nick. I wouldn't lie to you! This thing is far too important for us to play about with lies. People like me – us backroom boys – we're needed because we're fighting a backroom kind of war.'

He opened his legs and his hands gripped the front edge of the seat so he could shuffle and drag himself a couple of feet closer. I could smell the chocolate on his breath. I moved my head back a little so I could down the last dregs of mine.

He gave me his happy face. So close, it almost looked insincere, but his tone told me it wasn't. 'You see, this war, Nick, both sides would like to win. But to have the whole thing – and apologies for the pun – blow up like this, and become something that's out there, in the real world, for real, you know, that's kind of scary, and neither side wants it to happen. Once all that starts, it escalates, and . . . No, we don't want that. No, siree. And you don't want that, do you?'

I shook my head. 'Maybe you should play the whole thing online. That way no one gets hurt.'

He liked that. 'D'you know? That would be such a *great* idea. I might even suggest it when I get home. A *real* good idea.' He slapped his thigh in delight. 'No need even for drones. Thank you, my friend.'

The smile stayed, but the tone didn't. 'For now, though, we are fighting the new Cold War. Sometimes things happen that mean desperate actions are taken. I'm sure I don't need to tell you that, Nick. You, of all people. And this is one of them.'

'Just like the *Kursk* was?'

He moved his hand from side to side, as if he was rolling a ball or deciding what coffee to buy.

'Those *were* a couple of scary weeks. No one knew how that one would play out.' He ran a meaty finger back and forth below his bottom lip. 'And, y'know, this one . . . Well, this one is kinda just as bad.'

He gave the words a couple of seconds to hang about and establish their significance before he kicked back in. 'Look, Nick, we had ourselves a situation. The Russians have these gizmos that are . . . hmm, far more advanced than what we have. So of course we want them.

'But, hey, the Russians prefer us not to have them. So stuff happens. And you've seen for yourself how shit like that can get out of control. You've got to remember, the Russians respond very differently to problems like this. You know that, don't you, Nick? Russians, eh? What can you do?' He raised his hands as if to God, and maybe God would give him an answer. He wasn't going to get one out of me. 'Crazy world, crazy war, but there you have it.'

He wasn't wrong about that. We'd been delivered to him by the very people he was unwilling to trust. 'So why are you *here*? You're the enemy, aren't you?'

He sat back as I put my mug on the table alongside his. The only difference was, he'd left his three-quarters full. I picked it up and started to drink.

'I guess . . . And these guys,' he waved a hand behind him into the gloom, 'I don't even know them. But I think they don't like me that much.'

He got back into focus. 'Anyways, I'm here to calm everything down. Us, the Russians, everyone. Oil on troubled waters.'

He didn't apologize for that one.

'It could have been the other way round, and that's the way we play things.'

I was concentrating on his mug. 'Just like the Chechens. They cleaned up the mess?'

'Nick, you're catching my drift! I knew you would.' He pointed his finger and bounced it around, in time with his words, like he was conducting a kids' orchestra. '*I* clean up. *I* calm everything down. Before the real world knows what's going on, and we have our so-called leaders getting all excited and wanting to go to war. No one will find the icebreaker, or anyone connected to it, including your friends. I'm sorry about that. The whole world's been looking for that missing Malaysian Airlines aircraft for over two years. We know it existed, but . . .'

The chocolate had cooled, so I could take bigger gulps. I felt it furring my teeth. 'Well, did you get the gizmos?'

His happy face was suddenly overtaken by his sad

face, and he slowly shook his head. 'Nope. Maybe they're at the bottom of the sea. And if they are, we're never going to get them because the Russians will keep a sub down there twenty-four/seven, just to make sure. And if *they* got them back? Pah, they got them back. Tomorrow is another day.'

It sounded quite reasonable to me. 'So it's all sorted, then? Job done, war carries on. Time to shake hands and go our separate ways?'

The Owl would have made a great politician. He oozed another barrel of charm. 'I'm so glad you asked me that. That's a really important question. As soon as I got the *Lisandro* news, I wanted to get our people back – the ones who'd survived. Munnelly . . .' He switched back from happy to sad. The man was a walking emoji. 'He was a good man, a moral man.'

He stopped and looked at me, square on. 'But, unfortunately, I got you four instead.' The smile was still there, but his eyes broadcast disappointment.

I hadn't seen that emoji before.

I wanted to keep him away from Munnelly, the crew, the monitors. I wanted him to concentrate on us. 'Look, we're just a bunch of ex-soldiers heading for the Pole. I didn't know what Cauldwell was up to. But I know now we were used as a cover for this heap of shit.'

He was nodding and agreeing with every word. 'Yup. It took a while, the background searches, more footwork, help for Mr Cauldwell . . .' He tilted his head in the general direction of his temporary morgue. 'Look, sorry, but he had to go. Part of the clean-up. A quite important part.'

He leaned forward again. 'Did you know that it's

against the law to bury people here? Crazy? No. It's the permafrost. Keeps 'em all preserved. Anyhoo . . .'

Anyone who'd had any connection with any American, anytime, anywhere, knew that when you heard that, you were getting to the point.

'Anyhoo . . . You four present quite a problem. Real people in *our* world. Normally that kind of thing is dealt with, if you take my meaning. Car accident. Suicide.' He tried a little smile as if he'd just come up with some drunken innuendo.

'Nick, I just wanted my people back. To do that, I had to jump up and down, scream and shout like a two-year-old, you get what I'm saying? So I've got to continue. Show some dominance here. Follow through with my demands.' He clenched his fists and jabbed away in a very bad Muhammad Ali impression. He paused to let that sink in. 'After all, we are at war. We don't want to be. But sometimes it can't be helped.'

He paused again.

I nodded. 'Yup, I get it.'

'So, I need to get you guys out of my hair. But how do I convince the Russians you won't go tell on them? I kinda also need to know that for myself. You grasp my problem?'

I tilted my head back to get the last of his hot chocolate down my throat. 'I don't see it as a problem. I don't see it as a problem at all.' I'd never sounded so helpful in my life. 'There's going to be nothing coming out of our mouths. We've seen what you lot are capable of. We'll do anything that's required to get our lives back. Whatever keeps you breathing, right?'

The Owl reached over and slapped my leg. 'Thank

you for that, Nick. You're very . . . understanding.' Then he straightened. 'Say, I've got to go talk to my guys back there. How about you go talk with yours?'

He stood up and gripped his chair so he could take it back around the table. He tucked it nice and gently under the Formica top, remained where he was for a moment, then leaned across conspiratorially. 'You're not the only guys who've gotta stay here until we've sorted out this problem of ours. They won't let me leave either.'

His brow creased as my four-man escort came and indicated it was time to go back to my cell. 'I'm *sure* they don't like me.'

We passed the guardroom. At least the two girls were still having a good time.

78

All three of them were lying on their bunks.

'You're OK.' Jack was the first to sit up after the usual clank, rattle and buzz. 'Thank fuck for that.'

'Yup. All good.'

I kicked the still empty bucket out of the way and stood between the two sets of bunkbeds and told them what had just happened – leaving out the bit about Cauldwell. I'd work out what to do about that later.

Then I explained the problem the Owl and his kind had with us, the real people, and why we needed to sign up with whatever needed to be signed up. They all agreed. Why wouldn't they? I got Rio to come down off his bed and sit next to Gabriel, and did the same to Jack before gathering them all in really close, to within whispering distance.

'No way are we putting our lives in the hands of these fuckers. All we're being offered is words. They mean jack-shit. Even if we do get out of here, who knows what's going to happen next? Are we really going to put our destiny in the hands of someone who looks like a fucking owl?'

All three exchanged glances. What the fuck is he on about? Rio piped up. 'Well, yeah, course – but . . .'

'Look, I'm not too sure how we can get out of here yet. But I know how we can get out of the town, and then to Longyearbyen. I know where we can hole up and sort our shit out.'

Jack frowned. 'What shit do we have to sort out?'

'Let's get out of the cell first. Then the building. Then the town. Once we're out of the danger bubble—'

'Yeah, but what are we going to do? Even if we do get out of the building, we're not going to tab, are we? And we can't just flag down that minibus.'

'We're going to take a fire engine. They've got some Gaz-71s. Not far from here.'

They all knew what they were. Enemy-vehicle recognition and use were drilled into British soldiers pretty much from day one.

Rio had a brainwave. 'We'll start a fire. That'll get a Gaz down here, double-time.'

Gabriel stared at him. 'Shit for brains – how're we going to make a fire that's bigger than something we can put out with a piss? You're not thinking straight.'

We all heard someone coming in or exiting the main door, followed by the metallic clank of it locking down.

'We need to get out of here on a rolling start-line. We keep on going till we get to the fire station, and then all the way to Longyearbyen. Who knows? We might even be able to lift a Gaz without anyone knowing. I doubt they have a full-time crew hanging about. Anyway, the only way to find out is by getting out of here, and up that hill.

'If it goes noisy at any point, we'll just have to go for it, won't we? The station is on the high ground behind us. Me and Stedman passed it on the way in. You can't miss the fucking thing. It's new, and of course it's red. Lads, I've got nothing else for you because I don't know anything else – except that if we stay here, we've got no control over our wellbeing. So, how do we get out of here?'

Jack grunted. 'As quickly as possible! But it's not like we're the Fantastic Four . . .'

Gabriel jumped in. 'I'll get you sad fucks out of the cell, and then you can get me to the fuse box, or whatever's out there, and I can attack the main door. I'll be able to cut the power to it without anybody knowing, no problem at all. So over to you lot. I'm waiting.'

Rio gave his mate a wide grin, then regretted it as his cracked lips took the punishment. Gabriel poked his chest. 'You're not taking the piss now, are you? Not fucking heli fuse-box repair man shite now, am I?'

Rio took the jab. 'Mate, you haven't got us out of here yet.'

'So I'd better get to work, hadn't I?' Gabriel pointed to the mid-section of the door. 'Buzz, buzz. The lock's magnetic, right? I knew a twelve-year-old who defeated one of these things. It was a gate on the security fence, and he was trying to get into a Sports Direct warehouse – he was just pushing, pulling up, really quickly in unison.'

Jack had worked it out at the same time we did. 'Did you get what you wanted?'

Gabriel shook his head. 'Nah, I couldn't get in the main building. Just one pair of new Nike Air, that's all I wanted. I just wanted to be like my mates, know what I mean?'

I shook my head. 'No, mate. Too much noise. We wouldn't even make it to the main door without being compromised.'

Gabriel tapped a finger against his nose. 'Exactly. But I'm a fucking REME fuse-box genius, I know stuff. Fundamentally, that heap of Soviet shite the other side of the door is a classic traction electromagnet. The force between the bonding of the electromagnet and the armature,' he glanced at Rio, 'the strike plate, for thick fucks, varies, but based on its size, I'd say that one packs no more than a twelve-hundred-pound holding force.'

He turned to Jack. 'That's just over five hundred and forty kilos, for numerically illiterate Ruperts. And for stupid fucks like you,' it was my turn, 'the armature and the mag need to be in direct contact for its maximum force. The insertion of anything, any non-metallic material, is going to diminish that force. Even a leaf from a tree, between magnet and armature, can reduce the mag lock's holding force by about fifty per cent. So it'll still lock, it'll still close, but the holding force will be reduced.'

He pointed at Rio. 'Even you, with your gimpy arm, could push that open – so, you three work out how to get the door open long enough, and I'll do the rest. Then we'll just wait for things to calm down. Show me the mains box, I'll cut the power and we're off.'

Gabriel unzipped his Gore-Tex trousers and eased his stump from the socket. Next, he ripped the zinc-oxide tape off his dressing, tore it into strips and lined them up carefully on the bed frame.

79

Jack was up for it. 'You two,' he gestured at me and Rio, 'stay where you are, so you're not presenting a threat. I'll deal with this. You.' He pointed at Gabriel. 'You'll be up here with me, won't you? You need to do your stuff.'

'Don't you worry.' He rolled the double *r* in a way I'd not heard before. He was getting more Scottish by the second. Maybe it came with becoming a twelve-year-old all over again.

Jack checked to make sure it was safe to go and Gabriel gave him a nod. Jack headed for the door and started banging on it. 'Hello? *Please?*' There was real pain in his voice.

Gabriel took up position to his left, the opposite side of the door to the hinges, a strip of zinc-oxide tape in his hand.

It wasn't long before we heard movement in the corridor, then the buzz and rattle that might be our passport out of there. Beer-gut stood in the frame, with two of the escorts a pace behind him. None of them looked like they'd enjoyed being torn away from the calendar girls.

'Cigarette? Please? Cigarette?' Jack was half pleading, half charm, as he mimed the first stage of trying to give yourself lung cancer.

Gabriel nodded and agreed, leaning against the doorframe with his hands behind him, as if he was supporting himself. He'd left the Gore-Tex open, and was showing a bit of prosthetic. Even I was convinced: nobody was going to worry about a cripple. He turned back to us. 'What's the Russian for cigarette?'

Beer-gut knew without me telling him. 'Ah! *Sigareta.*'

No matter where you were on the planet, the two common bonds were football and nicotine. Anyone who'd experienced the need for a smoke understood it immediately in others. This was Beer-gut's kind of emergency.

The two heavies powered down now they knew what the door-banging had been about. They hung back in the corridor as Beer-gut muttered something and pulled out a pack, flipped it open and offered Jack one.

Jack added most-grateful-man-on-earth to his list of Oscar-nominated roles.

Gabriel asked for one too. Beer-gut nodded and Jack fished out a second. He put the first into his mouth and did the classic move as the disposable lighter came up. He cupped his hands around Beer-gut's, as if he was shielding the flame from a force-ten gale, established eye-to-eye with his saviour, took the first drag, then nodded his appreciation. There was immediate bonding, and Jack tried to keep it in place while Gabriel still had his hands behind his back.

Gabriel finally did a big thanks as Jack turned the cigarettes around, lit the other one for him and passed it over. They all stood there, a convention of Smokers Anonymous, the worker bees sharing an emotional bond.

Gabriel took another drag. Beer-gut saw the leg and couldn't help his curiosity. He gently touched it with the toe of his boot. '*Voyna?*'

Gabriel looked like every hole in his head was exhaling smoke as he spoke. 'Afghanistan. Taliban.' He pointed to Jack's leg as well. 'Helmand.'

Beer-gut pursed his lips, as if to say, 'Life's a bitch.' Maybe he'd seen it happen to one or two of his own mates. Afghan had been no fun for them either.

Jack and Gabriel stayed where they were as the door closed, still thanking him effusively as it gave a reassuring clunk, just not as firmly as before. The chorus of thanks had masked it.

We held off talking for a while as they made their way back to the beds. Gabriel picked the zinc-oxide strips from the steel frame and stuck them onto his left arm.

Jack took his last deep drag of the very sweet and strong Russian tobacco that had contributed to the gulag's signature aroma when we'd arrived. Then he stubbed it out on the wet pitted concrete beneath his foot. 'That was good.'

Gabriel was ready to do the same. He'd smoked his right down to the filter. There was another hiss. 'How long?'

Jack went misty-eyed about the good old days. 'Just over four years. I still miss it.'

Gabriel sighed as he headed back to the door. He jabbed a finger at Rio. 'Come on then, fuckhead, do your bit. Let's see if you've got enough lead in your Jamaican pencil.'

All four of us moved to it for one last listen.

I gave a final run-through from mains box to Gaz. 'If it all goes noisy, it's out of the building the best way we can, turn left, up the hill directly behind us, and you won't miss the station. First one to get the Gaz started heads down here to pick up any sick, lame and lazy.'

'Sorted.' Jack zipped up the last couple of inches of his duvet, like it was body armour and that was all the prep he needed. 'Apart from a couple of RPGs, of course.'

I had to agree with that. 'Let's hope they don't have any, then.'

80

Rio put his shoulder against the door and applied gentle pressure. Too gentle, from the way Gabriel rolled his eyes and tutted. Rio pushed harder and the door popped open.

Jack grabbed the edge to stop it rattling. Gabriel retrieved the tape from the armature plate, ripped it in half, and put it with the rest of the strips lined up on his arm.

I took control of the door and poked my head out into the corridor. There was no sound, apart from the low murmur of the TV. The voices were mournful and the music full of high drama. The corridor was still as gloomy. The forty-watt bulb was doing its best, and its best suited us just fine.

There was nothing tactical about what we needed to do next, apart from getting on with it and making distance. I moved towards the main entrance until I reached the turn. The noise of the TV had got louder, but it was still muffled. I hoped that meant their door was closed. Why wouldn't it be? Cold air was whistling through the building, and Beer-gut wouldn't want to spend the night supplying Jack and Gabriel with cigarettes.

I went into a crouch and checked round the corner. Their door was closed.

I moved along the passageway, the sound of my footsteps masked by love, hate, fear, you name it – all the ingredients of a bad Russian soap. I heard the rustle of Gore-Tex behind me as I took two more paces and stopped by the mains cabinet.

Gabriel bent down and examined the botched DIY job in front of him. Rio was checking the main door. You never knew.

Gabriel carefully lifted cables here and threw switches there, running through his geek routine. Two women started shouting at each other in the room beside us. The guards took sides and joined in. It was sounding less like *EastEnders* and more like the Champions League.

Gabriel unravelled two cables that had been cobbled together under the cloak of fresh insulation tape. Holding one, he took a couple of paces towards the guardroom to check he had the length, then signalled to Jack to come and hold it. He stooped and peeled off a few strips of the oxide tape, using it to attach the bare end of the cable to the metal handle of the metal door. He went back to the fuse box and threw a switch. With a big grin on his face, he went back to work on the wiring.

The soap went quiet for a second or two, and so did the guards. So why could I hear mumbling? I glanced at Gabriel, and then Jack, but they hadn't suddenly gone verbal. I held up a hand, then put my index finger to my lips. They went absolutely still.

It was coming from the conference room further down the corridor. Then an unmistakable 'Jeez . . .'

The others had heard it too. Jack mouthed, 'What the fuck?'

I motioned to Gabriel to carry on working, and then to Rio to follow me. As I reached the open door and peered inside, I saw a familiar figure at the end of the room. The Owl had his back to me, arms splayed, staring down at the desk. He was reading something. The two mugs stood at his elbow, beside a red Thermos flask.

'Oh, *Jesus* . . .'

This was something that had to be taken advantage of. All we had in our goodie bag right now was a Jock electrician and a Gaz-71 whose keys we hadn't yet got our hands on.

He mumbled away to himself, lost in his own troubled world. He wasn't a happy man but was just about to be a whole lot unhappier. I leaned back and whispered into Rio's ear, 'Just back me.'

I crept forward as quickly and quietly as I could, then rushed him once I'd drawn level with the Formica-topped table. He swivelled his owl-like head.

He opened his beak and made a noise that was somewhere between a cough and a gasp.

'Sssh! *Quiet!*' I grabbed his arms and pushed until his back slammed into the wall and I had him sandwiched against it. 'It's OK. I'm not going to hurt you. But make a noise and I will. Just listen.'

I held his arms tight against the wall at either side of his body, and pushed against him.

He gave a whimper, but not loud enough to be heard above the faint sounds of the soap opera drifting towards us from the guardroom. He started to shake. I let him settle for a few seconds.

The greeter's grin had disappeared, that was for sure.

'Calm down and listen in. We're going to do you a favour. We're going to do our own thing. All right?'

He opened his mouth to speak but I didn't need his input.

'No. No need. We're going to make ourselves security blankets. A record of who we know, what we know, where it happened and when. And you know what's going to happen next, don't you? They'll be out there for whenever we get in the shit. They'll get exposed and the families of the dead will take it from there. Politicians, the media, they'll be all over you like a rash. All those families who want to know where their loved ones are. And we know exactly where they are, don't we? Latitude 89.4235, longitude 87.1141.'

He nodded very slowly.

'Mate, it'll make WikiLeaks look like a comic.'

I heard Rio behind me, unscrewing the Thermos and helping himself to a brew. He really could have made it to the Pole in shorts and flip-flops. He came and stood beside me.

'So, here's the deal. I know that this lot here will come looking for us. Leave them to it. Take a break. Stay in the Radisson. We'll come and find you. And because we're about to do you a very big favour, you're going to want to do one for us.'

He kept his eyes on my shoulder, like I had a tarantula dancing on it.

'All you've got to do is convince the Russians we're good lads. There's no way we're going to be gobbing off about this shit – unless, of course, anyone comes for us.'

I got a nod. The tarantula still gripped him.

'We also need to get off the island, and get our lives back. You'll be able to do that for us, won't you?'

He nodded again.

'That's good. Because then you can be sure that none of this shit ever gets out. We don't want anything to do with it. And for me, no more ice. It's the Caribbean every time.'

There was no scare in him that had kept him quiet, he just wanted to make sure I felt in control. He knew it was time to look up and get eye to eye. 'Nick, how am I going to do that? They'll think I'm part of it.'

'That's easy. You're about to become a front-room boy.' I pulled back and took half a pace to my right, but gripped his shoulders so they were as tight against the wall as his chest had been.

'Rio, drop him.'

Rio threw his forehead straight into the Owl's face. I wouldn't normally have delegated, only I'd done enough of that shit recently and my brain hurt.

The back of his skull hit the wall. I kept hold of him as he went down so he didn't injure himself more than Rio had already.

He started to howl. I'd never heard anyone make so

much noise just from a broken nose, even if there was enough blood for him to tell war stories to his grand-kids for ever.

Jack appeared at the door. 'What the fuck?' This time he didn't just mouth it. It had gone noisy.

And then some.

81

We charged out into the corridor as the shouts and screams of the guards intensified. But they weren't going near their door. They wouldn't make that mistake again.

'No need to be subtle about it now, is there?' Gabriel sounded almost pissed off.

He grabbed one wire from the mess of cables and gave it a sharp tug. The lights went out, the soap came to a halt mid-sentence, and there was a hard clunk as the door demagnetized. We surged outside. There was nothing out there, except cold and wind and something that wasn't darkness and wasn't really light.

I swung left, skirted the building and started pounding uphill, shoving and kicking my way through the snow to try to carve an easier path for the legless behind me. I checked over my shoulder. Rio had taken the rear and was almost pushing them up the gradient. My throat was dry but my circulation was in overdrive.

My fingers and feet were starting to pulse with warmth and energy.

As I got further up the hill the bright red steel roof of the station began to fill my horizon to my left. Below and to my right was the town. Bodies already out and about, getting ready for another murk-filled day. What that might mean for us, I wasn't too sure.

I stopped about twenty short of the building. The Gazes weren't outside on the concrete, as I'd been hoping, but that wasn't a problem, depending on how many bodies were inside.

The rest caught up, gulping in the air, feeling the wind fire icy droplets into their skin, like frozen gravel.

Rio was enjoying the other two suffering. 'Don't like the puff now, do you?'

'I'll go do a quick recce.' I left them and moved to the station, towards the windows on the side of the building, although there were no lights shining out. I could make out the two red wagons in the larger of the two areas inside.

On the other side of the building there was a wall with a number of doors, which were clearly the offices. I moved round the front and passed the wide and closed roller-shutter, and to the right of it was the office space. There was a light trying hard to shine through the window on the other corner of the building, and there was a people door.

I moved out onto the concrete to get a better angle through the glass. A TV was working overtime at the back of what must have been a command room. I could also see a steaming kettle, a brew kit and a couple of radios on a work surface directly beneath the single overhead lamp. They'd gone for something more high-tech than the naked-bulb look in the gulag, but forty watts still seemed to be the rule.

There was one body in a swivel chair and she had her back to me. Her hair was pulled into a ponytail that swung from side to side as she followed every detail of whatever was happening on her screen.

Did that mean she was the watch? That the crew only came when she called, rather than being ready to slide down a pole at a moment's notice? I hoped so. We were about to find out.

I ran back to wave the rest of them in. 'It looks like there's just the one on stag. We have to go via her office. I'll bang on the door, we grip her, and take it from there. Can anyone drive one of these things?'

Rio stepped up. 'Got a fucking Warrior licence, mate. But . . .' The other two wouldn't be able to either. At least, not on their own.

'OK. Jack and me, we're going to grip her. You two, follow us in, head straight out to the vehicles and get one moving.'

I didn't wait for them to confirm. This wasn't brain surgery. It was about making distance.

The woman in the command centre was still rooted to her chair. The soap must have been the same one our guards had been watching, from the high-octane music I could now hear through her door.

I gripped the handle and tried to turn it. No luck. She obviously didn't want just anyone interrupting her viewing. I banged on it with my fist, hard, quick and desperate. It seemed to take her for ever to tear herself away from the drama, but finally I heard the scrape of a chair. She was on her way.

A bolt slid back and the door opened inwards. As soon as there was a gap wide enough for me see there was no security chain, I barged my way into the boiling hot room. The woman rocked back, lost her footing and tumbled onto the floor. Jack hobbled straight over to her, made calming noises, showing her two flat hands.

It was pointless miming if there was anyone else inside the building. She could give a yes or a no; she could be lying or telling the truth.

Rio and Gabriel pushed their way through the door on our left into the vehicle area, as I started to grip the woman. She was no older than a teenager, now that I had the chance to look at her. So I gave her a smile as I turned her onto her stomach and got my knee stuck into the small of her back, holding her down as Jack searched for something to contain her. It was a fire station: brand-new yellow fire-suit tops and bottoms were hung up in a neat row, trailing wide elasticated braces. 'Jack – on the wall . . .'

I left her as soon as we'd tied her wrists and ankles behind her back. She was in tears, despite trying her hardest not to be, but she didn't shout or scream. No one would hear her anyway. And she'd be found and released when they came to investigate why the Gaz was burning up fuel.

I heard the gentle electric whine of the shutters, then the growl of an engine. We legged it to the nearest Gaz, which Rio had sparked up. It gave a belch of diesel fumes before settling into a steady rhythm.

Rio was in the left seat of what turned out to be a two-man cab. He was shouting and beckoning through his open door, but I couldn't hear a word. It didn't matter. I ran round the front, with Jack just behind me, and saw Gabriel trying to fold himself onto the centre console.

I climbed over the track and into the right-hand seat and Jack scrambled in too. He ended up half on me and half on Gabriel when the wagon staggered forward.

There was a fair amount of lurching and jerking as the tracks ground their way over the concrete base of the maintenance area, but who gave a fuck? We were mobile.

Jack closed his door on the third lurch and as we kangarooed the first fifty metres I could see why this wasn't the smoothest ride at the fairground. There were two of them at the controls.

The Gaz was no different from any other tracked vehicle. The accelerator was down below, the engine was automatic, and there were a pair of tillers to slow, stop and turn. Rio gripped the left-hand one with his good arm and Gabriel, lying on the centre console, had the right. Rio was getting impatient. As far as he was concerned the jerkiness was Gabriel's fault. 'Gently! Just pull it gently!'

I left the two of them to it and pointed through the screen. 'We're heading north-east. I can't see a compass. We've got no sun. So just keep the sea to the left. We OK for fuel?'

Rio was busy bollocking Gabriel, but took time off to bollock me too. 'It's full, isn't it? Why have a fucking fire engine that can't get anywhere? How far are we going?'

'About fifty-five, sixty Ks from here, maybe more.'

I tried looking behind me but couldn't see a thing, and there were no mirrors.

Jack wasn't fussed. 'Don't worry about it. If anyone follows us, we'll just turn and crush them.'

The other two nagged each other endlessly as the Gaz started to pick up speed on the snow, but gradually hit a steadier rhythm.

82

Rune's grey wooden box
Latitude: 78.2119 North
Longitude: 15.6426 East

Jack was seated at the table in front of the laptop's camera, finishing off his statement. He was trying hard not to move his hands now. We'd had to shout at him every time he got pissed off and gesticulated at the camera.

'That is all I know. That is all I saw. That is all I heard. End of statement.'

He was the last to film his security blanket. All four of us had covered the who, the what, the where and the when, from our respective points of view. It was now his turn to copy his performance onto all six of Rune's USB sticks. He tested each one in turn to make sure it had successfully transferred.

Rio and Gabriel were sprawled on the sofas, drinking good coffee now that Gabriel had repaired the machine. As he might have reminded us, he was a REME genius. He knew stuff.

Each of them was digging handfuls of dry Axa Go'Mix out of a carton. Rune seemed to have cornered the market in the stuff, like he'd been anticipating some kind of muesli apocalypse.

Gabriel also had a rifle on the floor alongside him, its bolt-action open and exposing the ten rounds in its mag. I had another, closed, with a round in the chamber, resting across my lap.

I regularly scanned the approach road through the slight gap in the shutters at the front of the house. It wasn't as if we were going to make a quick getaway – half the team had removed their legs to sort out their bloody and swollen stumps – but it felt good to know that if shit came our way, we could send a bit of it back.

We'd dumped the Gaz in dead ground about three Ks out of town, and tabbed in. That was the final nail in the coffin for the legless. They'd taken a battering over the last few days. But we'd got to the house and sorted ourselves out. From here on in, the plan was simple.

I'd track down the Owl, and he'd get us off the island. We'd leave one of the USBs hidden here, maybe somewhere in the house. It meant we had some security between now and when we landed back in the real world, in case the Owl had second thoughts about our get-out-of-jail-free card.

Each of us would have a copy of all four statements, to secure as we wished. The last would go to Claudia Nangel in Zürich: she'd tuck it away for any of us to have access to it on a rainy day. After all, she was almost family, and always ready to help.

We still hadn't sorted out what we were going to do about the dead members of the team, how we were going to frame that for consumption. We might need the Owl to help us. The easiest way, I guessed, was to say that they'd fallen down a lead and that was it, we'd lost them. They were somewhere at the bottom of the Arctic Ocean. Not the first. And very probably not the last. Whatever and wherever, we all had to get our story straight, but that wasn't on today's agenda.

I still hadn't told Jack yet about his dad. Sorting out the living was more important than sorting out the dead.

So that was it.

A simple plan.

Except that nothing in life was ever that simple.

The way we saw it, now was not the end. It wasn't even the beginning of the end. But maybe it was a few steps past the end of the beginning. We were halfway through the last part of this fuck-up. We might get out. We might not. We all knew that. But for the moment, at least, we were on solid ground and breathing.

Jack finished checking the USBs and threw us one each. 'So, what now?'

Gabriel caught his in an outstretched hand and tucked it into a pocket. 'You know, I've been thinking about the missus and kids. If we really do get out of here, I'll have been given a third life. However long it lasts, I'm going to try not to fuck this one up. I'm going to go back and see if the family will take me in. What do you reckon?'

Rio caught his in his lap because he couldn't be arsed to move. 'Same here. The girlfriend – well, the ex – she's got a new man now, but you never know, do you? If we make it home, I'm going to get to know the kids. Kids need their dad, right? Even if he's not all there.'

Jack had a question for him. 'Talking of women, Biyu, Chinese TV . . . did you really?'

Rio gave the widest cracked-lip smile of the trip so far. 'No, mate. She fucked me off before I even crossed the starting line – but at least I got to wind up the REME, didn't I?'

Gabriel snorted with laughter and threw a fistful of Go'Mix at him.

Jack turned to me. 'What about you, Nick? What's on the cards?'

'I've been thinking I might start up a little security business. Might even ask the Owl if he can throw some work my way now and again. He seems to have plenty of it. One thing I've discovered – you really are better off inside the tent pissing out, than outside pissing in. Especially if it's forty below.'

Rio and Gabriel immediately wanted in.

I grinned. 'We'll see. Who knows?'

I was relieved that they liked the idea because I wouldn't have considered setting it up without them. They might not have the correct number of limbs for that sort of work, but that didn't matter. What they had was commitment and brains, and that counted for more than anything else. I was excited by the idea; who knew what we could get up to?

Rio even had a name for the new company. 'We could call ourselves SNS, Special Needs Service, get it?'

It got a laugh from me and Gabriel but Jack was deep in thought. Gabriel threw what was left of his Go'Mix at him to bring him back to earth.

'What about you, mate? Maybe the four of us? What do you reckon?'

Jack came halfway out of his trance. 'Of course. Great idea. Count me in. Without a doubt.'

But Rio knew he wasn't really there. We all did. 'Mate, what's going on in that head of yours?'

It took him a while to answer. 'You're right. If we *are* given a third life, I'm not going to waste it. I think it's time to bury the hatchet with the old man. He doesn't deserve it, but my mother does.'

I caught Gabriel's eye and signalled for him to take over stag. I needed to grip this.

I stood up and Gabriel took my place. I took one last look out at the approach road before turning back to Jack. 'Mate,' I said gently, 'there's something you need to know about your dad.'

The unstoppable Nick Stone is back in

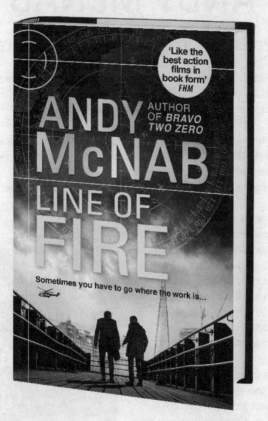

'Like the best action films in book form'
FHM

ANDY McNAB
AUTHOR OF *BRAVO TWO ZERO*

LINE OF FIRE

Sometimes you have to go where the work is...

Out Autumn 2017, available for pre-order now

DETONATOR

ANDY McNAB

THE HEART-STOPPING NICK STONE THRILLER

Ex-deniable operator Nick Stone has spent a lifetime in harm's way – but when someone he cares for very deeply is murdered in cold blood, he can no longer just take the pain.

A high-level internecine conflict at the dark heart of the resurgent Russian Empire and an assassin's bullet on an isolated Alpine pass propel him from an apparently run-of-the-mill close-protection task into his most brutal and challenging mission yet.

As the body count increases, Stone becomes one of Europe's Most Wanted. He must evade the elite police forces of three nations in his pursuit of faceless men who trade in human misery, and a lone-wolf terrorist who threatens to unleash the western world's worst nightmare.

Vengeance of the most explosive kind is top of Stone's agenda. The fuse has been ignited – but who really holds the detonator?

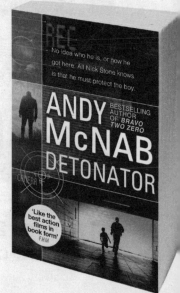

No idea who he is, or how he got here. All Nick Stone knows is that he must protect the boy.

ANDY McNAB

BESTSELLING AUTHOR OF BRAVO TWO ZERO

DETONATOR

'Like the best action films in book form'
FHM

SORTED!

THE GOOD PSYCHOPATH'S GUIDE TO BOSSING YOUR LIFE

Dr KEVIN DUTTON & ANDY McNAB DCM MM

Over thirty different examples of situations and ideas to show you how you can change your approach and change your life . . .

Looking to nail an **INTERVIEW?**
Want to make a better first impression on a **DATE?**
Trying to make your **MONEY** go further?
Bet you never thought being a bit more **PSYCHOPATH** could be the answer.

Time to grab that bullsh*t by the horns!

Dr Kevin Dutton studies psychopaths and his latest subject is SAS hero Andy McNab. He's a bit different, he's a **GOOD PSYCHOPATH.** Andy can control qualities like decisiveness, ruthlessness and fearlessness to get the **BEST** out of himself and life. Together, this unlikely duo has established what they call the **SEVEN DEADLY WINS**, the good psychopathic quirks that can help make you more **SUCCESSFUL.** And now it's time to put their theories to the test.

SORTED! THE GOOD PSYCHOPATH'S GUIDE TO BOSSING YOUR LIFE offers a new approach to the everyday to help you get more out of life than it gets out of you.

RED NOTICE
ANDY McNAB

Deep beneath the English Channel on a Paris-bound express, a crack team of East European **terrorists** has taken four hundred **hostages** at gunpoint – and declared war on a British government with more than its own fair share of **secrets** to keep.

One man stands in their way. Tom Buckingham, an off-duty **SAS** soldier, is on-board the train. He is **the only chance** the passengers and crew have of survival. With only a failing mobile to contact the outside world, he must use all his **tradecraft** and know-how to take out the enemy and secure the train.

But the odds are stacked against him – twelve **battle-hardened**, tooled-up veterans of a bitter civil war to his one, **unarmed** and injured. And little does he know that someone on his own side is determined that no-one will get out of that tunnel **alive** . . .

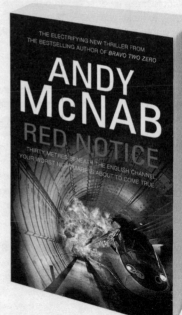

THE ELECTRIFYING NEW THRILLER FROM THE BESTSELLING AUTHOR OF BRAVO TWO ZERO

ANDY McNAB

RED NOTICE

THIRTY METRES BENEATH THE ENGLISH CHANNEL YOUR WORST NIGHTMARE IS ABOUT TO COME TRUE